Dear Reader,

Summer days are long and lovely at Crescent Cove's Beach House No. 9, but there's just something about those summer nights that will make your visit unforgettable! Even as the sun goes down, there's plenty of heat left in the most enchanting bungalow on the sand. Join me to see what the magic is all about....

Not so far from the cove is another unique place you'll visit in *Bungalow Nights*—"avocado country," where the hills are covered with the deep green-leaved trees that bear the prickly product sometimes known as the fertility fruit or the alligator pear. It's another part of California I'm pleased to show you. After all, everything goes better with a little guacamole on the side, doesn't it?

Combat medic Vance Smith has no idea of all that's on the menu when he makes his visit to No. 9. Only when he meets pretty, brown-eyed baker Layla Parker does he get an inkling of the sweets within his grasp. The two struggle against their growing feelings for each other—they both have wary hearts—but fighting love is as useless as fighting an incoming tide. I hope you'll root for their happy ending.

Here comes the sun!

Christie

CHRISTIE RIDGWAY

BUNGALOW NIGHTS

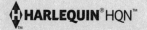

Recycling programs
for this product may
not exist in your area.

ISBN-13: 978-0-373-77745-7

BUNGALOW NIGHTS

Copyright © 2013 by Christie Ridgway

Printed in U.S.A.

This book was written when I was virtually bed-bound due to a fractured leg that required surgery (plates! pins! screws!) followed by three months when I wasn't allowed to put weight on it. My loyal and loving husband came home at lunch every day to make me a good meal and followed that up with dinner every night. That's not to mention all the other household tasks that he took over or the many times he cheered my spirits, including when he drove me to visit the places that inspired the Beach House No. 9 books. So, my darling Rob, this one is for you. Again. Always.

BUNGALOW NIGHTS

Every lover is a soldier.

—Ovid

A family is a place where minds come in contact with one another. If these minds love one another, the home will be as beautiful as a flower garden. But if these minds get out of harmony with one another, it is like a storm that plays havoc with the garden.

—Buddha

CHAPTER ONE

VANCE SMITH HAD FACED down Taliban bullets with more cool than he felt sitting on the beachside restaurant's open-air deck. He was here to meet his companion for the next month, and not that he'd admit it to anyone, but there was an undeniable film of sweat on both palms— sweat he couldn't even swipe against his jeans thanks to the fiberglass cast that bound one wrist and the soft brace that was fastened around the other.

Sometime during his short hospital stay, a dumb-ass private with Picasso pretensions had taken a Sharpie to the pristine polymer wrapping on his left arm and drawn a big-busted, half-naked warrior princess, de- tailed enough that Vance had been forced to beg his cousin Baxter this morning for some help in disguising the X-rated image. He was meeting an impressionable young person, after all.

Grimacing, Vance glanced down at his cousin's solu- tion, then back at Baxter himself, who was sitting across the table, nursing a club soda. "Really?" he said to the other man, not bothering to blunt the edge to his voice. "A tat sleeve? That's the best you could come up with?"

Baxter blinked. In their youth, people had mistaken the two of them for twins and they still had the same blond hair and blue eyes. But while Vance sported a soldier's barber cut and casual clothes, his one-year-

younger cousin had a salon style and looked the epitome
of his nickname, All Business Baxter, in a conservative suit and tie. His gaze dropped to the nylon fabric
stretched over Vance's cast. "I say it's inspired. And I
could have made a worse choice, you know. As it is,
you almost blend in."

Vance grunted. He supposed Bax was right. The
sleeve's design wasn't demonic, or worse, straight out
of a prison documentary. Instead, the images were in-
tricate and colorful weavings of tribal signs, tropical
flora and curling waves. Nothing to scare off a child.

"Snuggle up closer with Teddy if you're still worried," Baxter advised. "Then your new little friend
won't even notice them."

It wasn't embarrassment but annoyance that burned
Vance's skin. "Shut up," he said, adjusting the toddler-
size stuffed bear on his lap. A big blue satin bow was
tied around its neck. "And remind me why you're not
at work again?" His cousin managed the numbers end
of the family business, Smith & Sons Foods, that grew
avocados and citrus in a fertile area about sixty miles
southeast of here. "Shouldn't you be counting packing
crates or something?"

Baxter tilted his head and seemed to consider the
question. "Good point. I *am* very busy. But I'm also
the only relative who gets more than the rare two-line
email from you. My three sentences confer a certain
responsibility upon me."

Vance looked toward the ocean to avoid the censure
in the other man's gaze. The restaurant was situated at
one end of Southern California's Crescent Cove, a gentle
curve of land that created a shallow cup for the gray-
blue Pacific water. Today's bright July sun scattered

gold discs onto its dappled surface. A beautiful sight, and as different as could be from the stark landscape of Afghanistan that he'd been gazing upon for months, but he didn't find it soothing. There was that kid in his future. Four weeks playing father figure to a stranger.

"'Confer a certain responsibility,'" he muttered, taking his uneasiness out on his cousin. "You've turned pompous, you know that?"

"It must be those sixteen hours a day I sit behind a desk," Baxter replied without heat. "Not everyone has spent the last half year or so dodging IEDs and getting in the middle of firefights."

"It's my job." He was a combat medic, and though it wasn't what he'd originally planned for himself, Vance held no regrets about being the one to aid his fallen brothers on the battlefield. He did it damn well. Lives had been saved.

And some not.

"Uh-oh," Baxter said now. "Stay with me, fella. You look ready to bolt."

"I'm not going anywhere." He could still hear his grandfather's voice in his head. *A man never breaks a promise.* And Vance lived by that. His fingers absently played with the ends of the stuffed bear's satin ribbon. "When her dad was dying in that godforsaken valley, I swore to him I'd give Layla a vacation to remember at Beach House No. 9."

The injured colonel had carried the details of his planned trip in the interior webbing of his combat helmet, where it was common for soldiers to tuck valued letters and precious photos. Like Vance, he had learned of Crescent Cove from Griffin Lowell, an embedded journalist who had waxed poetic about his childhood summers at the place to anyone who'd listen. Those idyllic reminiscences had served as an escape for all of them from the drudgery and brutality of war, but must have struck a particular chord with the officer, because he'd arranged the cottage rental for his upcoming leave and stashed the particulars with the photo he carried of his little girl.

Hiding behind a straw-and-mud wall, while Vance was doing his best to stanch the bleeding from the older man's multiple wounds, Colonel Samuel Parker had one thing on his mind—his daughter. As death closed in, he'd extracted from Vance a promise to act as stand-in tour guide during Layla's month-to-remember. Vance considered it a point of honor to obey the good man's final order.

"Hey." Baxter jerked in his chair, his attention riveted over Vance's shoulder. "Is that…?" He wiped a hand across his mouth. "It couldn't be."

Alarmed by his cousin's sudden loss of urbanity, Vance glanced around. "Oh," he said, relaxing. "It's Addy. You remember Addison March—her mom is friends with our mothers, she grew up down the road from our ranch—"

"I know who she is," Baxter interjected. "But why is she here? Why is she coming toward us?"

Vance once again glanced over his shoulder. Addy, a small, curvy blonde dressed in a pair of flat sandals and calf-length pants, was crossing the deck toward their table. She didn't look the least bit worthy of the thread of distress in his cousin's voice. "I hired her to act as a nanny. I couldn't very well be alone with a little girl. I ran into Addy when I was checking out the cove a couple of days ago and—"

"But you said you'd never heard of this place before that reporter mentioned it. *I've* never heard of it before. Of all the gin joints," the other man muttered, pushing out of his chair with agitated movements. "I've got to go."

"Hello," a female voice said from behind Vance's back. Addy had arrived. "Leaving already, Baxter?"

His cousin froze and his panicked expression would have been comical if it wasn't so out of character. "You feel okay?" Vance asked him.

"I'm fine. Fine," Baxter muttered, sinking back into his seat. "Never been better. Not a care in the world."

"Whatever you say." Vance gestured toward one of the free chairs at the table. "Sit down, Addy. You're right on time. Layla should be here any minute."

"With her uncle?" the young woman asked.

"I suppose." The arrangements to meet today had been made via email through Phil Parker, the contact he'd been given by Layla's father. If you asked Vance, the man came off a bubble short of level, his often-vague replies free of punctuation and peppered with irrelevant references to kismet, fate and surfing. Each email ended with *namaste,* whatever the hell that meant.

"The stuffed animal's a nice touch," Addy said.

The mention of Teddy irritated Vance all over again, so he slipped the photo he carried out of the breast pocket of his sports shirt. Yeah, he'd sort of dressed up for the kid, too. His best jeans and a short-sleeved button-down, straight from the dry cleaner's plastic. He slapped the picture onto the tabletop. "Her father had this with him. It's what gave me the idea."

Layla Parker stared up at the three of them. She was sitting on a short flight of concrete steps, one of her knobby little-kid knees sporting scabs. Her long hair was in pigtails tied below each ear, revealing a wide forehead over big brown eyes. She appeared to be approximately ten years old and she stared into the camera, a little smile curving her lips as her skinny arms hugged a potbellied teddy bear to her middle.

"Ah," Addy said, smiling. "Cute."

"Yeah." Her dad's fingers had been trembling when he fished out the picture. *Isn't she beautiful, Vance? You've got to do something for her. You've got to do something for my girl.* What choice had there been? The husky emotion in the mortally wounded man's voice had impelled Vance to say he would.

He'd also done everything in his power to save the colonel, but it hadn't been enough. Too soon he'd been gone, leaving Vance alone with his pledge to fulfill the fallen officer's final wish.

"I've got to go," Baxter said again.

"Sure." With Addy on scene, there was another person at the table to smooth over the awkwardness of the initial meeting with young Layla. He angled his head toward his cousin. "Thanks for—"

Vance broke off as the breeze made a sudden shift, blowing a cold breath across the nape of his neck. The small hairs on his body—even the ones surrounded by the infernal cast and brace—went on instant alert as if eager to escape. He tensed. Soldiers learned to rely on their gut, and Vance's was suddenly shouting that the person who should be leaving was him.

But though he'd been scared shitless a hundred times, since joining the army he'd never ducked his duty and he wasn't about to start now. Anyway, what could possibly endanger him in this sun-drenched civilian world?

That weird breeze chilled him again, and Vance jerked his head in its direction. Sunlight dazzled him. Something dazzled him, anyway, and he was forced to blink a couple of times before bringing into focus the deserted hostess stand across the deck and the lone figure positioned before it. It was a very pretty woman, probably in her mid-twenties, wearing a silky-looking dress of swirling jewel colors that hit at midthigh and was belted around her slender waist. Medium-brown hair waved past her shoulders and her forehead was covered by a deep fringe of bangs.

A new feeling tickled him. He should know her, he thought, frowning. And not just in the way any red-blooded man would want to know a woman that hot. She looked familiar.

And nervous. Her fingers combed through the ends of her long hair as she went on tiptoe to scan the area. When she settled back on her heels, she bit down on her bottom lip.

God, didn't he know that mouth?

He wouldn't have forgotten kissing those lips, would he?

Still puzzling it out, he narrowed his gaze. He was thirty and she was about five years younger, which crossed her off his list of high school hookups—even if one might have coincidentally ventured here, an hour from home environs. As for more recent conquests—until six months ago he'd been in a yearlong, serious relationship. Meaning if this lovely little mama was part of his past it would have been in his wild and crazy years…wild, crazy and *hazy*.

He glanced over at Baxter, who had been his partner in crime—okay, he'd been the designated driver—

whenever Vance could pry him free of his Aeron office chair. "Cuz."

Baxter started. He'd been watching Addy, who'd been watching the waves curl toward shore. "Uh, what?" His hand smoothed over the tasteful stripes of his preppy tie even as he slid a last look at the blonde seated beside him.

Vance couldn't cipher what was going on there, not when he had to determine the identity of the leggy girl at the hostess stand. "Don't be obvious, but check out the woman waiting for a table." He saw his cousin lift his gaze in the right direction. "Do I know her?"

Bax's eyes flicked back to Vance's face. "Huh? How would I be aware of all your acquaintances?"

"It's a long shot, but…" But he had this dreadlike feeling that she wasn't a mere acquaintance. He fought the urge to ogle her again, though the guy in him was clamoring for a second look. It was a bad idea, though. If she was a former…interest of his, he didn't want to attract her attention. He'd become a little classier—and a lot less of a party animal—over the past few years, and it would only embarrass them both if she attempted reacquaintance and he was forced to admit he'd forgotten her name and how he knew her.

How well they might have known each other.

Could I really have forgotten that mouth?

Hooking a foot around a leg of his chair, he gave it a little twist, presenting more of his back to the brunette. "Never mind."

"Um," his cousin said, his gaze drifting over Vance's shoulder again. "I guess she's given up waiting on the hostess. She's walked onto the deck and it looks as if she's coming in this direction."

Hell! Vance did a rush shuffle through his memory banks. In college, he'd double majored in hedonism and procrastination until dropping out to join the army. Returning to California after his four-year stint, he'd briefly gone back to his bad boy ways. Though he'd soon straightened up and begun a relationship with a woman he'd thought was his future, it still left time for him to find then forget the wavy-haired woman he could practically feel from here.

He took a chance and glanced back. She was standing still again, scanning the restaurant's patrons with a hint of anxiety in her expression. He hoped some asshole hadn't stood her up. As he watched, her eyes started to track toward their table and Vance hurriedly turned his head. Sliding lower in his seat, he made to grab a menu from the table to use as a shield, then froze.

What the hell was he doing? If he hid behind the vinyl folder, Addy would think he was addled. Bax would laugh his ass off. Vance considered himself an idiot just for having the craven impulse.

Anyway, no chance I would have forgotten that face.

Preparing to start some relaxing small talk with his companions, he cleared his throat. Addy and Baxter both looked at him and then, as one, their gazes transferred to a spot above his head. Vance's belly tightened. A delicately sweet scent reached him on another of those cold, cautionary breezes.

"Vance?" a throaty, feminine voice asked. "Vance Smith?"

That slightly scratchy timbre goosed him somewhere deep inside, waking his previously snoozing sexual urges with a start. Shit, he thought, tensing. Now wasn't the time for this. Now was the time for Layla Parker to show up. And if the girl arrived this very minute, then an awkward encounter with the female he'd forgotten could get lost in the flurry of meeting the colonel's daughter. His libido would settle back to its deep sleep. Without moving a muscle, he waited a beat for his wish to come true.

When his hope went unfulfilled, Vance swallowed his sigh of resignation and slowly half turned in his seat.

"So...The Breakers?" he asked, naming one of his old hangouts as he shifted. "Or was it Pete's Place?"

"What?" she asked.

He made himself look into her eyes. They were big and a soft brown, circled with thick dark lashes. Damn, Vance thought, those eyes, that mouth, the whole package stirred him up.

And stirred a memory, but for the life of him, he couldn't place it.

"I'm trying to recall where we met," he clarified. There was nothing to do but confess, though the way his body was responding it seemed unbelievable her identity wasn't burned in his brain. "I'm sorry, but I don't know..."

"Oh." She shook her head, and a pair of gold hoop earrings swung. "We haven't met. I took a guess. You have the shortest haircut out here." Her lips curved just a little and—

It clicked. That tiny smile snapped the missing piece into the puzzle. It was the same one worn by the bear-toting kid in the officer's photograph.

His gut knotted. *Hell,* he thought, stunned. *Oh, hell.*

She was right; they'd never met, but he knew her all the same. As a matter of fact, he'd been waiting for her. *Yes, Colonel, she* is *beautiful.*

So damn beautiful Vance felt a little sick.

The sexy woman standing two feet away was none other than Layla Parker. Layla Parker, the "little girl" whose dreams he'd been charged with making come true.

Good God, he thought. This changed everything, didn't it? The little girl was all grown up.

VANCE WAS SO UNBALANCED he didn't get to his feet, he didn't speak, he might not have been breathing. Baxter's manners kicked in, thank goodness, and it was he who shepherded the colonel's daughter to the empty chair beside Addy. Layla let herself be led away from Vance and gave her attention to his cousin and the woman he'd hired to live at Beach House No. 9 with him and the little girl.

The little girl who wasn't a little girl in the least.

Still trying to come to grips with that, he let Baxter and Addy initiate introductions and continue the conversation. Layla smiled and spoke, even as Vance didn't hear a word she said.

Her big browns kept stealing glances at his face. She was clearly puzzled by his continued silence, but he couldn't do more than try to ignore his body's reaction to her while thinking of the speediest way to put an end to this impossible situation.

A server, apparently noting every chair at their four-top was occupied, hurried over to discuss the menu and take requests. He considered telling the aproned girl they wouldn't be sticking around that long, but Baxter—who'd apparently changed his mind about leaving—and the others were already making decisions and communicating food orders. There was nothing he could do but ask for a sandwich and iced tea.

So they'd have lunch. Share a meal before bidding goodbye. Layla was more than twice the age he'd expected and surely she had better things to do than hang out at the beach with a virtual stranger.

Just as he had the comforting thought, she addressed him. "My dad wrote me about you."

Vance blinked, looking up from the photograph he'd tossed on the table before, now half-obscured by a place mat. "He did?" They'd known each other, of course—the officer had held a keen interest in the men under his command and he'd been deeply respected and admired in return—but their real closeness had come on that fateful day when Vance had been one of the patrol accompanying the colonel across the valley to his meet with a tribal elder. Fighting to save someone's life brought about a profound intimacy.

Her gaze dropped to the stack of thin metal bracelets circling one delicate wrist. She spun them one way and then another. "He sent me long letters, describing the people he worked with, the scenery around him, that sort of thing."

Vance thought of the stingy emails he tapped off to his family and for the first time experienced a pinch of guilt. "Ah."

"He was a good storyteller," she said in that sweet rasp of hers. "If he hadn't been a soldier…"

Her words dropped away, leaving behind an awkward pause. The fact was he *had* been a soldier and they all knew how that had turned out.

Addy broke the uncomfortable silence. "What is it you do?"

Yeah, Vance thought, *good lead-in.* Layla would want him to know she had a life that made spending four weeks at Crescent Cove inconvenient, if not downright impossible.

"Karma Cupcakes," she answered.

Karma cupcakes? He didn't know what the hell she meant, but it reminded him of something else. "Where's your uncle?" he asked abruptly. For God's sake, surely the man should have realized Vance had been operating under a misconception. *I was expecting a ten-year-old, Phil!*

Layla shrugged. "About now? When he can, he practices tai chi in a city park from noon to one."

Didn't that just figure. *Namaste.* It only solidified Vance's burgeoning belief that the man was flaky enough not to pick up on the oddness of the situation he'd arranged for his *grown niece.* No wonder Layla's father hadn't entrusted his last request to his brother. "And after that?"

"He drives the cupcake truck." Glancing around at their confused expressions, she released a laugh.

A little husky. Young.

Yet dangerous miles more mature than the laughter of the female he'd been expecting to entertain at Beach House No. 9. God, what a joke.

"We operate a mobile bakery, Uncle Phil and I," Layla informed them.

Addy looked interested. "Gourmet food trucks are the new big thing."

"Exactly," Layla said, nodding. "We're called Karma Cupcakes, and we make the batter and bake the cakes in our truck. Then we sell them at various locations in Southern California. We have a regular schedule of farmers' markets and popular stopping points. Our customers happen upon us or track our whereabouts via social media."

Baxter straightened in his chair. "I read this article in *Commerce Weekly*—"

"That's got to keep you very busy, Layla," Vance said over him. He'd moved into Beach House No. 9 that morning, but because he'd let go of his apartment upon being called up, since returning to Southern California he'd squatted in the second bedroom at Bax's city town house for a few days. It was more than enough time to know that the other man devoted himself to business twenty-three-and-a-half hours out of twenty-four. His cousin could go on forever about some dry article he'd read in a financial journal, only postponing the understanding at which Vance and Layla needed to arrive.

The understanding that they'd part ways as soon as he took care of the lunch check. "And summer's probably a hectic time of year for you," Vance added.

"Sure," she agreed. "But we have it worked out so I can stay at Beach House No. 9, if that's got you worried."

Of course that had him worried, dammit.

"Uncle Phil can make friends in a minute, including with the couple who owns this restaurant. Once they heard our story, they agreed to let us park the truck overnight in their lot adjacent to the coast highway. In the mornings I'll do the mixing and baking as usual, in the afternoons, we can..." She shrugged.

We can... Oh, God, he was a bad man, because the *we can*s instantly spread across Vance's mind like a set of erotic playing cards. Blame it on the dearth of female companionship a combat tour offered. Blame it on the train wreck that was his last romantic relationship. Hell, place the blame squarely on the beautiful young woman who was sitting a tabletop away, the summer sunshine edging her feminine figure. Who could blame him for his sudden and sharp sexual response? She was big eyes and a tender mouth, soft tresses and golden skin. Nothing could stop his gaze from tracing the column of her throat to the hint of cleavage revealed by the V neckline of her dress.

Unbidden, he pictured himself nuzzling the fabric aside with his mouth, tasting the sweet flavor of her flesh, finding her secret points of arousal and exploiting them with his hot breath and wet tongue. Her long legs would move restlessly, creating a space for his hips, and she'd open to him with a blissful sigh of surrender that was the single best turn-on a man could experience.

A man who'd made promises to her father.

Dammit!

His gaze refocused on the little-girl photo on the tabletop. "This isn't going to work," he said, emphatic.

"What do you mean?" she asked.

Vance stifled a groan and met her eyes. "Look, I didn't expect you—uh, it to be like this."

She stared at him, clearly perplexed. "But you said my father spoke about it. About me being here."

"Yes, yes. You were in his thoughts at the very last. However…" Vance could feel Addy and Bax looking at him like he was a monster, but hell, he felt like a monster. Juiced up on sex and ready to grab the fair maiden and abscond with her to his deep, dark den. As a reaction it was near violent and damn embarrassing. "Maybe we could meet for a walk someday and talk about it. Or perhaps a phone conversation would be better. I know, I'll tell you the whole story in an email."

"You said July at Beach House No. 9," Layla insisted, her brows meeting over a small, straight nose, betraying she had more backbone than he'd assumed at first glance. "That was my dad's request—it was his last wish and I think I should fulfill that. It's what you said you wanted, as well."

Yeah, he could certainly understand that the colonel's daughter felt compelled to follow through with what her father had asked of them. It was something he took very seriously himself. But…but…

I thought you were a little kid!

He'd have to find some way to let her down easy. What kind of man would admit he was afraid of getting behind a closed door with her? It would have to be some other excuse, an emergency, or…

He was considering and discarding options when the server reappeared, a tray of drinks in hand. She rearranged items already on the table, scooting the photograph closer toward Layla to make room for a sweating glass of tea.

Layla's gaze landed on it and her brows came together in another small frown. *Shit.* Deciding he'd only feel more foolish if she knew of his misunderstanding, he shifted forward to grab the picture before she could connect the dots.

Only to realize he still had a lapful of teddy bear. Wonderful. He was worried about his dignity while sharing a chair with ten pounds of stuffing and fake fur. What else could he do but get rid of it?

"I forgot," he said, half standing to thrust it in her direction, "this is for you."

Layla stood, too, automatically reaching for it, then froze, Teddy clutched between her hands. Her gaze flicked to the photo, flicked back to the bear, flicked again to the photo. A flag of bright pink appeared on each cheek. "Oh," she said, her voice going small. "Oh, God."

Consider dots connected, Vance thought. Grimacing, he reached out with his casted arm to snatch the picture off the table.

Now she was staring at the colorfully covered plaster wrapped around his hand and wrist, her face losing its pretty blush. "How…how did you do that?" she asked slowly.

He looked down. Damn Baxter. "They're not real tattoos."

She made a little face. Her mouth wasn't wide, but it was top-heavy, the upper lip more prominent than the lower.

Sue him, he found it fascinating.

"I know *that,*" she said. "I meant…how did you get hurt?"

He hesitated.

"I heard… Uncle Phil said…" She swallowed. "It was while you were trying to save my father, right?"

"It was while I was trying to get us both out of the danger zone," he admitted, never wishing more that the attempt had turned out differently. "To my deep, deep regret, I wasn't successful."

Layla sank back to her seat.

Vance shot a glance at Addy, who immediately scooted closer to the other woman. "Are you all right?"

"Of course." But Layla's gaze didn't move off him, even as he dropped back into his own chair. "Now I understand why you're worried about our month together, though."

He was pretty certain she didn't have a clue that his concerns ran to the limited power of cold showers over a suddenly raging, adolescent-like libido. "Yeah," he said, anyway.

"Well, you don't have to be concerned any longer."

"Good." She must understand it wouldn't work, he thought. And if *she* decided against the plan, he wouldn't have to feel guilty about the cancellation.

"Your injuries won't affect our month together at all, though." Her shoulders squared as if she was shrugging off her earlier embarrassment. "Because, of course, I'll help you while we're together at Beach House No. 9."

Oh, damn, she didn't understand anything. "Layla, no."

"It's only right." She'd gone from soft gold to steely spine. "You were hurt while trying to save my father's life. So now it's my turn."

He frowned as another blast of premonitory chill wafted across the back of his neck. "I don't know what you're talking about."

"It's karma," she said, and a little dimple fluttered near the corner of her mouth. "You took care of my father, so for the next month I'll take care of you."

CHAPTER TWO

LAYLA HURRIED FROM the restaurant and headed across the parking lot toward the Karma Cupcakes mobile bakery, grateful for the breeze against her hot face. The lunch that started awkward had ended awful and even the cheery pink-and-kiwi paint scheme of the food truck didn't raise her mood. Uncle Phil had positioned it close to the Pacific Coast Highway to catch the attention of passersby. Its awning was popped open to shade two tiny bistro tables and to reveal the glass cases displaying the baked goods she'd prepared that morning.

As she drew nearer, a car pulled into the lot and parked nearby. A woman rushed to the counter and walked away with a half dozen of Karma Cupcakes' most popular flavor, a rich devil's food enhanced with cinnamon and cloves that they called Chai Chocolate.

Layla's uncle met her eyes as their latest customer drove away. "Been here less than ten minutes and made four sales already," he announced, rubbing his hands together. "A month at Crescent Cove could turn out to be an excellent business decision."

It should have been a happy thought. Instead, misgiving was squeezing her heart like a cold hand. *A month at Crescent Cove. A month with Vance Smith.*

Layla frowned at her uncle. "I can't believe you didn't tell him I'm twenty-five," she said.

"Uh...what?" Uncle Phil looked like a professor emeritus of Surf Culture 101 in his khaki shorts, Guatemalan-weave shirt and stubby gray ponytail. "What's wrong?"

"He was expecting a ten-year-old." Recalling her moment of comprehension, another wash of heat crawled up her face. As the server made room on their table, Layla's gaze had landed on a photo of her much younger self. Suspicion had dawned, only to be confirmed scant moments later when Vance had thrust Teddy into her hands. "A *ten-year-old,* Uncle Phil."

His expression turned guilty. "I didn't realize. I was just so pleased you'd have this vacation...you know, some time to socialize with a young, uh, person about your own age."

Some time to socialize? Surely Uncle Phil wasn't trying to matchmake!

He avoided her narrowed eyes and gestured toward the fuzzy bear. "I suppose the age confusion explains the stuffed animal."

She frowned at the oversize toy clutched in her fist. Yes, when Vance had passed it over, she'd finally fathomed the mix-up—and wished for a sinkhole to open at her feet. "And *he* should have told *you* he isn't old enough to be my father, either," she grumbled.

Uncle Phil's eyes widened in what seemed to be faux-innocence. "Oh?"

Too irritated to call him on it, Layla threw herself into one of the folding chairs set out for customers who couldn't wait to sample their purchased confections. "He must be around thirty." Rangy, but with powerful shoulders and biceps. Blond hair. Eyes a startling blue. Likely in possession of a nice smile, but she wouldn't know because he hadn't found a single reason to send one her way.

Who could blame him? "He hired a *nanny*." Addy March herself had revealed that tidbit, then waved off Layla's apology for the confusion. The other woman was a graduate student researching the movie studio that had made silent films at the cove into the 1920s, and she'd voiced her intention to still use Beach House No. 9 as a home base.

Which meant Layla's own impulsive offer to "take care" of the man with the two hurt arms was wholly unnecessary. Yes, she'd embarrassed herself like that, too…though wouldn't anyone feel a certain obligation under the circumstances? He'd been injured trying to save her father. But with Addy there, if he needed to open a pickle jar or fish something from a cupboard, he didn't need Layla to lend a hand.

She glanced over her shoulder at Captain Crow's restaurant, a little shiver tracking down her spine as she remembered the moment the afternoon had gone completely haywire. While attempting to sign his credit card receipt, Vance had fumbled the pen. It had rolled across the table toward Layla and when she'd scooped it up and offered it to him, their fingertips had met.

Hers still burned.

She rubbed them against the silky fabric of her dress and directed her focus to the ring on her left index toe. It was hammered gold embedded with a tiny mother-of-pearl quarter moon. "What would you say if we just close shop and head up the highway? We can drive to Zuma. The Malibu crowd loves our cupcakes."

"I thought you were going to move into Beach

House No. 9 this afternoon," Uncle Phil said, sounding puzzled.

"Maybe I should drop the idea." That was Vance's intention. *No,* he'd declared about their upcoming month together, even after she'd invoked karma. *Not gonna happen.* Then he'd mumbled something about her father apparently forgetting she was all grown up. She'd been prepared to persist until that moment when they'd touched.

A car whined past on the nearby highway, then she heard the squeak of the food truck's door and the muffled scrape of her uncle's hemp sandals on the asphalt. He lowered himself to the opposite chair. "But we talked about all this. When he contacted me, you said yes."

"I knew it's what Dad wanted, so it's what I wanted, too. But that was before I met Vance."

Uncle Phil straightened in his seat. "He did some—"

"He didn't do anything," she said. "Nothing like you're thinking." It was what she'd done—how she'd reacted to that simple touch. It felt as if her soul had attempted to jump out of her suddenly scorched skin. She didn't like it.

"He's rattled you," Uncle Phil observed. "That's a first."

Exactly. At twenty-five, she didn't have a legion of exes, but she'd had her share of relationships. They'd been enjoyable and ended amicably, due, she believed, to her training as a soldier's daughter. She was accustomed to goodbyes, absolutely aware that tears didn't solve anything, and she didn't foolishly hope to have a long-term lock on anyone. Dating had been casual and fun, and not once had she felt as though her nerve endings had been set on fire.

Now she was proposing to spend a month at the

beach with the one man who lit her flame. A man who was a soldier to boot.

"I'm just thinking the plan's a mistake."

Uncle Phil merely raised a brow. He rarely gave out advice, and she loved that about him—that and how he'd stuck around all those times her father was deployed when she was a kid so she'd have clean clothes in her drawers and three meals on the table. He might not always have the strongest grasp on details—which might go some way to explaining why her father had instead picked Vance to carry out his last request—but her uncle had managed to sign every one of her permission slips. Maybe now she could return the favor.

"You've been going on about your trip around the world for years and my month in Crescent Cove was postponing your departure date," she said. "If I bail now, you can leave right away."

"My passport's expired."

"I saw the application in the food truck. If you pay extra they'll expedite it."

Uncle Phil rubbed a palm over the silvery whiskers on his cheek. "Well, if you're going to renege, you better get down to that beach house and let the man know."

She hesitated. Even though Vance had told her their month was off, he'd also told her he had some things of her father's to hand over. Maybe Phil could take care of that for her.... But look what had happened when she'd left him in charge before! "You're right," she said, rising. "I'll go see him."

For the final time.

VANCE HAD GIVEN Layla written instructions to Beach House No. 9 that included a hand-drawn map. The bun-

galow was situated at the opposite end of the cove from
the restaurant, which meant she had to get back on the
highway, then turn off it again onto a narrow road that
led to an even narrower track. The path of crushed shells
was only wide enough for one car and took her along
the backside of the enclave of unique homes, all of them
stuccoed or shingled in natural colors and accented with
shades that reflected the poppies, bougainvillea and
tropical greenery thriving in the summer sunlight.

At the end of the route was the place she was looking
for. It was larger than most in the cove, two stories of
dark brown shingles and rough-sawn trim painted the
blue-green of mermaid scales. Layla parked her com-
pact in the driveway that led to a double garage, then
was forced to give herself a stern talking-to in order
to exit the car.

Even then she didn't head straight for the entrance
to Beach House No. 9.

Instead, chin down to keep her profile low, she sidled
between it and the much smaller cottage next door. A
few breaths of clean ocean air would brace her for the
conversation ahead. She didn't flatter herself that Vance
Smith would wilt with disappointment because she was
leaving without further argument, but she also didn't
want him prying into the reasons for her acquiescence.
What would she say?

You make the back of my knees sweat.

I'm allergic to so much sex appeal.

How could I possibly sleep *under the same roof as
you?*

When Layla felt the give of soft sand beneath her
feet, she continued onward, not stopping until she
reached the angled shelf of damply packed grains left

by an outgoing tide. Only then did she lift her gaze, and her heart stuttered a little, overwhelmed by the beauty of her surroundings.

On her left was a craggy bluff that reached like the prow of an ocean liner into the gray-blue water. Behind her and to her right sat the charming abodes of Crescent Cove, maybe fifty of them, stretched along the sand or nestled against the vegetated hillside. In front of her was the expanse of the Pacific, an undulating surface that drew the eye toward the horizon. Above that, the sun hovered like it did in a child's painting, an unabashed yellow orb against a sky so deep an azure it appeared one-dimensional.

Her father had wanted to bring her here.

Layla's throat tightened as she heard his voice in her head. *I'll help you build an entire city of sand castles someday,* he'd promised her once when they'd had to cancel a planned beach outing due to an emergency at the base. *We'll have weeks together,* he'd told her on another occasion as he'd packed in preparation for heading back into combat. *Time to relax with a clean wind on our faces and the cool Pacific at our feet.*

It would never happen now.

Ducking the truth of that was exactly why she'd allowed Uncle Phil to handle the communication with Vance, she realized. By taking herself out of the loop, she'd put a layer between herself and the reality of her father's death.

The reality that he was never coming here to Crescent Cove. That he was never coming back anywhere.

You weren't the child of an active-duty soldier without contemplating the fact that your parent might not return alive. Her father had loved his work—the army was his passion, his identity, his occupation, his preoccupation. He'd accepted the risks. And dutiful daughter that she was, she'd responded with years of cheerful goodbyes, newsy letters and upbeat emails.

If anyone had asked, she'd have said she was as prepared for what might come as anyone could be, though she didn't dwell on potential disaster. The life of an army brat—and the tutelage of Uncle Phil—had also taught her it was better to go with the flow, to live for the moment and, while acknowledging that the other shoe might drop at any time, not to hold her breath waiting for it to happen.

But the shoe had fallen six weeks ago and she didn't think she'd taken in oxygen since.

Not to mention the daily emails she'd been sending to the account of a man no longer able to receive them.

"Are you all right?" a voice called. Vance's voice.

"Stupid wind," she said, dashing away a hot tear with the back of her hand. "I'm fine."

She felt him come up beside her and steeled herself not to make any sudden moves. He was inches away, but her skin still twitched, some kind of sexual startle response, despite her damp lashes and clogged throat.

This was why she wouldn't fight to stay with him.

Vance made a short, awkward gesture with his cast. "It's a beautiful spot."

"We always lived inland. I have a duplex northeast of here by forty minutes if the traffic's not beastly. But my dad and I talked for years about vacationing right on the beach." And this was the place he'd planned for them. It was where he'd still wanted her to come as he lay dying. Where she supposed he wanted her to say farewell.

A seagull screeched and wheeled too close, causing Layla to stumble back. Vance sidestepped, using his big body to brace hers so she didn't fall. The sensation of his broad chest against her shoulder blades sent a ripple of pleasure through her and she closed her eyes. "Layla," he murmured, his warm breath touching her temple. "Things will turn out all right."

Would they? Wrapping her arms around her waist, she forced herself to move away, planting her heels firmly in the sand and keeping her gaze focused on the horizon. How could they when she was still sending messages ending with "Love, Layla" into the ether? When she was letting herself be run off from fulfilling her father's last request?

She hugged her body tighter, reconsidering her urge to escape. Perhaps there was another, truer source of her disquiet, she mused. Maybe her reluctance had nothing to do with Vance Smith. More likely, her imagination had conjured up a heated reaction to him as an excuse not to stay.

It made so much sense. She'd dreamed up the medic's appeal in order to avoid saying her final goodbye.

That avoidance would disappoint her father, she knew. He wouldn't want her clinging to sadness through emails that were never answered and commitments she eluded. He'd made arrangements for her to spend this month at Beach House No. 9—alongside the man with whom he'd spent his final moments—and that's what she should do. What she *would* do, she decided, hauling in a long, deliberate breath.

No over-the-top and surely imaginary sexual attraction would scare her away.

She took in more air, then turned to Vance. He was

staring out to sea and she didn't give herself a moment to appreciate his handsome profile. "I'm staying," she said. It would mean Uncle Phil couldn't embark on his trip for a few more weeks, but she knew he'd understand.

Instead of moving his body, Vance shot her a sidelong glance. "I thought we'd decided."

Layla stepped close, her voice going fierce. "*We* didn't decide."

He turned to look at her now. "Layla—" he started, shaking his head.

"Doesn't keeping your word mean anything?"

At that, he stilled, his gaze dropping to the sand. She could tell he was warring with himself, but she didn't care what the fight was about as long as the battle ended her way. She took another step, getting right in his face. "You *promised*."

His eyes jumped to hers, their blue hot and bright. A moment passed. "I did, and that's important," he finally said, a muscle ticking in his jaw. "All right. Okay."

"Okay?" A ray of sunshine seemed to brighten her bereaved heart. She smiled, even as another mortifying tear blinked from her eye. When she reached to wipe it away, her fingers tangled with Vance's, which were bent on the same mission. They both froze this time, and the drop was left to roll down her cheek and off her chin.

Feeling awkward and awful all over again, Layla broke away from him. "I...I'll go get my things," she said, hurrying away as she mentally composed yet another undeliverable email. *Dear Dad, I hope I haven't just made a huge mistake....*

LAYLA WAS MISSING WHEN Vance emerged from his bedroom the next morning. She'd moved her stuff into the beach house the day before as the sun began to set and he'd left her to it when she assured him she didn't need his help. His dinner offer had been waved away, too, so he'd wandered down the beach for another meal at Captain Crow's.

When he'd returned, the door to the bedroom she'd selected had been shut. He'd been relieved, of course, and not alarmed.

But now, with dawn coloring the sky the pearly gray-pink of the inside of an abalone shell, worry niggled at him. Her bedroom door was ajar but she wasn't inside. The pristine kitchen testified she'd not even made a cup of coffee.

Addy wasn't any help. He trudged upstairs and knocked on her door, but she clearly wasn't a morning person and was just as clear that she had no idea where to find Layla.

Where the hell had she gone? And why the hell hadn't he been able to quash the deal yesterday? Not only had he found himself keeping to the plan of a month with her at Crescent Cove, he'd even assured Big Brown Bambi Eyes that "things will be all right." As if that would happen when he couldn't even keep tabs on the woman!

Christ. He had to steer clear of this promise business.

After fumbling through the brewing of a carafe of coffee, he managed to down a cup and then headed toward the beach. The briny air dampened the denim of his jeans, and his leather flip-flops kicked up a trail of cold sand behind him. Everyone else in the cove appeared to be asleep except for himself…and Layla, wherever she was.

He walked northward, trying to tamp down his concern even though he'd noted her car was parked in the driveway and her clothes still hung in the bedroom closet. Frustrated, he made to shove his hand through his short hair and cursed when his cast clunked against his skull, knocking some sense into him.

"I'm an idiot," he told the clutch of sandpipers playing a version of Red Rover with the surf line. They didn't look up. "She'll be at the bakery truck."

He'd assure himself of that, he decided. Get a glimpse of her, then return to No. 9 without giving away he'd been worried.

She was all grown up, wasn't she?

Dammit.

It was the aroma that reached him first. Even before his soles hit the parking lot's blacktop, he breathed in something sweet and delicious. His mouth watered and, though that could have been enough to confirm Layla's whereabouts, he continued toward the food truck parked by the highway, lured like the Big Bad Wolf after Little Red's basket of Grandma goodies.

Just a quick peek, he told himself, and then he'd hightail it home.

Swirls of pink-and-green paint in a paisley design covered the surface of the vehicle and Karma Cupcakes was blazoned in black letters that appeared vaguely Sanskrit in style. It should have been advance notice, he supposed, but he still started when a spare figure appeared from around the side of the truck. *"Namaste,"* the man said, pressing his palms together and giving Vance a shallow bow.

"Yeah," Vance answered. "Uncle Phil, I presume?"

The man wore baggy cargo shorts, a Che Guevara T-shirt and a puka shell necklace. Cocking his head, he grinned, then came forward with fingers outstretched. "You must be Layla's Vance."

"No!" Jesus, he wasn't Layla's anything. "I mean, uh, I am Vance Smith." The hand-to-brace shake over, Vance stepped back. "But I was just leaving—"

"Not without a conversation first," Phil said, still smiling. "It comes with coffee and cupcakes."

Hell. What could he do but agree? In seconds he found himself sitting at a small table for two positioned on the asphalt, a steaming cup of coffee in front of him as well as a paper plate filled with a selection of unfrosted bite-size treats. Their smell said oven-fresh.

"You don't play fair, Phil," he muttered as the other man sat down.

"What's that?"

"I…" His words trailed off as the food truck's order window slid open.

Layla leaned out. Her face was flushed—by an oven maybe?—and she wore a pink-and-green paisley kerchief over her hair. "Uncle Phil," she began, but then her voice died, too, as she caught sight of Vance.

She frowned, her gaze shifting under those luxurious mink lashes. *"Uncle Phil,"* she said, a warning in her voice.

"We're only eating cupcakes," her relative answered, all innocence.

She blew out a breath from her bottom lip, stirring the fringe of bangs that skimmed her eyebrows. "I'm concerned he's uncovered a latent meddling streak," she cautioned Vance. "Don't let him give you the third degree." Then she disappeared.

Layla gone was good. Much of the problem when it came to her was that Vance's mind muddied in her proximity, those tender brown eyes and pretty mouth just too diverting. Per usual, after a brief delay, his stalled brain reengaged. *He's uncovered a latent meddling streak.*

It was his turn to glare at the older man. "You should have meddled a little harder. What were you thinking? I could have been some freak! You set up your ten-year-old niece—"

"But she's not ten," Phil pointed out. "I didn't realize you thought so."

"I told you in the emails I was going to hire a nanny."

The older man shrugged. "Whoops. Sometimes the particulars pass me by."

Vance ground his back teeth, not sure if Layla's uncle was really that clueless or just playing the part. "Phil—"

"Anyway, I knew you were a friend of my brother's."

That overstated the case. "I—"

"Clearly he trusted you."

Shit. "Maybe he shouldn't have," Vance muttered.

Phil pushed the plate of cupcakes closer. "What makes you say that?"

Instead of answering, Vance selected a cake that was pale blond on the sides and golden on top. Vanilla, he figured, popping it into his mouth. But when it melted on his tongue it offered up a surprising wealth of flavor. Warm milk and brown sugar, he decided, and the luscious taste left him speechless.

"On the menu board it's Dharma Dulce—a *dulce de leche* cupcake," Phil said in response to his unspoken question. "And for the record, I didn't agree to let her spend a month with just anyone. I have my ways of discovering the truth."

Vance grunted, unwilling to open his mouth and lose any of the sweet taste still lingering on his tongue.

Phil sat back in his chair. "At twenty-three, you dropped out of college and joined the army. Spent four years as a combat medic, then you were out for a couple before being called back to active duty through the Individual Ready Reserve. You were in Afghanistan for seven months when you were injured in the process of saving my brother."

Now Vance was forced to speak. "Didn't save him," he corrected, though hell, it was painful to say the words aloud.

"No one could expect—"

"I expected!" Startled by his own outburst, Vance looked away, staring off across the parking lot. "Look, it's…"

"It's…?"

Vance shook his head. "I had a good run all those years, okay? I never lost anyone on the battlefield."

"Is that right?"

Yes, it was true. "Every time I reached a fallen man I told him the same thing. I'd say, 'I'm going to get you out of here, soldier. I'm going to get you to the best doctors and nurses we have available.'"

"And you did?"

"Every time," Vance said. "That's not to say I didn't see death while racing to the wounded. And there were guys I patched up and got onto the choppers who didn't make it out of the hospital alive. But I…I fulfilled my battlefield vow to all of them."

Phil regarded him pensively. "All of them?"

"Except one," Vance answered, closing his eyes. A small sound had them flying open again. His gaze found Layla. She was standing in the open doorway of the truck, a hand over her mouth, her brown eyes wide. Their expression transported him to the day before, to that moment when she'd passed him the errant pen and his fingers had found hers.

He held himself rigid, remembering the jolt of heat, that blast of purely physical sensation that had dried his mouth and dizzied his head. Even under its influence he'd known the reaction was trouble. The last thing he needed was some unwelcome and hard-to-control chemical combustion.

He'd been wild in his younger days, acting on impulse and always riding an edge of danger, but years at war had finally leeched that from him. Plenty of soldiers came back from combat with adrenaline still flooding their system and no place for it to go. Those were the guys who operated at the whim of their cocks instead of their common sense, and he sure as hell wasn't going to be one of them.

Because he was smarter than that now.

And because he'd made promises. Though the colonel's daughter deserved more than a horny bastard who'd do better waiting out his return to service by tossing back beers on a Mexican beach than by babysitting an enticing woman he couldn't in good conscience touch.

He probably scowled, because Layla made another little sound and then disappeared inside the cupcake truck.

"Shit," he said. "I wish she hadn't heard that."

Phil appeared unconcerned. "Now she understands

you have your own reasons for being here." He nudged the plate of cupcakes closer. "Try the one we call Berry Bliss."

Strawberry? Raspberry? Cherry? His taste buds couldn't pinpoint the exact flavor. But it definitely tasted like bliss.

"So," Phil said, "I understand you have family in California?"

Oh, yeah, Vance thought, nodding as he swallowed the cake. Layla's uncle was cannier than he initially let on. Because Vance did have a family, one with tighter connections than many, because his father and his uncle had married twins and lived in side-by-side houses on a compound at their sprawling avocado ranch about an hour from Crescent Cove. William and Roy Smith continued to lead the business together, with Vance's older brother, Fucking Perfect Fitz, and their cousin Baxter being groomed to take over.

Thinking of all that made him scowl again, as old bitterness mixed with new disquiet. Bax was sworn to secrecy, but it worried Vance that he might not be able to keep his return to the area quiet. He was determined to avoid a face-to-face with any other members of his family, including his mother.

That brought on a new thought and he shifted his gaze toward the other man. "Phil, where's Layla's mom? Her father implied he was divorced, but his ex—"

"Is in the wind. She left her marriage and her daughter behind when Layla was two. My niece has only me now," Phil said. "And for the next month, you."

"Me?" She sure as hell didn't "have" him.

Then Vance thought of finding her on the beach yesterday afternoon, how the instant she'd known she was being observed she'd brushed away the telltale tear. The save-face gesture had found some soft spot inside him. Then she'd said, *Doesn't keeping your word mean anything?* and the question had burrowed deeper.

But the truth was, she'd gotten under his skin from the moment he'd turned his head at the restaurant and glimpsed that stunner of a face. It didn't bode well, not when he'd been sure his years of rash impulses and hasty reactions were well behind him.

"Things will turn out all right," Phil said.

Vance shot him a look. That had been his line yesterday, and he still regretted it.

"You won't let her get hurt."

What could he say to that? Of course, he couldn't deny it. It was never his intention to hurt her, and the truth was, his final promise to her father had been—

"As a matter of fact," Phil went on, "you might just make her happy."

Good God, Vance thought, his chair legs scraping against asphalt as instinct sent him into full retreat. He wouldn't be trapped into giving his word on *that*. Make Layla happy?

He was the Smith family's black sheep. He'd never been able to do that for anybody.

CHAPTER THREE

WITH THE BAKING DONE for the day and having waved off Uncle Phil as he embarked on a morning-to-mid-day route that included stops at two public libraries and two parks popular with the Mommy and Me set, Layla headed back to Beach House No. 9. At the sand, she paused to remove her gladiator-style sandals, then carried them hooked on a finger as she strolled southward.

Unlike the early a.m., she didn't have the beach to herself. Little kids dug holes near the surf, bigger kids splashed through the shallows, adults lounged on towels or tossed footballs and Frisbees. She ambled, the sun striking the left side of her body, its heat tempered by the cool breeze buffeting her right. The air tasted salty and clean and she took in great gulps of it, letting it refresh her lungs and clear her head.

For fifteen minutes she was lost in the sensations of sun, sand and surf. Then Beach House No. 9 came into clear view, its windows thrown open to the breeze, a red, white and blue kite attached to a fishing pole on the second-floor balcony spinning in circles, and on the beachside deck below, the figure of a man stretched on a lounge chair in the shade of a market umbrella.

Vance Smith, denim-covered legs crossed at the an-kles. What looked to be a classic pair of Ray-Ban Wayfarer sunglasses concealing his eyes. Nothing covering his chest.

Layla's feet came to a sudden stop. *Oh.*

Oh, wow.

Maybe it was the cast and the brace, she thought. They drew attention to his heavy biceps and the tanned, rugged contours of his shoulders and chest. She knew the amount of gear combat soldiers regularly carried on their backs; those muscles of his hadn't been honed in a gym but had been carved by regularly transporting sixty to a hundred pounds of weaponry and essentials.

Her skin prickled under the soft knit of her cotton sundress. The breeze fluttered the hem, tickling the backs of her knees and making her hyperaware of her sensitivity there. Dismayed, she told herself to blink, to move, to do *something,* but she was powerless against her reaction. He'd bewitched her, and her body was struck still by the powerful sexual response she'd told herself yesterday was nothing more than her psyche's excuse—and not at all real.

Wrong.

"Watch out!" a voice called from behind her, but her preoccupation inhibited her reaction time. A body bumped Layla's, knocking her forward two unsteady steps.

"Sorry, sorry," a woman said, catching her arm to keep her upright. "The Frisbee toss went long. Are you okay?"

"Fine," Layla answered. She shot a glance toward the deck, hoping Vance hadn't witnessed her clumsiness. "It was my fault. My mind was, uh, somewhere else."

The other woman followed Layla's gaze, tossing back her hair for a better look. Then she grinned, her white teeth a match for the bikini top she wore above a pair of hip-riding board shorts. "Can't blame you there. That's some distracting man candy."

"Man candy," Layla echoed.

"He's a handsome guy," the other woman said. "No harm in looking, is there?"

No harm in looking. "You're right." Layla smiled, her alarm evaporating. There was no harm in looking and nothing particularly unusual about the fact that she wanted to. If Vance caused another woman to do a double take, then Layla's own response was perfectly normal.

Like admiring a…a pretty butterfly.

She stole another glance at him, taking in the wealth of sunbaked skin. "It's not just me, right?"

The stranger grinned again. "Hey, I'm here with a posse of firefighters," she said, turning to fling the Frisbee down the beach, "and your guy caught my eye."

Layla diverted her attention to the handful of young men pushing each other aside in order to retrieve the plastic disc. Weren't they photo spread–worthy as well with their bright swim trunks and athletic builds?

"Man candy, too," Layla pronounced, and with a farewell wave, turned toward the beach house, a new lightness in her step. Any woman alive would experience a little quickening of the blood. It was nothing uncivilized, nothing to be anxious about, and now that she'd indulged in her short session of Vance-gawking, she was even over admiring him.

The man in question sat up, pushing his sunglasses to the top of his head as she mounted the steps from the sand. She gave him her best bright smile. "Hey!"

His eyes narrowed. "You're cheery."

"I'm a morning person," she confessed. Not to mention that she'd defeated her apprehension. Thousands upon thousands of attractive men populated the world, dozens of them on this very beach even, and there wasn't anything special about her brief fascination with this particular one's appearance.

Everybody liked butterflies.

He frowned. "Butterflies?"

Oops. Had she said that out loud? "Sorry, I do that sometimes. Talk to myself when I'm, uh, developing recipes."

"Butterflies?" he asked again, more skeptical.

"Or buttermilk." She waved a hand. Then, because he still radiated suspicion, she perched one hip on the cushion at the level of his knees, all casual friendliness. Looking him straight in the eye, she smiled. "So...how do you like my cupcakes?"

His face went strangely still. It gave her a moment to study him, though from the very first she'd tried to avoid a detailed examination. Even while being dispassionate about the whole thing—as she insisted to herself she was—his looks were striking. His dark blond hair was thick and sun-lightened a brighter caramel around the edges. He had strong cheekbones and jawline, with straight, sandy-colored brows over summer-sky eyes. The face was saved from pretty by the firmness of his mouth and the strong column of his neck. Those tough-guy shoulders dispatched the last of any spoiled playboy impression left by the golden hair and angel eyes.

Weird, how her heart was racing again.

"Your cupcakes?" Vance cleared his throat, and just for a second, his gaze flicked to a spot below her neck, before quickly jerking up again. "I like your cupcakes just fine."

Oh, jeez. She felt the skin between her collarbone and modest décolletage go hot. Her "cupcakes" tingled inside the cups of her bra. Why hadn't she used a more innocuous phrase like *baked goods?* she thought, burning with mortification. "Um—"

"Oh, hell," he said quickly. "I apologize. Forget I said that. Forget I looked… Just for a second my brain went stupid."

It was the first time, she realized, she'd seen him disconcerted. Even when she'd shown up at the restaurant, unexpectedly adult, his cool demeanor hadn't broken. It was an army thing maybe, because her dad had been like that, so good at projecting chill one could suppose he had an ice tray in his chest where a heart should be.

"It's all right," she murmured, willing the warmth on her cheeks to fade.

"It's not." He shook his head. "It's… Call it combat-conditioning. Before coming back to the States I lived in the crudest of circumstances with a bunch of guys who could make *me* blush."

"I get it. It's okay."

"Nah." A sheepish grin quirked his lips. "It's not."

It was the grin. That sheepish grin. Her skin flushed hot all over again as she felt her pulse start to pound at the tender skin of her wrists and at those sensitive hollows behind her knees. She could only stare at him and the lingering rueful smile on his face.

Vance didn't seem to notice. "What can I do to make it up to you?" He reached out and casually touched her hand.

He shouldn't do that, she thought, unable to move.

Something was going on here, a situation she didn't have control over, and she'd never wanted to believe this kind of thing would happen. You couldn't choose? Without your permission this…this fever overcame you, or rather, reached out to you, or rather, exploded all around you…and you were at its mercy. Layla began to tremble.

His long fingers curled over hers. The edge of his cast pressed into her skin but she barely registered it over the hot-cold shiver that shot toward her elbow. "Vance…"

"I'm sorry," he was saying, his voice light. "I'm a bad man."

And then her hand slipped from his to press his cheek. Why? Because he wasn't a bad man, that was certain. There was a slight bristle against her palm, gritty, masculine, and the sensation pinballed more tingles to her toes and then to the top of her head. She didn't move. She just held her soft flesh against the hard plane of his cheek.

Their gazes met.

She didn't try to read anything into his because his expression had shut down and *she* wished she didn't feel this way. Knowing what was going on in Vance's mind didn't seem like any kind of win for Layla. "Hey…" she finally said. Her voice was so hoarse she had to stop and lubricate her throat. "Um."

"Yeah?"

Her hand slid away from his face. She saw his cheek muscle jump. "I have an idea." She swallowed again. "A good idea."

"Oh?"

She stood, jolting upward so fast she swayed a little. He reached to steady her, but didn't make contact.

Good. "We're here for the month. My father wanted that. But we don't have to…to…be in each other's pockets."

His gaze was so blue it should have steadied her.

But it was only more heat, not a cool, calm blue at all anymore. "Layla—"

"We'll live in the same house, but there's plenty of room. We'll go our separate ways. Live, uh, totally separate lives."

Now he touched her. The back of his fingers skimmed the flesh of her forearm. She felt it to the marrow. "No," he said. "We can't do that. If we've come this far, we've got to do it right. Because I made another promise, too."

VANCE CURSED HIMSELF for the wary look on Layla's face. What the hell was wrong with him? He knew damn well her father wouldn't approve of him messing up the agenda he'd laid out with this man-woman complication. The colonel had still considered his daughter a little girl, and Vance should be seeing her as the same.

Except she'd been sitting so close a few minutes before, her womanly hip against the denim of his jeans, her pretty face smiling at him, so that when she'd said "cupcakes" his baser self had reared its prurient head and, well…

Checked out her cupcakes.

He didn't allow his gaze to stray in that direction again, but his memory worked just fine and yes, she had very nice cupcakes.

As if she could read his mind, she shuffled back a step, and he swung his feet off the lounge and onto the planks of the deck. "Let me explain—"

"Not necessary," Layla interjected. "Really. I think my ships-in-the-night plan is a good one."

Vance stifled a sigh. It was all his fault. He should have made an effort to get laid between leaving Afghanistan and moving into the beach house, but it honestly hadn't occurred to him. Six months had passed since he'd opened Blythe's Dear John letter, and it had served as an effective sexual appetite suppressant until yesterday. Until he'd caught sight of a certain soft-eyed brunette who just happened to make his mouth water.

"You should hear me out," he said, keeping his expression harmless and his voice mild.

Layla was already edging toward the house. She touched the handle of the sliding-glass door. "Not—"

Addison slid it open from the inside. "There you are!" she said, stepping onto the deck and effectively pushing Layla toward Vance again. Addy had a yogurt cup in one hand, a spoon sunk inside like the business end of a butter churn. "Our host was looking for you earlier, knocking on my door in the dead of the night."

"The sun was up," Vance said, and tried signaling her with his eyes. *Go away, Addy.*

The message went unheeded. She crossed straight to Vance's lounge chair and, much as Layla had done minutes before, plopped herself beside him. He could barely remember Addy as a kid, but she was a curvy fairy now, with a fluff of platinum hair ringing her small head and tip-tilted green eyes. Her mouth seemed always ready for a mischievous smile.

Vance gave her a second look. If his libido was re-awakened, how about Addy? She smelled like strawberry soap, was sexy in a handle-with-care kind of way, and he'd made no pledges to her papa. Maybe she'd consider a summertime fling....

"Why are you looking at me like that?" Frowning, her green eyes crossed. "Is there something on my nose?"

"Just a sprinkle of freckles," Vance said, shaking his head. "They're cute." But they did nothing for him, he realized, damn his perverse horny urges. Punishing him for his misspent youth, he supposed, through an uninvited and inconvenient fixation on Layla.

As if on cue, the brunette cleared her throat. "I'm glad to have a chance to talk to you, Addy. I have some free time on my hands and I was thinking I could spend some of it helping you with your research."

Addy halted her spoon midtwirl and looked up. "You're interested in the silent film era?"

"Uh...I could be."

Vance decided Layla was more nervous than he thought warranted. He hadn't been *that* out of line. One little cupcake comment that he'd followed with a light-hearted apology shouldn't send her screaming for the books. He narrowed his eyes and saw her throw him a quick nervous glance, her face coloring.

She cleared her throat again. "Tell me some more about what you're investigating."

With her spoon, Addy gestured around the cove. "This place was magic in the heyday before the talkies. All the palm trees and tropical vegetation? Trucked in. Coastal California hillsides are normally sage scrub and manzanita. Thanks to the creek running through here, though, everything from the banana plants to hibiscus bushes took hold. *Et voilà,* a South Seas atoll for pirate stories, a rainforest for cannibal movies and, in one particularly famous case, Cleopatra's ancient Egypt."

Obviously Addy was enthused by her subject. Using her spoon again, she pointed down the beach. "There's a small room attached to the art gallery beside Captain Crow's that's an archive for business papers and memorabilia from Sunrise Pictures—the company that operated out of the cove. I'm the first scholar given access to all of it."

"Fascinating." Layla darted another glance at Vance, then her tongue came out to touch that top-heavy upper lip.

Off-limits, he reminded himself. *And you're way past your days of reckless rule-breaking. Even if the rules are of your very own making.*

Layla smoothed the skirt of her dress with her palms. "Well, if you could use me, I'm free after my morning baking's done." Again, she slid him a look.

Huh, Vance thought, not knowing what to make of the strange vibe he was getting from her. It wasn't just wary, it was...

"While I'm here, I'd like to keep myself very busy," she continued. "Very, very busy." This time she studiously avoided his gaze.

And then he finally got it.

Hell, he thought, surprised by his own thickheadedness. He could probably blame that on Blythe, too—it was only natural to distrust his instincts when it came to women after receiving that letter from her ending with "and I hope this won't cause any unpleasantness between us."

But now he couldn't ignore what his gut was telling him. The lust bug that had bitten him so bad? Looked like it had sunk its teeth into Layla, too. This hot-for-you thing went both ways.

Dammit.

"So what do you say, Addy?" Layla asked. "Can you use my help?"

The other woman shrugged. "If you want, but are you sure you'll have time with what you and Vance have on the calendar?"

Layla's blank look said what he didn't have to. Addy groaned. "Vance hasn't told you about that yet." She turned to him. "I'm not normally so stupid, you know. It's Baxter."

Vance's brows rose. "What does my cousin have to do with it?"

Addy jumped to her feet and started muttering. "I saw him yesterday, okay? Well, you know that. It's just, he… Never mind."

Still muttering, she stalked back into the house, slamming shut the glass door behind her. Vance and Layla both stared after her, and then he shifted his attention to the colonel's daughter once more. After a moment of tense silence, she met his gaze.

Her tongue touched her top lip and he worked not to notice it. "Do I want to know about this 'calendar'?" she asked.

"It's nothing bad," he assured her. "And not so time-consuming that you can't hang with Addy if you want, or just spend time soaking up the summer air."

Layla stepped a little closer to him, her wariness apparently lifted for the moment. "That sounds nice," she admitted. "I haven't taken any days off from cupcakes since we bought the truck."

"Your dad said you deserved a vacation. He wanted this one for you on the beach."

She drew closer, her eyes searching his face. "You… There was time? He really had time to talk to you about me?"

"Yeah." Vance softened his voice. "He wasn't in physical pain, Layla. I was able to make sure of that."

He saw her swallow. She stepped closer yet, sank again to the cushion beside him and pushed her hair away from her temples with both hands. Then they dropped to her lap. "What's this calendar all about?"

Her father's face flashed in his mind, sweat-streaked and pale, but determined as he fumbled with the precious papers in his headgear.

Isn't she beautiful, Vance? You've got to do something for her. You've got to do something for my girl.

He'd sworn he would, and nothing as temporary or as ill-advised as surrendering to his baser urges would get in the way of keeping his word. "Your father gave me a piece of paper he always kept with him—a list of things he wanted the two of you to do together. Things he thought he'd put off for too long."

"Oh, Dad." Her thick lashes swept down to hide her eyes. She brought the back of her hand to her nose. "I'm not crying. Tears always upset him—Uncle Phil, too— so I don't do that."

She was worming her way under his skin again, this stoic little soldier. Under other circumstances, Vance would have put his hands on her. As a medic, he understood the comfort of human touch. But right now it didn't seem wise. "I pledged to take his place—to do them with you," he said.

She slanted him a glance. "And what are they exactly?" she asked, her voice thick.

"A surprise. Are you okay with that?"

Her laugh sounded more sad than amused. "He liked surprises, the goof."

This time Vance allowed himself to reach out. His fingers caught in her hair and he managed to tuck a piece behind her ear. "He called it his 'Helmet List,'" Vance said, softly. "And I promised to share it with you."

As his hand fell, Layla caught it with hers, squeezing. And God, the sexual thrill was there, undeniable, but the buzz that goosed his libido also sent an electrical current toward the center of his chest. It was some kind of weird sorcery. Because the heart he thought Blythe had stomped dead thumped once. Twice. In that instant reanimating, like Frankenstein's monster bolting upright on the table.

CHAPTER FOUR

BAXTER SHOT HIS CUFFS, smoothed his palm along the silk of his striped tie and then peered around the door-jamb into the small room. Narrow windows ran along its roofline and the walls were decorated with framed movie posters and black-and-white stills, all looking to be from the silent movie era. At the room's center sat chairs arranged around a rectangular table, a closed laptop resting on its surface. No one was inside. He frowned. The salesperson of the adjacent art gallery had directed him here.

It was where he was supposed to find Addison March.

Baxter's glance landed on his Cordovan loafers and he frowned again, noting the dry film of fine sand along their shiny tops. It took him just a moment to withdraw his white handkerchief from his back pocket and dust the particles away.

When he straightened, he saw movement across the room, at the closet entrance he'd missed on first inspection. Backing out of it was Addison March's ass.

Addison—Addy, she'd told him she liked to be called all those years ago—March had a very fine ass, and he leaned one shoulder against the doorjamb and allowed himself a moment to admire it as she dragged a carton into the main area, her body bent nearly in half, her feet shuffling backward, her denim-covered bottom leading the way. He wasn't aware he did anything to give himself away, but suddenly Addy froze. A moment passed. Then, instead of rising to a stand, she turned her head and glanced around her bent elbow.

Her green eyes caught Baxter's gaze.

With a yelp, she leaped a couple of feet into the air. Upon landing, she spun to face him, her hand covering her heart. "You scared me!"

Oops. He should apologize, Baxter thought. That's what he'd come to do, after all, though not for startling her. He'd come to talk about That Night. That Night he'd thought he'd purged from his mind until seeing her yesterday afternoon.

She frowned at him. "Aren't you going to say anything?"

He took a step into the room. "Hello?"

Without a greeting of her own, she returned to dragging the box from the closet. It was unclear how heavy it was, because Addy was such a little thing he figured a ream of copy paper could make her break a sweat. His mother had worked hard to instill in him good manners—even though he might have ignored some of them after That Night—so now he moved quickly to come to her aid.

"Let me help," he said, reaching around her. She ignored him, though, her backward trajectory putting that cute ass on a collision course with his crotch. It was Baxter's turn to leap.

She gave him another around-the-elbow glance. "I've got it." With awkward tugs, she dragged the carton toward the room's table, then left it to return to the bowels of the dim closet.

He followed her, noting the stacks of cartons inside. "Do you want all of them out?"

Rather than answering the question, she said, "I've got it." Again.

It annoyed him. He was here to make things right between them and her stubbornness wasn't helping. His arm bumped hers as he shouldered past. "Just point to the one you want."

At her silence, he threw a glance over his shoulder. "Well?"

She had an odd expression on her face. Then she cleared her throat. "Honest, I don't need your help. They've been in there a long time, Baxter. They're dirty."

"I'm not afraid of a little grime."

"Really?" She tilted her head. "Because you look a little...prissy."

Insult shot steel into Baxter's spine. He played mean and stinky roundball with his old high school buddies on Saturday mornings. He regularly signed up for 10K races—beating his own time the past five outings—and just last month he'd participated in the Marine Corps' mud run. Nobody he knew had caught him taking that yoga class and he'd only agreed to it because the woman he'd been dating at the time had promised banana pancakes afterward.

Wait—were banana pancakes prissy?

The internal question made him glare at Addy, even as he noted the self-satisfied smirk curling the corners of her mouth. Without a word, he turned back around and started stacking boxes and hauling them from the closet.

"That's enough," she finally said. "This is a good start."

He paused. After the first few he'd stopped to remove his suit jacket and roll up the sleeves of his white dress shirt. His hands, as she'd predicted, were gray with filth and there were streaks of it on the starched cotton covering his chest. Addy, on the other hand, was hardly marred. With a pair of colorful cross-trainers, she wore soft-looking jeans rolled at the ankle and a T-shirt advertising a film festival in Palm Springs. Her white-blond hair stood in feathery tufts around her head and her cheeks were flushed, but Baxter thought that was Addy's normal state.

She'd appeared...excitable to him from the very first.

As if his regard made her uncomfortable, she shifted her feet. "Don't blame me if you're mucked up. I told you this wasn't work for a guy in business wear."

He blamed her for things, all right—sleepless nights, a guilty conscience—but not for the state of his clothing. "What exactly is all this stuff?" He popped the lid off the nearest box and eyed a stack of yellowed paper. "Why would you be interested in it?"

Her pale brows met over her nose. That feature was small like the rest of her and he repressed an urge to trace it with his forefinger. "You must have been in another world yesterday afternoon," she said.

"Huh?" Baxter knew exactly where he'd been yesterday afternoon. Face-to-face with the woman who had been his singular out-of-character event. His lone antimerit badge. The one and only time he'd gone off the BSLS—Baxter Smith Life Schedule.

She shrugged. "I talked about all this at lunch and I suspected then you weren't listening. Vance calls you

All Business Baxter, so I suppose while your body was sitting at Captain Crow's, your brain was back at your desk or something."

Or something. His brain had actually been recalling a summer night nearly six years before. The night of the Smith family's annual Picnic Day, a noon-through-night celebration at their avocado ranch. Open to the public, it featured food, drink and a dance band. Lights were strung everywhere…except in the dark shadowy corners where kisses could be stolen.

And peace of mind lost.

Addy gave him a strange look, then bent to ruffle through the box he'd opened. "I'm a grad student in film studies. My thesis focuses on the history of Sunrise Pictures—the company famous for its silent films made here at Crescent Cove."

She peeked into another box, then lifted it onto the tabletop. "That closet is supposed to hold everything from the studio's business records to the original scripts to the correspondence from movie stars of the time. That's what I've been told, anyway."

"Oh."

"I made a deal with the descendant of the original owner of Sunrise. I'll spend the month cataloging what I find in return for unlimited access to the material."

"Oh," Baxter said again, because he wasn't listening with any more attentiveness than he had yesterday. Then, he'd been unbalanced by the flood of memories seeing her had invoked. He hadn't liked the feeling. He was a sensible, rational, always-on-an-even-keel sort of man. Seeing Addy had reminded him of the night that impulse had overridden common sense. The night that he'd done things and said things without considering the consequences. With no regard to the Schedule.

Afterward, the memories had preyed upon his conscience. Finally, he'd managed to assuage the reawakened guilt by promising himself he'd right things with her someday. The very next time he happened to see her.

Which had taken much longer than he'd expected to come about.

But that time felt too short now because broaching That Night with this near-stranger didn't seem as if it would be an easy thing.

With a little cry of pleasure, she yanked out a handful of old-looking postcards, the ends of her hair seeming to vibrate with enthusiasm. Six years ago, she'd had masses of the stuff, curling like crimped ribbons away from her scalp and then floating in the air toward her elbows. The slightest breeze had wafted the fluffy strands over her features and across her chest, and he'd had to part it like clouds to find the heart shape of her face.

She wore a different style now, and he recognized an expensive cut when he saw one. The platinum locks had been sheared to work with her hair's texture, the curled pieces a frame for her smooth forehead, her pointed chin, her amazing green eyes. It was short enough to reveal her dainty earlobes and her graceful neck.

As she dug back into the box, he saw her swallow, the thin skin of her throat moving in the direction of her collarbone. A dandelion, he mused, with that fluff of hair and slender stem of neck. One wrong breath and he'd lose her on the breeze.

As if she heard his thoughts, she jerked her head toward him. "What?" she asked, catching him staring.

His brain scrambled for something he could say. He

couldn't just launch into his apology, could he? "Well…" Glancing away from her questioning expression, he took in the boxes and tried remembering what she'd told him about them. "What made you pursue…uh…film studies?"

She was staring at him.

Had he gotten it wrong? "Or, um, film studios?" God, he sounded like an idiot.

"Film studies." She returned her attention to the box. "I love movies. Always have, since I was a little kid."

"I remember that."

Her head whipped around. "You couldn't. You didn't know me then." She looked anxious at the thought he might.

Baxter couldn't figure out why. He frowned, searching back in his mind for a picture of Addy as a schoolgirl. But his memory stalled on her at nineteen, heat rushing to his groin as he pictured her blushing cheeks, her sun-kissed shoulders, her—

Stop! he ordered himself, shaking the images from his head. He shoved his hands in his pockets and cleared his throat. "I remember you getting a boatload of DVDs as birthday presents. Your parents threw a big bash for one occasion and invited the entire neighborhood. Vance and I breezed through…" His words trailed off as her face turned scarlet.

She rubbed her palms on the fabric of her pants. "It was my thirteenth. I can't believe you came to it."

"We were probably hoping to score some cake and make our mothers happy." He studied her still-red face. "The memory doesn't seem to be a pleasant one for you."

"I didn't like being the center of attention at that age."

Baxter frowned, thinking back again. "Yeah, I remember the party, but I don't remember you there."

"Good," Addy said, her voice fervent. She half turned from him, her focus back on the box.

The bare nape of her neck drew him closer. Six years ago, it had been hidden under all that hair. Her skin was so pretty there, smooth and vulnerable. "Which means," Baxter murmured as he moved in, driven by some undeniable impulse, "that I owe you a birthday ki—"

"No!" She spun to face him, so close their toes were an inch apart. Her voice lowered and her gaze dropped away. "No."

His attention focused on the pink perfection of her lips. They looked soft, too, and as vulnerable as that sweet spot on the back of her neck. He wanted to taste both.

"You don't owe me anything, Baxter."

He froze. Oh, God, but he did. That apology! He'd come to square things between them so he could erase her from the "Owe" side of his personal ledger book. More kissing would only add another entry.

Dammit all.

Clearing his throat again, he stepped back. "You're right. What I came to do, to *say* that is—"

"You found everything!" a female voice exclaimed.

Both Baxter and Addy swung toward the slender brunette striding into the room. She wore a man-size shirt, the tails brushing just above her knees and the ragged hems of her long jean cutoffs. On her feet were a pair of faded, shoelaceless Keds. On her face, not a stitch of makeup.

Her smile died as she caught sight of Baxter. Her gaze darted to the other woman even as she halted in her tracks. "You're all right, Addy? He's not bothering you?"

"No, no! This is an old, uh, family friend. Baxter

Smith. Baxter, this is Skye Alexander, the descendant
of the movie studio owner I was telling you about. She
manages the Crescent Cove properties."

He didn't reach out to shake her hand. Something
told him she wouldn't appreciate the contact. "Nice to
meet you."

"He was just leaving," Addy put in.

Baxter frowned at her. No, he wasn't. He had that
apology to deliver and being deterred would mean he'd
only have to face her another day. "Addy—"

"Look at this," she said to Skye, ignoring him as
she brandished a sheet of paper covered with spidery
writing. "I think it's the inventory of props from *The
Egyptian*. That's the famous Cleopatra movie we were
talking about."

Skye skirted Baxter to peer at the list in Addy's hand.
"You located it already?"

"I can't claim any special powers. The film's name
is right here on the outside of the box." Addy smiled.

Baxter had forgotten her smile. But how could that
be? She had an elfin kind of grin, the curve of her mouth
tilting the outside corners of her bright green eyes. A
dimple in her right cheek teased him.

He felt himself going hard again.

No.

To get his body under control, he tried thinking
of arctic swims, dental drilling without Novocain,
scratches in the finish of his beloved Beemer. But his
gaze didn't drift from Addy and the animation on her
face as she chattered away, something about the infamy
of the movie and the rumors of a jeweled collar that was
associated with it, a gift to the married starring actress
from her leading man-slash-lover. Scandal had ensued

and the priceless necklace had gone missing all those years ago. Rumors of its existence persisted to this day.

"The starring actress…" Skye said, quirking a brow.

"Edith Essex, my great-great-grandmother."

"Yep. And her husband was the owner of Sunrise Pictures—as well as the man who discovered her." Addy cleared her throat. "About Edith's infidelity—that could only be a story."

"But it's a relentless one, just like that of the missing necklace."

"Very, very valuable necklace." Addy hesitated. "Are you…are you still okay with me looking into those rumors? I'm interested in uncovering what made Sunrise shut down—whether in expectation of the takeover of talkies or bad business dealings or perhaps the destructive power of an extramarital affair."

"Go ahead, I'm okay with it." Skye shrugged. "Broken hearts are nothing new to the cove."

That last comment gave Addy visible pause. She shivered a little, and Baxter saw her jaw tighten.

Which gave him pause.

This clearly wasn't the time for them to talk, he decided, moving toward the exit. They needed privacy for that, and Addison March in a relaxed frame of mind.

Or better, he thought, glancing over his shoulder. Maybe with a little more time and space he could talk himself out of having such a conversation with Addy altogether.

On her second morning at Crescent Cove, Layla again walked down the sand on her way from the bakery truck to Beach House No. 9. It was another beautiful day, the sun warming the air, the breeze cooling her skin.

The waves hit the sand with an unceasing rhythm, the ocean's steady breathing.

She moved with purpose, winding her way around scattered "camps" on the sand delineated by colorful towels, beach chairs and baskets stuffed with sunscreen, magazines and sand toys. Then her gaze caught on the weaving and bobbing Stars and Stripes kite flying from the second-floor balcony of the last house in the cove. Her insides mimicked the flutter of the red, white and blue fabric and she pressed her palm against her stomach, cursing her sudden jittering nerves.

That were anticipating seeing Vance again.

This was *so* not the way the month was allowed to go, she scolded herself. They were together to fulfill a promise, nothing more. He was a soldier, on leave from war, and he'd be back to it once he healed, out of her life and out of her reach as surely as her father. *Remember that.*

Straightening her spine, she forced her feet to forward march. Letting herself develop an emotional attachment to Vance wasn't smart—and would only serve to make her soft. And ultimately…hurt.

Anyway, he wasn't interested in any sort of connection between them himself. Why would he be? It was her father's wish that had Vance staying at Beach House No. 9, not his own choice. And yesterday, after explaining to her about his commanding officer's Helmet List, he'd seemed to extinguish the sexual spark that had singed her before—almost enough to convince her it had been her imagination.

But then she'd brushed past him in the kitchen when she and Addy were putting together an easy dinner. The flash of heat she'd felt had made her stumble a little, and Vance had caught her elbow…and then his fingers had lingered on her bare flesh, his thumb stroking the tender inner skin at the joint. She'd shot her gaze to his, and he'd smiled a little, given a shrug and let her go.

Just one of those things, that casual shoulder movement had seemed to say. *Whatcha gonna do?* He'd proceeded to comment on the precise way she'd arranged the cut-up fruits and cold salads on a platter, teasing her like a pesky sister or that ten-year-old he'd expected her to be.

After dinner he'd sprawled his big body on the sofa and conked out with a baseball game playing on TV, as if her presence in an adjoining armchair didn't register. A situation which, once Addy retreated upstairs, allowed Layla the guilty pleasure of stealing glances at his long limbs and handsome features while she pretended to herself she had an interest in the outcome of the nine innings.

Game over, she'd done the courteous thing and shaken him awake. He'd responded with the same good manners, rousing himself and wishing her a polite goodnight as they peeled off into separate rooms down the hall. Not by a single blink betraying any awareness that she was a woman who'd be sleeping a mere few walls away and that he was a healthy and virile single man whose thumbprint she still felt like a new tattoo at the bend of her arm.

Layla's feet halted once more as her gaze took in the figure of a woman standing near the short flight of steps leading from the beach to No. 9's deck. She wasn't dressed in the swimsuit-and-cover-up uniform of the other females on the beach, but was instead in cropped pants and an oversize sweatshirt. Layla might have thought she was an occupant from one of the neighboring cottages, but Addy had shared that an elderly gentleman lived in the residence behind No. 9. For now, he was visiting his niece in Oxnard. As for No. 8, this month it housed a middle-aged couple on a spiritual retreat that prescribed an all-green diet and no verbal exchanges between themselves or anyone else.

Was the stranger here to see Vance then? Maybe his cool composure last night was because he wasn't single, after all.

As she approached, the other woman's gaze remained focused on the house and Layla realized the sand was muffling her footsteps. She cleared her throat to make herself known. "Can I—"

A half-swallowed shriek rent the air as the stranger spun around. Her eyes were wide and her fingers clawed at the neckline of her long sweatshirt as if the ribbed fabric was intent on strangling her. "Oh," she choked out. "Sorry."

"My line," Layla said with an apologetic grimace. "I didn't mean to scare you."

"No, no." The stranger took a breath and tucked her long, coffee-colored hair behind her ears. In her mid- to late-twenties, she was swathed in too-large clothes that did nothing to camouflage the high-cheekboned beauty of her face. "It's all my fault. I usually walk around with one eye over my shoulder, but my mind was somewhere else."

On Vance? Layla wondered.

"I'm Skye Alexander." The brunette held out a slender palm.

"Layla Parker." She shook hands, then nodded toward the beach house. "I'm staying here for the month," she said, then hesitated. If this was Vance's girl, she should probably clarify the nonsexual nature of the situation. "I don't know if Vance told you, but I'm here with him because—"

"You don't need to explain. I'm the one your father made the original arrangements with," Skye put in. "And I'm the one who Vance contacted about the change in circumstance. I manage the cove's rental properties."

"Oh."

Skye touched Layla's arm with cool fingertips. "Please accept my condolences on your loss."

Loss, Layla thought. *My loss.* Her father was gone, wasn't he? The truth dug deep again, pain stabbing the center of her chest, a burning, breathless ache. She fisted her fingers, her nails biting into her palms. *He's really gone.*

"Are you all right?" Skye asked, and her gaze darted toward the house. "Should I get Vance?"

"No." Reaching out to him when she felt vulnerable was the dumbest idea yet. "I'm good." Layla inhaled a deliberate breath, then let it go. "Just fine."

When she could almost believe that, she again addressed the other woman. "Is there something I could help you with?" At Skye's quizzical glance, she added, "You were staring at No. 9 when I walked up."

"Preoccupied with old memories," Skye admitted. "And some new ones." She smiled, and it transformed her classic, cool beauty. She looked younger, more… relaxed.

"Good memories," Layla guessed.

"I grew up at the cove." Skye made a small gesture with an arm.

"Addy March told me a little of its history. You're a descendant of the original owners?"

"That's right. My great-great-grandparents owned the property and operated Sunrise Pictures from here into the late 1920s. Its colorful history doesn't stop there, though. During Prohibition, rumrunners were known to use it as a drop-off point. Later, my family rented out the property to families during the summer. Finally, we sold off some plots for residential use—though most of the cottages we still own and lease as vacation rentals."

"My father heard about Crescent Cove from a journalist that was embedded with the troops in Afghanistan."

That radiant smile lit her face again. "Griffin Lowell."

Aaah. "Special friend?"

"Griffin and his family spent every June through September here when we were kids. Idyllic summers."

Layla nodded. "Like I said, special friend?"

Skye blinked, then shook her head. "He has a twin, Gage—" She stopped, a blush rising on her neck. "Both of them are friends, but not special like you mean."

Sure, Layla thought, *keep telling yourself that.*

"Griffin's getting married next month, to a woman—Jane—he met right here at No. 9." A small smile curved her mouth. "I warn you, there are people who claim the cottage is magic—like the love potion."

"You don't say." Layla didn't buy such romantic drivel.

Skye buried her hands in the front pouch of her sweatshirt. "But I stopped by because the party who signed for August failed to pay the balance of the deposit. I can't seem to reach them through their email address, so it's possible the house will be free next month."

"You can rent it to someone else."

"Technically, yes," Skye said. "Though I'm thinking I'll leave it open. If it's left vacant, fine, that will work with this brilliant idea I have. And if the money comes through late, I'll take it—but in exchange for the use of the house for one very important day."

"Do you want to come up on the deck?" Layla asked, finding herself curious.

Skye looked pleased. "Just the invitation I was hoping for."

Layla led the way. It wasn't the first time she'd trusted her instincts and warmed to a stranger. The transient lifestyle of an army brat had taught her to size up people in an instant, separating ally from enemy. It was a useful ability, that of forging the right friendships quickly, because military kids knew relationships weren't destined to last long.

So you also learned to let them go just as easily.

Skye came to a stop in the middle of the deck, and she seemed lost in thought again, her gaze traveling about the space. "It's perfect," she murmured.

Settling on one of the chairs surrounding a round table topped by an umbrella, Layla looked over. "Okay, I'll bite. Perfect for what?"

"A wedding."

"Let me guess." It wasn't very hard. "Griffin and... Jane?"

Skye nodded, then crossed the deck to take another chair. "I'm going to call them today and suggest it. They don't want to wait long to get married but have yet to find the right venue."

"And you think here will do," Layla said.

A smile once again curled the other woman's mouth. "Can't you just picture it?"

"Uh…" Maybe it was the result of being raised by two men, one her army officer father and the other her new-age uncle, that as a little girl Layla had been given compasses and canteens, prayer flags and polished rocks instead of paper dolls and princess clothes. Sure, she'd found her feminine side, but she'd never developed a full-blown bridal fantasy. Sharing a childhood with a pair of perennial bachelors had meant she never thought much about matrimony at all.

Perhaps it was the permanence of the idea that made it seem so foreign.

Skye wasn't waiting for her input. Instead, she was already waxing on about the upcoming nuptials. "Here's what I'm thinking. Rows of white painted chairs. An aisle created by a spread of sand on the deck. The backdrop for the bride and groom will be the view of the Pacific. Pretty, don't you think?"

"Sure." Layla shrugged, again aware of her lack of matrimonial imagination. She knew most girls honed the ability to envision romantic tableaus of frilly lace and fancy rings from an early age. "I mean, I guess it would be just fine."

"The ceremony right before dusk. White pillar candles everywhere, each one protected from the wind by hurricane glass." Skye's expression was dreamy. "Picture it…we can wrap the deck railing with swathes of white tulle and hang buckets of flowers from each post."

"Uh-huh." Layla voiced the rote agreement, though she was as unmoved as before—and felt just the slightest bit superior about that. She slouched in her seat and let her head rest against the back of the chair. Her eyes drifted shut. The candles, the flowers, the white frothy fabric had just never clicked with her.

And then, suddenly, they did.

All at once, Layla *could* picture it. The chairs, the guests, golden sand creating a wide aisle on the painted surface of the deck. Roses in buckets. Fat, sunset-colored blossoms and glossy green leaves. The tulle would ripple in a breeze that would lift the bride's veil, as well, tugging it away from her face, which would be glowing in the candlelight. The groom would catch the filmy material, his fingers trailing her cheek as he bent toward her for a kiss…

She and Skye sighed at the exact same moment.

The sound woke Layla from the beguiling daydream. Her eyes snapped open and she stared at the other woman as if she might be a witch. "You're dangerous," Layla said. "I'm not given to flights of fancy."

Skye shook her head. "It's not me. Maybe you've been touched by the magic of Beach House No. 9."

"Hey, ladies."

Vance's deep voice was a welcome intrusion into the hearts and flowers that still seemed to float about the deck. Grateful for the conversation he started up with the property manager, Layla took time to blink away the ridiculous fairy dust that lingered in her eyes.

The masculine rumble of his laugh brought her feet straight back to earth. Thank God. Mushy marriage stuff was not for her. Returned to her normal, practical self, she glanced over at Vance.

She couldn't imagine him in groom wear. Instead, he looked right at home in a pair of beat-up jeans, leather flip-flops and a short-sleeved cotton shirt that matched his eyes but was rebelliously wrinkled. The tat sleeve covered his cast.

His real-man persona blew the last of the romantic cobwebs from her brain. Yep, she absolutely felt like herself again, the unsentimental soldier's daughter who didn't believe in anything more magical than the alchemy of baking powder and heat that caused a cake to rise.

Her spine straightened, and she sat up in her chair. At the movement, Vance glanced over. He smiled.

A bubble of apprehension hiccupped in her chest. Her nerves danced again.

No.

She was too strong for this. Too unsentimental. Too smart to go soft, despite that gilded daydream Skye had painted with her words. *We've already gone over this,* Layla reminded herself.

"Hey," Vance said again, meeting her gaze. "What's up?"

"Nothing." Layla jumped to her feet, deciding she needed coffee or a shower or space she didn't have to share with the handsome combat medic. The door to the house was just a few feet away and surely she could make it there without incident.

"Hold up."

Gritting her teeth, she turned, walking backward now.

Vance caught her arm, though, and tugged her to him. At his touch, her imagination went wild once more, filling with candlelight and flowers and now naked bodies twining. A hard thigh sliding between two smooth ones. A long finger brushing a tight nipple. The aggressive thrust of a tongue.

Oh, God, Layla thought, feeling heat climb her face. Time to go!

"Too late," Vance murmured, and she realized she'd spoken aloud. "We have a date with an amusement park ride."

CHAPTER FIVE

"THE SANTA MONICA Pier?" Layla asked.

"It's the closest Ferris wheel," Vance replied. "Number one on your dad's Helmet List." Without glancing at her, he pulled his Jeep into a spot in the parking lot across the street from the famous landmark that included restaurants, shops and a designated fun zone built on a wide, pillar-supported platform extending into the Pacific Ocean.

That was his strategy. Not to look at her too long, talk to her too much or even breathe too deeply of her sweet perfume.

He'd hit upon it last night, when they'd settled in to watch a baseball game together. Hyperaware of her every move, he'd finally closed his eyes and willed himself into sleep. It was an ability soldiers developed, and he'd been grateful for it, though it had been a near thing when he'd awoken to find her leaning over him, her hand on his shoulder, the ends of her hair tickling his forehead. For a critical fifteen seconds he'd struggled against dragging her down to the couch, his libido clamoring for action.

He'd resisted then; he'd resist her now. The important thing to focus on was ticking off entries on the Helmet List, and that made the Ferris wheel poised at the end of the pier their destination.

And not looking at her too long, talking to her too much or breathing too deep in her presence his policy. It required maintaining some decided personal space, but even that shouldn't be overly onerous. They'd beat feet down the three hundred or so yards to the ride at the end of the pier, circle beneath the sun a time or two, then reverse the process and return to Crescent Cove.

No harm, no foul, no inappropriate thoughts or actions.

Avoiding Layla's perfume didn't appear to be a problem—as they crossed beneath the arched entrance, they entered an olfactory atmosphere that was a heady combination of sunscreen chemicals, fruity sno-cone syrup and salty sea air. But that cacophony of scents also heralded the fact that they weren't the only people in Southern California who'd decided on a visit today, and the throng of bodies streaming onto the pier almost immediately carried his companion away from him. Helpless to stop the outgoing tide of humanity, Vance caught a glimpse of her wide eyes as she glanced around for him.

With a groan, he surged into the crowd after her, his gaze following the top of her head, but he lost even that when a pair of rollerbladers cut across his path. Forced to a halt, he turned in a circle, searching for the lacy camisole she wore with a denim skirt. *Damn.* It was stupid to feel panicked, but a shot of sick worry coursed through him, anyway.

What the hell had Colonel Parker done, putting Vance in charge of his darling daughter? He'd been "that rowdy and reckless Smith boy" from the age of four onward, and even though he'd grown out of most of that behavior—finally—Blythe's defection had made it clear he still wasn't responsible enough for any kind of commitment.

Hell, he obviously couldn't hold on to a woman for fifteen minutes! With quick strides, he made his way to the wall beside the entrance to a small shop. Plastering his back to it, he peered down the long crowded walkway, trying to catch sight of Layla again.

Then he felt a hand pinch the sleeve of his T-shirt and yank him around, into the little store. It was littler than little, almost a closet, and filled with decals, keychains, cheap sunglasses and the woman he sought.

"There you are." Layla was laughing softly, her voice breathless. "I thought I'd lost you."

Annoyed by how relieved he felt, Vance grabbed up the darkest-of-dark lenses he could find, slipping them on his face to obscure her loveliness. Then he reached into his back pocket for his wallet and forked over five bucks to the clerk on the other side of a glass case that held Disney watches. Fakes, most likely. "You're the one who wandered off," he groused. He'd bet his bad temper showed on his face. "You need to stay in sight."

He could feel her roll her eyes. "Sorry, Grandpa Vance. But I promise to find a nice policeman or another adult I can trust if we get separated again."

"That's not gonna happen." With that, he took a firm grip on her hand and towed her back out into the sunshine.

"Hey," she protested, her fingers wiggling like fish on a line, but even with the clumsy bulk of the wrist brace impeding his grip, he didn't let go.

"Come on," he said, tugging her into the mass of visitors.

With the two of them attached, though, they made

less progress than before. The swarm of people was just that hard to navigate, or maybe it was Layla, who seemed to hang back even as he tried to move forward. He glanced down at her, noting the sudden faraway look on her face. Was there a problem?

Then it hit him. She had to be missing her dad. This was something she was supposed to be doing with him, after all. Vance couldn't blame her for finding him a poor substitute.

He leaned nearer, close enough for the scent of Layla to reach him. It was her shampoo, he decided, as the wind stirred her hair and a lock of it caught in the bristle of whiskers on his unshaven cheek. He brushed it away with his free hand, the silky strands caressing the inner surfaces between two of his fingers. "Is everything okay?"

Pausing, she glanced up. Their faces were close, her mouth near enough to kiss. "Vance, I…" She shook her head. "I'm fine."

Of course she wasn't. Her head turned away from his again and he saw she was staring at a boardwalk game, one of those carnival contests that gave you three chances to win for a dollar. He didn't think she was actually seeing it, but an idea came, anyway. "Hey," he said. "Would you like to try that?" He'd planned to hustle her down to the wheel ride, but now that seemed the wrong move. "You could win a stuffed animal."

She slid him a look. "I already have a teddy bear."

"You could win *me* a stuffed animal." He squeezed her hand. "They've got Garfield the cat. My favorite."

Before she could reply, he was steering her toward the booth. Money changed hands and the old guy running the game passed over three baseballs to Layla. Her expression bemused, she focused on the targets, three neon-painted cartoon figures just waiting to be knocked down. "You really want a Garfield?" she asked. "Because I'm pretty sure it's going to cost you."

Vance could see a little smile quivering at the corners of her lips. "Positive," he said. He positively wanted to see that smile let loose, no matter what the price.

It took twenty-two dollars and the mercy of the game operator. By the time she finally clutched her prize, that grin he'd been after came with a touch of more-fool-you. "We could have bought one of these for half that much at the toy store," she said, presenting the orange feline to him.

"Wouldn't be the same," he said, tucking it under one arm and reclaiming her hand. "Because this guy comes with the indelible knowledge that you have the throwing arm of a girl."

She punched him in the shoulder as they headed down the pier again.

"You do that like a girl, too," he said. "When you hit somebody you should curl your thumb over your fingers, not put it inside your fist."

"Really?" She blinked. "I never knew that."

"That's why boys are so much better than girls." He smiled at her little *harumph* and lowered his voice to murmur in her ear. "Stick with me, baby, I'll teach you everything you've yet to learn."

Her feet stumbled. Her gaze jerked toward his.

Just like that, the crowds evaporated. The sun seemed to shine on Layla like a beacon, burnishing the rich brown of her hair, adding a glow to the smooth curve of her naked shoulders. There was a flush on her cheeks and her mouth glistened when her tongue wet her top lip, then the bottom one.

Hell, Vance thought, a surge of lust coursing through him. It wrapped around his balls like a caress. His cock went heavy, then hard, and all he could think of was sex. Sex with Layla.

"Let's go back to the car," he murmured. There he could get his hands on her, run his fingertips against her throat, lick the slope of that golden shoulder, press his face between her breasts. His gaze flicked down to them and he saw the tight buds of her nipples pressing through her bra and the thin cotton of her top.

His belly tightened as he imagined turning his cheek and taking a nipple into his mouth, wetting the material with his tongue as he sucked it inside. "The car," he said again, his voice low and tight. "We could be there in ten minutes."

Her eyes widened. "And skip the Ferris wheel?"

The Ferris wheel? Oh, hell. *The Ferris wheel.* He was supposed to be playing Boy Scout and fulfilling a promise, not letting his imagination and his sex drive run wild.

Cursing himself, he dropped her hand like a hot potato and resumed striding onward, reminding himself of his earlier strategy. Resist her, dammit. And don't look at her too long, talk to her too much, or breathe too deeply in her presence.

And for God's sake, *no touching!*

Without glancing right or left, he led the way to the attraction at the west end of the pier. It had been the backdrop in movies and TV shows and maybe that added to its appeal. For whatever reason, the line was a zigzagger, one that would take some time and patience to get through. Resigned to it, Vance planted his feet behind the last group in the queue and prepared to endure.

"I guess it's going to be a wait," Layla said.

Vance grunted, keeping his gaze on the blue crown of the Dodgers baseball cap the guy in front of him was wearing. It was safer to pretend she wasn't even there.

"Are you all right?" she asked.

The question instantly made him feel like an ass. It wasn't her fault that he was horny and she was lovely. He shoved his hand through his hair, welcoming the clunk of his cast against his forehead. The small pain was not even close to what he deserved. "I'm fine," he said, finally glancing over at her.

She was looking up at him with those big eyes of hers, puzzlement putting a crease between her brows. "Then what's the problem?"

He wanted to bash his head all over again. Instead, he signaled to a vendor walking past and without asking first, bought her a paper cone topped with pink candy the height and consistency of a 1950s beehive hairdo. "Here," he said, thrusting it at her. If she had something to eat she wouldn't have a chance to question him further. He wouldn't have to search for some half-baked answer to explain his mood.

Of course, fate was still conspiring against him. He supposed he could have bought a worse item for her to consume—a corn dog maybe?—but watching her pluck pieces of spun sugar from the cone and slide them into her mouth wasn't soothing his lust any. After waving off an offer to share, he went back to staring at the Dodgers cap and shuffling his feet forward as the line moved ahead.

He was doing damn well with his not looking/not

speaking/not breathing policy and then it was their turn to step into a rocking bucket. Vance climbed in first, then he glanced over as Layla lifted her foot…and froze. Her stricken gaze jerked to his face.

Uh-oh. "What's the matter?"

"I…" She swallowed, hard.

The attendant steadying their seat spoke with the tone of experience. "Ferris fear," he announced. "Strikes all kinds, all ages. You can exit over there," he added, pointing with a finger.

Layla stared at Vance, her head shaking back and forth. "I have to do this."

"Of course you don't," he assured her, starting to rise.

"I have to do this." Though her face was pale and now her gaze was trained over his shoulder.

Vance glanced back and saw that the view—which gave the impression they were suspended over the ocean—wasn't helping her any. "Layla—"

"Please, Vance. It's on the list. Dad's Helmet List."

He couldn't resist the plea. "All right, all right." He slid down the molded plastic seat and reached for her hand. "Look at me. Now take a step inside. I won't let go."

She landed beside him with a gentle plop that sent the bucket swaying. Her free hand clutched his thigh.

"Look at me," he directed, angling her chin so her big brown eyes didn't leave his face. "Just keep looking at me."

"Okay," she said, and a little tremor ran through her.

He brushed at the bangs that were tangling with her long eyelashes. "You're afraid of heights?"

She made a face, both sets of fingers still clinging to

him. "I don't know. Maybe so. Or maybe it's just like the man said, Ferris fear. This is my first ride on one." Her breath caught as their bucket moved upward in order to let other people into the next on the line.

Over Layla's shoulder, the view was incredible as the ride continued to slowly revolve and the buckets were filled. The Pacific was far below them, boats gliding across its surface, leaving white trails on the glassy water. Antlike people crawled across the sand of Santa Monica Beach, some of them playing in the lacy edges of the waves. Vance didn't dare direct her attention to any of it.

Instead, he slung an arm around her shoulders and didn't flinch when she nestled closer to his chest. She was cool to the touch, and he let her snuggle close, noting that her long lashes were squeezed tightly together.

"Do you know why they call this a Ferris wheel?" he asked.

Her head moved in a short, negative shake.

"It was named after the designer, one George W. Ferris, who came up with the idea for the 1893 World's Fair in Chicago. The organizers wanted an attraction to rival the Eiffel Tower, which had wowed visitors in Paris four years before. The ride is based on the water-wheel he remembered watching move in the river near his childhood home. He completed it in four months' time and with some of his own money because no one had any faith in him."

Vance knew how that felt, didn't he? No wonder he'd always held a soft spot for ol' George, whose wife had ultimately left him and who had died penniless.

He glanced down. Layla's eyes were open now, but again fixed on his face. "How do you know all that?"

"Report in the sixth grade." With his forefinger, he

tapped his temple. "The facts never left me. Best grade I ever got on anything until I joined the army, though I never told my folks a thing about it."

Layla frowned. "Why not?"

He shrugged. "Fucking Perfect Fitz had the honor roll role already sewn up."

"Who?"

"That would be my older brother. Never a hair out of place, a grade less than A, the slightest smudge on his permanent record."

"A big brother?" She sighed a little. "I always wanted one of those." Then the wheel lurched into motion again, but instead of stopping shortly, it became a smooth revolution that took them even higher.

Layla made a little squeak and burrowed closer, her face turning into him, her mouth touching the side of his throat.

Vance sucked in a breath, trying to ignore the almost-kiss. "How about I be a big brother to you then, during this next month," he proposed, keeping his voice light. "I'll teach you how to throw, how to punch, how to survive your fears."

Of course, he didn't feel like any kind of brother to Layla at all. And damn, she felt good in his arms, despite the contact being everything he'd tried to avoid. He felt good, period, he decided with some surprise. Until now, the month had struck him as an obligation, not the least like his own vacation. Huh.

Propping his chin on the top of her head, he allowed himself, for a few minutes, anyway, to just enjoy the ride.

As the sun sank toward the horizon, Baxter climbed the steps from the beach onto the open-air deck of

Captain Crow's, his gaze sweeping the space. Looking for Addy.

He'd tried releasing his guilt. He'd tried to tell himself he could let the past go, that his effort at talking to her two days before was enough to clear it from his conscience.

But he couldn't stop thinking about the fluffy-haired female—and it was affecting his work.

All Business Baxter couldn't have that.

So he'd called Vance, and he'd not even begun to fish for the woman's whereabouts before his cousin had extended an invitation to spend the Fourth of July evening at the beach house. Baxter had quickly accepted.

Not that he'd intended to stay for long. No, he headed to Crescent Cove with the purpose of getting Addy alone and once and for all addressing what had been said and done—and then ignored—That Night all those years ago.

But upon arrival at No. 9, he'd learned the woman he sought was meeting some friends for drinks at the restaurant on the sand. Waiting for her return smacked of stalling, so he'd taken himself up the beach. Once he spotted her, he'd pull her aside and spit out the apology that had to be made.

His gaze caught on Addy's bright hair. Then he took in the fact that she already had male companionship. Surrounding her at a table were four guys in scruffy-casual: cargo shorts, T-shirts and beat-up running shoes. Baxter didn't allow himself to feel overdressed, even though his khakis and sports shirt were pressed. So what that his leather sandals were Ferragamo?

The soles of them were silent as he came up behind her. The fivesome didn't notice him as they passed around a pitcher of beer and continued their discussion. The topic of the moment was Sunrise Pictures, what Addy had discovered so far about it, how much material there was for her to sift through.

One of the men leaned close to her, his narrow fingers wrapping around her glass to top off the beer. "Sign of the jeweled collar?" he asked. His neck was skinny and his complexion pale, made sallower by the contrast to his faded black T-shirt.

Addy shook her head. "It could just be old Hollywood gossip, you know."

"It's gotta be," another of the group concurred. "Priceless treasure still undiscovered after all these years? Not a chance."

"You should let me help you look for it," Skinny Neck said, scooting his chair closer to Addy's. "I have some free time. I could be here every day." He put his hand on her arm.

The gesture made Baxter move forward. "Addison," he said.

Her head whipped around and she turned in her chair, causing the man to release his hold on her. "Baxter!" She said it with such enthusiasm he couldn't help but suppose she didn't like Skinny's touch.

Baxter didn't like it, either.

"What are you doing here?" she asked.

He yanked a free chair from an adjacent table and insinuated it between her and the guy in the black T-shirt. The other man didn't move an inch, but Addy obligingly shifted her chair to give Baxter room. "Do you mind if I join you?" he asked, when it was already done. He smiled genially about the table. "I'll buy the next pitcher."

He'd learned a thing or two about managing people over the years. Ask for permission after the deed was already done. Never overlook the opportunity to buy a round of drinks for your friends...or enemies.

Holding out his hand toward Skinny, he gave him a full-wattage Smith smile. "Baxter. Addy and I go way back."

Introductions garnered him the knowledge that the others at the table hadn't known her nearly as long. They were fellow students from her undergrad years, and all seemed to still hold a passion for film. Two worked in the industry, one was in law school, Skinny put in part-time hours as a barista while monitoring a chat room dedicated to all things movie.

And he was itching to get into that small archives room with Addison.

"Listen, Addy, I'm serious about the offer," he said, after the waitress delivered the pitcher of brew that Baxter had ordered. "I got the time, you got the access." He leaned over the table to send her a smile that was close to a leer. "We could have some fun."

Baxter glanced at Addy, then went with his instincts. "I don't think so," he told the guy.

"Huh?" Skinny frowned at him.

Sliding an arm around Addy's shoulders, he tugged her closer to his body. "Let me explain..."

What could he possibly say? Six years ago they'd had one intense night together when, for some reason he still couldn't explain to himself, he'd gone off the BSLS. He was only here now to apologize for what he'd said then and what he hadn't done afterward. Once that was over they were never going to see each other again.

"Fine," the man said, as Baxter hesitated. "I get it.

You're bumping boots with Ad. That doesn't mean I can't help her out with her research."

"Bumping boots!" Addy bristled.

Baxter cursed himself. This wasn't going the way he'd expected. He had no business laying claim to any kind of relationship with her. He was trying to lay the past to rest. *Get on with it, Smith. Get it out, then get yourself out.*

The pitcher of beer was making the rounds again and under the cover of that Baxter turned to her, sliding his arm from her shoulder so he could take both of her hands in his. They were small and cool and resisted his grip until he tightened his fingers. "Listen," he said. "I'm…I, uh…"

Crap.

He took a quick breath. "I didn't mean to insinuate something to your friends."

Her eyes narrowing, she gave a careless shrug. "Why are you here, Baxter? It can't be a coincidence. Shouldn't you be at the office?"

"It's a holiday." He actually had been at the office, but she didn't need to know that. "And it's after five." Though he often stayed at his desk beyond 8:00 p.m.

"What do you want?"

He opened his mouth, then shut it, staring as her face started to flush. Or was that merely from the pinkish cast of the lowering sun's light? In either case, it distracted him, and he chased the color downward, aware for the first time of what she wore. It was a dark blue sundress of a gauzy fabric that bared her shoulders and cupped her breasts.

Nothing good could come from allowing his gaze to linger there, so he jerked it upward, noticing the wire-

and-beads headband that was half-hidden by her curling hair. The small seeds of glass were colored red, white and blue.

It was the Fourth of July, he reminded himself, and he was here to claim independence from That Night that had been shadowing him for years, staying tucked behind his shoulder until it was clear no amount of paperwork and meetings and conference calls could keep his brain occupied enough to forget it.

"Look," he said quickly. "I'm here because we really need to talk. What happened six years ago, what we did, what I said... It should have been resolved differently." It hadn't been resolved at all, that was the problem. The things that had come out of his mouth as he held her in his arms... Sweet Lord.

His last words had been the assurance that he'd be calling her and yet he'd never dialed her number, sent an email or even posted on her Facebook wall. He didn't even know if she had an account.

"Will you accept my apology?" he asked.

She blinked, those green eyes of hers expressing... what? Christ, he couldn't read her. Six years ago she'd been an open book.

"I don't know what you're talking about," Addy said. "I...uh, *what?*"

"I don't know what you're talking about," she repeated. Her brows came together and she looked perplexed. "Six years ago? We did? You said? It doesn't ring any bells."

Baxter may have been gaping at her. She didn't recall? She didn't remember That Night? Okay, she'd had one beer, but he didn't think she'd been drunk.

Not drunk enough to forget being with him.

To forget he'd taken her virginity. And what he'd said after the fact.

As he tried to wrap his mind around her apparent forgetfulness, she turned away from him to respond to one of her college pals. Banter circled the table as they told old stories, brought up shared classes, dissed clueless professors.

Rocked by the revelation that what had eaten at him for six years apparently didn't rate a single memory in her brain's filing cabinet, Baxter sat frozen. After a few minutes he reached into his pocket for his smartphone, but even calling up his email and checking for voice messages didn't shore him up.

Work always shored him up. Routine. Sticking to the BSLS.

He only tuned back into the conversation when Skinny Neck spoke up again. He leaned around Baxter to address Addy. "As I mentioned," he said, "I can help you with your research. I have a lot of free time."

Baxter didn't like the guy on sight and even less now that he wanted to "help" Addy with such insistence. But he steeled himself to stay silent. Heck, if she didn't remember him from That Night six years ago, he shouldn't stick his nose into her affairs.

"Well?" Skinny prodded.

"Steve…" Addy hesitated, looking down, then her lashes swept up and her gaze touched Baxter's face.

He could read her well enough now, he thought. And she was clearly saying, *Help.*

Before he could even think it through, he had his arm around her again. "She doesn't need anything from you, Sk—Steve. You see, I've already volunteered my services. When Addy needs an extra hand, it's going to be mine that comes to her aid."

Then he shined his smile on her, the foundation firm beneath his feet again. If she'd forgotten what they'd been to each other, he now had a reason to be around her to remind her of it.

After that he'd apologize and put That Night to bed.

He winced, not sure if it was because of his mind's turn of phrase or the sneaking suspicion that his logic held a serious fatal flaw. But her warmth at his side felt too good for him to reason it out now.

CHAPTER SIX

LAYLA FIDGETED IN THE KITCHEN, rotating the plate of cup-cakes she'd frosted in red, white and blue as the dessert for the Fourth of July dinner she'd thought she'd be sharing with Vance and Addy. But the other woman had gone to Captain Crow's to meet some friends for a quick drink and she'd yet to return. Vance's cousin Baxter had arrived at Beach House No. 9 not long after Addy had left, and he'd headed straightaway after her. He was still MIA, as well.

That meant Layla was alone with Vance, who was seated on the couch in the adjacent living room, staring out the sliding glass door that led to the deck and then the ocean beyond. Over the past couple of days, being by herself with him was a circumstance she'd done her best to avoid. Taking her gaze off him, she played once again with the placement of the baked treats, her twitchy nerves making it impossible to keep still.

Unable to help herself, she stole another glance at Vance and wondered about his mood. Was he edgy, too? Without other company as a buffer between them, the atmosphere in the house felt heavy with tension and her nerves stretched thin enough to snap. As if sensing her gaze, he turned his head and she quickly redirected her attention to the cupcakes. Boy, were they fascinating.

Not. Even as she pretended an interest in them, she could tell that Vance continued looking at her. The nape of her neck went hot beneath the long fall of her hair and her sundress, a patriotic red with white polka dots, suddenly seemed to cling too tightly to her ribs. The nervous shuffle of her feet made the hemline tickle the sensitive spots at the back of her knees.

As more minutes passed, her breath bounced back at her from the old-fashioned tile backsplash, sounding much too loud. And was it just her, or were the walls now closing in?

Layla spun away from the countertop. "I'm going to find Addy."

In a move just as abrupt, Vance shoved up from the couch. "Sounds good to me."

He was going with her? She wanted to refuse his company, but that would only seem rude and... immature. God knew she'd appeared childish enough when she'd clung to him during the Ferris wheel ride. She couldn't help that the height of the metal contraption had triggered a bout of panic, but it only had added to her humiliation that he'd been prompted to offer up his services as her big brother.

Big brother! He was a step or two ahead of her now as they descended the stairs from the deck to the beach. The thin fabric of his short-sleeved, white chambray shirt fluttered against the strong muscles of his broad back. His ancient Levi's had a rip in one rear pocket, which drew her eyes and made her all too aware of the way only a man could fill out a pair of jeans. She heaved a sigh.

He glanced around at the sound, just in time to see

her trip on the last step. Her neck blazed hot again as his hand shot out to steady her.

"I'm fine," she bit out, jerking to avoid his touch. "I don't need a keeper."

Then, sucking in a breath, she started striding along the sand in the direction of the restaurant. Okay, maybe she sounded as if she needed a keeper.

Or a big brother.

Gah!

The mere fact that he'd mentioned it on the Ferris wheel proved he'd managed to bury what she'd thought was a mutual attraction. Or perhaps on his end it had evaporated all on its own. In any case, clearly she'd morphed in his mind from sexy to sibling.

Great.

She was still grinding away on that when they approached the deck at Captain Crow's. It was a much different place from where she'd eaten lunch a few days before. Then it had been relaxed. Quiet. The tables half-full.

Now a rock band was playing in one corner. People were sitting, standing, dancing. Drinking.

As they entered the throng, a man let out a loud whoop and lifted a scantily clad woman to his shoulders, where she swayed to the heavy beat. Vance leaned into Layla and spoke directly into her ear. "This place is nuts. Let's go back."

For another session of her nerves on the torture rack? No, thank you. Pretending not to hear him, she side-scooted around another piggyback-dancing couple. Addy had to be around somewhere.

A guy with curly blond hair, wearing board shorts and a tan, grabbed her arm as she went by. He swung her onto the dance floor, a good-natured grin on his face. "I'm Ted," he shouted over the guitar licks. "I bet you like to dance."

She opened her mouth to reply, but a different hand found her wrist and spun her away from her would-be partner. It was Vance. Her back to his front, he held her against his body with his half cast and used the other arm as a shield of sorts to push them through the throng and toward the bar.

He had the devil's own luck, or maybe it was his set expression that had two stools opening up just as they approached. He half lifted her onto the leather-strapped seat and then took the other. It was quieter here than near the dance floor, so she didn't have to resort to lip-reading to hear his opening remark. "This was a bad idea."

She frowned at him. "I might have wanted to dance, you know."

"What? With that surfer dude? He was drunk."

Her chance to retort was interrupted by the bartender, who slapped a couple of napkin squares in front of them and asked for their orders. Vance wanted beer. Layla put in for a margarita.

It didn't add to her dignity that the guy pouring drinks followed up by requesting her ID and from the corner of her eye she saw Vance smirk. Ignoring him, she fished her license out of her sundress pocket and at the bartender's satisfied nod reiterated her desire for a margarita and tacked on an order for a tequila shot, salt and a slice of lime.

Vance made a noise. "Do you think you should—"

"It's a patriotic choice," she hissed at him.

"Today's July Fourth, not Cinco de Mayo," he said as their drinks were delivered.

Instead of answering him, she grabbed up the salt-shaker that had been placed in front of her. With her tongue, she wet the web of skin between her left forefinger and thumb, sprinkled salt on the damp spot, then traded the shaker for the shot glass. After licking at the salt, the tequila went down fiery and hot, and she chased the flames by biting into the tangy citrus pulp of the lime.

Then she smiled at Vance.

His expression didn't tell her anything. He watched her coolly over his bottle of beer, unnerving her again, so she turned to the margarita and took a hefty swallow. The chill of the blended drink mitigated the burn in her belly, the combination creating a warm glow that traveled through her blood.

Feeling more relaxed than she had in days, she lifted her margarita glass again.

"Maybe you should take that slow," Vance warned.

Before she could even roll her eyes, someone on the other side of Layla spoke up. "What you doing drinking with such a Danny Downer, pretty lady?" a man's voice said.

Two guys crowded near her left elbow, both holding beers and wearing smiles as bold as the Hawaiian shirts they were wearing. "Hey," the one in the orange shirt said, nudging his friend in blue. "That's more than a pretty lady. That's the cupcake girl. Remember, we bought a dozen from her this morning after surfing?"

The second man's eyes went wide. "Hot damn, you're right." He leaned in closer, whispering as if he had a secret to tell. "Never tell my mom I said this, but you beat out anything she ever baked for me."

Layla laughed, then lowered her voice, too. "I'll keep that between the two of us."

"Wait just a minute," his friend protested, tapping his own chest with his half-full bottle of beer. "*I* saw her first. *I* realized she was Cupcake Cutie. No sharing sweet nothings with my woman."

Layla laughed again as they started squabbling about the rules of first flirtation rights and who'd ignored those very same rules just last Saturday night with the "awesome red-haired babe" at "that bar on Second Street." Clearly, the pair spent a lot of time together cruising for female companionship.

As the not-quite sober, almost entirely serious discussion continued, the blue-shirted man paused the conversation to address Layla. "Excuse us for just a minute," he said. "We'll get back to you as soon as we sort this out."

Layla could only smile at them. They were clearly harmless and actually quite good-looking if you weren't blinded by the ultraloud shirts. "I'll be right here waiting."

"Oh, God," Vance muttered. "Don't encourage them."

She turned to him. "What's the matter, Danny Downer?"

His eyes narrowed at the nickname. "They're idiots," he told her. "Boozed up and bored. They're the kind of men you should give a wide berth."

Oh, yeah, he was going all big brother, wasn't he? Doling out unsolicited advice and treating her as if she'd never been to a bar or handled a couple of flirtatious men.

Maybe he didn't think she was appealing enough to

actually have been approached by the male species before, she thought in annoyance, taking another swallow of her margarita to cool her snap of temper. "I've dated before, Vance. Kissed men. Even—don't faint—had sex. I know what I'm doing."

His mouth tightened. "Not with guys like that you don't."

Layla glanced over her shoulder at them. They were still engrossed in arguing the finer points of bro etiquette. In her judgment, their XY was of the nontoxic variety. They'd had a few beers, but so what? Yet her escort continued scowling in their direction.

She shook her head at him. "Listen, every person isn't a Boy Scout, Vance."

He turned his frown on her. "What?"

"I'm talking about you," she said, gesturing toward him with her glass. "Just because you're a squeaky-clean, always-in-control ice man—"

"Actually, I was the rowdiest party animal you'd ever have the misfortune to meet."

"What?" Layla blinked in surprise.

"You heard me." He set his beer onto the bar. "I excelled at wild and stupid from the day I bought my first fake ID until I was well into my twenties."

Her mouth dropped, then she swallowed. "What happened then?"

Vance shrugged. "Cleaned up my act."

There had to be more to the story. "Because…?"

"Because I grew out of stupid. Then I met a woman who made me…made me think. Eventually I asked her to marry me."

Layla thought her eyes might pop out of her head. "You're engaged?"

He retrieved his beer and took a swallow. "*Was* en-gaged, until about six months ago. But the point is, I recognize your friends Tweedledum and Tweedledee. That was me. Going nowhere good fast."

She still considered him too harsh on the other two, but that didn't concern her now. *Vance had been en-gaged.* And not that long ago, either. For some reason she couldn't pinpoint, the idea irritated her as much as or more than his big brother act.

Shouldn't he have told her he'd wanted to marry someone? Shouldn't she have sensed it? He'd presum-ably been in love with the woman. Was he still in love with her?

The question was on the tip of Layla's tongue when the clack of a shot glass against the polished wood sur-face in front of her redirected her attention. "Top shelf tequila," the bartender explained, then nodded at the pair in Hawaiian shirts. "From your buddies." He also slid over another wedge of lime and nudged forward the salt.

"I'll take that," the guy in orange said, scooping up the shaker and shouldering his friend away from Layla. Catching her eye, he lifted his hand and made a loose fist. Then he wet the skin between his thumb and fore-finger with his tongue. "Lick the salt off me, Cupcake Girl, it'll make your tequila shooter so much tastier."

A strangled sound came from the other side of Layla. Vance reached across her, snatching the shaker from the other man. He was standing now, drawn to his full height of six foot three, all the muscles he had from packing pounds of equipment and weapons radiating threat. "Can it, buddy. The only man she'll be licking is me."

She might have laughed, but he didn't seem the least bit aware of the suggestiveness of his remark. Neither Hawaiian-shirted guy found it amusing, either. Hands up, they backed away, murmuring all the while. "No offense" and "Sorry to bother you" and "Didn't mean to trespass."

Layla turned her head toward Vance. Even though the innocuous duo was walking away, he didn't relax his posture. He stood there, glaring at them until they disappeared in the crowd, all junkyard dog.

Or older brother.

Her ire rose as he settled back onto his stool. How dare he…

She couldn't decide exactly how she wanted to end that sentence. She only knew she couldn't stand his guardian act any more than she could stand his cool control any more than she could stand this ridiculous attraction to him she couldn't seem to stifle—and he'd been engaged just a short time ago! He was in love with someone else!

Her gaze settled on the saltshaker that he'd placed in front of her. *The only man she'll be licking is me.* Without giving herself time for second thoughts, she grabbed it up at the same moment she grabbed Vance's left hand. The cast covered part of it, but she didn't let that stop her. Before he could have a chance to yank away, she leaned down and licked a wet line across his knuckles. Then she dashed the salt there, tongued up the granules and knocked back the tequila.

Feeling triumphant, she dropped the empty glass, bit into the lime and met the gaze of her "big brother."

Her mood died as she saw the bright smolder in his eyes. The wedge of citrus fell from her limp fingers as she watched him reclaim his hand. Without breaking her gaze, he ran his own tongue across his knuckles, licking up the remaining salt granules—taking the same path as hers.

She shivered, his gesture like a stroke of wet velvet against her own skin. Goose bumps rose on her spine and feathered along the ticklish skin covering her ribs. Her intent had been to poke at him. To shake him up like he'd shaken her at the idea that he'd been engaged. That he was in love with some other woman. She'd wanted to rattle him because she despised being looked upon like a little sister.

But the blue fire in his eyes told the true story. Vance didn't think of her as a sibling any more than she thought of him as a brother.

He was just better at hiding it.

ALONE, VANCE STRODE from Captain Crow's toward Beach House No. 9. Addy had been located and she'd shared the information that Baxter had recently departed for home and that she'd be returning to No. 9 just as soon as she gave her old college pals a brief tour of the Sunrise Pictures memorabilia stash. Layla was trailing in Vance's wake, but he wasn't inclined to slow for her. He needed to put distance between them.

Again.

On the way to the bar, he'd thought the buffer of the crowd would provide that distance, but then he'd caught sight of the raucous mob. Instinct had warned there was trouble brewing. Someone was going to spill a drink on Layla, he'd thought. Or a fight would break out and she would get caught by an errant fist.

Hah.

The fight had been with himself, trying to keep from snatching her bodily away from those two aloha-shirted ass-hats on the make. As for the fist… Vance looked down at his hand and remembered her soft tongue sliding across the bumps of his knuckles, lapping delicately at him like a cat. His fingers curled, his nails biting into the hard surface of his cast as heat started smoldering in his belly.

Dammit! He had to find a way to smother this sexual fire that kept flaring up between them despite his best intentions.

Suggesting he play big brother had worked for shit. So…what now? Maybe he should initiate a civilized conversation about the situation and lay out the exact boundaries.

We're just going to be friends.

There's no point in getting any more intimate than that.

You stomp out your sexual sparks and I'll stomp out mine.

All very calm. All very polite.

He took a deep breath of damp ocean air and released it, his stress starting to ease. The straightforward approach would work, right? Honesty was always best.

His gaze narrowed as he caught sight of Beach House No. 9 just ahead. There was a male figure standing on the deck, his facial features indistinct in the dusk. But Vance didn't need to see the face to recognize who it was.

The very last person he wanted to see.

A bitter cocktail of emotions poured like bile into his belly and adrenaline blasted through his blood, once more tensing his muscles to battle-readiness. He was going to kill him, Vance thought, surging forward as his fingers again curled into fists. He was going to knock the bastard's head from his shoulders and—

No.

God, no, he decided, coming to a sudden halt. That reaction would only prove he cared a whit about the betrayal. No way would he give the guy the satisfaction. *So chill,* he told himself. *Be chill.*

Forcing a second long breath into his tight chest, he allowed himself another moment to calm. Then he mounted the stairs from the sand and confronted the man leaning against the deck railing.

"What the hell do you want?" he demanded of his brother. Because being chill didn't mean being polite.

Fucking Perfect Fitz stared at him in silence. His chiseled features hadn't changed since Vance had seen him last. He still looked as if he'd been born with a label reading Most Likely to Succeed.

"You *were* wounded," he finally said. Running his hand over the smooth layers of his nut-brown hair, he cleared his throat. "You were really hurt."

Vance ignored the comment. "How did you find me?" he asked, then made a disgusted sound as the obvious answer presented itself. "I'm going to kick Baxter's ass."

Fitz shook his head. "Not Bax— Wait, Bax knows?"

Vance pressed his lips together.

"It was Addison," his brother said, crossing his arms over his chest. "She told her mother where and with whom she was staying. I guess Mrs. March missed the memo that it was a big secret you were hiding out here at the beach, a mere hour away from your family home, and injured to boot."

"I'm not injured." He was never going to admit to Fucking Perfect Fitz that he'd been hurt by anything… or anyone. "I'm fine."

Fitz was silent another long beat, just staring at Vance as if assessing that for himself.

Impatient with the examination, Vance huffed out a breath. He didn't know how long he could keep his temper in check, so this show had better get on the road. "You never answered the question. What do you want?"

"Go visit Mom, V.T."

He found the use of the old nickname his brother had coined—V.T. for Vance Thomas—rankled as much as the order. But he stayed silent.

Fitz sighed. "She's upset."

"And Dad?" The question slipped out before Vance could haul it back. Then he shook his head. "Don't bothering answering. I'm disappointing him. What else is new?"

Fitz pushed away from the railing to stand at his full height, an inch and a half less than Vance's. "Do you know what it's like for them—for us—when you're in Afghanistan? It was bad enough the first round, after you enlisted—"

"I had no choice this time, you get that, right? They called me up, I had to go."

Fitz ignored the point. "You should have told Mom in person that you had to return—and then that you were back in California, safe. For God's sake, you should have let her know you'd been wounded."

"Yeah, because that would have eased her mind," Vance scoffed.

His brother shook his head in obvious frustration. "You forget she's accustomed to seeing you banged up."

That was the thing with family. Their ammo never ran out, making them the most formidable of combatants. Sure, Vance had once been young and stupid, but man, didn't Fitz see how it had been? His brother had done everything so older son–ideal that a guy had needed to carve out a different place for himself.

Or maybe he'd just been an immature idiot.

The thoughts only further frayed the tether on his anger. "I don't want to be having this conversation with you, Fitz."

The ambient lights around the deck clicked on, activated by the deepening darkness. In their glow, Vance saw an unfamiliar, uncertain expression cross his brother's face. "Look, V.T., about—"

"We're done talking." A few minutes more and he'd lose it. Hell, he was itching to deck his brother and he'd do so without a qualm if it wouldn't reveal how close to the bone Fitz's betrayal had cut.

"We're going to have to clear the air," Fitz started again. "We're family—"

"No," he answered, his voice turning sharp. "We're not. Not anymore."

"Vance."

Just his name in that censuring, self-righteous tone unleashed his temper. "That's it," he bit out, moving forward. "That's *it*."

One hand was reaching for the collar of his brother's shirt and his other arm was drawing back for the first punch when a tipsy female voice called up from the sand. "Va-ance," it sang. "I talked to Addy and we both want more margaritas."

Oh, God. Layla. The thought of her checked his momentum and his hands dropped. He'd forgotten all about the woman, he realized in surprise. His brother got him just that riled up. Spinning around, he saw her reach the top of the steps. She stood there, swaying slightly, her big eyes blinking against the light. It illuminated her flushed cheeks, her breeze-tousled hair and her dainty sundress. One of its skinny straps had slid down her arm and she carried both sandals in her right hand, giving her an appearance that was both innocent and suggestive.

Like she'd just finished playing a round of blanket bingo on the beach—or was about to go to bed in Beach House No. 9.

Obviously—as he should have suspected—she was a lightweight when it came to alcohol. During the short walk down the beach it must have caught up with her. One blended icy drink and those two shots had left her a little blurry around the edges.

She smiled at him, apparently oblivious to the other man on the deck. "You do know how to make margaritas, don't you, Vance? Vance-Vance-Smartypants?"

He winced. Under his watch, she was never being served tequila again.

"'Vance-Vance-Smartypants'?" Fitz murmured.

"Shut up," he said, glancing back. He was still a hairsbreadth from clobbering Fitz. It was only the presence of Layla that kept his brother's handsome face intact. "You don't get it."

"Oh, I get it very well," the other man responded. "I've met her before, or girls just like her, dozens of times. Color me unsurprised to find you're back to your old ways of picking up random beach honeys in bars."

Sanctimonious jerk. "That's no random beach honey," he gritted out. "That's Layla."

Fitz didn't appear to recognize the name. Which meant Mrs. March didn't know or hadn't shared the whole reason Vance was here at Crescent Cove.

His brother still wore a disapproving expression as he glanced at the tipsy woman, then back at Vance. "Layla, Leila, Lila, Lola, they're all the same to you. I thought you'd grown out of this kind of behavior, though. Is this because of Blythe? Because of Blythe and—"

"Layla's not a pickup, Fitz," he said, furious all over again. He couldn't stomach his brother seeing Colonel Parker's pretty daughter as some replaceable and inter-changeable temporary bed partner, just as he couldn't bear him bringing up Blythe. "We're…we're…uh…"

Fitz rolled his eyes. "Oh, sure. You're the big 'uh' to each other. Do you even know her full name?"

"Parker," Vance said from between his teeth. "It's Layla Jean Parker."

"June," his housemate corrected in a helpful tone. "Layla *June* Parker."

Fitz snorted a derisive laugh. "See—"

"You don't see anything," Vance shot back.

"I see you with yet another of your one-night stands."

Red tinged the edges of Vance's vision. "She and I aren't only together for tonight," he said. "We're liv-ing together."

Fitz's jaw dropped. "You're *living together?*"

His brother's shock revealed his misinterpretation of Vance's words. "I don't mean—" But then he halted. Why not? Why not let Fitz believe he was shacking up with a beautiful woman?

Even though part of him felt guilty for the deception, still he crossed the deck to Layla. At least the fib would prove he wasn't pining after someone he couldn't have.

He curled his arm around the colonel's daughter, at the same time catching that drooping strap and drawing it onto her shoulder. "Sweetheart," he said, wondering if he had a chance of her getting the message he was trying to send with his eyes, "this is my brother, Fitz." *Did you hear what I said, Layla? We're* together. *Play along.*

"Fitz?" she repeated in a low, sweet voice. Leaning into Vance's body, she looked owlishly up at him and then over at his brother. "He doesn't look so fucking perfect to me."

The affront on Fitz's face was priceless. All at once, both Vance's tension and his temper evaporated and he didn't know if he wanted to laugh out loud or kiss her silly. Then he remembered the conversation he'd told himself that he and Layla needed to have—*We're just going to be friends. There's no point in getting any more intimate than that. You stomp out your sexual sparks and I'll stomp out mine*—and settled for keeping her close to his side.

"I'm sure you have plans for tonight," he remarked to his brother. "Don't let us keep you."

Thank God Fitz didn't try to delay his dismissal. He strode toward the deck steps, but paused before descending. "This isn't over, V.T. Before you leave this place, you and I—and the rest of our family—are going to have it out once and for all."

"No, we're…" But the other man was already gone. *Hell.* Vance let his head drop back, staring at the stars just starting to poke through the dark blue canvas of the sky. Fucking Perfect Fitz was like a dog with a bone, dammit, and for the next month he knew exactly where to find Vance. Which meant more potential confrontations...and that his impulsive Layla-lie might have unpleasant repercussions.

Cursing himself for his rash words, he squeezed her shoulder. "Sorry. I shouldn't have involved you in that."

"I went right along with you," she said. "It was that Layla, Leila, Lila, Lola speech. If brothers are that judgmental, I don't want one, after all."

"It's Fitz's specialty," Vance murmured, gazing down at his companion. There was something different about her now. She glanced up, looking decidedly more sober—which struck him as highly suspicious.

He frowned. "Did you really just arrive, or were you down there on the beach eavesdropping?"

"I was giving you privacy, not eavesdropping," she said primly. "But then it sounded as if the conversation could use some redirection and you could use some backup."

He stared at her. Right as Vance was about to haul back and slug his brother, thus exposing the dent in his own pride, Layla Parker had sensed the danger and come to his rescue. He, the Black Sheep Smith, had a champion.

Scarcely aware of moving, Vance turned into her body so they were chest to chest. He nudged her chin higher with the same knuckles she'd licked earlier. Her breath hitched, and her breasts brushed his chest as he crowded closer. "You're not drunk, are you?" he asked, looking into those long-lashed eyes.

"Not even a little bit." A small smile quirked the corners of her mouth. "Uncle Phil claims the Parkers are special. He knows this from forty years of surfing trips down the coast of Baja. Our constitutions have a natural resistance to tequila."

"Unfortunately," Vance murmured as his mouth lowered, "I don't seem to have a natural resistance to this."

If he'd been in the mood for lying again, he might have told himself he meant only to brush his lips against hers in gratitude. But there was nothing but naked honesty in the compulsion to have his first taste of her. Her lashes swept low and he touched the tip of his tongue to the center of her lush upper lip. A sharp tremor ran through her body, but her mouth opened on the smallest of sighs. Vance slid into the tart, sweet taste of her.

God.

Fire flashed over his skin. The half-casted arm slid around her hips to yank her closer. Her body molded to his and he lifted her onto her toes, his sex—already hard—pushing into the juncture of her thighs.

It was too hot, it was too fast, it was wrong for some reason he couldn't quite dredge up now. Layla threw an arm around his neck and he angled his head to take the kiss in a different direction.

Harder. Deeper.

She stroked her tongue against his, sending his head spinning. His fingers slid over the curve of her ass, cupping her close and tight. She shuddered again, and he lifted his mouth, giving them both a moment to breathe. "Layla," he whispered, then his lips were on her again, testing the softness of her cheek and the edge of her jaw.

Her fingers dug into his shoulders as he nuzzled the hollow behind her ear. He took her mouth once more, easier now, tickling the ridged roof, teasing her with soft touches to the slick inner surfaces of her lips. From deep in her throat came a frustrated noise and he smiled, amused by the sound of it.

Her nails bit once again into his skin, she thrust her tongue into his mouth, and nothing was funny anymore.

Under the influence of that deep, hot kiss, he caressed the bare skin of her arm to her shoulder, then flicked the thin strap of her dress toward her elbow. The back of his knuckles traced its path, then slid around to brush the top slope of her breast. Layla went breathless; he could feel her sudden stillness. Her anticipation.

He let her wait a moment, then used two fingers to catch the nipple jutting through the fabric. Her body sagged into him and her head fell back. Sweet God. Her response only made his fire jump higher. He dragged his lips down her neck while toying with the hard peak of her breast.

She clutched at him, her ragged breathing loud in the night, even over the *shush, shush, shush* of the incoming waves. But then he heard something else.

Footsteps on the wooden stairs.

His head shot up and he glanced back. Addy's curly blond hair came into view. *Dammit.*

He looked back at Layla. "Sweetheart, I—"

But she was already stepping away, her stunned gaze on his face, her palms covering her red cheeks. "Uh-oh," she said.

It almost made him smile. *Uh-oh* was right. He was pretty sure he'd lost his chance to have that straightforward conversation he'd planned to stymie all this.

Which meant he had a problem. And, he remembered, it got worse.

Because as far as his family was concerned, he also had a girlfriend.

CHAPTER SEVEN

THE SOUND OF BAXTER'S whistling warned Addy of his approach. In the small room designated as the Sunrise Pictures archives, she froze, torn between wanting to run to her purse for lipstick and a hairbrush and wanting to just…run.

She didn't want him back in her life.

Not that he'd ever left it, if she was honest with herself. For years, he'd been her comfort crush, something she'd turned to like she'd turned to cookies and potato chips from the age of five until eighteen. Lonely? Bask in the memory of being in Baxter's arms. Low? Call up the memory of the effervescence flooding her bloodstream as he swung her onto the dance floor. Who knew Baxter Smith could two-step? But he had, and he'd deftly taught her the rudiments, as well, shuffling the two of them through and around the other couples as the country band played "Like We Never Loved At All."

The same Faith Hill/Tim McGraw tune Baxter was whistling now as he stepped into Addy's workspace. The sound cut off as she turned to face him.

Her heart stuttered. Oh, wow. He was a gorgeous specimen of a man. Most of the males in her world were hungry-looking grad students, with hair barbered by their mothers or their girlfriends and clothes that came straight from laundry baskets that were filled straight from dryers, without any folding in between. Baxter had left the jacket to his suit behind, but his dark olive slacks were pressed and his white shirt starched. The leather of his dress shoes and matching belt gleamed.

By contrast, Addy felt nearly naked in her nylon running shorts, tank top and lightweight hiking boots. She wasn't taller than five foot two, but it seemed there was an awful lot of bare skin between her ankles and the tops of her thighs.

Baxter appeared to be studying every inch.

She cleared her throat and his gaze took a lazy path upward. When his blue eyes met hers, he smiled. "Hey."

"Hey." Her heart fluttered again. Oh, she was in such big trouble! She knew better than to like something too much—say, donuts or ice cream—and that applied to Baxter, as well. While he might be fine in the abstract, in the flesh there was the danger that she might find him addictive.

And wallflowers-by-nature like Addy March would only be heartbroken by hoping for something real and lasting with ideal men like Baxter Smith.

With that thought pinned tightly to her mental bulletin board, she returned to stuffing her backpack with supplies for her planned hike, including a couple of water bottles and a sandwich bag half-filled with raw almonds. "If you're looking for Vance, last I saw him he was in the kitchen at the beach house."

"I'm not after Vance."

Then what was *he after?* She wanted to scream the question, but she wasn't a nineteen-year-old who'd never been kissed anymore. Self-respect demanded she maintain a hold on her dignity. So she faced him again and lifted inquiring brows, feigning a cool indifference. "Oh? Then—"

"You know why I'm here, Addy." He leaned against the doorjamb, his hands in his pockets, a faint smile on his impossibly handsome face. "You know exactly what I want."

Oh, yeah, she knew. He'd tried going there yesterday. For whatever reason, he didn't want to let that…that interlude between them go unacknowledged. Why? Did it not count as a bedpost notch if she pretended it never happened? She frowned at him, wishing his ego wasn't demanding she speak her secrets aloud.

You were a wonderful first lover.

My girlhood dreams all came true that night.

I've never forgotten a moment of it.

Those were the truths she held close to her heart. But she was keeping them there, unvoiced. They were hers, and no one else's.

Striding for the door, she brushed past him. "I'm sorry, but I don't have time for conversation," she said.

He caught the back of her shirt, halting her forward movement. "I want to help you out, Addy. Remember? I promised that at the bar."

At the bar, when she'd turned to him, looking for a way out of Steve's insistent offer. Though she'd known that guy for years, his avid interest had struck her as a little creepy, and she hadn't wanted to accept—nor had she wanted to say that to his face. Some stupid instinct had made her glance toward Baxter, and he'd immediately stepped up with a promise of his own.

"Thanks for that," she said now, without looking at him. "You helped me out of a tight spot, but I didn't take you at your word."

"Of course you didn't."

A grim note in his voice had her glancing back at him. He let go of her shirt, and used that hand to smooth his already-smooth golden hair. "But I meant it," he said. "I'm volunteering my services."

She shook her head. "I appreciate it, but I'm actually just on my way out. I'm going to hike around the cove this morning, scouting out locations used in the Sunrise movies."

"I'll go with you."

"You're dressed for a board meeting, not a tramp down the beach and a scramble in the hills."

He was already unbuttoning his cuffs. Then he loosened his tie and began stripping out of his dress shirt. As she watched his hands, the past reared up, image overlaying image. In the darkness, Baxter toeing out of his shoes. Baxter yanking his shirt over his head. Baxter's hands at the buckle of his belt.

His delicious scent had been in the air, she remembered. It had already transferred to her skin during their heated kisses, a sophisticated sandalwood cologne that she'd breathed in while trying to steady her triple-timing heart. Her nervous trembling had seemed to shake the entire bed and her skin prickled with chill... until he'd lain on top of her, his bare chest against her now-naked breasts, his erection nudging the notch between her thighs. "Addy," he'd groaned, the word hot against her ear.

"Addy," Baxter said now, standing before her in his slacks and a V-necked white T. "Ready?"

She shook her head, trying to return that old memory to its usual high shelf. "You..." Her voice was so dry she had to try again. "You can't go like that."

"Of course I can," he answered, his voice full of the confidence only the Baxter Smiths of the world could claim.

The kind of confidence that drew the Addy Marches of the world—and that clearly would be a waste of breath to argue against. She sighed. "C'mon, then," she said, digging through her backpack as she led the way outside. Finding the tube of lotion, she tossed it over her shoulder to him, certain he'd make the catch.

"What's this?"

"Sunscreen. You better use it. You look a little pasty."

Addy didn't pause to hear his response or stop to let him apply the stuff. However, a few moments later he tugged the backpack from her to stow the lotion. "Pasty, huh," he said, slinging the strap over his own shoulder. "And I looked prissy just the other day."

She didn't glance at him as she took a path along the lower edge of the bluff. He wasn't pasty or prissy, of course, but wallflowers developed a defensive edge. They didn't always let it show—mostly never—but when their backs were too tight to the wall... Now Addy felt as if her shoulder blades were jammed against thick plaster.

Trying to ignore the sensation as well as the man who brought it on, she focused on her original plan. Her first stopping place was a short ten-minute walk. Once she found the vantage point she sought, she paused to enjoy the view. They were halfway up a footpath on the hillside that rose behind the beach. The surrounding grasses were knee-length and well on their way to going from spring-green to September-blond.

"I'll take the backpack now," she told Baxter. As she unzipped the largest compartment, she noticed the sand sprinkling the tops of his loafers. Their slick soles had slid on the path's silty dirt. Pulling free her camera, she glanced up at him. "Really, Baxter, go back. You don't have the right equipment."

"Oh, I think you know I do," he said.

The ocean breeze cooled her suddenly hot cheeks. Instead of responding to that, she dropped the backpack and brought the viewfinder to her eye. With flicks of her finger, she took a shot of the stretch of ocean to the west, another of the cliff at the south of the cove and then a northward view that included that tangle of tropical vegetation planted a century before.

"What are you doing?" Baxter asked.

"Seeing if I can match some establishing shots to those in the Sunrise Pictures iconic movies. The first filmed here at the cove told the story of two strangers washed up on a deserted island. They landed on the beach with the detritus of a shipwreck and had to find a way to survive…as well as fight a fierce attraction, of course." She smiled as she focused the camera on a stretch of sand that she thought was the exact location where dashing Roger and innocent beauty Odelle had built their encampment.

When she drew the camera away, she saw that Baxter was staring at her again. Embarrassed by his scrutiny, she hitched the pack over her shoulder and set off once more, trying to pretend he wasn't dogging her footsteps. It didn't help, however. At each stop Baxter inquired about her purpose. So she ended up telling him the storylines of *The Courageous Castaways, Penelope and the Pirate* and *Sweet Safari.*

"For that one, they managed to truck in an actual

elephant. When it wasn't being used in a scene, they tethered it to a stake driven into the sand on the beach."

"That must have been quite a sight," Baxter said, rubbing the sweating side of one of the water bottles she'd brought over his forehead.

She tried not to stare as he unscrewed the top and chugged the liquid. But from the corner of her eye she watched his throat move with each swallow. "It *was* quite a sight, especially for some hapless men out for a pleasure sail from Newport Harbor one afternoon. Apparently they'd been drinking and lost track of time... and they thought possibly longitude and latitude as well when they spied the pachyderm nestled among the banana plants and palm trees."

"Did they put in for land to discover the truth for themselves?"

She nodded. "So the story goes. They were quite relieved to find themselves still in California and then thrilled to meet the famous film star Edith Essex."

"Skye's ancestor."

"A great talent," Addy said, as she turned back the way they'd come. She had enough photos for today.

On the return trip, she found herself telling Baxter more about one of the silent film era's most notable actresses. "Edith left a hardscrabble life with her family in Arizona and headed for Hollywood when she was still in her teens. Though she had ambition, she didn't consider herself particularly attractive, but on-screen...on-screen she glowed. She eventually married Max Sunstrum, the head of Sunrise."

"You've seen all her movies?" Baxter asked, keeping pace behind her.

Addy nodded. "I like imagining how much fun she

had in her acting career. I'll bet through childhood she'd escaped the reality of a large family and little food by fantasizing she was someone else, someplace else. Then finally here she was, in this beautiful location, playing characters who found adventure, battled villains and won the love of worthy men."

Baxter held a door open for her and she blinked, realizing they'd made it back to the archives room and that she'd been chattering about Sunrise Pictures and Edith Essex the entire time. "Well," she said, feeling Awkward Addy all over again as she crossed the floor and dropped her backpack on the table, "I guess you learned more about Crescent Cove's silent movies than you ever wanted to."

He shut the door, enclosing them in the small space. "I enjoyed all of it," he said. "Were you like Edith as a kid? Did you get lost in your imagination?"

She hesitated. Would he think it was weird of her?

"Don't bother answering, I can read it on your face." Smiling, he came closer to toy with the ends of her short hair. "Who would have thought Addison March had such a wild fantasy life under these pretty curls."

Addy told herself she wasn't blushing again. "I suppose that means you didn't entertain yourself by making up stories as a kid. I knew we didn't have anything in common." He was Golden Boy Baxter. His real life was ideal, ordered and full of people who cared about him. She was the girl who'd spent her childhood with imaginary friends and other solo comforts.

"That can be a good thing," Baxter said. "For example, without a woman like you I wouldn't be improving on my pasty complexion today. I can't remember the last time I took this much time away from my desk on a workday."

"Really?" The Smith family owned an expansive and successful avocado ranch and, according to her mother, had their hand in other businesses, as well. "Don't you regularly go out and, I don't know, walk among the trees?"

He shook his head. "It's not really necessary for me to do my job. Avocados are no different to me and my sixteen-hour workdays than if they were sponges or soap or birthday candles."

Addy could smell that enticing sandalwood scent of his again, so she was taking shallow breaths that made her head a little woozy. "Sixteen-hour days," she murmured. "You must enjoy your work."

"Sure," he agreed, and he lifted his hand to again play with the ends of her hair. "But I don't have the passion for it that you express about the movies."

Addy walked right into it. "What do you feel passionate about?"

Baxter's white smile grew slowly.

She hastened to step back, but he wasn't having that. Instead, he cupped her face between his hands. "I remember a passionate night," he said quietly. "Have you really forgotten it?"

"I..." Her heart was in her throat, thrumming fast. She was supposed to be maintaining her dignity, she knew that, but suddenly every instinct she had was urging her to break free. Leaping back, she slammed her hip into the table. Its legs screeched against the floor, but she ignored the sound to grab up her backpack and flee for the door.

Yet when she reached it, she paused. To hell with

pretending. She had to make sure that Baxter understood where things were between them. "Look," she said without turning around. "The past is past. I know there's no future between us."

"Oh, good," Baxter said.

She barreled through the door, but the rest of his remark followed her out into the narrow hall.

"Because that leaves the present wide-open."

LAYLA LINED UP THE CUPCAKE ingredients on the small counter in the food truck, hoping to find inspiration for a new recipe. Getting lost in the creative process would be a welcome diversion and she'd left off her usual food prep gloves in order to touch the silky smoothness of the flour and rub the fine granules of sugar between her fingertips. The results of this baking session wouldn't be sold to the public, so she could "play" with the food, and now she took hold of a sunny lemon. She rolled its cool skin between her palms, trying to focus. Lemon cakes with coconut icing? Strawberry lemonade topped with a clear glaze?

She moved to her laptop, thinking to locate her Ideas file, but when it came to life, her email program popped on-screen. It displayed the message she'd started typing in the middle of the night.

The door to the food truck squeaked open and Uncle Phil stepped inside. Layla clapped her laptop closed and swung back to contemplation of her ingredient row.

"Uh-oh," Uncle Phil said.

Uh-oh. That's what Layla had said on the deck of Beach House No. 9 as she moved out of Vance's arms the previous evening. And the why of those two syllables was what she'd been trying to distract herself from thinking about now. Vance had kissed her. They'd kissed.

Oh, how they had kissed.

At the memory of how quickly things had escalated, her skin flushed and felt stretched too tight. It had been no tentative experiment, no first-time fumbling to find the right fit. His lips had touched hers and she'd thrown herself into the wonder and the heat without worrying for an instant about the subsequent burn.

That, she'd done for about half the night afterward, reliving those moments.

"Let go," Uncle Phil murmured.

Startled, she blinked, noticing he was trying to wrestle the lemon from her grasp.

"You're going to strangle the innocent thing," her uncle said. When she still didn't release it, he tugged again and her fingers finally loosened. He glanced down at the rescued fruit, then cocked a brow at her, his expression half-humorous. "You know what Buddha would say."

Reading the direction of his mind, she made a face at him, then glanced up at the statue of the spiritual leader sitting high on a shelf above them. "I was lost in thought—lost in thinking up a recipe. I don't have an attachment to that lemon, Uncle Phil."

"Buddha tells us it's not good to have an exaggerated attachment to anything…or anyone."

She slid a guilty glance toward the laptop. Had he seen the address line on the email? Weeks back, she'd admitted to him that she'd been typing messages to her dead father. "I know it seems crazy, but—"

"Layla," Uncle Phil said quietly. "I miss him, too."

Ignoring the press of tears behind her eyes, she

smiled softly, suddenly remembering sitting between her father and Phil at the kitchen table, playing hearts. The two men, so different in temperament and ambition, had come together seamlessly over one thing— Layla. They'd both cheated like crazy to ensure she always won.

On impulse, she hugged her uncle, and he gave her an awkward pat on the shoulder then moved away.

She watched as Uncle Phil took a seat at the small table adjacent to the baking area, drawing close one of his travel guidebooks. He opened it, but she didn't think he was seeing the words any more than she'd absorbed her cupcake lineup.

Her uncle grieved for her father.

And it made her ache not only for him, but for what was going on between Vance and his brother. Sure, Fitz hadn't been particularly polite to her, but the expression on his face as he'd looked at "V.T." had spoken of something deep and painful running beneath the surface.

Of course, Vance hadn't shed any light on the situation.

Of course, she hadn't pressed, either. She had basically attached her hip to Addy's and counted the minutes until she could escape to her room and try to figure out what came next.

Did he assume they'd share more kisses…and beyond?

Or were they going to pretend that night never happened?

Layla liked the latter option. It avoided embarrassing conversation. It was safe. Because no matter how attractive the man, how hot the kisses, two things stood out.

He was a soldier. And at the end of the month he'd be out of her life.

She glanced over at Uncle Phil. In a month, where would he be? He seemed to be more attentive to his book now, and was making notes in the margin. His lifelong dream of world travel was almost in his grasp.

When he left, who would Layla have?

Her mother had gone away long ago.

Her father was never coming home again.

A dark desolation threatened to sweep over her. She straightened her spine, holding steady against it. *Don't think about being alone,* she told herself, pressing her fingertips to her forehead to contain a rising sense of panic. *Instead, think about...think about Vance and his brother.*

Fitz's attitude and Vance's near-violent tension told her there was great emotion there. A bond. And didn't she, with so little family remaining, know its value? Instead of focusing on her loss, maybe she could do something to heal the rift between the combat medic and those who cared for him.

Crossing to her laptop, she flipped it open and gazed on the email she'd written to her father.

Dear Dad,
Did you send Vance to me for a reason?

Her fingers flew over the keys, altering the question.

Dear Dad,
Did you send me to Vance for a reason?
Love, Layla.

Then she clicked Send.

THOUGH HE'D BEEN WAITING on Layla's return to Beach House No. 9, Vance jumped when she pushed open the sliding glass door and entered the living room from the deck. "Jesus," he muttered.

"Did I scare you?" she asked.

He would never admit it. Instead, he grunted, lifting the newspaper in his lap and pretending absorption in the headlines. "You've made yourself scarce all day." The sun was now low in the sky and as usual she'd left the house not long after dawn.

That's when he'd finally managed a little sleep. In the dark hours of the night, when normal people took their shut-eye, he'd lain awake staring at the ceiling.

The only noise in the house had been the wet rush of the waves against the sand, but he could have sworn he heard Layla breathing, as well.

He'd imagined it, anyway, her breath warm on his bare chest as they lay entwined in his bed. The weight of her head on his shoulder had been nearly palpable, as well as the silky coolness of her hair between his fingers as he toyed with it in postcoital contentment.

Yeah, he'd imagined that, too—the whole thing, from foreplay to afterglow.

So the truth was, she scared him all right. Because, of all the promises he'd made her father, getting naked with the man's daughter wasn't one of them.

As Vance still pretended avid interest in the news of the day, the sofa cushion beside him bounced. Glancing over, he confirmed that Layla had taken the seat beside his.

That was good, he guessed, directing his attention back to the paper. He'd been concerned when she hadn't arrived back at the house after her morning baking,

afraid awkwardness over the kiss had driven her to
avoid him. But she looked unruffled. Serene. Apparently she wasn't embarrassed, nor was she experienc-
ing the same aftereffects as he.

So, yeah, good. It made him effing thrilled to know
she wasn't suffering from the I-want-mores.

"I need a taster," she said, in that slightly scratchy
voice of hers.

His whole body jolted, the *L.A. Times* in his hands
rattling. A *taster?* Her mouth? Or— Dropping the newspaper, he whipped his head around.

Her expression innocent, Layla gazed on him, a plate
of small, two-bite cupcakes in her hands.

I'm a very bad man, he thought. *I'm a very bad man
and an idiot.* He cleared his throat. "What do you have
there?"

"A new flavor," she answered, holding the plate
closer. "Tell me what you think."

*What I think? I think you're incredibly beddable,
with those big brown eyes and that lush, top-heavy
mouth and—*

"Vance?"

With a grimace, he reined back his wayward mind. If
Layla could waltz in, apparently unaffected and feeling
no residual weirdness, surely he could act like a civilized human being. Blessing the newspaper that hid his
overeager hard-on, he reached for one of the treats. His
nose told him… "Lemon?"

"With a hint of candied ginger."

He took a bite. Tart yet delicate, the flavor spread on
his tongue and was so delicious he resisted swallowing
for a moment. Then he popped the rest in his mouth,
chewing as he reached for another.

"Good?" she asked, a hint of laughter in her voice.

"Great." Possibly addictive.

Now she did laugh. "Slow down. You're getting crumbs all over yourself." Her hand reached out and her fingertips grazed his bottom lip.

Vance stilled. So did Layla, her gaze shifting upward to lock with his. They stared at each other and their kiss played out in his memory once more. He recalled the sweet warmth of her mouth, the smooth skin of her shoulder, her moan that he felt on his tongue as he thrust deep.

The walls seemed to close in, the room becoming a bubble that contained only him and Layla. And a driving need for sex.

Of all the promises he'd made her father, getting naked with the man's daughter wasn't one of them.

Slowly, as if a sudden movement might shatter his tenuous restraint, Vance returned the cupcake to the plate. Her hand dropped from his face, but her big eyes remained trained on him.

It was up to him to end this dangerous intimacy.

"We need to go outside," he said. "I'll get a blanket. You put on a sweatshirt."

She blinked. "Why?"

"Time to put another check mark on the Helmet List."

It was the plan he'd come up with when he'd woken, bleary-eyed and nearly strangled by the disordered sheets. Getting on with the Helmet List would remind them both of their purpose at Crescent Cove.

Which wasn't to forge an unwanted closeness.

He snagged a bottle of wine and a couple of plastic glasses. They weren't elegant, but the alcohol might blunt the edge of his need. Just beyond the deck steps, he spread the blanket on the beach, then settled himself on it, assuming Layla would join him there when she was ready.

But after a few minutes he found himself impatient and he glanced around, just in time to see her put her foot on the sand. She wore a pair of stretchy exercise pants that clung to the slender length of her long legs. A matching zippered sweatshirt covered her top half. They were a striking shade of blue-green and with her wavy brown hair sliding against her shoulder, she looked like a landlocked mermaid.

Jesus, she was sexy. The way she walked gave her hips just the slightest sinuous swing, and it made his belly clench. What worried him more was the accompanying gnawing want that he found harder and harder to ignore. He'd spent years indulging every reckless urge: fast cars, extreme sports, hard drinking. He was much less practiced at self-denial.

It'll be good for your soul, he told himself. *You'll be a better man for it.*

But the man in him wasn't any better once Layla gracefully settled onto the blanket beside him. He stared at her bare ankles and toes and thought about her legs twined around his hips and those pretty feet crossed at the small of his back, bringing him deeper inside the wet and heated softness of her. Closer. As intimate as two people could be.

Damn.

He put several more inches between them, then snatched up the bottle of wine and poured two glasses. Without looking her way, he passed one over, then drank deeply of his own. Her gaze was on his face, he could feel it, so he gestured toward the horizon with his wine. "We're here to see the green flash at sunset." An object of myth and superstition, the flash was a real but rare optical phenomenon. As the trailing edge of the sun appeared to hit the water, a green light could sometimes be seen shooting upward.

"Oh." She was silent a long moment. "I've never caught sight of one. Dad—" She broke off, her breath a little hiccup that was almost a sob.

The sound made his chest ache. He looked over at her. "Honey…"

"I'm fine," she said quickly, straightening her posture as if under inspection. Her attention was focused westward, at the sun already half-hidden by the horizon line. The wind fluttered the ends of her hair. Then, as he watched, a single tear crested her lower eyelid, turning gold as it caught the last rays of light.

Vance didn't even think before sliding close and then circling her waist to draw her against him. It killed him when she lifted her shoulder in a quick surreptitious gesture to blot her cheek.

So intent on hiding her emotions. In a professional soldier's household any sentimental display had likely been looked upon as weakness.

She cleared her throat. "My father told me about one he witnessed in Iraq," she said, her voice a deeper rasp than usual. "You can see them over the tops of mountains and even clouds, did you know that?"

Vance shook his head, struck by the beauty of her face as a second golden tear rolled down her skin. His fingers itched to touch it, to brush it away, but suddenly that seemed like the most intimate act of all.

Her hand lifted her glass, but she lowered it before taking a sip. She stared at the sun as it sank lower. "Jules

Verne said that a person who sees a green flash gains special powers. They can't be deceived because they can read others' thoughts."

He grunted, alarmed by the idea. Good Christ, it would only be trouble if Layla started reading his mind.

"But according to sailors," she continued, "when the flash appears, it means a soul has crossed over."

According to Layla, too, Vance realized, watching her so-serious face. She wanted to believe she was here to see her father's soul pass on.

So Vance turned westward, as well, willing it for her with all he had. When the wind died and the final fingernail rim of the orange sun slipped into the ocean, though, there was no coinciding emerald burst of light. No souls crossed that night.

He thought *he* might just cry at the lack. Another long silence followed, the dusk deepening around them. Lights came on in the windows of the other houses in the cove, but their glow didn't touch them here, at the south end and under the darker shadow of the looming cliff.

Finally, Layla lifted her glass for a sip of wine. "Vance, can I ask you something?"

"Sure." *Ask me if I saw the flash. I'll lie my ass off and say yes if it will make you believe the colonel's peacefully passed on. Anything. Any damn thing to make you happier.*

"I have a couple of questions for you, actually." She went quiet again, as if gathering her thoughts. "First, about last night…"

His groan was swallowed back. "Maybe it would be better to leave that alone." He started to shift away from her, but she placed her hand on his thigh.

"Okay," she said easily enough. "Then answer my other question."

Darkness came swiftly once the sun was gone. Her features were already obscured, and it made him uneasy. "If I can," he said, cautious now about his promises.

She took a breath. "I wondered what the problem is between you and your brother."

He blinked. "Fitz?"

"I know you were angry at him last night and maybe I was miffed, too, but the fact is, he seemed upset—"

"I've changed my mind, Alex," he said. "I'll take About Last Night for two hundred dollars."

She let out a little startled laugh. "Really? You won't tell me why—"

"About Last Night for one thousand dollars."

No way in hell did he want to discuss the situation with his brother. Talk about personal. And intimate. Telling that story would be like plunging a fist into his belly and pulling his guts from his navel.

Yeah, he'd talk about kissing Layla and everything it shouldn't mean all night long, rather than that. But then she was silent long enough for him to think she'd abandoned uncomfortable topics altogether. Whew.

The relief came too soon, however. Because finally her head swiveled his way and words tumbled out. "I wondered—worried that you felt…well, guilty, or, I don't know, disloyal because we kissed."

"What?" He frowned. "Disloyal?" He'd felt aroused and agitated and like a goddamn saint for putting her away from him.

"Because of that woman." She took her hand from his thigh. "The one you wanted to marry."

Vance let out a short, bitter laugh. "Oh, baby, you do ask the funniest questions."

"You said you'd answer."

Oh, what the hell, he thought, and found himself laying it out for her, something he hadn't told anyone, not even the guys whom he considered brothers, the men he would have bled for, died for. The men whose wounds he'd bound. "I don't feel the slightest bit of loyalty to Blythe. That's the name of the ex. She sent me a Dear John letter a month after I'd returned to Afghanistan."

Looking up at the sky, he laughed again. "Two weeks later I received another letting me know she was already dating someone else. My brother. The one and only Fucking Perfect Fitz."

THE MORNING AFTER THE fruitless wait for the sunset's green flash, Layla was stepping into Beach House No. 9 from the sliding glass door when she heard knocking on the front entrance at the other side of the house. Because she'd been at the food truck since dawn, she was unsure of the whereabouts of the other inhabitants, and hurried forward, only to see Vance place his hand on the knob and pull open the door.

Whoever was on the other side caused him to freeze. Curious—the visitor was obscured by his wide shoulders—she continued toward him and peeked around his body. An attractive middle-aged blonde was staring at him, her blue eyes wide.

Vance released a sigh. "Mom, what are you doing here?" he asked, his tone aggrieved.

"I…" Her gaze flicked from her son's face to his cast and brace and she swallowed. "My car broke down."

"And you just happened to be at Crescent Cove when you experienced your little automotive malfunction."

"Well…" The woman's slender back straightened. She wore a simple white T-shirt and a pair of jeans, and as Layla watched she seemed to plant her sandaled feet a little firmer on the concrete stoop. "Yes."

"I'll call you a tow truck."

"I took care of that," his mother said hastily. "I just need a ride back to the ranch."

Vance radiated tension. "Absolutely not."

An expression of anguish flickered over the woman's face. Layla flinched in sympathy, but then she took a silent step back. This was none of her business. After what Vance had told her on the beach last night, she'd sworn off efforts at facilitating a Smith family reconciliation. Not now that she'd heard the details of his breakup with his fiancée.

Two weeks later I received another letting me know she was already dating someone else. My brother. The one and only Fucking Perfect Fitz.

He'd said he no longer felt loyalty to the ex. As if he didn't still love her.

Layla was having a hard time believing a word of it.

Without daring to breathe, she took another step back, but the movement must have caught the eye of the woman on the other side of the door. Tilting her head, she met Layla's gaze and stretched out slim fingers. "I'm Vance's mother, Katie Smith."

Her son turned to glare at Layla as she moved forward to shake hands. Well, what else could she do? "Layla Parker," she murmured, then sent Vance a swift glance. "Uh, excuse me. I was just on my way to—"

"Surely you have a few minutes to chat," Mrs. Smith

said, propelling herself past her son. "You can show me around this pretty bungalow."

Behind her, Vance groaned. "It's rooms and a view."

His mother tucked her arm in Layla's elbow and steered her farther into the house. "I'd love to see them."

"Don't bother resisting," Vance called out, trailing behind. "She's a bulldozer. Mom, three minutes, and then I'm calling you a cab."

Ignoring her son's remark, she came to a halt in the sunny living room. "Oh," she said, staring out at the ocean. "It's beautiful." Wearing a smile, she swung around to face Vance. Her gaze dropped to his injured arms again, and this time her cheery expression died. She put her face in her hands.

Layla's heart twisted. Even Vance softened a little. In two strides he was at his mother's side. Pulling her against him, he gave her a rough pat on her shoulder. "I'm okay, got it? Perfectly fine."

One more quick squeeze, then he moved her away. "Let me get you a glass of water," he said, disappearing in the direction of the kitchen.

Katie Smith turned to Layla, her expression still distressed. "Is he really all right?" she asked, her voice low.

What was she supposed to say to that? Physically, he was on the mend. But that rift with his brother, and maybe his father—*I've disappointed him,* she'd overheard Vance say—clearly ate at him. Her lesson had been learned last night, however. The answers to her questions had only served to reveal the complexity of the problem...one that wasn't hers to solve.

"It's not my place to get involved." With relief, she saw Vance come back in the room, bearing a tall glass. "I'll leave you two alone now."

"No," Vance said quickly. "Don't run off."

Her gaze leaped to his and she couldn't miss the entreaty in his eyes. Great. It didn't take a genius to realize that now that his mother had made her way into the house, he wanted to use Layla as a buffer. But when she'd played that role during Fitz's visit, she'd ended up being claimed as Vance's girlfriend. Surely he didn't want his mother to get the idea that—

"Please," Katie Smith said now. "I want a chance to get to know the woman in my son's life."

She already had the idea.

"Bigmouthed Fitz," Vance muttered.

Taking a seat on the couch, the mother addressed her son. "I can't tell you how happy I was to hear you've moved on. After the situation with Blythe—"

"Layla doesn't want to hear us discuss that old business, Mom."

Meaning he didn't want to dwell on that old business, Layla decided. For herself, she vacillated between a desire to not think about the ex and a desire to scratch the woman's eyes out if she ever had the chance to meet her.

Katie placed her glass on the table beside the couch. "What does it matter? If you have someone new in your heart—"

"What will it take to have you drop this?" Vance interrupted.

"A ride home," his mother promptly answered. "I promise to steer clear of any topic you like if you'll drive me there."

A muscle in Vance's jaw ticked. "Why?"

"I need to see your feet on the ranch's soil," she said.

Her honest emotion hit Layla's chest dead center again. She shot a glance at Vance and saw him wince.

He was going to give in and Layla hoped it worked out well for him.

"All right," he said, grudgingly. But as Layla moved in the direction of her bedroom, his fingers snagged the sleeve of her shirt. "You're coming, too."

"Me?" she asked, dismayed.

"Yes," he said, gaze intent. "I don't go anywhere without my girl."

"Coward," she murmured.

"Katie can put the fear in me," he agreed, whispering.

So with a sigh, Layla acquiesced. Still, she was determined to keep herself separate from Smith family business during the hour ride southeast. They left the beaches behind for the inland mountains, where the temperatures weren't moderated by the ocean breeze. Though the interior of Vance's Jeep was air-conditioned, the window glass was hot to the touch.

Vance deflected his mother's probing by telling her she'd only get two pieces of Layla's personal information that he himself provided. One, that she baked and sold cupcakes in her own gourmet foot truck, and two, that she'd met Vance through a mutual army acquaintance. Layla did add that she'd never visited Vance's home territory, the region of California known for horses, citrus and avocados, because upon exiting the freeway it felt as if she'd entered another world.

Here, roads wound over and around hillsides planted with orchards of oranges and tangerines or covered with lush groves of tall thick trees with low-hanging branches and dark green leaves. Creek beds ran alongside the pavement and sometimes the roadway itself ran through the creeks. Mostly dry now, they still provided enough water to sustain beautiful oaks, their leaves creating a canopy overhead. Every so often a side road would branch off, and she saw signs for horse breeders and another for a gourd farm.

As they took one of the smaller roads, Katie pointed out items of interest—a llama against a fence, a handful of horses and riders cresting a hill—and Vance lapsed into a heavy silence. His mother had taken the backseat, so Layla slid him a sidelong glance from the passenger side.

If he felt her regard, he didn't betray it with a flicker of expression. His face could have been carved in stone and his lips were pressed firmly together. They stayed that way until he slowed the car around yet another bend—this one more hairpin than the others. Then he glanced in the rearview mirror at his mother and uttered a single word. "Dad?"

"Not expected back until dinner. But, Vance—"

"You made a promise," he said, pulling into a gated driveway.

Katie went silent, and Layla found she couldn't speak, either, her voice stolen by the beauty around her. Wrought-iron gates stood open and up the paved driveway were two massive mission-style homes arranged around a spacious courtyard with a tall fountain in the center. Behind the buildings, a hill rose, covered in those thick-foliaged trees. To the left of one of the two dwellings was an expansive spread of land shaded by a grove of tall oaks. In the distance beyond them was another, smaller dwelling similarly styled to the other buildings. Though they'd passed other homes of different sizes and styles along the way, the Smith compound stood alone in its lush setting.

To get a better look, Layla pushed the button to unroll her window, and a blast of warm air, scented with leaves and cool water, rushed into the car. "It smells so…green. It's beautiful here." She glanced back at Katie Smith, noting the woman's attention was focused on her son's profile.

Layla whipped her head toward Vance, and for all her vows to not get involved in his family business, she was still struck by the naked longing on his face as he gazed upon his childhood home.

VANCE BLAMED IT ON LAYLA. He'd intended to keep the car running upon reaching the compound. With his foot on the brake, he'd pause just long enough to let his mother hop out and then they'd be making the return trip to Crescent Cove. But the first person out of the car had been Colonel Parker's pretty daughter and his mother had encouraged her to explore the grounds.

Hell. He couldn't let her wander without an escort, could he?

She trailed her fingers in the water showering from the courtyard's fountain, then teasingly flicked drops in his direction. "You actually grew up here?" she asked. "It's paradise."

He shrugged, glancing around. No sign of any other Smiths, thank God. His father and uncle could be anywhere, from the grove located behind the house to any of the others they owned in the area. Fitz was likely at his office in the packing house a few miles away. Baxter kept to his high-rise city offices, where he managed the numbers side of Smith & Sons Foods. Neither one of the younger men was much interested in getting his hands dirty, so they hired an independent consultant for grove management.

A waste of money in Vance's mind, and something his grandfather would have frowned upon....

His train of thought derailed as he saw Layla bend over to pick up something at her feet. She wore cuffed shorts that rode up in the back, high enough to make his mouth go dry. It wasn't accidental, he decided. She was out to make him nuts with that display of long, smooth legs.

"What are you doing?" he demanded.

She straightened, a piece of paper in her hand. Frowning, she stared at him over his shoulder. "Excuse me for objecting to litter in this lovely place."

Looking around, he realized that while his mind had been preoccupied, she'd wandered away from the compound and that he'd trailed her to the stand of massive oaks that had been their childhood go-to place for games of hide-and-seek, cops and robbers, astronauts and aliens. For a moment he saw their ghosts: Fitz and Baxter and Vance, their skinny boy bodies darting from tree to tree. Long-ago laughter echoed in his ears, causing sudden pain to pierce his chest.

Still frowning, Layla came closer. "Are you all right?"

He didn't want her to read his mood, so he ducked his head and snatched what appeared to be a flyer from her hand. "What's this?"

Bold lettering spelled out PICNIC DAY across the top.

Another pang stabbed him. His fingers crumpled the paper, but Layla pried it free before he could turn it into a ball.

"'A Smith family tradition. Thirtieth annual celebration,'" she read aloud. "'Food, dancing, fun for everyone.'"

"It's a yearly summer thing," Vance said. "They open the ranch to the public, give tours, sell stuff like barbecue and corn on the cob, bring in some ponies for the kids."

"The date's coming up," Layla said.

"Yeah," he agreed, then strode away from her as if he could distance himself from those memories, too. Didn't work for shit, because he could see his grandfather in his mind's eye, a spare and straight Clint Eastwood look-alike, welcoming visitors with a smile and a slice of buttery avocado on a long toothpick.

Vance, his shadow from the time he could toddle, standing at his elbow, feeling all cock of the walk as one of the successful Smith family. Never seeing ahead to a time when he'd lose his promised future among them.

"I don't think I've ever been this close to an avocado tree," Layla said, a little breathless, he thought, from trying to keep up with him.

Again, Vance had to glance around to ascertain exactly where he was. They were standing at the edge of the grove that was closest to the family compound. Without being aware of it, he'd picked his way across the now-dry creek that ran behind the houses. The trees began right there, an old growth that reached up and over a low mountain.

Layla took a step forward and peered into the deep shade caused by the leaves. The trees were planted between fifteen and thirty feet apart, but their spreading branches created a roof overhead and swung low to the ground. The pebble-skinned fruit were plentiful and about the size of a woman's fist, ready for harvest at any time. They only ripened once picked.

"I bet you could get lost in there," she said, taking a step into the shadows.

"Or caught by spiders and trussed up for their next meal."

It was more shriek than squeal that erupted from her mouth and the next thing he knew, he had a warm and very pretty woman cuddled against his chest. Her fingers clutched his T-shirt. "Tell me you lie."

His mouth twitching, he shook his head. "Well, they might have trouble capturing a grown woman, but I brought some girls here when I was a teenager who swore they just escaped with their lives."

Without putting a breath of air between them, she shot him a look. "Oh, I understand your ploy now. Scare the ladies into your arms."

He slid one around her waist without a twinge of guilt. She felt that good against him and being here, back at this place that had once been everything to him, had made him feel just lousy enough to need the distraction. He breathed in the scent of her hair as she turned her head, gazing into the grove again with cautious eyes.

"Still," she said, "the idea of great big spiders could put me off guacamole forever."

"Oh, don't deny yourself one of life's great treats," Vance said.

A smile curved her lips. "I admit it's a weakness of mine."

That mouth of hers could be his, Vance thought. "You know, avocados were once known as the fertility fruit. Decent women refused to eat them."

Her dark eyebrows came together. "Uh-oh. I've been indulging for years. What does that make me?"

Tempting. Delicious. Irresistible.

Maybe she read the words on his face, because she stepped back, putting a breeze-worth of distance between them. "I don't know how you could leave this place," she said, turning in a circle to take in the oaks, the avocados, the sprawling houses in the distance.

"I didn't leave," Vance said without thinking. "They threw me out."

Layla spun toward him, her mouth dropping. "No."

"No," he conceded. "It didn't exactly go like that." But the result had been the same. The spoiled young prince banished from the kingdom.

"How did it go, exactly?"

He tilted his head, staring up at the blue sky. "My grandfather bought a small grove as a young man—this grove right here—and kept buying more land as he prospered. Avocados weren't as popular then as now. He also grew tangerines and oranges—we still do—and the smell of their blossoms is as much a part of my childhood springtimes as the pollywogs swimming in the creek."

"Sounds wonderful."

"Was," Vance agreed. "And I always assumed I'd be part of the Smith ranch just like my dad and his brother. My grandfather taught me everything he knew about growing our products and I assumed I'd go into that end of the business. Bax was a business guy—he always says he might as well be counting pencils as pieces of fruit—and Fitz…Fitz just likes being in charge."

Mentioning his brother made him restless again, so Vance began walking once more, heading back in the direction they'd come. Layla dogged his heels. "So, what happened?" she asked. "Why are you on the battlefield instead of in these fields?"

He grimaced. "Short answer—at twenty-three, after my grandfather died, I demanded my place in the business. My dad refused to allow me in."

"What's the long answer?"

His smile held no humor. "Long answer is that I was too reckless to trust. I was the anti-Fitz as a kid—liked recess instead of reading, sports instead of studying. Then adolescence arrived and I perfected that position, becoming the absolute best at playing, partying and generally screwing around."

They'd made it back to his car. Layla leaned against the side and he followed suit. "Lots of kids take a while to find their place," she said.

"I *lost* my place." He tried shrugging off the deep anger welling inside of him. He was never sure who he was angrier at—himself or the rest of the Smiths. "But my grandfather had made me a promise. I expected that my father would honor that. When I realized he wouldn't...I joined the army."

"Vance..." Biting her lip, Layla looked over. Her warm fingers found his beneath the cast, and she squeezed. "I'm sorry."

Embarrassed, he disentangled their hands and stepped away to study his rear tire. "Jesus, *I'm* sorry for spilling my stupid sob story that way. You'll think I'm..." He didn't know what. A fuck-up? A whiner?

"You're my hero," she said.

He sent her a sharp glance. *"What?"*

"Vance." She smiled, and it was as sad as heartbreak. "You are, you know that, right?"

"No." He was the black sheep. Trouble. The man who had failed to bring her father home. "Don't say such a thing."

"You saved me from the spiders, though. I really was about to walk inside there."

Her obvious conversational bypass relieved him, bringing out a reluctant grin. "All right. I guess I should get a medal for that." He looked around, noticing that it was afternoon now and he didn't want to chance running into his father. "Let's go."

"I need to say goodbye to your mother first."

He nodded. "That will get you your own commendation."

Layla tilted her head, and he tried not to notice the sweet curve of her cheek. "For the girlfriend thing," he clarified. "Thanks for going along with that. It gets Mom off my back…and makes her happier, too."

With her own nod, Layla turned toward the house where he'd grown up. When had he last sat down in there for a family meal? Suddenly, he didn't want to count the years. With jerky movements, he let himself into the driver's seat.

C'mon, Layla, he thought. *I want out of here.*

The place evoked too many memories, too many regrets, too many disappointments. All of them hurt so damn much. Back at the beach he'd be able to breathe without pain again.

The front door to the house opened and Layla and his mother both stepped out. Yeah, he supposed he needed to say his own goodbye. The look on his mom's face when she'd seen his cast and brace at Beach House No. 9 was only another memory he wished he could erase.

Layla climbed into the passenger seat as his mom

came around to his window. "'Bye," he said to her, surprised by the gruffness of his voice. "I'll try to remember to give you a call before I return—"

"On Picnic Day," his mother said, beaming. "Layla and I have it all figured out."

"What?"

"Just following through with that girlfriend thing," the young woman beside him murmured. "Your mom came up with the idea that I should bring the cupcake truck."

"We have the barbecue caterers coming, and the taco truck, but nothing for dessert."

"Mom—"

"It's a great opportunity for her. Don't you want to support your girl's business?"

His jaw fell and he glanced over at "his girl."

She merely shrugged. Smiled. And Vance realized he was screwed. He'd be back at the ranch before he knew it.

And that, too, was all Layla's fault.

LAYLA HEARD VANCE curse under his breath as they turned out of the Smiths' driveway and onto the road. He glanced back in the rearview mirror. "Girlfriend," he said, like the word tasted bad.

"Hey," she protested, "it wasn't my idea." And it was a dangerous label for what she was to him. Saying it too much, playing that role too often, well, it could make her care for him.

Or make her care for him more. Because when he'd said, *They threw me out,* in that calm, cool voice, she'd stared at his expressionless face and fought the urge to wrap her arms around him.

"I need a drink," he muttered, and he took a turn she didn't remember. In short minutes they'd reached a crossroads with a mom-and-pop gas station attached to a small convenience store. Kitty-corner from them was a cozy-looking tavern beside a small parking lot.

Once inside the building, she realized it was bigger than she'd thought. Beyond the bar was a stylish dining area, and though it was a little after four o'clock in the afternoon, the seats were already filling up.

"Outside of a bag of pork rinds and a six-pack of beer in the back of your pickup, this is the only place to get food and drink without leaving avocado country," Vance explained as they were shown into a booth. "Sit here long enough and everybody who knows the difference between a Hass, a Pinkerton and a Fuerte drops by."

He grinned at her bewildered expression. "Varieties of alligator pear."

"Huh?"

"Just another name for avocados." He appeared to relax as their drink orders were delivered. A beer for him, a diet soda for her. Then he asked for guacamole and chips.

When a basket and a ceramic bowl of dip were slid in front of them, Vance cocked a brow Layla's way. "You'll share with me, won't you?"

She rested her elbow on the table and propped her chin on her hand. "I don't know if that's wise." He'd taken two long swallows of his beer and his earlier tension seemed nearly evaporated, which made her mood lighter, too. "Somebody told me recently that your alligator pears are the fertility fruit. Would that make the green stuff an aphrodisiac?"

He stilled for a moment, then a sparkle came into his blue eyes. Mimicking her pose, he placed an elbow on the table. Using his other hand, he picked up a chip and scooped some guacamole. "Maybe we better test that theory."

What could she do but open her mouth? Still, it was unavoidably intimate, she discovered, to have him feed her.

And even more so, when he touched his thumb to a spot at the corner of her mouth, ostensibly dabbing up a dot of guacamole. Her mind leaped back to the day before, when she'd made to brush cupcake crumbs from his lips. Her fingertips prickled at the reminder, recalling the distinction between the soft flesh of his mouth and the golden stubble edging it.

Layla felt herself flush, then go even hotter as she watched him lick the smear of dip from the pad of his thumb.

He pretended to study her face. "You look...warmer," he said.

She, in turn, pretended that consuming the chip made it impossible for her to respond. But it was fascination that kept her silent as his long fingers delved into the basket again. He loaded another chip with guacamole and then popped it into his mouth. Chewing, he tilted his head as if considering.

Considering *her*, because though his eyes were half-closed, they were focused on Layla's face. Her skin prickled with another rush of heat and under the table she pressed her thighs together, trying to contain the rising sexual ache there.

Her nipples tightened and he must have sensed that, because his gaze slid lower. She didn't dare look herself, but she knew the hard points could be seen through her T-shirt.

"Definitely arousing," he murmured.

Oh, no. Physical desire was as dangerous as an emotional attachment. Pressing her spine against the back of the bench seat, she put distance between them. Her hand scooped up her cold drink. It might have been more effective to dash it on her skin, but she made do with a long, icy swallow.

Vance's eyebrow rose again and he stretched his long legs until denim from his jeans brushed the inside of her naked calf. When she twitched in reaction—that sexual startle response she'd yet to contain—a little smile prodded the corners of his mouth. "You okay, sweetheart?"

Layla scowled at the endearment. And his obvious enjoyment in teasing her. With careful movements, she edged her legs away from his. "Remember? I'm not girlfriend material."

His smile became even lazier. "I didn't say you weren't girlfriend *material*..." The word trailed off as his gaze shifted over her shoulder. "Shit," he said, straightening in his seat.

She glanced back. Strolling into the dining area was Vance's brother, Fitz. And beside him was a beautiful woman, her platinum hair and classic features like an ice sculpture of a royal princess. Layla turned back to Vance and he was wearing that nonexpression expression again.

She sent me a Dear John letter a month after I'd returned to Afghanistan.

And here "she" clearly was, with the brother she'd taken up with next. That had to hurt. And if Layla wasn't mistaken, Vance would stab himself with a fork before he'd want anyone to know that it did.

Reaching across the table for his fingers, she turned in her seat to catch the eye of the blonde's escort. "Fitz!" she said, pasting on her sunniest smile. "Fancy meeting you here. Can you join us?"

Without giving him time to reply—or anyone time to object—she patted the banquette seat beside her. "And, Blythe—you are Blythe, correct? You've got to sit right next to me so the two of us can get acquainted."

The other couple seemed so astonished by the invitation that they dutifully followed her directions. Vance had a tight grip on her left hand, but that didn't stop her from extending her right to the elegant woman now seated beside her. "I'm Layla Parker," she said. "Vance's girlfriend."

"Oh," the other woman murmured, with a quick blink followed up by a brief, polite clasp of fingers. "I'm happy to meet you."

Then she flicked a glance across the table. "Hello, Vance," she murmured, her voice even fainter.

Vance didn't twitch a muscle. "Blythe." Whatever his feelings, they'd gone deep undercover.

The two brothers sat side by side, both wooden-faced. A swell of panic curdled the cola and guacamole in Layla's belly, but she managed to calm herself as the waitress paused to take the newcomers' orders. She'd told Vance earlier that he was her hero and it was true. He'd tried to save her father at great personal risk and she was determined to pay him back for that as best she could. Helping him hide his broken heart seemed a good place to begin.

When the requested drinks were placed on the table,

she tacked on another sunny smile, supremely aware that Vance and Fitz were each pretending the other wasn't sitting an elbow away. "Blythe, I bake cupcakes for a living, if you can believe that. How about you? What's your line of work?"

Blythe was an interior designer, Layla learned. The other woman answered readily enough, even though she kept sneaking glances across the table, whether at Fitz or Vance, it was impossible to tell. Upon closer inspection, Blythe was also not any less attractive than Layla had originally thought. She wore her straight hair in a ballerina bun at the back of her head and was dressed in a tailored khaki skirt and white silk shirt that would be appropriate in an executive suite—or for decorating one.

By comparison, in her shorts and T, Layla felt like a camp counselor after a sweaty day of weaving lanyards and making name tags from popsicle sticks and macaroni letters. Still, she didn't let her lack of self-confidence show on her face. Instead, she shared stories about starting up Karma Cupcakes, their current flavor offerings and that she'd be bringing the food truck to the upcoming Picnic Day at the Smith family ranch.

Fitz, who'd been silent up to now, slid a look at his brother. "Picnic Day?"

"Yeah," Vance said. "Mom came by the beach house. We ended up driving her home."

"I'm glad she had a chance to see you," his brother said stiffly.

Vance shrugged. "She got to meet Layla." He idly played with her hand now, his lean fingers sliding up and down against the sensitive inner skin of hers.

Layla flushed again, she couldn't help it, and when

she shifted her legs restlessly, Vance caught them between his. Her head jerked up to find his gaze on her face. It felt like a caress.

Before the warmth of it had died, a stranger came up to the table. "Vance!" he cried in happy greeting and then immediately launched into some remember-when conversation that made clear they were long acquaintances. The other man brought Fitz into the discussion, as well, and soon it turned into something about baseball that—to Layla—was indecipherable. While the brothers each spoke to the newcomer, it was obvious they weren't speaking to each other.

The sensation of being watched tagged her consciousness and she turned her head to see that Blythe was staring at her. Layla saw her swallow. "He's a really good man," the other woman said, under the cover of the men's talk.

Layla couldn't help but give a little dig. "Fitz?" she said, tacking on an unspoken *You mean the guy who stole his brother's girl?*

Blythe dropped her gaze. "Vance."

"That's right," Layla said, with a light snap of her thumb and middle finger. "You two, uh, dated for a while."

"So much contained energy," the blonde said. "All that life buzzing under his skin."

Oh, yeah, Layla thought. Even when he was quiet, even when he acted as if he had ice in his chest like her father, there was a force to him, a leashed power that said he was prepared to uncoil in an instant and launch into battle. Fight hard. Take no prisoners.

It was attractive.

Exciting.

Then she thought of the Vance she'd seen at the ranch. The one who'd envisioned himself managing the groves. Growing things on the land instead of patching up men on the battlefield. She could see that, as well. He'd be decisive then, too. His hands gentle on the fruit. His natural vitality infusing each root, each branch, each leaf.

She supposed it would be a healthy, good way to employ the innate restlessness that had driven a little boy to make mischief.

"The fact is," Layla murmured, half to herself, "the big bad combat medic is a nurturer." And why did that feel like such a dangerous thought?

Blythe frowned a little. "I'm not sure he'd approve of that description."

"What description?" Vance said, from across the table. The friend who'd occupied him was moving away.

The two women glanced at each other. Then Layla smiled at the man who was running his thumb across the top of her knuckles. "That you're a handsome, generous studmuffin," she said. "*My* studmuffin."

His lips twitched, and he glanced at the now-empty bowl of guacamole. "How much of that stuff have you eaten?"

She waggled her eyebrows at him. "Wouldn't you like to know?"

"Yeah," he said softly. "I would."

And it was as if the other couple had slid beneath the table. Actually, there was no one else in the restaurant. Only Vance and Layla remained, smiling into each other's eyes. Clasping each other's hands. The heat captured between their palms shot up her arm and tumbled over her body.

"Time to go," he said, still holding her gaze.

They murmured their goodbyes to Fitz and Blythe, who seemed relieved to see them leave. Vance slid his arm around Layla as he led her toward the door. His mouth nuzzled her temple. "That was great. Thanks for being such a good…friend," he murmured in her ear. "Just one more scene, okay?"

"Huh?" she asked, but instead of answering, right at the door, in view of everybody at the restaurant including his brother and his ex-fiancée, Vance laid his lips against hers.

Claiming her. Cementing her position as his girlfriend.

It was just a role, she tried reminding herself, as she opened her mouth to the gentle thrust of his tongue.

A role that had turned even more dangerous than she'd supposed, she thought, shivering against him. Because right now it didn't feel like playacting at all.

CHAPTER EIGHT

ONE LATE AFTERNOON, following several hours spent poring through dusty boxes, Addy headed back to Beach House No. 9. Strolling along the sand, she caught sight of Skye Alexander up ahead, her attention on something in her hands.

Addy picked up her pace. Now was as good a time as any to provide a report on the progress she'd made cataloging the Sunrise Pictures archives. As she neared the other woman, the sole of her flip-flop found a pod on a string of rust-covered kelp. The bulb popped, the noise loud over the whisper sound of the surf.

Skye startled, dropping the papers in her hands. "It's you," she said, clapping one palm over her heart.

"Sorry," Addy replied, grimacing. Then she bent to pick up the scattered sheets. Lined paper was covered by a distinctly masculine scrawl. "I didn't think anyone wrote letters anymore," she said, passing the missive to Skye.

Wearing a small smile, the other woman carefully brushed at the grains of sand clinging to the pages. "He's overseas and doesn't always have access to the internet. Our old-fashioned correspondence isn't as instantaneous as email, but I like it. It feels more... personal."

"I get it. A person's handwriting can suggest their

mood." Addy grinned. "And there's always the option of writing your response in purple ink to convey your passion."

Skye's gaze shot up. "Passion?" She laughed. "No, we're just friends. Old friends from childhood."

"You've been pen pals since you were kids?" Addy thought of all the letters she'd fantasized writing when she was a girl. Each one addressed to the beautiful blond boy who lived down the road.

Skye shook her head. "He used to spend his summers here—in Beach House No. 9 as a matter of fact—but we started writing to each other less than a year ago. Gage—Gage Lowell—is a freelance photojournalist."

And Skye's secret crush, Addy decided. She might claim they were just friends, but the careful way she was handling that letter said that its future lay in a special box alongside the others the man had sent her.

Of course, that could just be Addy's overstimulated imagination. The hours she'd spent searching through the souvenirs of the silent film era and Edith Essex had made her preoccupied with love affairs and all their attendant complications. "You know," she told Skye now, "I've been unsuccessful in finding any letters between Edith and her husband, Max. I thought they might tell a truer story than the gossip rags of the day, which said she married the owner of Sunrise Pictures for what he could do for her career."

"But you think…?"

"I don't know." Addy sighed. "Later, there was also speculation that Max got out of the movie business to punish her for the affair and that flamboyant gift of jewelry…while also putting out the word he wouldn't tolerate anyone else hiring her."

"Not too nice."

Addy shrugged, then shoved her hands in the pockets of her cropped white jeans. "She stayed with him, though, and they had a couple of kids in quick succession and then, only five years later, after giving birth to their younger daughter, she got pneumonia and died. Did she resent her husband's actions? Did she regret the loss of her acting career to her dying breath?"

"The only family lore I can add is that my great-great-grandfather never remarried," Skye said.

Addy sighed again. "Well, you told me Crescent Cove has had its share of broken hearts."

Skye gave a lopsided smile. "I did, didn't I? Though to be fair, there is—" She broke off, her eyes brightening as her gaze moved over Addy's shoulder. "Teague," she said, in pleased surprise.

Addy glanced around. A dark-haired man was heading for them, barefoot and dressed in shorts and an unbuttoned short-sleeved shirt. Its edges fluttered in the breeze, revealing a chiseled chest and a pack of ab muscles worthy of a magazine spread. "Wow." She looked at Skye. "I think one of us should start exchanging passionate letters with that guy."

"Are you really interested?" the other woman asked, her eyebrows rising. "Though we'll need to take his romantic temperature first—he had a recent disappointment."

"Maybe." Addy shrugged. Because perhaps a summer fling was what she needed to purge her lingering and girlish infatuation with Baxter. She hadn't seen him since that day when she'd told him the past was past. But, dammit, his response continued to echo in her head. *That leaves the present wide-open.*

Not that he'd made any inroads into her present since then, she thought with a scowl. He'd likely found some svelte beauty that was the same twelve-on-a-scale-of-ten as himself. Someone he could picture in his golden life and golden future.

With an effort, she morphed her scowl into a smile as the good-looking guy joined up with them. He had a warm hand and a firm grip.

"Teague spent his summers here, too," Skye explained after introductions were made. "Along with Gage and his twin brother, Griffin."

"And their sister, Tess," the man added.

Maybe it was her imagination going wild again, but the way he said the name made Addy suspect this Tess was the source of the blow to his heart.

Skye confirmed the suspicion when she sent him a pointed glance. "Are you okay?"

"Getting there," he said. "I'm back to the beach, aren't I? First time since she left."

Addy felt a little embarrassed to hear this bit of personal business until he turned to her with a rueful grin. "I'm trying to exorcise a ghost, I guess. Last month I fell a little too hard for a lady who was already taken."

"Already taken by a husband and four kids," Skye put in.

"Yikes," Addy murmured. "Four kids?"

"I like rug rats," Teague said, and she gave him credit for not being at all abashed about the admission. "Comes from a childhood as a lonely only."

"Lonely only?" Addy repeated. "Hey, me, too."

"Yeah?" Teague's gaze sharpened.

"Yeah." Addy took in his handsome features, the dark hair tousled by the wind, the ripple of muscles.

She had someone she wanted to exorcise from her life, as well, and why the heck *not* with this dark-haired hunk? "I'm a little lonely now, too, as a matter of fact."

He smiled, revealing the deep crease of a dimple in one cheek. "This might be my lucky day." Then his eyes shifted over her shoulder. A glint of humor kindled in them. "Or not."

Addy turned—and took a quick step back, almost stumbling. "You."

"Hi," Baxter said.

As usual, he looked as if he'd come straight from a hard day at the office. His tie was loosened, his shirt's collar unbuttoned. Its cuffs were folded back to reveal his strong wrists, the left one banded with a steel watch.

The wind tugged at the cuffs of his trousers, but didn't dare ruffle his golden hair. The sun burnished the perfectly cropped layers, though, making him seem to glow. Addy swallowed, trying to appear unaffected, even as the memory of a naughty boss-secretary dream she'd been having lately bloomed in her mind. *Miss March, I found four typos in this memo...*

"Uh, hi," she said, cursing the blush creeping over her face.

He frowned. "What's going on?"

Addy crossed her arms over her chest. *I'm preparing for an exorcism.* It was imperative. She was certain of that now because it wasn't healthy for a woman to go weak-kneed when some man arrived out of the blue. Some man who'd said, "That leaves the present wide-open," but who'd then ignored her for several days thereafter, only showing up in her subconscious at night.

Miss March, come into my office and close the door.

"Addy?"

"Nothing's going on," she said, then slid a glance in Teague's direction. "Just making a new friend."

Baxter's blue eyes narrowed. "Is that right?"

The dark-haired man held out his hand, his expression still good-humored. "Teague White," he said. "I'm a nice guy, honest. Skye can vouch for me."

"He's a firefighter," Skye added. "Can't get more wholesome than that."

A firefighter? Addy sneaked a second look at the man. *Wholesome* wasn't the first word that came to mind, especially when the firefighter in question was absolutely hot and incredibly handsome. Maybe the exorcism thing could really work.

Baxter was frowning as if *wholesome* didn't ring true to him, either.

He shook the other man's hand, then glanced at Addy. "Look, can we go—"

"I was just about to ask her to have a drink with me at Captain Crow's," Teague put in.

Baxter didn't look away from her face. "She can't," he answered flatly. "We have plans."

The liar. "What plans?"

He stepped into her, so close his loafers were an inch from the toenails she'd painted a bright melon as a pick-me-up when he hadn't called or stopped by. How silly she'd been to believe he might. She'd been smart enough to have no expectations of him before and she shouldn't be harboring any now.

"I'm sorry I haven't been in touch." The back of Baxter's hand slid along her cheek. "I had to take an emergency business trip."

The caress sent a line of fire running from her face, down her throat, between her breasts. Addy couldn't breathe. "I don't… You don't…" She had no idea what words were coming out of her mouth.

Damn the man! He scrambled her brain, garbled her good intentions, messed with her mind with just a look from his blue eyes.

His hand slid from her face to the back of her neck. His palm covered the tender skin there, more fire racing along her scalp and down her back. Panic added to the heat in her blood. She couldn't want him like this.

In childhood, she'd had her defenses—coping mechanisms to smother her feelings or escape her surroundings. She'd worked hard to eradicate the unhealthiest of them, but now she found herself still vulnerable. Baxter—wanting Baxter—could take her back, take her down, making her that weak girl again who lived in her fantasies instead of living her life.

He leaned close, his voice for her ears only. "I've thought of you." The thumb of the hand that was curved around her nape stroked the edge of her jaw, just under her ear.

Oh, God. She shouldn't listen. He had the power to make her yearn. After a childhood of pining for things she couldn't have or couldn't make right, she knew better than to let herself long for Golden Boy Baxter. Six years ago, despite how breathtaking the experience, despite the things he'd said afterward, she'd never let it become more than a blissful night of wish fulfillment.

She'd never expected there to be more.

The Addy Marches of the world never got to have a Baxter Smith. Not really.

But he seemed to be offering something now…and even if it was only something temporary, it was still tempting.

She should shut him down. Turn away and then purge him from her life so she wouldn't pine for him.

"Addy," he murmured, that caressing thumb seducing her again.

Seducing the wallflower. Wallflower Addy, who after years of hiding herself away had finally learned that when her shoulders were flat against a hard surface, it was time to push back. "All right," she said, making a sudden decision. She shot an apologetic glance at the attractive Teague, then focused on Baxter once again. "Let's go to your place."

He blinked. "What?"

There was a way to exorcise him other than running off with another man. She and Baxter could have sex again. Maybe the problem was that her experience with him was squarely in the sentimental category of first times and girlish dreams come true. Now, older and more experienced, she'd realize he was a mere man.

And that there wasn't anything especially captivating about Baxter's tab A sliding into her slot B.

She'd purge all right. All the stupid stars from her eyes.

BAXTER DIDN'T KNOW WHAT was going on in Addy's mind, but he knew one thing for sure. They were *not* going to have sex.

He'd done that with her way too soon six years before. So when he opened the door to his condo and ushered her inside, he reminded himself he was no longer a twenty-three-year-old hothead. Which, actually, was a weird reminder in itself, because he'd never been a hothead. Not at fourteen, not at eighteen, not at twenty-three. Baxter had been focused on the BSLS. Hotheadedness was Vance's domain. The only time Baxter had been driven by impulse was that particular night six years before.

So, no, this wasn't going to be a repeat of that rash act. There was plenty of safe daylight left. It was summer and just past six o'clock, the perfect hour to have a reasonable, adult, getting-to-know-you interlude over a bottle of wine and some appetizers on his twentieth-floor balcony.

Because he *did* want to get to know her better. It was much too hasty to be considering a serious relationship according to the Baxter Smith Life Schedule, but there was nothing wrong with furthering their acquaintance. After that hike around Crescent Cove, he'd found himself charmed by her enthusiasm, entertained by her tales of the silent film era and completely unwilling to merely settle for her acknowledgment of and his apology for That Night.

Because she did remember it.

As he watched her move out of the entryway and into his living room, that six-year-old memory welled in his own mind. Addy was crossing the carpet to approach the sliding glass doors and the city view they afforded, but in his inner vision they were at the family ranch. The summer's night air was redolent with barbecue, watermelon and beer. The deep rural darkness was held at bay with strings of small bulbs edging the rooflines, wrapping around the trunks of the oak trees, crisscrossing above the designated dance floor. Still, even though larger spotlights illuminated the players in the band and the booths providing food and drink, there were plenty of pockets of warm darkness.

Baxter had taken to one, his shoulder braced against

the heated stucco of his parents' house, listening to the country performers who did damn good covers of the latest hits. He'd been watching the dancers when, through the circling couples, he'd spied a pixie. In a pale yellow sundress a near color match to her hair, she'd been standing on the edge of more shadows. He might have missed her, except that she was moving to the beat, just the tiniest bit, the swaying of her belled skirt catching his gaze.

Without thinking, he'd been on the move toward her.

He was on the move now, making his way into the galley kitchen. "White wine okay?" he called to Addy.

"Sure," she said, turning from the vista of skyscrapers and SoCal traffic to follow him into the small room. "What can I do to help?"

He glanced over. Froze. At the beach he'd noticed what she'd been wearing. White jeans, a simple pair of flip-flops, a thin white-and-turquoise-striped tunic-type shirt that fell to her thighs and buttoned down the front. Then, it had been fastened to her throat.

Now it was open near to her navel.

No, not even close really, but damn, from certain angles it would reveal the top curves of her breasts. Like from his angle. He was tall enough that when he looked down he couldn't miss the pale mounds of her skin. His mouth went dry, and his fingers curled toward his palms as impulse poured like adrenaline into his bloodstream. *Touch,* it insisted, while his common sense tried negating the thought.

Bad idea, it reminded him.

Addy stepped nearer, and he pressed the small of his back into the countertop. She reached around for the cupboard behind him. "Glasses in here?" she asked, going on tiptoe.

It was as if she didn't realize she was nearly plastered against the length of his body. That if he moved his head just a fraction, his mouth could find the soft skin of her temple and from there slide down to the pink warmth of her mouth.

Baxter sucked in a breath.

And on her perfume, was taken back in time.

He'd slowly made his way around the dance floor to where the pixie had staked out her place in the half shadows. She hadn't seemed to notice his approach, as absorbed as she was in watching the couples spin and turn. Some of them actually knew how to dance. Others were just using the music as an excuse to touch, hand-to-hand, hip-to-hip.

Baxter had tugged on the ends of the pixie's long hair. She'd started, turned, then, even in the dim light, he'd seen the deep rose color overtake her face.

And he'd fallen back. Crap. *Too young?*

But he was nothing if not polite, so he'd introduced himself. She'd nodded, said her own name and, half afraid and half relieved, he'd attempted the all-important calculations. Because he knew Addison March, or at least *of* her. She'd lived down the road and surely…if his memory was correct… Then, Baxter Smith, a day away from leaving town to enter a world-renowned MBA program, was forced to ask a question because his brain was too muddled to add for himself.

"How old are you?"

Frankly, nineteen had still felt too young. Disappointed, he'd meant to make his excuses and walk away. But she was staring at him with big eyes and still wearing that pretty blush. Somehow he'd found himself asking her to dance.

She didn't know how to two-step.

It was pretty evident from the way she trembled against him, from the way her breath came so shallow and fast, that Addy didn't know how to do two-anything. Another clear warning to him.

They were just going to dance.

"Are you all right?" Addy asked now.

Yanked back into the present, he jolted, moving away from her tempting scent and penetrating gaze. Did she know what he was thinking?

"Would you like a soda instead?" he choked out. Yeah, they were adults and all, but surely alcohol wasn't safe to add to this mix.

Addy shrugged. "Wine is fine. Or beer—if it's light. I only drink light beer."

She'd had one that night. It wasn't Baxter's fault. Somebody else had actually given it to her, she'd told him, a bottle of golden brew with a slice of lime from the Smith family ranch shoved into the neck. Before they'd danced, she'd set the empty down at her feet. And after the dance, seduced from his good intentions by the perfect way she'd fit in his arms, he'd tasted the citrusy tartness on her lips, tasted the smoky yeastiness of the beer on her tongue. Yeah, he'd kissed her.

He didn't think she'd been tipsy. One beer hadn't incapacitated her.

But he'd been drunk. Drunk on her kiss, her petite body, on the spontaneity of it all. So off-the-Schedule.

As they'd walked arm-in-arm toward the bachelor house on the other side of the oak grove, the spacious quarters that had separate suites of rooms for him and

Fitz and Vance, he'd been just a little high on doing something he hadn't planned beforehand. It had felt like falling in love, wild and impetuous and completely out of control.

Addy approached him now, her footsteps steady on the kitchen's hardwood floor. Baxter tensed, unwilling to be the victim of his urges once again. They were supposed to be getting to know each other like grown-ups. In a responsible way. He was supposed to be considering whether he wanted to casually date her, which was the only option available at this time according to the BSLS.

"Baxter," she said, shaking her head. There was a very adult look in her eye. An adult note of admonition in her voice.

"What?" he asked, fiddling with the end of his tie.

She took that hand. Placed it down at his side. Then, her knuckles brushing against his ribs, she grabbed the tail of silk and yanked him toward her.

"Wait," he said, his other hand on her shoulder. "What are you doing?"

She blinked. "I have to tell you?" There was a very sensual, very knowing look in her eyes.

A look he'd put there. Six years ago, she'd been as ignorant about sex as she'd been about the two-step, and he'd taught her how to do both. Sweet Lord. What a turn-on.

"I didn't want it to go this way," he murmured.

Her brows rose, not in doubt but in challenge. "Is that right?"

His hand was no longer pushing her away, but instead caressed that small cap of her shoulder. He was supposed to be the master of his urges, but looking at her, at that tinge of a flush breaking across her cheek-bones, at the darkness of her pupils almost swallowing the green of her eyes, he realized that while he might be the master of *his* urges, he was no match for hers.

She stepped away. But his tie was still gripped in her small hand and he moved with her as she backed out of the kitchen. Without asking, she found the interior hall, still taking him with her.

With a slight shake of his head, he indicated they should pass the first door on the right. "Extra bedroom."

Her feet moved past the bathroom that came after that.

Then they were at the end of the hall and inside the big master bedroom. Dropping his tie, she looked around her, taking in the king-size bed, the large chest of drawers, the flat-screen TV on one wall. Her gaze landed on the sliding glass doors that afforded yet another view. It was still plenty light in the room even though the drapes were drawn. At this height, they weren't really necessary for privacy, so he'd chosen only the sheerest fabric. He started his days early.

As Addy continued to stare at them, yet another memory rose in his mind.

He hadn't taken her to the bachelor house with the focused intention of getting her into bed. After three dances in his arms, she'd mentioned she was cold and he'd volunteered to find her something from his closet. He would have dashed back to get a sweatshirt and then returned, but she'd offered to accompany him.

She'd already shared kisses with him at the dark edges of the dance floor. He'd not been averse to making out more.

A few more kisses couldn't hurt.

Once inside the empty bachelor house, he'd found her a soft fleece jacket that she'd draped over her shoulders before draping herself on the couch. Though he'd taken a seat several cushions away, in moments they'd been in each other's arms again. Her perfumed warmth against him, her cloud of hair in his hands, her pretty face upturned.

The bedroom then, like now, had been her idea.

Her small tongue in his mouth had melted all his objections. Within seconds of her proposing they go there, he'd ripped off his metaphorical merit badges and led her to his big bed. Six years ago, an expression of doubt had crossed her face as she first glimpsed the smooth bedspread and stacked pillows. The same one she wore now.

So he sought to reassure her in the same way. "Hey, we don't have to do this."

She responded with the exact same words. "Turn off the lights."

Then, he had. Now he couldn't. "Addy, there aren't any on. It's the sun."

Her gaze turned toward the filmy covering on the glass sliders and her teeth worried her bottom lip.

"Addy…" He crossed to her and put both hands on her shoulders. "Look, second thoughts are fine."

"Second chances don't always come around," she muttered, then whirled to face him. "Kiss me."

His thought was to take the heat down a notch. To turn the fire down to simmer, so that they would have clearer heads with which to reconsider. But when his lips touched hers she kissed him the way he'd taught her, mouth instantly opening to reveal the hot, sweet juiciness inside.

His body hardened and when she pressed against it she moaned. Damn, he thought, his hand sliding down to cup her ass, she was as determined as she'd been six years ago. As dangerous to his defenses.

They were still dressed when they stretched out on the bed. Her scent surrounding them, she crawled over him, kissing his mouth, sucking on his neck. He breathed her in, he reveled in her taste, his body imprinting on hers so that he worried he might end up following her around for the rest of his life like a baby duck after its mama. For a while he let her have her way—he'd done that six years ago, too—but then he had to touch.

He ran his hand along her sleek spine under her shirt, then slipped his palm beneath the denim of her white jeans so he could knead one curved cheek. "Let's get these clothes off you, sweetheart."

She glanced up, her mouth still on the bare skin of his chest. She'd unknotted his tie and unbuttoned his shirt; her pubic bone was pressed deliciously tight to his erection, but it wasn't enough.

With his free hand, he began to draw up the hem of her long shirt. "Please," he said, feeling more than a little desperate.

Instead of cooperating, she rolled away. Her hands went to his belt. "I want to see you naked first."

Who was he to complain? He let her fumble for a couple of moments, then decided that was too much torture and made quick work of it himself. As he tossed his shirt aside, getting completely naked, she grabbed at his tie, eyeing it, then eyeing him.

Uh-oh.

That wasn't a game he'd taught her, nor one he'd

played before. Vance called him stuffy and he supposed, with the exception of that mad night of passion with a near-stranger six years before, that he was pretty conservative when it came to sexual matters.

Okay, he wasn't kinky.

But hell, maybe he could be. Baxter swallowed. "You want me to tie you up?"

She shook her head.

He swallowed again. "You want to tie *me* up?" That would be more of a challenge.

But that wasn't it, either. She kneed her way over to him and pressed the silk fabric against his eyes. "Please, Baxter." Tilting her head, she put her mouth to his as she made a knot at the back of his head. "Let's do it in the dark."

And like on that first night, he couldn't refuse her anything.

He didn't need his eyes to undress her. He didn't need his eyes to touch her silky skin, to palm her full breasts, to urge her over him so he could tongue her nipples. They hardened, and he grunted at the goodness of that. She writhed against him, her denim pants abrading his shaft and he grunted again, rolling her over before any damage was done.

Finding the button and zipper of her jeans was easy. Feeling her wriggle out of them while he thrust his tongue into her mouth over and over was a kind of painful bliss.

Then there she was, flush against him. Bare.

Full frontal nudity.

He didn't need to see anything to feel the ripe softness of her between her legs, that sweet, wet, swollen flesh that was because of his kiss, his touch. Him.

Any man could put a condom on with his eyes closed. But then Addy "helped" him, and his fingers fumbled when he felt her hot breath on the flesh of his belly. She laughed, he cursed, they both went searching for the errant rubber.

Of course she found it first. She could see.

So he groaned again as she rolled it over his length. He lifted into her touch, his hips ready to plunge, to take, to have her. Have Addy.

But once sheathed, he pressed her to the mattress again. Used his mouth to Braille his way from her lips to her nipples to the soft center of her. Holding her legs wide, he kissed her there, too, tongued her, loving the bite of her fingernails in his scalp. As she began to quake in climax, he slid up and inside her, letting her muscles clench him in rhythmic bliss before surging himself, thrusting, until he came.

Breathing hard, he pulled away and flopped to his back beside her. After a second or two, he dozed.

When he came awake, it was night.

No, no. It was his tie, still blindfolding him. He left it there another moment, trying to think. Now that he wasn't under the influence of driving lust, he wondered what the silk fabric's purpose had been.

She wanted to keep him in the dark? If that was the case, it had worked. He was as confused about them as ever and concerned about why his intentions were so easily derailed. Days ago all he'd wanted was to apologize.

Not for making love to her six years ago, but for the reckless things he'd said afterward.

I think I'm in love with you.

I'll call you tomorrow.

He'd said that, though that very tomorrow he'd had plans to head off to business school across the country. As for Addy, after taking a post–high school gap year, she'd been signed up to begin college classes in a month's time. Neither of their future plans had stopped him from saying more, however.

And we'll find a way to be together. We have to be together.

But the next morning, as he packed his belongings in his car, Baxter had recalled the BSLS. This was not the time for a girlfriend. This was not the time to be dating, even. And for pity's sake, he was much too young to be thinking about love. So he hadn't picked up the phone, he hadn't written her, he hadn't left her any message... and then had agonized over not doing so during the entire three-thousand-mile trip.

Beyond that, too. For six years. Yet still he'd not made amends.

He fingered the soft swathe of material covering his eyes. She should have choked him with the damn thing while he was sleeping.

Great. So his little getting-to-know-you time had turned into a disaster. They'd gotten as close as two bodies could be, but the blindfold had kept her hidden from him.

It had allowed her an opportunity to escape him, he thought.

And, he realized when he stripped the tie away, she'd done exactly that.

He was once again alone.

CHAPTER NINE

IT WAS FOUR DAYS FOLLOWING their visit to the ranch before Vance suggested that he and Layla make another attempt at witnessing the green flash. Before that, an unusual July fog had rolled in, obscuring the view and wrapping the beach house in a gray blanket. Outside, the visibility was down to a mere dozen feet and it might have made the interior of No. 9 feel too couple-cozy except that Layla spent most of the days with her uncle Phil at the food truck—apparently gray skies didn't stifle cupcake cravings in Southern California. In the evenings, Addy was in the mix for dinner and a baseball game on TV or dinner and a girl-movie on TV, depending upon how the postmeal coin toss went.

To be honest, Vance had been grateful for a reprieve from Layla's exclusive company. After their time at the ranch and then their stop at the tavern…well, he felt a new strain to the relationship. She knew things about him now he hadn't intended to tell her. There'd been something in that kiss in front of his brother and his ex that went beyond role-playing.

A little distance seemed a fine way to smooth out the new edge, and he suspected she'd been keeping herself busy for the exact same reason.

But he'd made promises, so the Helmet List could

not be ignored. With the sun once again visible in the sky, they were going to watch it set.

As they left No. 9, Vance had a new appreciation of Crescent Cove's clear air and the boundless vista of open ocean. Instead of doing their sunset-viewing from a spot on the sand, he proposed they climb to the top of the cliff directly south of the beach house. There were several footpaths snaking up its rock-and-shrub surface, and he trekked along one of the easier routes behind her, telling himself he was watching her butt to make sure she didn't fall.

Yeah, right.

Because even with Layla out of the house during the day and Addy in the house at night, his awareness of Colonel Parker's lovely daughter hadn't been deactivated.

She was beautiful, of course, in nothing more elaborate than a simple pair of cropped sweatpants and matching long-sleeved T-shirt, but he also couldn't put from his mind how she'd gone to bat for him when his mother had made her appearance. And then again with Fitz and Blythe at the tavern. That first meet with his ex could have been hellishly awkward, but Layla had smiled them all through it. And instead of focusing on the blonde who'd dumped him, Vance instead had been hyperaware of the sexy, sunny brunette who'd been sitting across from him.

Which went a long way toward explaining the incendiary quality of that kiss in the tavern, though didn't for a second lessen the simmering sexual tension. At that thought, he looked at her, only to catch her glancing over her shoulder at him. They both quickly diverted their attention.

He sighed. Yes, there was definitely a new strain to things between them.

Upon reaching the cliff's summit, he led the way toward a level spot that, while well away from the edge, was at the farthest end of the promontory jutting into the ocean. Water surrounded them on three sides, and when he settled beside Layla on one of the blankets he'd spread, she gave him another quick glance.

"From here, it's like we're the only people in the world," she said, draping a smaller throw over her lower legs.

"I could sign up for that," Vance said. "You'll do all the cooking and cleaning, of course, and I'll do... whatever manly things need to be done."

"I wonder why I'm highly suspicious of this proposed division of labor," Layla replied, a thread of welcome humor in her voice. "Oh, maybe it's because you can't come up with any of your own duties besides 'manly things.'"

"Hey," he said, spreading his fingers. "I'm the soldier."

"If we're the only two people in the world, it occurs to me we won't have need of your combat skills."

"Until there's spiders to manage," he reminded her. "Or killer dolphins."

"Killer dolphins," she scoffed. But she was smiling and the tension between them eased even more. He smiled back, his spirits lifting, too. Maybe they'd meet with success tonight.

According to sailors, when the flash appears, it means a soul has crossed over.

As if she caught his train of thought, her smile died and she went silent again. Her expression pensive, she turned her attention toward the horizon. The sky was a wash of pinkish-orange, the water the gray of gunmetal, the round sun glowing like molten lava. Vance breathed deep again, and over the shush of the ocean tossing against the rocks at the bottom of the cliff, he heard Layla sigh.

He turned to her. The wind had caught her long hair and it swirled around her face. He grabbed a long skein of the stuff and tucked it behind her ear. "You okay?"

"Hmm." She drew up her knees and linked her arms around them, then flicked him a quick look. "This morning I spoke to your mother about Picnic Day. Details. How many cupcakes she thought we might need, what time we should get the truck to the ranch, that kind of thing."

He swallowed his groan. "I thought we were the only two people in the world," he said. "In which case there is no upcoming Picnic Day."

"Nice try," Layla said. "But you can't bury your head in the sand."

Why not? It was effectively what he'd done when he'd joined the army all those years ago. With relations between him and his family in shambles, he'd buried himself in the sand of war. Stretching out his legs, he fumbled in the pouch of his ragged sweatshirt. The flask he'd stashed there clunked against his cast, and he pulled it out, glad he'd thought to bring it.

"Whiskey," he said, unscrewing the lid with his unencumbered right hand, thanking God for his renewed mobility. He'd put the brace away three days before. A hefty swallow of the liquor went down smooth. A clean burn of unpleasant thoughts. "You want?"

She eyed him. Then took a sip, sputtered.

"Sorry," he said. "I forgot you're only good with tequila."

As if she took the remark as a challenge, she tipped the flask for a second sip. Color flushed her cheeks as she passed it back.

Jesus, she was something. She *did* something to him, with that soft skin, the top-heavy mouth, those long-lashed eyes that now faced forward again. As he watched, her back stiffened.

"Here we go," she said, groping for his hand.

After four days of avoidance, he keenly felt her touch. It was as if the small fingers twining with his also had some clutch hold on his heart. Trying to ignore its ache, he turned to the horizon. The sun slipped lower, moving fast now, as if it had suddenly remembered a previous engagement. A golden reflection of it spread against the dappled water and the wind suddenly died. The breakers seemed to quiet, too, as if nature was holding its breath.

Vance knew he was. Tightening his fingers on Layla's, he leaned his shoulder closer to hers. She trembled a little, and he pressed against her, sharing his warmth. His strength.

The orange orb dropped. And dropped. The top edge seemed to spread and flatten as it slipped the final bit. And then—

Nothing.

His heart twinged in more sympathetic pain, and he damned the thing. It had been nicely numb after Blythe's defection, but thanks to Layla it now seemed determined to mirror his every mood. Her every mood.

He glanced over. "I'm sorry, sweetheart."

"Yeah," she said, her gaze on the now-empty sky.

"We'll see it next time. I'll pick the right sunset, and then we'll see it." God, once he started on the promises, he couldn't seem to stop.

"Sure."

The melancholy on her face made him nuts. "We'll make a wish on it then," he said.

She turned her head, perking up a little. "A wish?" Her lips curved.

"Yep. That's a bit of folklore I picked up." He touched the pillow of her bottom lip with the tip of his forefinger. The surface was unbearably soft. "Tell me, lovely Layla, what does your heart desire?"

Her smile fell. Her lashes swept down to hide her eyes. And Vance cursed himself. Her heart's desire? *It would be to have her dad beside her right now, you idiot, not some substitute.* Pissed at his own stupidity, he fumbled again for the flask and took another drink. "Sorry," he mumbled. "Just ignore me."

Instead, she took the whiskey from him and sipped, grimacing as if it was medicine. "What about you, Vance? What would you wish for?"

"That you wouldn't be sad," he said, and meant it to the marrow. "That I could take the pain away for you."

Her head bent as she seemed to consider it. "Maybe you should save that wish for yourself," she replied after a long moment, lifting her gaze to his. "You're sad, too."

"Me? No." He had annoyances. Grievances. Frustrations. But sadness? "Not that."

Layla took another sip from the flask. "Come on. Fitz and Blythe…"

He snatched the liquor from her. "I don't want to talk about them." It was another reason he'd spent four days avoiding her. There was no need to dig around in that old nonstory.

"We're going to have to."

In the waning light, he frowned at her. "I don't see why."

"Because we'll be at your family's ranch." She hesitated. "Look, I know we've been stepping over the elephant in the living room, but we can't do that forever. If we're going to do the pretend girlfriend/boyfriend thing again on Picnic Day, I need to have a better understanding of—"

"What, you haven't had a boyfriend before?" he asked, throwing the question out like bait. Anything to redirect the conversation.

She made a face at him. "I told you. I've had experience. I've kissed. I've been in relationships."

Ah, yes, thank you, God. His little fish had gone right for the worm. "Forgive me for finding it hard to see your tough-as-nails father allowing you to kiss anybody." Even as he said it, he worked hard to put *their* kisses from his mind, the sweet plumpness of her top lip, the soft velvet of her tongue.

Her laugh was rueful. "Okay, I admit it. He was an impediment in my younger teenage years. I wasn't allowed to attend many parties or go out on one-on-one dates. I thought I might die a ninety-five-year-old virgin."

Vance wasn't surprised that the colonel had tried to shelter his only daughter. "But in your older teenage years?"

"I had more freedom." She found the flask that he'd dropped on the blanket between them. "I was a freshman in college when Dad's latest deployment left me with an empty house—Uncle Phil was at a meditation center for the weekend. So I devised a battle plan to put an end to my untouched status."

It was almost dark now, but he turned toward her, anyway, intrigued—no, appalled. "A *battle* plan?"

"A strategy, if you will," she said. "An agenda. An approach to finally learning what it seemed as if everyone else in the world my age already knew."

Wow, Vance thought. No romantic daydreams for this girl. No getting swept away by emotion or even hormones for Layla. The soldier's daughter thought in terms of tactics and maneuvers to get what she was after.

She swigged some more from the flask. "Here's the truth. I'd had exactly one date that ended in exactly one kiss before the night I engineered to experience the whole shebang."

"Shebang," he echoed. "She-*bang?*"

"Whoops." Layla released a husky, half-tipsy giggle. "Bad choice of word."

He snatched the metal canister away from her. "I think we can leave it at—"

"So I had this battle plan," she continued. "I'd been to the doctor for birth control, I had condoms, I bought a slinky nightgown, I picked a guy who seemed respectful and who I kinda liked."

"You *kinda* liked him?" Vance asked, now almost aghast.

"Well, no," Layla admitted. "I actually liked him okay, but I amended it later…when, you know."

A chill rocketed up his spine. "No, I don't know." *And how can I find this asshole?* "Did he…what did he do?"

"He just didn't do it for me." Layla was silent a moment. "And then he seemed somewhat irked when I pointed that out."

Good God. Vance rolled his eyes skyward, to see the first stars shining above them. On the heels of a single kiss, she'd attempted the full monty with all the sentimentality of an officer drawing up combat plans in a war room. No wonder she'd been left unsatisfied. By a guy she liked *okay*.

"Frankly, now that I think of it, he probably wasn't any more experienced than me. He'd moved around a lot, too, which cuts down on a person's ability to get close to others. But I figured, as another army brat, that meant he wouldn't become too attached to me."

Good God, Vance thought again.

"Now you," Layla said.

"Me…what?"

"Your first," she said, sounding disgruntled. "I shared. Isn't that what boyfriends and girlfriends do?"

Ignoring the boyfriends and girlfriends remark, he forced his mind away from Layla's story and thought back. His first? "It wasn't nearly as well planned as you're describing, that's for sure."

"No?"

"It was more…impetuous. I had a rubber, mind you, and managed to remember to roll it on, but I'd had months of fooling around with Marianne Kelly before we did the deed when we were sixteen."

With a little smile, he lay back on the blanket to stare up at that star-studded sky. Layla was hovering over him, her features obscured by the darkness. "Maybe that's where I went wrong," she said, a mournful note in her voice. Then she positioned herself beside him, her head pillowed by one arm, her shoulder brushing his. "No fooling around before doing the deed."

Vance could guarantee it. Still smiling, he thought of those heady hours with his high school girlfriend. No empty houses, no satiny nightgowns, no cold-blooded arrangements. "We snatched time together wherever we could. In the front seat of my first car. On the couch at her house, with her parents just a room away. She even braved the avocado grove once."

"No," Layla said, clearly disbelieving. "No girl gets naked when there're spiders around."

He clucked his tongue. "Layla, Layla, Layla. There's fun to be had over clothes. Or by sneaking a hand under them."

They were lying so close and it was so quiet that he heard her breath catch. His body went on sudden alert as she shivered. He rolled his head toward her. "Cold?" he asked, his voice low.

She shivered again. "A little."

He reached for the second blanket that was puddled near their feet and pulled it upward, over their bodies. As he drew it toward Layla's chin, the side of his pinkie brushed her breast. She twitched, and her breath hiccupped again.

Vance's hand stilled. A breeze found the back of his neck but it was nothing against the new heat pouring through his body. He should stand up now, he thought. It might be a little awkward with the sudden stiffness poking at the placket of his jeans, but the two of them should probably leave here, where they felt as though they were the only two people in the world. Return to Beach House No. 9...

Where, since Addy was out for the evening, they'd be the only two people within the four walls.

Still, maybe between the cliff top and the confines of the house, he'd manage to corral this irrepressible lust, this shouting, insistent, reckless need to touch her, kiss her, teach her what he knew.

Hell! His good sense knew he couldn't afford that complication.

But then Layla made the internal argument moot.

Her fingers found his. Not to brush them away, but to press them to the sweet, swelling mound of her breast. *Sweet Christ.* Four days of avoidance, four days of good intentions and four days hoping to cool the smoldering tension disappeared in a burst of steam.

With a groan, he surrendered to the goodness of her under his hand. He rolled to his side, ignoring the awkwardness of the forearm cast between them, and fastened his mouth to hers. She opened instantly, and he painted the inner surface of that heavy upper lip with his tongue. Her body arched, and the stiff jut of her hard nipple was evident under her shirt and bra. He circled it with two fingertips as he kissed her more deeply, plunging now, driving into the wet heat.

She angled toward his body, offering herself to him. His lips drew away from her and traveled across her cheek, finding the hollow behind her ear. He was breathing heavily and when he touched his tongue there, he could feel her reaction to his hot breath. Her skin rose in goose bumps and he roamed over them, wetting them.

"There's fun to be had over clothes," he murmured again. "Or by sneaking a hand under them." Then he slid his hand from her breast and burrowed it beneath the hem of her shirt.

She jerked as his touch found the bare flesh of her midriff. Her head twisted, her mouth seeking his. Her kiss was desperate, full of gratifying need, as he finger-walked up her ribs. One of his knuckles touched the underside of her breast and they both moaned.

Her bra was of a thin, stretchy material. He skated across it until he found the upper edge. Then, in a quick yank, he pulled the fabric beneath the plump rise. Layla stilled, and then she arched toward him, sucking on his tongue when he thrust it inside her mouth.

Her intense, instant reaction was heady stuff. He loved the way she clutched his shoulders, the bite of her nails testament to her need. He thumbed the bare nipple, then gently pinched it between two knuckles. Layla's legs moved, restless, and he threw his top thigh over them, making her his captive. She moaned, her body thrashing a little as if to test the bond, but he didn't give way.

The restraint seemed to accelerate her desire. Little sounds came from deep in her throat, short moans that were their own demand. Vance knew she wasn't going with any plan right now, wasn't thinking of tactics or strategy; she was moving on impulse, letting her yearning build to a heedless pace, finding the power in being passionate. Impetuous.

Like he had been for so long, Vance thought. And it wasn't always bad, was it? But he was in control now, fascinated, and also committed to nurturing the craving he felt in the thrumming quiver of her lovely body.

"Vance," she moaned, then bit at his lower lip as if she couldn't help herself. "Oh, God."

He damned the awkward arm cast. There were so many places he wanted to touch her! Pushing her flat to her back again, he shifted under the blanket, then stopped teasing her breast to raise the hem of her shirt. His mouth found the naked nipple and he licked it, reveling in her husky groan.

The vibrations of it went through his fingertips as he insinuated them beneath the waistband of her sweats. Her stomach muscles jittered at his touch and she went still again. Vance jerked his mouth from her, needing to suck in some harsh breaths as he found the elastic band of her panties, riding low on her hips.

"Oh, God," Layla said again, lifting into his touch.

He allowed her to part her legs, and then he pressed the weight of his thigh back across them. She stilled again, and he could sense the need building inside of her. "That's right," he whispered against her breast. "Let me touch you. Let me make it good."

Complications. The word whispered through his mind, but he pushed it away. This was simple. So simple. Her heated skin beneath his fingers, against his tongue. Her desire, which she'd tried to experience through agendas and arrangements, under his control now. He teased it, stoked it, blowing on the flame to create the fire that would sweep over her.

It was a…a kindness. Not a complication.

His tongue curled around her nipple as his fingertips slid beneath her panties. He parted her for his sure touch, stroking into the soft, layered petals. She moaned when he discovered her wetness. He reveled in it, his heart pounding hard and fast, his fingertips drenched in her liquid heat. Driven himself now, he yanked his hand from beneath her sweatpants and took it to his mouth, tasting her essence.

She made an urgent, almost panicked noise.

"Shh," he soothed, then swiped his tongue against his fingertips once more. He shifted to kiss her again, sharing the flavor of her need. She went a little wild, her body arching high, and he pressed his thigh more firmly against her twitching legs. That urgent noise came from her throat again, muffled now by his mouth, and he took the hint, sliding his hand low again, against her belly, under her panties, to the knot of nerves at the apex of her sex.

He rubbed there, circled, toyed, tapped. Then rubbed again.

And she went wild.

It was a beautiful thing, all he'd wanted for the woman who'd never fooled around. Who had efficiently sought out sex without being driven by the hot-blooded need to climax. He took her orgasmic cries into his mouth as her body shook against his.

He gentled his kiss and his touch as she calmed. Her breathing slowed and her lashes swept up, her gaze on his face. They looked at each other, and reality whomped Vance on the side of the head.

Oh, hell. With a silent groan and an aching body, he rolled to his back beside her, no longer touching her. What a way to lose his head!

She was so sweet and tempting and desirable and…

He gritted his teeth. And off-limits.

Layla cleared her throat, a nervous sound. "Um, hey. Do you… Don't you…" Her fingers brushed his arm. "We can—"

"No," Vance said. "I— No."

"But—"

"It just seems smarter to keep it simpler, don't you think?"

She cleared her throat. "Sure, but it doesn't seem fair—"

"I'll be fine." Tortured, but he deserved it. With a surreptitious movement he made an adjustment to his still-tight jeans. Yeah, he was going to hurt for a while, but it was a fitting punishment for letting his own impulses get away from himself. For allowing Layla to come, thus creating only more complications.

MIDMORNING OF PICNIC DAY, Layla let Vance drive the Karma Cupcakes truck to the Smith ranch and wished she'd roped Addy into attending, as well. If the other woman had also been in the vehicle, Layla would have had a cheerful companion. Someone to talk to.

Someone who wasn't brooding in silence.

The silent brooder was Vance, of course, and she might entirely chalk it up to the upcoming interaction with his family if he hadn't been in a distinctly preoccupied mood since that night they'd watched for the green flash. Her stomach tightened at the memory of what had gone on under the blanket, and she snuck a look at the stony-faced man behind the wheel.

Okay, she glared at him a little. It wasn't that she could blame him for a moment of it—well, of course he was responsible for every kiss, every caress, every jolt of sweet satisfaction—because the true guilty party wasn't a person at all. It was the magnetism that had pulled them together from the very first. That attraction that had burned her fingertips and made her insides melt like heated marshmallows even now.

As if he felt her gaze, he glanced over.

Just like that, it happened. A string seemed to tether them together, and it pulled tighter the longer they looked at each other. Her belly clenched again, and Layla pressed one leg against the other, trying to dissipate the ache between them. Vance's jaw tightened and she saw his lips press into a taut line.

Unfortunately, that only sent her mind to the incredible moment on the cliff when he'd taken his fingertips straight from her body to his mouth. He'd made a little sound of appreciation as he'd absorbed her taste, and her skin had flamed with both a deep embarrassment and an almost uncivilized surge of desire.

God, she thought now, feeling an echo of that heat radiating from her bones outward. The unselfconscious lustiness of the gesture had been so...so *male*.

As Vance directed his attention out the windshield again, she allowed herself a little shiver. She needed some outlet for the sensual pressure bottled inside her.

Vance cleared his throat. "You're cold? I can turn down the air-conditioning."

"No." She almost laughed. He'd posed that question before, and she hadn't been trembling due to the chilly temperature then, either. It was as if she had a sexual furnace inside her, one that was constantly stoked by the smallest things. The flex of his long thigh muscle as he braked into the next sharp curve. The gold tips of his hair, longer than it had been when they'd first moved into No. 9. The look of his lean fingers as they gripped the steering wheel. His right arm was lifted to the two o'clock position, while the left, the one with the cast, lay in his lap. Two fingertips rested on the bottom curve of the wheel.

She imagined herself sucking them. Then sucking him.

Shocked by the thought—in broad daylight! In the

*cupcak*e truck!—she made a little noise. When he glanced over, she whipped her head toward the passenger window.

"Are you okay?"

"I'm fine."

Maybe she should just get it out into the open. *You put strange thoughts in my head. I woke up last night hot and restless. I want to taste you.* His quiet mood didn't invite confessions, however. And he hadn't mentioned anything about their sunset interlude himself since that night when he'd thought it "simpler" for the sexual satisfaction to be one-sided. She'd agreed, and then, in silence, they'd picked their way down the cliff in the starlight.

She supposed there wasn't much more to say, anyway, but…

Had he decided it should stop there because he was concerned she'd make too much of it? Did he worry she might get too attached?

"I'm fine," she told him again.

Because she didn't make too much of anything, ever. And army brats knew better than to count on permanence.

Soon they were approaching the Smith ranch. In deference to the expected traffic, she supposed, there were temporary caution signs set up along the way. It made sense, given the hairpin turns, though Vance navigated them smoothly, and soon they were pulling into the sprawling courtyard that lay between the two big houses. At the center was a low stage already crowded with musical instruments and audio equipment. Nearby were long rows of adjoined picnic tables, sunshades erected above them. Vance steered the truck beyond, to the stand of massive oaks. There was enough room between the trunks for vehicles to park, and it was here that the food vendors were setting up for the event. Already she caught a whiff of meats being tended over large grills. Vance set the parking brake and then took a breath. "Showtime," he murmured.

Layla slid him a sidelong look. He couldn't be looking forward to this, but you wouldn't know it from his calm posture. He sat in the seat in his worn jeans, navy blue single-pocket T-shirt, and a beat-up pair of running shoes. Apparently Picnic Day was a casual affair.

She'd counted on that, though she was wearing a dress instead of shorts for this second visit to the ranch. It was a soft cotton, halter-style sundress, with a swirling pattern of umber and gold colors that she thought set off the light tan she'd gained from her days at the beach. She didn't wear much makeup, opting for a double layer of mascara and a sheer lipstick that held just a hint of bronze.

Flipping down the visor overhead, she checked her face in the mirror.

"You have to know how pretty you are," Vance said, as if it was a personal insult.

She turned to him, frowning, and he winced, apparently catching his harsh tone. "Sorry," he said. "I just want this damn day to be over."

"My sentiments exactly," Layla agreed. Then she hauled in a deep breath and blew it out. "Shall we get moving then?" *Yeah, let's just get this damn day over with.*

They were ready by the noon opening. The awning was erected, the small bistro tables and chairs set out, the cupcakes transferred from the bakery boxes she used for transport to the glass display cases. She and Vance worked well together and he did all that she asked, but the quarters were close and she realized he was being careful not to touch her—or even get too near.

Katie Smith came toward the truck just as the first visitors arrived, dragging a garbage can behind her. Vance hopped out to take it from her. Her face lit up at the sight of him. "You're free of the wrist brace," she said, and then her smile turned teary as he bent to kiss her cheek.

"Mom," he admonished, shaking his head, but she only let out a watery laugh and pushed him away.

"Go find a good place for the can. I want to see your girl's wares." Then she perused the selections with great interest. "These look delicious."

"Would you like one?" Layla asked. The "your girl" had sent her pulse stumbling. She'd had second and third thoughts about Picnic Day and had even considered bowing out altogether, Vance's cool detachment making it even more difficult to pull off a pretend relationship.

But she'd sympathized with his family dilemma and she'd made a promise to his mother, so she pinned on a smile. "We have our famous devil's food cupcake, a new lemon flavor that I just started featuring and, in honor of today, a vanilla-avocado cake with milk chocolate frosting."

Katie blinked in surprise. "Avocado in a cupcake? We've used it with zucchini to make a bread, but I've not attempted a lighter crumb."

So she bakes, too, Layla thought, inordinately pleased. "It works. It's a fat replacement, really. I'm pretty happy with the results."

"Let me get Vance's father over here," Katie said. "He'll love an avocado cupcake…and I'm sure he wants to meet you."

"Sure. Great," Layla said, not letting go of her smile. Facing the Smith patriarch had to be done, she knew. The uncomfortable day wouldn't be over until she'd made that acquaintance. But before her nerves had a chance to really get jangling at the idea, there was a line in front of her, four deep.

Slipping into the rhythm of taking orders, making change and delivering desserts, she barely looked up when Katie reappeared at the window. "William," she said, turning to the figure behind her, "this is Vance's girlfriend, Layla…"

"Parker," Layla finished for her, and stripped off her food prep glove so she could shake the man's hand. He stepped up and her heart stuttered. *Oh.* There was Vance, thirty or so years from now. Though the golden hair had turned silver, father and son shared the same tall, lean body and the same blue eyes. The same guarded expression.

"Pleasure to meet you," he said, with polite reserve.

"And you, too," she replied, then glanced around the interior of the truck. "Hey, Vance, your dad…" He'd ducked out, she realized with a frown. Intentionally avoiding the situation, she was sure. She turned back and pretended not to be annoyed. "I'm sorry. He was just here."

An expression crossed the older man's face and now she saw his son Fitz in him, too. The two men were similarly bad at hiding their troubled emotions when it came to the younger Smith brother. "I'm sure I'll

catch up with him sooner or later," William Smith said.
"Thank you for coming."

"You're welcome. It looks to be a great event."

"Yes. Sure." He shoved his hands in his front pockets. "Well, uh…" He looked as if he wanted to ask her
questions but didn't know where to start.

In the distance, a voice shouted his name, and relief
crossed his face. "I'm sorry, maybe later we can…"

She was already smiling again and waving him away,
and then she was quickly consumed by managing the
clamoring crowd when the event really started swinging. As the temperature climbed, she heard a fiddle and
a banjo break into a bluegrass tune. Somebody whooped
as they walked by with a plate of ribs and an ear of
bright yellow corn.

Vance reappeared and once again pitched in. She
managed to corner him for a moment, noting his grim
expression. "Are you all right?" she asked.

He was silent as he studied her face. "Do I need to
apologize for being a moody ass?"

His rueful smile melted her. "Memories bringing
you down?"

"I'm just trying to float on top of them," he said,
then brushed her cheek with a knuckle and went back
to work.

The hours flew by. When there was a brief lull in demand, Vance left the truck and returned with platefuls
of food, as well as the teenage daughter of a neighbor.
The girl took Layla's place at the counter so she could
eat. There was a heaping mound of potato salad, skew-
ered strips of barbecued chicken, tortillas and beans.
Thick slices of creamy green avocado speared by long
toothpicks had been drizzled with a vinaigrette.

Though Vance wandered off to consume his meal—still trying to avoid her when he could?—Layla took a stool near her temporary helper. It was while she was sitting that she caught sight of Fitz and Blythe in the distance. The blonde looked as though she belonged at the country club instead of in the country. Her tailored, sleeveless shirtdress was silk, her long platinum hair tied back in a sleek tail.

She's so lovely I want to stick a pin in her, Layla thought, instead stabbing a chunk of potato with her now-empty avocado toothpick. Then she noticed Vance sitting against a tree, his gaze on his brother and his ex, and stabbed another, with more viciousness. Was he still floating on top of the memories or had he fallen into pining after the elegant beauty?

The thought made her a little bad-tempered as she returned to duty. Vance stepped inside, and praise be, his mood seemed improved—by the food or perhaps because he saw the end of the day in sight. Unfortunately, Layla only became more irritable when she ran out of lemon cupcakes, then the avocado ones, just as it was turning dark. She'd been so sure she'd baked enough of every flavor to make it through the entire event.

"Won't this day ever be over?" she muttered, as she tried breaking into a shrink-wrapped package of napkins.

Opening the darn thing seemed impossible. "Great," she complained aloud. "Now they're childproofing paper goods."

Vance approached, and in the truck's well-lit interior she saw he held a small knife in his hand. She glared at him. "You can put your weapon down, okay? I'm not actually dangerous."

He raised a brow. "I was going to offer to get that open for you."

"I've got it." Still seething, she snatched at the knife. There was a sense of pressure, a quick slash of heat, and then she was staring at the shredded fingertip of her glove. And blood.

"Oh," she said. It all caught up with her: the tension, the frustration, the long hours on her feet. She felt her knees go soft.

From far away she heard Vance curse. Then he had an arm around her to hustle her toward the sink. He flipped on the water, stripped off the glove and thrust her hand under the flow. She shivered in reaction to the cool liquid on her skin as the cut began to throb.

Vance cursed again. "You have bandages in here?"

But her dizzy brain couldn't formulate an answer. With another muttered curse, he wrapped her finger in a paper towel. His arm still around her, he hustled her down the steps.

"Wait," she protested, "we can't leave the truck."

"We're leaving the truck," he said, but he set her in one of the bistro chairs while he lowered the awning and locked up. Then he had her back on her feet and was helping her toward the courtyard.

Next thing she knew, she was sitting at one of the pic-nic tables beside the dance area, surrounded by people talking, eating and laughing. Vance had found an elas-tic bandage somewhere, and he was hunkered down, bent over her wounded finger. The strings of fairy lights overhead caught the gold threads in his hair. Bemused, she watched him unwrap the paper towel with tender care.

"I'm fine," she said.

He glanced up. "Drink the cola."

She blinked, realizing he'd brought along a can with the first-aid equipment. Her free hand circled the sweating aluminum and she tilted her head to take a long draft of sugar and caffeine—nearly half of it in one go. "Good," she said, and pressed the cold container to her throat.

Vance wrapped the bandage securely about her finger, then looked up again. "Your hand's fine—"

"Told you."

"—but you need to hydrate. Finish that and I'll get you some water."

She made a face. "Yes, Grandpa Vance."

One brow rose. "My grandpa switched me when I sassed."

"Liar." With the cola almost finished, she was feeling much better. Or maybe it was because he continued to cradle her hand. It was the closest they'd been to each other since that night on the cliff. "Bet your mom would confirm it."

His eyes narrowed. "That doesn't mean I won't spank you."

Some imp invaded her body. Spoke through her mouth in a soft, teasing tone. "But not because you're mad at me."

He abruptly stood, and she rose, too, drawn up by his hand. His gaze dropped to where they were joined, as if he'd just realized he still had her in his grasp. In the next moment, the band started playing again. No bluegrass now, but a country ballad. Love gone wrong.

"Dance with me," she said, another impulse she couldn't stifle.

"We could go now," Vance replied, his expression

guarded. "Back to the beach house. We've more than put our time in."

That's what she'd wanted all day. For this command performance to be over. Until now.

"Dance with me," she repeated. And without waiting for an answer, tugged him toward the couples who were already moving to the music under a canopy of crisscrossed lights.

With a sigh, he let himself be led. Then he released another as she moved into his arms, his big male body sheltering her in a way that made her acutely aware of her feminine differences. They swayed together, their feet barely moving, her arms around his neck, his fingers linked at the small of her back. He rested his chin on the top of her head.

Layla's body started to hum, a force pulsing under her skin. It made her feel edgy in Vance's arms and at the same time as if she'd found the most comfortable place on earth. The thought startled her, and she instinctively tried to retreat, shuffling back.

She glanced up as Vance tightened his hold.

Their eyes met and she couldn't look away. Or move away, either.

He groaned softly. "I've tried everything I can to control this…"

Well. They were finally going to address the issue.

"…but it continues to be a problem."

"It's not my fault," she protested.

"I didn't say it was." The fingers at the small of her back rubbed a little, and the pulse beneath her skin turned into a throb. Low in her belly, heat clenched like a fist, then released, sending fiery sparklers of sensation through her body. "I keep thinking it's *my* fault," Vance continued.

She shook her head. "It isn't. It's a force of nature, like…like the green flash."

"I looked that up, you know. It has to do with the atmosphere's density gradient and refraction."

What? Her brain was too tired for science, and she wouldn't allow him to change the subject now. Vance's leg moved between hers. It was rock-solid and the denim scraped deliciously against sensitized skin. "That doesn't make a bit of sense."

"Neither does this," he grumbled.

"Don't think I commemorated it in my diary with big happy letters," she shot back, a little insulted. "I wasn't prepared for this…this attraction thing to just show up. I assumed I'd have more of a choice."

He rolled his eyes. "Don't think sex is always like that time you strategized your own deflowering."

Now she narrowed her own eyes. "Yuck."

"Exactly what I thought when you told me about it." He heaved another sigh. "The truth is that yeah, sometimes it does just happen—the flash, the flare, the…"

"Burn," Layla supplied. So he'd felt like this before… with someone else? With Blythe? In her belly, a green-eyed monster twitched its tail.

"The burn. Jesus, Layla," he said under his breath. "What only you can do to me."

Only you. The monster subsided and, feeling a bit smug, Layla found herself smiling at Vance.

Which made him glare at her, though she detected an answering smile deep in his eyes. "Hey. I find it extremely inconvenient, lady."

What could she say to that? It wasn't as if she found

it any easier to deal with than he. So she closed her eyes and kept dancing. The band segued into another slow song—more heartbreak—but Vance didn't stop moving. Instead, he pushed her head against his chest and she nestled her cheek there and breathed him in.

The sexual fire settled a little, as if it could be banked when he was this close. Her gaze took in the other dancers, the twinkling lights, the beauty of the warm night. Picnic Day had likely looked this same way thirty years before. "This event's gone on every year of your life," she murmured.

"Mmm. We have photos of me from the first one, being carried around in a baby backpack."

She allowed her fingers to sift through the short hair at the back of his neck. "What's the best Picnic Day you remember?"

He was quiet a long moment. "Actually, this one's turned out not so bad."

"Yeah?" Surprised and a little pleased, her head came up.

Vance looked down at her, his lips curved. "Yeah."

Had she wished the day could be done? Layla thought. Not anymore. Right now she wanted the night to last forever.

And Vance was about to kiss her, she could read the intent in his eyes, so she lifted her chin to make sure he knew she'd welcome it. To shorten the distance between their lips, she even went on tiptoe.

But then she fell to her heels when Vance's brother appeared beside them, Blythe at his elbow. "Shall we switch partners?" Fitz said.

CHAPTER TEN

IF DANCING WITH LAYLA hadn't made his brain mush, Vance would have seen the trap coming and taken evasive maneuvers. As it was, Fitz had already moved off with the colonel's daughter—what the hell?—and he was left looking into Blythe's irrefutably beautiful face.

Blythe, who was his ex, and his brother's girlfriend.

Didn't that make him feel stupid? Vance shoved his hands in his front pockets and tried wiping his face of any expression.

"You're looking well," Blythe said, color rising up the pale skin of her neck. "I didn't really get a chance to talk to you at the tavern the other day, but you, uh, you looked well then also."

"Thanks," he said tersely, recalling that afternoon and how he'd fed Layla chips laden with guacamole. He'd been in a shitty mood then, too, until she'd teased him about the dip's aphrodisiac qualities. Thinking of that laughing light in her eyes, he almost smiled.

"So…" Blythe said, drawing his attention back to her and the present. She made a vague gesture with her hand.

Unlike Layla, Blythe had never been much of a chatterbox. God, their dates must have been made up of many long silences. He'd probably found it restful.

Now it struck him as too quiet. Passive.

Boring.

"Vance, I…" she began.

"Yes?" He could play polite.

Another moment of quiet plagued his patience. "I thought we should talk," she said, and then more words seemed to elude her.

Talk? *How about not,* Vance thought. "Go ahead," he replied, anyway.

But Blythe went mum for another long ninety seconds. "Well…" she finally said, swinging out one graceful arm.

Vance followed the movement, and his gaze caught on Layla and Fitz. They were, indeed, dancing, and he saw his brother's hand on her delicate shoulder. His stomach roiled as he watched her hair brush the back of the other man's knuckles. Something bitter-tasting coated his tongue.

Even more than he didn't want this conversation with Blythe, he didn't want Fitz's hands on the colonel's daughter, Vance decided. He could still feel her against *his* chest, could still feel the trusting curl of her fingers against *his* palm, could still feel the balm of her smile invading *his* heart. *Mine,* a voice whispered in his head, the single syllable as hard as steel.

Moving past Blythe with a murmured excuse and without a backward glance, he strode into the crowd of dancers, his gaze on Layla. *Mine.*

The primitive possession in the word poleaxed him. He halted, suddenly shocked by his fierce response. *Shit,* he thought, quickly backing off the dance floor. Had he actually thought *mine?* "Shit, shit, shit," he muttered to himself as he avoided everyone by returning to the oak grove.

The other food vendors were already packed and gone, leaving the area dark except for the spotlight on the Karma Cupcakes truck. He leaned against its metal side, blessing the solitude. Just what he needed. Some quiet alone time to recoup from the hormones that must have supercharged his system while he'd danced with Layla.

Sweet God, she slayed him, and even the awkwardness of facing his ex, the beautiful Blythe, hadn't yanked him to the straight and narrow.

Yet it was imperative he clear his head, he thought, sucking in oxygen. Screw it on right. Regain his cool so he could go back to Beach House No. 9 with Layla and leave behind this craving to screw her brains out.

A few quiet minutes passed, calming him. Okay. He was solidly centered again, he decided. Feet firmly planted, common sense reestablished, wayward inclinations leashed.

With his composure regained, he decided to ready things for their return to Crescent Cove. He transferred the few leftover cupcakes to the pink boxes they'd arrived in, stored the bistro tables and chairs in the truck then moved toward the garbage can sitting nearby. Just as he pulled the liner free, a man walked out of the shadows and into the light. Vance started, gave an inward groan, then wiped any reaction from his face. *Don't lose your cool.*

"Dad," he said with a nod. Before this moment, he'd intentionally kept his distance from the older man—and suspected William Smith had done the very same thing. It was the coping mechanism they'd used the rare times they were forced together over the past years. As casually as he could, Vance tried tying off the bag, but his cast made him fumble and he cursed.

"I'll do that," his father said, reaching out.

Vance tightened his grasp on the plastic. "I've got it."

"Don't be ridiculous," the other man snapped, getting ahold of the bag. "Let go."

Looking down at his father's fingers, a sudden memory bubbled in Vance's brain. He'd been, what—four?— and learning to ride a bike on the long driveway here at the ranch. His dad had been running alongside him, keeping a steadying clasp on the handlebars. But Vance hadn't wanted steadying. He'd wanted to fly under his own steam and he'd been fierce about it. "Let go!" he'd shouted. "Let go!"

His father had acquiesced, and Vance had taken off, legs spinning as he sped away on a wave of exhilaration. He remembered grinning. *I'm a big kid now.* The new independence spurred him to pedal even faster....

Straight into the fence post at the end of the drive.

He'd lost a tooth, busted his lip, split open his chin. It was his first visit to the E.R. After stitching him up, they sent him back for X-rays twice. But it was only soft tissue damage, turned out. Broken bones came later.

Now, to prove he'd matured a little, he released his grip on the garbage liner.

It left his father holding the bag and staring at the cast on Vance's arm just as his mother had done back at Beach House No. 9. "Well..." the older man said, pulling a long breath into his lungs. "Well."

Vance didn't like the way his chest was beginning to tighten. *Keep that cool.* He ignored the feeling and tried for politeness. "How are you, Dad?"

His father tied an efficient knot in the plastic and

set it down at his feet. "Tired," he said, sounding irritable. "About this time every year it occurs to me what a damn lot of work we go through for Picnic Day and I swear this will be the last one ever."

Vance thought his father did look worn. He'd made a brief stop at the house eight months ago—on the eve of his latest deployment, as a matter of fact. His imminent leave-taking had gone unannounced—instead, he'd broken the news in a brief email once he was already out of the country, sparing himself the discomfort of witnessing his mother's certain dismay. Sitting in the kitchen with her that night, drinking coffee, he'd had a glimpse of his father. The other man had come in, they'd exchanged nods then he'd gone back out.

Though the contact had been brief, Vance was sure the spokelike lines bracketing the outside corners of his father's eyes were deeper now. He looked thinner, too, the wear in the leather belt around his 501 jeans testifying that he'd cinched it to the next hole. "You should get Fitz and Baxter to do more of the work. I ran into Uncle Roy and he said Bax didn't even show today."

"It's my ranch," his father replied, his voice tight. "My decision."

"That's right." Vance worked hard to hold back any flicker of reaction. "It's always been up to you."

Then he turned to the truck, his chest feeling as if it was wrapped by a belt fastened even more tightly than his father's. *Breathe,* he told himself. *Be calm.*

"You've hurt your mother," his father called out.

Old news, Vance thought, suddenly as weary as the other man claimed to be. "I'm sorry for it," he said. "When I go back, I'll try to send a few more emails."

"Emails." His father made a sound of disgust. "Is nothing serious with you?"

Vance hung on to his calm with everything he had, even as he spun to face his father again. "War is pretty serious. I take it that way."

The older man's mouth set in a harsh line of disapproval. "You're determined to go back, then?"

Vance hesitated. Under the circumstances, he could request a medical discharge, dispensing with the remainder of his service obligation. But then what? Right now it was a question he didn't have an answer for. "I'm going back."

"What about your girl?"

What about her? he almost asked. Layla had no place in his future. "It'll give her a chance to dump me," he said, pissed at how bitter he sounded. "There's a precedent for that, as we both know."

His father winced, then his voice took on an almost conciliatory tone. "Vance, your brother…"

"No." Just like that, the calm was gone, a spike of rising anger in its place. And all the bitterness he'd kept at bay flooded him, his fingers curling into fists. He couldn't listen to his dad defend Fucking Perfect Fitz. Not now.

Not ever. God, Vance thought, he never should have returned here for Picnic Day.

His father appeared pained. "Look—"

"I don't want to talk about Fitz." Vance's chest was tightening again, but now the pressure was all from the inside. His temper was lava-hot and ready to blow. "Or about that."

"But you landed on your feet, son, like you always do. You're with Layla."

Layla. Thinking of her did nothing to reduce that suffocating heat building inside him. *Just admit to it,* he urged himself, *because you've always been a lousy liar. Tell him she's nothing to you. Clear up this stupid charade.* "Layla is—"

"I hope you're about to say something really nice," the woman herself put in, emerging from the gloom into the circle of light surrounding the cupcake truck.

Surprised by her sudden appearance, Vance stared at her. All day, even when he'd held her in his arms on the dance floor, he'd avoided really looking at her. Now here she was, in a little dress the color of fertile earth and decorated with swirls of gold and bronze. Her shoulders were bare, her long legs revealed from an inch above the knee down to her gold-strapped sandals. Her skin gleamed with a light tan. *You have to know how pretty you are,* he'd told her when they'd arrived.

"So damn pretty," he murmured now.

She smiled at him. "That will do." Then she turned to his father. "Your wife said you might enjoy an avocado cupcake. We ran out earlier in the evening, but I managed to set aside a couple for you."

Before his father had a chance to answer, she ducked into the truck, and then was out again, a square of pink cardboard in hand. "I hope you like them," she said with another smile.

William Smith looked down at the box, then up at Layla. Vance almost laughed. Clearly he wasn't the only Smith whom she could disarm. "I...uh, thank you."

"You're welcome."

Vance's father hesitated, glanced at Vance. "I should get back. Help your mother." He stepped toward the shadows, then turned around. "Son…" Words seemed to fail him.

"Yeah?"

"If I—" He stopped, started again. "If I don't see you before you…return, stay safe."

Vance gave a curt nod.

His dad now turned to Layla with a ghost of a smile. "And you, young lady. Word of caution. Be careful with this one."

Hearing it as an insult, Vance bristled. "That's right. My father never could bring himself to trust me not to do the wrong thing."

The other man shot him a look, his own temper clearly kindling. "You never gave me much—"

"I trust him," Layla said, her voice emphatic. "You should know why."

His father blinked. "What?"

Vance stared at her. *What?* "Don't—"

"He was wounded trying to save my father's life," Layla said. "You should know that. Your son's a hero."

"I…" The older man glanced between Vance and Layla.

"But before that, my dad wrote me letters. He was a colonel, and he told me about the men under his command. 'There's something special about his hands.' He wrote that to me about Vance. 'Or maybe it's his heart that makes the difference,' my father said. 'He's saved soldiers I thought would never survive.'"

Jesus. More emotion roiled in Vance's belly. *Saved.* That was all gone now, wasn't it? He'd lost his fucking battlefield luck like he'd lost so much else. The ranch, his family, the fiancée he'd been sure would meet with their approval. A right move, for once. His body vibrated with the tension of holding back the urge to punch the daylights out of something. He'd take off running, he would, if he thought he had a hope of escaping the mess that was inside him.

His father was staring at Layla now, clearly non-plussed. "Well. I'm sorry to hear about your loss."

"Thank you," she said.

With a quick glance at Vance, he grabbed the tied-off bag of garbage. "Good night."

She smiled up at him, guileless. "Goodbye. I won't forget meeting you, Mr. Smith."

And at that—a kind word regarding Layla's dad, but nothing nearly as nice for his son—Vance's father left. Left them alone.

Left Vance with the war that was raging inside him. Left Layla, who looked as if she hadn't a care in the world.

In seething silence, Vance climbed into the food truck. She followed suit. In the driver's seat he sat for a moment, the fingers of his right hand tight on the steering wheel as he tried to separate the tangle of feelings coursing through him.

A skirmish with his father. Fitz and Blythe. Layla in his arms, slow dancing to "Love Gone Wrong."

He's saved soldiers I thought would never survive.

Glancing down at his "healing" hands, he tightened his fingers on the wheel. "When we get back to the beach house," he told Layla, his voice thick, "you stay clear." He was ready to blow, past the point where he could extinguish flames.

"Why?"

He didn't dare look at her. They might not make it as far as Crescent Cove if he did. "I'm on the edge of

control. You get too close and it's going to be the green
flash, baby. Our very own unique natural phenomenon."

She sucked in a quick breath.

"Yeah," he said, answering the unspoken question.
"We'll both burn."

VANCE DROVE AWAY FROM the ranch without waiting for
Layla's response. His muscles were tense, his mind
whirling, a maelstrom kicked up by the day. His companion stayed silent, but that didn't mean she was quiet.
In the darkness the sound of her breathing brushed
down his spine like a touch. She squirmed in her seat,
moving restlessly and, Jesus, he swore he could detect
the soft swish of smooth flesh on smooth flesh when
she crossed her legs.

It made him sweat.

Instead of driving the truck to the parking lot of
Captain Crow's, he took it straight to No. 9, bumping
along the crushed-shell track, then braking in the driveway. He jumped out and on fast feet headed around the
side of the house toward the surf line, churning up the
soft sand.

He didn't stop when he reached the hard-packed
stuff. Nor when the first wave washed over the toes of
his running shoes. Ignoring the icy wetness, he kept
wading forward, drenching his calves, his knees, his
thighs.

"Are you crazy?" a voice yelled from the beach.

He ignored Layla, going deep enough to baptize his
private parts. His feet were steady on the bottom of the
ocean, tonight's surf rolling in without any real force.

"I said, are you crazy?"

She sounded closer now, and he glanced back. The

moonlight revealed the woman. Her sandals were discarded on the sand and she was up to her ankles in the water. A striped beach towel lay over one arm. "C'mon out. You're going to freeze."

It's what he wanted. To put his feelings on ice. To numb every emotion the day had wrought, from lust to hurt. "Leave me alone."

"As soon as you get into the house."

Didn't she understand? Inside those walls, he'd be dangerous to her. Addy had said she'd be out for the night, which left just him and Layla. Alone. Alone with his temper that was as reckless as he'd once been and poised to find a convenient outlet.

"Vance."

He gritted his teeth, fighting the need to turn to her. To take her in his arms and use her to forget the events of the day. The feelings had to go somewhere, and it was either freeze them into submission out here in the ocean, or drag her back to a bed and bury them—and himself—inside Layla.

Fingers touched the small of his back. He whirled, shocked to find she'd waded this far, too. Ocean water swirled around her midriff, and the skirt of her dress rose up, floating around her. "Let's go inside," she said, her teeth already chattering. "Please, Vance."

And it was as if his brain thought she was pleading for something else. Because suddenly he moved in on her, his uncasted arm at her waist, bringing her close. His fingers tangled in her hair and he yanked back her head. Took the kiss he'd been wanting all night.

All day.

Every day since meeting her.

It wasn't gentle or seductive or kind. He thrust his

tongue deep, tasting Layla, that trademark sugary tartness of her, as if she'd just sucked a fingerful of lemon
icing. She pressed herself against him, not fighting for
her freedom, only fighting to get closer to him, he realized. One of her legs wrapped around the back of his.

Then another wave slapped at them, this one stronger
than the others. He stumbled a little. She lost her foot-
ing and slipped lower into the water, only saving herself from total immersion by latching both legs around
his waist and hanging on.

Neither of them broke the kiss.

But instinct had him moving toward the beach, even
as he feasted on her. She was wide-open for him, her
own tongue stroking inside his mouth, and he no longer
felt the cold. When he reached the shoreline, the wet
sand sucked at his shoes, but he didn't let it slow him.
Finally on firm ground, he lengthened his stride, making for the deck steps.

He halted, though, outside the sliding glass door.
They'd neglected to leave any lights on, but even in the
darkness he knew salt water was streaming from them.
Breaking their kiss, he looked down into her dazed eyes.
"I'm wet," he said. "You're wet."

"God, yes," she said, her voice fervent.

Wait. Did she mean...? Then she pulled on the back
of his neck and brought his mouth to hers for another
deep, hungry kiss. Her urgency was contagious. This
was just what he'd been waiting for, what he needed,
and his pulse started double-timing as he took in harsh
breaths through his nose. Yes, yes, *yes*. Sex would be the
vehicle in which he drove away all that troubled him.

Layla's fingers were at the hem of his sodden T-shirt.
He let her draw it up and off, even as he toed out of his

shoes. She muttered as she worked at his wet jeans. Finally, he had to push her hands away because her touch was only causing them to fit that much tighter. Between the damn cast and drenched denim it was awkward to get them off, but he managed, and even purloined the beach towel that she'd brought and wrapped it around his naked waist.

Now he turned his attention to the beautiful woman who stood before him.

Her big eyes on him, she was leaning against the door, her palms pressed to the glass. He thought about giving her yet another chance to back out. He thought about all the promises that should be standing between them. Between this.

But then he ran his forefinger along the slope of her bare shoulder and she shuddered, her lashes drifting low. Yeah, she was wet.

Screw second thoughts, his or hers. He couldn't wait to have her. It would suck the wildness out of him, purge him of the old betrayals and the new pain. He'd lose himself in her, thus lifting the heavy weight that being home had put on his soul.

His slow finger reversed, then moved around to the nape of her neck and the halter tie of her dress. He toyed with it a minute, giving himself a chance to appreciate how the soaked cotton material was plastered to her braless breasts. The tips were beaded to hard points and he imagined taking the cold nipples in his mouth. Warming them with his tongue.

She made an impatient sound, a husky little moan that came from the back of her throat.

"Shh, shh, shh," he murmured. "Easy."

"Vance, you should… We should… I think—"

"No thinking, Layla," he said, still playing with the bow. He'd be damned if she thought ahead this time. Plotted things out. No, not going to happen that way with him. "Close your eyes, baby. Just feel." Then, bending his head, he sucked her nipple into his mouth, rubbing his tongue over the fabric.

She made another sweet sound of urgency, and he tightened on that nub of flesh, then pulled on the tie. He lifted his mouth long enough to allow the fabric to fall and then he latched onto her again, her bare flesh now, more strong sucks that had her fingers clutching at his hair, holding him to her.

Her skin was cold and he rubbed his face against the fullness of her lush breast, then moved to the other, breathing on the chilled surface to warm her up. He was on fire already, that burn that she could spark in him roaring. He found the zipper at the back of her dress, and still caressing her with his whiskered cheeks, drew it down.

The dress dropped to her feet and he straightened.

Sweet Lord. Layla, with her long wavy hair, her big eyes. Slim limbs, heaving breasts, teeny tiny white panties that gleamed like an oyster shell in the moonlight.

His cock jerked against the terry of the towel. He rubbed his fingers there, calming it down, and she watched him touch himself, those eyes of hers wide again. Intrigued. Another shot of fire ran through him and he saw her lick her lips, her fingers curling into her palms as if to stop herself from reaching out.

She glanced up at him. "Vance?"

"You can touch me," he said, his voice hoarse. "Is that what you want?"

With a nod, she moved her right hand. It seemed to

take an aeon, but then her small fingers circled him, her palm cupping his shaft. He groaned, his head falling back as she moved it up and down. The damn arm injuries had prevented him from easing himself like this, and he'd needed it, so often, since meeting this brown-eyed girl.

He heard himself start to pant, the thrumming urgency turning to emergency as she continued to rub. His hips moved, bucking into her touch, and it was so good. So, so good...

Groaning again, Vance snatched at her wrist and held it away from him. Another second and he'd be making love to a towel instead of to the woman who drove him mad.

"Bedroom," he said, his voice guttural, and he spun her around by the shoulders. They made it inside and he flicked on a low light to guide their way to the hall and his downstairs bedroom. He kept one set of fingers on her shoulder, but then his gaze fell to her panty-covered ass. It wasn't a thong she was wearing, but French-cut panties that revealed the under-curves of her sweet bottom's rounded lobes.

Vance almost tripped on his tongue at the sight, and he inserted the fingers of his free hand under the elastic on the right side, holding it between thumb and fingers, allowing his knuckles to stroke the full softness with each of her steps. She glanced over her shoulder at him, wide-eyed again, and he hoped the baring of his teeth looked friendly. But oh, hell, did he want to take a bite out of her.

The room was dark and he flipped on the small lamp on the dresser, adding a soft glow to the interior. He thought, *condoms,* and hurried to grab some from the bathroom drawer. They'd been an autobuy during a toiletries run when he'd first returned, though he'd had little expectation of using them. Back by the bed, he ditched the towel, but she remained where he'd left her, wearing only that little scrap of Frenchified satin and her long hair hanging over her bare breasts.

He tossed the condoms onto the bedside table and moved close to kiss her again. Her taste should have made him mindless, but that mix of emotions inside him started boiling once more with the heat of her tongue against his. In his mind's eye he saw her going into Fitz's arms, he saw her handing his father cupcakes, he saw his father warning Layla about him.

Word of caution. Be careful with this one.

Vance didn't want her any less, but he wanted all the memories and conflicts and anger brought on by the day smothered, too. He pushed her onto the mattress and she scrambled back toward the pillows. He crawled after her, catching the side of her panties with his right hand so that the material slid down her legs as she moved toward the headboard.

Yeah. This was what he wanted. This was what he had to have, he thought, as he glimpsed the wetness between the pink, plump petals of her sex. He'd taste her, touch her, penetrate her, and he'd use his tongue and his fingers and his cock to banish the anger he felt toward his family.

Vance froze, startled by that last thought.

"What the hell are we doing?" he asked, a wash of guilt making him feel a little sick. "I don't want this."

She lifted a brow, her gaze sliding down to his eager erection.

"Okay," he conceded. "I want this. God, I *really* want

this. But I shouldn't be acting on it because of what happened today with them." He shifted to sit on the side of the bed and closed his eyes, his cock throbbing like a toothache.

"Them?"

He made a slashing gesture. "You know. My family. God, I'm pissed. And I shouldn't take that out on you. Like this."

The mattress dipped as she moved toward him. "They've disappointed you." Her voice was soft. "Today, they hurt you."

He didn't want to admit it.

"It's okay. I understand." Her hand touched his back, smoothed down. "My mother walked away from me when I was two years old. My father left me for good two months ago. I can get a little mad about those things."

"Ah, sweetheart…" Half turning, he gazed at her face. Her eyes were big, vulnerable pools in the darkness. He cupped her cheek with his hand.

She nudged her chin into his palm so her mouth could press a kiss to his flesh. "And lonely."

God, didn't that just hit him square in the chest? In a quick move, Vance pulled her into his lap, her nakedness against his. He was still angry and frustrated, not to mention stirred up by lust, but now tenderness infused him, too. Layla was lonely. Of course she was. And though it only added to his already-crowded emotional landscape, he didn't seem to have a choice.

Her arms went around him. "You know what, Vance?" she whispered.

"What?" he said, pressing a kiss to the top of her head.

"Sometimes...sometimes a person just needs to be held."

And like that, he took another blow. But the pain turned into a pulsing sexual ache as his mouth found hers and their tongues tangled and their skin heated. The decision was done, the die cast, the outcome destined. And it was okay now because he no longer was doing this only for himself.

Sometimes a person just needs to be held.

So he held her in a dozen ways. Her body against him. Her tongue in his mouth. Her pearling nipples between his lips. She took him in, as well. Arching when he slid a finger inside the wet clasp of her core. Crying out when he made it two, then three. He thumbed her clit until she was making those sweet, urgent sounds again, and then he turned her to her belly and used his tongue to paint the long valley of her spine and the sweet curve of her bottom cheeks.

The frantic clamor of need quieted the longer he had her under his hands and his mouth. The desire was still insistent, but he found finesse, and used it to nudge her in small increments toward the edge. Putting her once again on her back, he bent to her breasts, tonguing and sucking as his fingers moved to toy with the hard little knot between her thighs. He listened to her breathing, paid attention to the coiling tension in her body and, when he felt her rise up to his hand, her hips tilting toward him, he replaced his fingers with his sheathed cock. They both groaned as he began to thrust.

As his hips moved, he lifted onto his elbows and cradled her face in his good hand. "Lonely now, baby?"

Her low husky laugh sent heat up his spine and her

knees bent so the silky insides of her thighs clasped him. "No, Vance."

He kissed each cheek, her nose, her chin. "This is good," he said.

"So good," she agreed, and then she smiled.

He smiled back, but then turned serious as her internal muscles tightened on his cock. "Oh, God," he muttered.

She lifted into his next thrust. "Oh, now," she said.

He drew back, then pressed deeper, pushing into the melting, yielding, pulsing heat. "Now?"

"Now."

Reaching between them, he brushed the wet, upstanding knot of nerves and Layla jolted, her body jerking into his. She came around him, her muscles clenching his cock, her moans sweet music as he felt the new flush of heat crossing her skin and entering his.

He took her mouth then, pushing his tongue inside, penetrating her there, too, in a rhythm matching the carnal beat of his heart and the erotic demand of his desire. She surrendered to him, her arms and legs holding him against her as he groaned in climax.

Breath still moving fast in his chest, he rose up to look at her pretty, pretty face. Everything he'd felt all day was still inside him, but it was frosted with the sweetness of Layla's fine-grained skin and her swollen mouth. He'd gotten rid of nothing in the bedding of her, he acknowledged, but only added her flavor, her voice, the miracle of her coming around his cock to his memory. Filling him up instead of purging anything.

And at that moment it all felt too damn good to regret.

CHAPTER ELEVEN

LAYLA WOKE UP LIKE SHE never did anymore, in a room warmed by sunshine. Usually, dawn's gray fingers tickled her into wakefulness, the need to get to the cupcake truck and get to work foremost in her mind. But because she'd not known how late her Picnic Day duties would go, she and Uncle Phil had decided to take the day off, their first, and she stretched her toes along the sleek sheets and—

Shot upright in bed.

Vance's bed.

The place beside her was empty now. He'd been there all night long, though, his muscled male warmth, his even breathing. Sinking back onto the pillow, Layla let herself remember what that was like. The sex beforehand had been scary-wondrous, an experience that later she'd break down layer by layer, detail by detail in order to marvel over each and every one. But, oh, how sweet was the companionship in sleep, she mused, closing her eyes against their sudden sting.

While she'd never intended to get physically involved with Vance, last night seemed as right to her now as it had been when she'd been pulled, naked, into his lap. She had wanted to be held, he'd needed the skin-to-skin contact, too, and the results…well, who could complain about the results?

Not Layla. What's done was done and regrets were for women who didn't know how transient life could be.

The smell of coffee lured her from the covers a short while later. She dashed for her own room, showered quickly then pulled on shorts and a T-shirt. At the last moment she grabbed a baseball cap and tugged it low over her forehead, threading her long hair out the back gap. It would provide a shield of sorts.

Sure, she had no regrets, but she did have a healthy sense of self-preservation. Which meant she didn't want to give Vance a clear shot at reading her emotions on her face—not until she had a chance to assess his.

The kitchen was empty. Was he avoiding her like he'd avoided his famiily the day before? Trying to ignore the disappointing thought, she filled a mug from the coffee carafe and added a splash of half-and-half. Cocking her head, she listened for any sign of Vance, but though the toaster was still warm and a loaf of bread lay on the counter, the house was silent.

Her bare feet quiet on the hardwood floors, she drifted across the living room, drawn by the view of blue sky, gold-dappled ocean and the small waves flouncing against the sand like sassy little girls with white-edged petticoats. Then she saw Vance. Pleasured relief filled her as she took in his relaxed figure. In jeans and a T-shirt, he sat on the deck by the stairs that led to the beach. His back was propped against one newel and an empty mug rested beside his hip. As she watched, he broke off pieces of toasted bread and tossed them into the air.

Greedy seagulls had figured out his game and wheeled for them, somehow just managing to avoid midair collisions. Pigeons gathered, too, hoping for a missed crumb or two. Their tubby, sooty-feathered bodies waddled around the sand at the bottom of the steps, looking as out of place in the beach setting as the tourists who showed up wearing their dress socks with sandals.

She pushed open the sliding glass door, and the outside air washed over her, warm and salty and welcoming. Vance had yet to notice her arrival and she indulged in another moment of observation. He tossed another piece of toast into the air, his face lifted, and she saw the small smile on his face. It made her own lips curve.

He looked at ease, she thought, a rare state for him. Even when he was still, there was an alertness about him, as if he was waiting. Something like a runner braced for the starting gun at a race, she decided. Or, considering where he'd been and what he did, waiting for the sound of a real gun.

Her hand went to her belly as it suddenly jittered. Vance, at war. Her fingers curled and she moved the fist to the space between her breasts, cursing her hard-thumping heart. After the many times she'd waved goodbye to her father, she thought she'd learned how to manage these sudden bouts of anxiety.

Vance, at war.

Did she make a sound? Because his head swiftly turned and his gaze landed on her. He raised his half-casted arm and waved two fingers. "Hey." Layla held her breath, then released it as he followed that up with an easy smile. *Happy to see you,* it said.

Hot goose bumps skittered across her skin as she stepped farther onto the deck. "Good morning."

He glanced toward the surf, then back at her. "Looks that way. Sleep well?"

"Mmm." Without being able to help herself, she continued toward him, drawn by this new mood of his. Maybe they'd have more scary-wondrous sex, maybe not. For now it was enough to see that look of contentment on his face.

His fingers caught hers, pulling her nearer. He shifted around to face the beach, leaving a spot for her on the step. As she sat down, he purloined her mug and brought it to his own mouth, his blue eyes warm over the rim.

More hot chills burst over her skin and her nipples budded, remembering the heat of his mouth. Okay, for sure she wanted more scary-wondrous sexy times with him. And also moments like this, when they shared a morning and a cup of coffee.

Maybe she was beginning to believe in the Beach House No. 9 magic, after all.

"V.T.," a voice said, and a figure came around the corner of the deck, approaching from the beach.

Vance stiffened, and his fingers untangled from hers. "Fitz," he said, and the name sounded more like a snarl. "One dance with Layla and you can't keep away? Are you trying to steal another of my girls?"

The other man flicked a glance at her. She gave him a small nod. He hadn't said much during their dance the night before—a dance he'd clearly orchestrated to give Vance and Blythe a chance to clear the air, not that it had seemed to do much good—but she had more sympathy for him than maybe she ought. He *had* hurt his brother.

Fitz returned his attention to Vance. "We have unfinished business, V.T. Me and you."

Layla made to rise. "I'll go."

"Stay," the two men said together.

Great, she thought, but settled back on the step.

Fitz wore a pair of khakis and a white polo shirt. He hesitated a moment, then dug into his pocket for something he then tossed to his brother.

Vance's reflexes were good, but his cast got in the way of the catch. The small item bounced off the hard surface crossing his palm and arced toward Layla to land in her lap. A jeweler's box. Slowly, she picked it up and passed it to the man seated beside her.

He looked at it for a long moment, then flipped open the lid. A diamond solitaire winked in the sunlight. Elegant and classy, it suited a woman like Blythe. The lack of expression on Vance's face confirmed it had been hers.

"She's been wanting to return it to you," Fitz said. "Last night she had it with her, but you didn't stick around long enough for her to give it back."

The ring box shut with a snap and Vance looked at his brother. "She can keep it," he said, holding it out.

The other man shook his head. "No, she can't." There was another long hesitation. "Because as of early this morning, she's wearing *my* ring."

Oh, *no.* Layla froze, remembering the last confrontation between the two on this deck. There'd been bloodshed and bruises in the offing, she'd smelled it like brimstone on the breeze as she'd stood on the sand eavesdropping. And now that Blythe wasn't just Fitz's girlfriend, but his full-fledged fiancée...? She slid a cautious look at Vance.

He didn't move a muscle. "Congratulations," he finally said, his voice carefully neutral.

Fitz frowned. Clearly he hadn't been expecting felicitations. "Uh…" His gaze darted to Layla.

"I hope you'll be very happy," she said, suppressing her sigh. No matter what Vance's attitude appeared to be, this couldn't be happy news to him.

Fitz cleared his throat, shoved his hands in his pockets, withdrew them. At his obvious discomfort she felt another spurt of sympathy. This wouldn't bring the brothers any closer to the reconciliation that the older of the two so clearly desired.

His hands ran through his hair. "Look, Vance…"

An awkward silence welled up. Layla tried breathing through it, tried appearing as impassive as the man seated beside her, but one of her legs started moving, the knee bouncing up and down. She stole another glance at Vance, thinking of his earlier sunny mood. He wasn't tearing his brother limb from limb, so maybe it was still there, just waiting behind his stony expression. Just waiting for Fitz to be on his way.

"Well," she finally said, unable to bear the tension—and eager for the confrontation to end without bloodshed. "You've made your delivery. We don't want to keep you any longer." Her knee was pumping now, like a telegraph key under the fingers of an experienced operator.

Vance reached over and pressed the twitchy joint, stilling the movement. "I don't think Fitz is finished."

"V.T.…" His brother started, stopped again.

"Just spit it out," Vance said. "Layla's right. We have things we want to get to." He turned his head to nuzzle her cheek.

The touch of his lips on her skin, his breath on the shell of her ear made her blood run hot again. But Fitz was standing there, watching, so she managed not to melt into the floorboards. Instead, she covered the fingers Vance had on her knee with hers.

His brother cleared his throat once more. "I know… of course, I know about that letter she wrote you. Blythe's letter."

"The one breaking our engagement?"

"I'm talking about the second letter," Fitz said. "After you two were over. In it she said we had begun dating, though it was nothing serious."

"What?" Vance still sounded calm. "You thought I didn't guess it was more than that?"

"I…" Shrugging, his brother let the word drift off.

"Fitz, I know you. You're always serious. It didn't fool me for a second." Then he turned his head to press another kiss on Layla's cheek. "So, if you've finally gotten everything off your chest…"

Implying—and she wasn't sure if it was solely for his brother's benefit or not—that there were some scary-wondrous sexy times in the offing. Layla squirmed a little on her wooden seat, having mixed feelings about that now. Was she still just a prop to disguise his wounded feelings? Now that something real had happened between them, that didn't sit so well any longer.

Vance caught her chin and turned her face toward him, his gaze searching hers as if he sensed her new disquiet. "Go away, Fitz."

"Just one more thing."

Vance's sigh was warm against her face. "What?" he said, glancing toward his brother.

"Mom wants you at the engagement party. A brunch deal."

Vance stilled. "I don't think—"

"Please. We have to do this right for the family. You need to be there."

"I told you—"

"You told me you're with Layla now." Fitz lifted his arms. "What's the problem?"

"I'm returning to Afghanistan," Vance said. "Soon."

"That's why we'll have it soon. You're here at Crescent Cove until the end of the month, you told Mom. So the party's scheduled for the last Sunday in July."

"Fitz—"

"We picked that date just for you, Vance."

"For me," Vance repeated. "You're doing this for me."

"Hell," his brother said, spinning around. "Never mind. But you'll tell Mom you refuse, not me." He began to stalk off.

"Fitz!" Layla called out.

With a sigh, he halted. When he turned back, the misery on his face made her feel sorry for him all over again. "I forgot my manners," he said. "Goodbye, Layla."

Without looking at Vance, she twined her fingers with his and addressed his brother. "You tell us where and what time—we'll be there." She didn't dare look at the man sitting beside her, but she could feel his temper in his rigid posture and the way his hand tightened on hers. Still, it seemed like the right action to take, and if Vance couldn't commit to it, she'd do it for him.

Anything else was retreat, and her father had taught her to never tolerate such a thing.

Fitz glanced from her face to Vance's. "V.T.?"

"What the lady wants," he said, shrugging, then

lifted their joined fingers in order to kiss the back of her hand. "Whatever she desires."

When Fitz was gone, Vance dropped her like a hot potato and rose to his feet. Layla looked up at him, uncertain about what mood he might reveal next. Happiness again, she hoped. But it was a vain hope; she knew it when he ran down the steps, racing toward the surf. Two chubby pigeons twittered in alarm and fluttered out of his way. One of the seagulls he'd befriended sailed close on the wind as Vance drew back his arm.

The gull tried snatching at the ring box on its long arc toward the water. But it missed, and the splash was small and silent as Blythe's ring sank into the depths.

Vance was silent, too—though not small at all as he stalked back toward the house. His expression hard, he brushed past Layla to mount the steps.

"Are you all right?"

He grunted.

She scrambled to her feet. "What are you going to do now?"

"I'm going to hunt down a calendar."

Confused, she tried to keep up with him. "A calendar? Why?"

"In order to count down how many more goddamn days are left before I can get the hell out of California."

ADDY KNEW BAXTER had returned. Though she didn't look up from her laptop screen, she sensed him looming in the doorway of the Sunrise Pictures archives room. *I'll ignore him,* she thought. *Then he'll go away.*

She was done with him. She had to be done with him.

It's what she'd been telling herself since that day in his condo. She'd kept herself busy since then, working by day on the archives and then distracting herself in the evenings by visits with old friends. She'd even gritted her teeth and managed a dinner with her mother and then another with her father.

Thoughts of Baxter hadn't bothered her at all.

At least not as much as his silent presence was bugging her, as he continued to stand just a few feet away. "What are you doing here?" she groused, her gaze still focused on her computer. "Your reputation as All Business Baxter is going to be downgraded if you keep escaping your office like this."

Instead of answering, he moved into the room. From the corner of her eye, she saw him riffle through one of the boxes. She'd been sorting the paperwork, and had put what she termed the "numbers stuff" into its own carton. The ledgers were bound by olive-green, cloth-covered cardboard, and she'd barely spared them a glance before separating them from the business and personal letters that she hoped held clues to Sunrise's demise as well as the truth of the relationship between Edith Essex and her husband.

She'd scanned the correspondence page by page into her computer so she could examine it as much as she liked without damaging the originals. That process now done, she'd entered them into a database, arranged them by date and was now reading through them one at a time.

Baxter moved to stand behind her. "Have you found anything interesting?"

"No," she said, but continued on in hopes of quickly satisfying his curiosity. Perhaps then he'd go. "From what I can tell, Sunrise Pictures was fine financially— though I confess I'm not an expert at deciphering that side of things. But the letters between Sunrise and its various vendors and suppliers don't hint at money problems."

"What about the personal correspondence?"

That made her sigh. "There's a dearth of it, actually. I hoped to find letters between Edith and her husband, but so far, nothing. There are a few dozen from some of the leading men and ladies of the day to Max Sunstrum, Sunrise's president, and there's a nugget or two there. In between discussions of schedules and salary and availability I've found references to parties they'd mutually attended. As time goes on, however, more than one correspondent questions where Edith has been and why she's been absent from the Hollywood scene."

"Because there was trouble in the marriage? The affair that's rumored?"

Addy lifted a shoulder. "That's what I'm trying to find out. *That's why I'm too busy for interruptions.*" Now she glanced back to see if he got her unsubtle hint.

Damn. She shouldn't have looked at him. Of course, he'd come right from the office. His hair was in those impeccable layers, as smooth and shiny as golden fish scales. He wore his summer-weight suit like most men wore T-shirts and jeans. The tie around his neck had been loosened.

The tie.

Oh, God. She stared at the navy-and-white stripes, remembering the one she'd secured around his eyes so she'd have the courage to go to bed with him. And she'd gone to bed with him to get him out of her life.

"Why are you still here?" she demanded, frowning.

He frowned right back. "Why did you leave the other night without saying goodbye?"

Addy shrugged again. Not for a million dollars would she admit she'd been grateful he'd dozed off afterward so she could escape. He'd been her first, though not her only lover. A time or two over the years she'd looked into the face of a man she'd been intimate with and managed to make clear there wasn't going to be another encounter between the sheets.

So it shouldn't have been hard—once she was back in her clothes—to have said so long to Baxter in a way that made clear she meant it as a permanent goodbye. Except she'd slipped out instead.

"Was that payback for what happened six years ago?" he asked, his eyes narrowing. "Because I essentially sneaked away, you figured you should have your chance to do the same?"

She glared at him. "I don't know what—"

"Can the crap, Addy," he said. "I'm not buying for a second your story that you don't remember our night together then. You gasped in shock when I licked your nipple for the first time. I kissed the tears from your cheek when I entered you—your first time."

She opened her mouth to emit some matching sort of answer, but nothing came out. He was the one with the confidence to be so blunt. Addy March had nowhere near that kind of self-assurance, and being with Baxter only made her feel the lack more.

"I want to see you again," he said. "I want to find some way to make it up to you for—"

"Why?" she interrupted, exasperated. "I'm not expecting you to make anything up to me."

"But—"

"I didn't expect anything from you after that night six years ago."

Baxter blinked. He rubbed his palm along the length of his tie, a gesture she might label as nervous if he didn't always appear so annoyingly poised. "You really *don't* remember that night."

Addy rolled her eyes. Maybe he wasn't as intimidatingly smart as she'd always thought. "I just admitted I do, okay? I'd had a little crush on you for years, that's the truth. When you asked me to dance, you're lucky I didn't keel over at your feet. My heart was going so fast when you took me in your arms that I thought I might pass out."

"A crush?" He was smiling, the smug bastard. "I kind of knew the second half of that. Even with only those twinkling lights overhead, I could see the pulse at your throat. Racing. Your skin is so fragile there, so thin and sweet. It's the first place I put my mouth."

Addy swallowed, nonplussed again.

"It's racing now, too," he said quietly.

She spun back toward her laptop. "The thrill of near-discovery. I'm excited about unraveling the mystery of Edith, Max and Sunrise Pictures."

Baxter put his hands on her shoulders and began to knead. "You're so tense, Addy. I'm not going to let you down again. I don't want it to be that way with us."

"I told you, you didn't ever let me down. Why do you keep insisting you did?"

"The things I said, the promises I made—"

"Not for one minute did I expect you to follow through on any of those."

His hands stilled, then dropped away. "I didn't think I could feel much worse about what happened, but you just proved me wrong."

Surprised, she turned to face him again, the casters

on the chair legs squeaking in the quiet room. It wasn't something she'd said to hurt him, but the expression on his chiseled, nearly too-handsome face was pained. "Baxter…"

He threw himself into the seat beside her. It was wheeled, like hers, and he used the heel of one elegant leather shoe to push himself away from the table. "I guess I deserve that. Clearly I have an overinflated sense of my own integrity."

"What?" Addy stared at him. "I don't know what you mean."

"Despite what I did that night, I've always considered myself one of the good guys, okay? I'm ethical, I pay all my taxes, I always buy my mother her favorite candy on Valentine's Day."

Addy told herself not to be charmed. But he bought his mother candy on Valentine's Day! "You *are* one of the good guys…at least I've always thought so."

"But you say you disbelieved me that night…even before I had the chance to prove your distrust was well-founded." He groaned, and ran his palms over his hair. "I *am* a jerk."

"No, Baxter. I don't think you're a jerk. I didn't put any credence into what you said because…because I'm me, and you're you."

"The jerk."

"No." It was frustrating and more than a little humiliating to clear this up. "You're Baxter Smith," she said, waving her hand to indicate the hair, the suit, the shiny shoes, "and I'm me."

He frowned. "I don't get it."

"You're you, and I'm me. Pl—plain Addy." She'd almost said "plump," but no need to go into that. "Nose-in-a-book, eyes-on-a-screen, head-in-the-clouds Addy March."

He just stared at her.

"You know *Little Women,* the book by Louisa May Alcott? The 'little women' are the March sisters. I used to pretend that I was one of them. They performed plays and told each other stories and had their loving Marmee and Father." When Baxter continued to stare at her she thought she wasn't making herself clear. "I pretended I was pretend people. I could pretend I was pretend people for days on end."

He still looked puzzled. "If this is about swapping childhood stories, I should probably tell you about the BSLS."

It wasn't about swapping childhood stories, it was about why they were ill-suited for each other, but now she was intrigued. "All right, I'll bite. BSLS?"

"*The* BSLS. The Baxter Smith Life Schedule."

"Huh?"

"I'm a very, uh, goal-oriented person. Maybe a little obsessive-compulsive. Even as a kid, I made lists, developed agendas, tracked my progress on spreadsheets. The summer after eighth grade, I got into running. I had a target. In the twelve weeks before school started—and the high school cross country season began—I wanted to log five hundred miles."

"That was very ambitious." Not that she'd admit it, but that was the summer her crush had begun. She'd been waiting for fifth grade to start, dreading another school year where she'd be ignored, or worse, made fun of. Always a dreamer, she'd been ripe for falling for a teen heartthrob. The first time she'd seen him run by, it had been chance, but after that she'd sit in wait by her bedroom window, a box of Pop-Tarts and another of Cap'n Crunch beside her, munching and crunching until he passed her window as he left on his run. She'd be there on his return, too, a little sick on sugar and puppy love. "Five hundred miles."

"They weren't all logged on the road. My father and I assigned a mile value to other things—sets of tennis, a round of golf, laps in the pool." He shrugged. "I think it was the next year that I developed the BSLS."

"The Baxter Smith Life Schedule."

"Yes. I've kept it all these years…kept to it. It's a timetable of important dates and milestones. I listed my high school graduation date, college graduation. I already figured I wanted a year of work before getting my MBA. Then, after that degree, I'd go directly into a job with the family."

She nodded. Baxter would be ordered that way. Precise in what he wanted, knowing it early, sticking to it like glue. It was the confidence thing again. That innate understanding of himself and his place in the world.

The golden boy.

Using the heel of his shoe, he rolled his chair closer to Addy's. His left kneecap brushed her right one. She moved it quickly away.

"The BSLS didn't just cover career plans," Baxter continued. "I charted my future personal life, too, in a logical, sensible fashion. No serious dating until after business school graduation. No living with a woman until marriage. And no thought of matrimony, or even falling in love for that matter, until somewhere past my thirty-first birthday."

Addy could think of nothing to say, though for the first time he seemed a little more human. Because only a man would come up with a prescribed system like that one.

"Oh, and that falling-in-love part? It would take six months, minimum, of dating before I'd even think of spilling those words." Baxter slid his hand down his tie again. "So you see, what happened that night was just so…so antithetical to those plans of mine."

"Off the Baxter Smith Life Schedule."

He spread his hands. "Yes. And I've felt lousy about the way I handled things ever since I impetuously made those promises. I woke up the next morning, panicked, and for what it's worth, I guessed and second-guessed myself over not calling you after promising I would. It's eaten at me for the last six years."

Addy turned back to her computer screen. "Well, don't worry about it. I didn't take you seriously. Like I said before, I didn't pencil you into my life schedule then, not even for a moment. So we're clear."

An odd sound echoed in the small room. From Baxter? She turned her head, stunned at the frustrated expression on his face and the tufts of hair sticking up on his head. As she watched, his fingers speared through the golden stuff again, creating more disorder. Baxter was never disordered.

"What's the matter now?" she asked.

"I want to see you, Addy. You know, go out with you. Date you."

"No—"

"We could take our time. As a matter of fact, that's best, right? Get to know each other, figure things out…"

Break her heart, when he finally opened his eyes and figured out an Addy March was not a proper match for a Baxter Smith. "No," she said again.

He shoved out of the chair and started pacing the small room. Slightly alarmed, Addy watched his quick strides, his lean figure moving past the movie posters for *Country Caroline* and *The Ghost and the Girl* and then the wall of framed movie stills of Edith Essex as an intrepid explorer, a rising nightclub star, a heartbroken lover. He stopped in front of this last, staring at it, she thought, without really seeing it.

"Look, Addy, I can explore long-term relationships now."

"But I can't."

"That's ridiculous," he said. Then he spun to face her. "We deserve a chance to see where this could go, don't you think? Look, you know I've never forgotten you. And we're great together in bed."

"Baxter—"

"I've got a business trip coming up the first week of August. Seattle. Come with me and we'll make a weekend of it."

"Baxter, I can't." When he made to protest again, she held up her hand. "I'm leaving the country—I'll be spending the next year in Paris studying at the Sorbonne. I leave the first week in August, which means it's better we say goodbye now."

"Paris. For a year." He looked staggered by the news. She supposed the Baxter Smiths of the world were rarely stymied.

But she knew well how to handle giving up her heart's desire, so she merely said, "Yes," then turned away from him and focused back on her laptop. Still, she was hyperaware of him as he started moving again. His sandalwood scent reached her and she suppressed the desperate urge to turn toward it, ignoring the yearning she had to bury her nose against his neck and warm her suddenly cold face against the heat at his throat.

Goodbye, she whispered in her mind. *Live well. Be happy.*

"This box of ledgers," he said at length. "Can I take it with me? Page through them?"

"Sure," she replied absently, hardly aware of the question as her own misery closed in on her. Think of the Seine, she told herself. Of studying in the City of Light. Of some future French lover, dark-haired and seductive, who would whisper to her, demanding a kiss. *"Donne-moi un bisou."*

Except all seductive men in Addy's fantasies were golden-haired Americans who whispered, "Dance with me."

Desolate, she glanced over just as Baxter breached the exit. She'd wanted him gone, she reminded herself. Out of the archives room, out of her life. But then she noticed the box in his hands, the one she'd given him permission to take…and realized she'd also given him a reason to return.

CHAPTER TWELVE

VANCE FOLLOWED HIS NOSE across the parking lot of Captain Crow's toward the Karma Cupcakes truck. The scent of baking made his mouth water. An ocean breeze plastered the back of his shirt to his spine, displacing sweetness with a briny smell, and he wondered if he'd ever breathe in one or the other of those two aromas without thinking of this summer. Without thinking of Layla.

As he drew nearer, Phil Parker climbed out of the truck. Vance paused, a wave of guilt slapping at him. He hadn't considered having to face the older man this morning. With the single purpose of getting things back on track with the niece, he hadn't even remembered the uncle.

Phil glanced up as he seated himself at one of the bistro tables. He slid a dog-eared stack of travel guidebooks onto the tabletop. "Good morning," he called with an easy smile. "Come join me."

"I've come to collect Layla," Vance replied. "I don't really have the time."

Phil pushed out the chair beside him with a sandal-clad foot. "I'm sure you can sit for a moment or two."

Hell. Vance tried not to scowl as he lowered himself to the wrought-iron seat.

Phil smiled again. "So…how're you two getting along?"

More guilt. *Well, I got Layla to pretend to be my girlfriend. Worse, I ignored my scruples and listened to my inner horndog, Phil. I had wild monkey sex with your beautiful niece.* Except wild monkey sex would have been less disturbing than what had really happened. He'd stroked her, enjoyed her, *savored* her. Even now he could feel the satin of her skin against his fingertips, hear the sweet need of her husky moans.

Instead of expressing any of that, though, he cleared his throat. "What does she say?"

"She's been pretty quiet. I'm a little worried."

His gut tightened. Disturbed by that visit from Fitz, Vance had kept clear of her for a couple days. That wasn't exactly courteous behavior from a lover, no matter how temporary, how casual the hookup. But she hadn't complained.

Instead, she'd just gone ahead with her usual routine without ever taking him to task for keeping to himself even more than usual.

No, until now he'd thought it was only him that was all messed up, still smelling her on his sheets, even though he'd changed them. Still remembering her pebbled nipple on his tongue, the rhythmic clasp of her body on his cock. The silk of her hair wound around his fingers. When she was in the same room with him he couldn't think of anything but the taste of her.

That's why he'd struck upon today's plan. He was going to spin time backward, returning things to the way they were those first days at Beach House No. 9. They'd been two strangers then. On the forefront of his mind had been her father and fulfilling his promise to the man.

"The loss of my brother is eating at her," Phil said, almost as if he'd read Vance's mind. "Sometimes she goes still, and the sadness on her face…"

Damn, Vance thought, his gut tightening again. He didn't want to be wondering or worrying about the state of her heart. It wasn't his job to heal her in that way—in any way. His glance landed on one of the books in Phil's stack. It was a Lonely Planet guidebook to Nepal, the cover showing Everest and a string of prayer flags, and it reminded him of the older man's spiritual interests.

"You should talk to her," he told her uncle. "Don't you have some Buddha voodoo spell that will make it all better?"

Phil glanced down, picking at a frayed end of the macramé-and-wooden-bead bracelet he wore on his left wrist, then his gaze returned to Vance's face. "Something tells me I'm not the one who has the magic right now."

"Don't look at me," Vance said, pressing back in his chair. "What do I know about overcoming grief?"

"Buddhism teaches that you can't overcome it," Phil said.

"Thank you, Obi-Wan."

The other man continued as if Vance hadn't spoken. "And that there are two places grief can take you. Toward the negative—where you waste time desiring to undo the past or create an impossible future. Or toward the positive—where your grief gains you a new understanding of the transience of life. That gives you a greater appreciation for the world and a greater well of kindness for your fellow human beings."

"Like I said," Vance grumbled, "Buddha voodoo."

Phil smiled. "I—"

But the truck's door opened, interrupting him. Layla stepped out. Vance got to his feet. "There you are," he said. "I've come to get you."

In an instant, her expression turned guarded. "Why?"

Shit. Was Phil right? Her wary tone suggested there was something beneath the surface of her postsex laidback demeanor. Damn woman was just too good at hiding her true emotions.

He scowled because now he felt like an ass for not looking beneath the convenient facade. "We need to work on the list today."

"Oh," she said, then hesitated, as if she was considering refusing him.

"Please," Vance said.

Another hesitation. Then she sighed. "All right," she finally answered. "Do I look okay?"

He didn't bother checking. "You always look okay. Better than okay. You know that."

"I mean for what we're going to do." There was a hint of annoyance in her voice. "I wasn't fishing for compliments."

This time he let his gaze linger on her. She must have a closetful of little summer dresses, he decided. Each and every one designed to make a man unable to forget the tempting slope of her shoulders, the golden smoothness of her long legs. This one was bright blue, sleeveless, with a decorative zipper down the middle that ran from the scooped neckline to the full skirt.

"I'm complimenting you, anyway," Vance said gruffly, trying not to think of how easy it would be to peel it off of her. "You look great. Perfect for what I have scheduled."

"Which is?"

"A surprise."

She obligingly kept her mouth shut during the half-hour drive northward, though her gaze surveyed the snazzy beach town they entered with interest. That gaze became even more curious as he pulled into the parking lot of an elegant day spa just off the main boulevard.

"Beauty Day," he said, slanting her a look.

Her brows came together. "What?"

"I'm not making this up. It's an item on the Helmet List. Actually, I'm knocking off two. One is Beauty Day, and after that we're going to have tea at a shop around the corner."

Her confusion cleared. "Oh. Beauty Day." She swallowed, hard.

Shit. Vance thought she might be fighting tears. Apparently what he'd considered an odd entry for the gruff colonel to put on the list meant something pretty profound to her. "Let's go," he said, reaching for the door. "You shouldn't be late for your appointment."

But she poked along after him, so he was forced to twine his fingers with hers. It was the first time he'd touched her since that morning after they'd had sex, and the usual sexual zing fired through his blood, heating the back of his neck and stirring his cock. Trying his best to ignore the reaction, he pulled her into the spa's anteroom. It was quiet there, the only sound coming from a fountain in the corner, where water burbled over polished river rocks. The receptionist spoke in hushed tones and Vance followed suit, confirming Layla's appointments for a facial and mani-pedi.

His companion didn't say anything, but he sensed her amused surprise. "Mani-pedi," he repeated, turning his head to narrow his eyes at her. "Yeah, I said it. I even know what it is, because I have a brain in my head and because Addy set this whole thing up for me."

"I don't think I've ever heard a man say mani-pedi before," she mused, and then sucked on her cheeks as if she was trying not to smile.

"Twice," he reminded her. Then he pointed his finger toward the door that led to the treatment rooms. "Now go. I'll be here when you're done."

With a last amused glance at him, she followed instructions. Vance settled on a comfortable chair in the seating area and picked up a magazine. Her mood seemed more upbeat now, he decided, then frowned. No. Her mood was none of his concern.

He was supposed to be doing the job. Ticking off the items on the Helmet List. Being that same mere stranger to her he'd been on the day they'd met.

Ninety minutes or so passed and he'd leafed through almost all the magazines. They were the classy kind, not a how-to-drive-your-man-mad-in-the-sack article in the bunch. He read about meditation gardens, the ten best uses for truffle oil and the most popular book club picks. Clients had disappeared in the same direction as Layla. Others had come out, all checking text messages as they headed toward the exit.

He was skimming a story about antiaging herbs when a woman strolled from the treatment area, swaddled in a long, thick robe and wearing terry slippers on her feet. She headed for the magazines, then drew up short when she noticed Vance. He wondered if he'd missed a spot while shaving or was walking around with food on his face.

"Uh…" he said, shifting in his chair. "Is something wrong?"

"No." She started forward again, offering a smile. Her butter-yellow hair was pulled back from a cute face, with round cheeks and a dimpled chin. "I'm sorry. I was just surprised to see a man in the waiting area. I come here every two weeks and have never seen one before."

Vance smiled back. "I had to learn the secret pass code."

"Oh?" She laughed. The receptionist looked over, sending an admonishing look and the robe-wrapped woman lowered her voice. "And what *is* the secret pass code?"

He made a big show of glancing around as if he couldn't let it fall into the wrong hands, then leaned forward. "Mani-pedi," he stage-whispered.

She clapped a hand over her mouth to stifle another laugh. "I've never—"

"I know. Heard a man say that phrase." He relaxed into his chair again, grinning. The cutie grinned back, loosening him up a little more. After days of being over-focused on one woman, this felt good. Easy. Maybe he should ask for her number. Living at Beach House No. 9 with Layla didn't mean he couldn't go out for a drink with someone else.

The colonel's daughter wasn't his woman, after all.

Clutching the sides of the robe together at her throat and at her knees, the blonde perched on a nearby chair. "Are you here with your wife?"

Getting her number was looking better and better. "I'm not attached."

"No?" she asked, blue eyes definitely flirtatious. "You're here with your sister, then?"

Vance opened his mouth just as the treatment area's door reopened and another robe-wrapped woman stepped out. His teeth clicked shut as he stared at Layla. Her bangs were swept back with some kind of hair band, revealing the glowing skin of her pretty face. His heart lurched hard against his ribs.

God, she was something, he thought, staring. Like a dew-dampened rose.

"Not a sister," the blonde murmured, moving away from him.

"Huh?" Vance glanced at her, and then his gaze was drawn back to the colonel's daughter. "Are you okay?"

"Yes. Wonderful," Layla said, smiling. "My appointment ran a little long. The pedicure." She pointed one bare foot in front of her like a ballerina. He could see the nails had been painted a midnight-blue. In addition, a small half moon decorated each big toe, with a tiny jeweled star beside it. "I wanted to tell you I'll be out in a flash."

Then she was gone again, and Vance realized the blonde had left, as well. He'd lost his chance at her number. It didn't make him happy that he couldn't work up any disappointment.

Not after seeing Layla like that, lit up like a candle, her smile a thousand watts of energy. It had been as if the world was right again, with Layla looking genuinely delighted. He'd wanted to stand up, grab her, kiss her.

Which you didn't do to a stranger you planned to keep your distance from. That thought had him frowning after they left the beauty place and moved the car nearer to the tea shop. He shoved his hand through his hair as they walked down the sidewalk, groaning when the cast thumped against his forehead. "Jesus, you'd think I'd remember about that," he muttered.

Layla glanced over. "Was it the spa? Did too much estrogen put somebody in a bad mood?" she teased.

"I'm not in a bad mood." It was just that he'd missed his opportunity to get that blonde's number.

"Cranky, then."

He shot Layla a glare. "And I'm *not* cranky."

She only laughed as she preceded him into the tea shop. In moments, they were seated at a small table set near a bow window. It was covered by a floral cloth and held a centerpiece of fresh flowers. Layla sniffed at the blossoms, clearly still in a happy frame of mind.

Good, he thought. Maybe she was permanently over her dark mood.

Nothing that happened next changed Vance's opinion. A waitress in a flower-printed apron came by. She seemed a bit nonplussed to see a man prepared to partake of tea, but he murmured his new fail-safe, "mani-pedi," and though the girl just blinked, this time Layla laughed.

A pot of Earl Grey was delivered to them, and then a selection of tiered plates that held tiny sandwiches, little tarts and bite-size scones. He hadn't expected to get full on the stuff, but there was plenty for both of them. The tea itself wasn't terrible.

Layla looked at him over the rim of her delicate china cup. "I didn't peg you as a hot tea drinker."

"It's not so bad," he said with a shrug.

Setting down her cup, she looked about the room. "This is all so much better than not bad. Better than the place we went for tea on my twelfth birthday…the party my dad missed."

"Ah," Vance said. The colonel hadn't explained about that.

"Instead of taking four girls to tea, he went—" She broke off, shook her head. "I don't remember now."

"And Beauty Day? He skipped out on that, too?"

"No." Her lips curved. "I think he added that entry because I was always after him to paint my fingernails and toenails when I was little."

"Somehow I don't see the colonel hunkering down with a tiny bottle and brush."

"But I didn't have a mom to do those things, so I persisted. It was one of the few times he out-and-out refused me." She sighed, then picked up her cup, studying the contents as if she could read the scattering of leaves on the bottom. "But he made up for it today."

"Yeah."

She lifted her chin to meet his eyes. "*You* made it happen for me today. Thanks, Vance."

There were tears in her eyes. They didn't brim over, but they made those eyes shine, and it was like looking into freshly washed windows. Vance felt as if he could walk straight through the glass.

And he could see straight inside…of Layla. There was a chilly breeze on the back of his neck, a cold premonition of trouble ahead. But it didn't impede his vision. There, plain as the nose on her face, was Layla's tattered, vulnerable heart. Aching. So he ached, too.

Damn. He'd been trying to wind the clock backward…but come to think of it, perhaps he had. Because the fact was, it had always been like this between them, even when they *were* two actual strangers. There'd been the cold wind on his neck, the pretty woman with the big brown eyes, the attraction and the connection he'd felt from the instant they'd met.

VANCE WAS STILL BROODING over his afternoon with Layla when Baxter showed up at Beach House No. 9 that night. He greeted his cousin with a nod, then led the way into the living room. It was dark beyond the sliding glass doors. The sky was clear, and he noted the half moon and the bright star to its right. Hell. As if he needed another reminder of the colonel's daughter.

Baxter glanced around the room. "Uh? Addy? Layla?"

"They went for a drink at Captain Crow's. Girls' Night or something with Skye."

It was too damn quiet with the women gone. But Vance had been all for it, shooing them out before the dinner dishes were done. Layla had studied him with those soft Bambi eyes of hers, and he'd turned away from the scrutiny. He didn't want her catching a hint of the turmoil inside of him.

For some inconvenient, unfathomable reason, the exposure of her soft side only pulled harder at his sexual side. Yeah. That glimpse of her heart had made his cock hard and nothing he thought or did convinced the bad boy to lie down and behave.

"Classy, huh?" he murmured.

"Are you talking to me?" Bax asked. "And why haven't you offered me a beer?"

His cousin's testy tone caused Vance to give him a second look. Whoa. His cousin wore beat-up jeans, a T-shirt that was decorated with—paint splatters?—and a pair of rubber flip-flops. "Who are you and what have you done with Baxter Smith?" He waited a beat. "On second thought, just leave him wherever you stuffed him. You look a lot more fun."

Baxter sent him a sour look. "I've never been fun."

"We should do something about that right away," Vance said, and headed for the kitchen. He ducked his head in the open door of the refrigerator. "Uh-oh. Out of brewskis."

Hovering in the doorway, Baxter groaned. "Don't tell me that."

"No worries," Vance said, and pushed his cousin back into the living room, toward the sliding doors. "We've got libations just up the beach."

"Captain Crow's?" Baxter frowned. "And interrupt Girls' Night?"

"We won't interrupt," Vance said. "We'll just have our own Manly Night. We'll discuss sports stats and porn stars."

Baxter rubbed his hand over his unshaven chin. Those whiskers were completely out of character. Something was definitely bothering his cousin, something bad, and Vance couldn't in good conscience let that lie. That's why he was going to take that hike up the beach. It wasn't about getting closer to Layla, not at all.

Because he was still determined to ignore his clamoring libido. That he couldn't evict her from his thoughts didn't mean he had to pull her back into his bed.

It took little time to reach Captain Crow's. Twinkling lights framed the roofline and the railings of the restaurant/bar. It was Surfing Saturday, according to the chalkboard set up at the entrance. Two TVs over the bar were playing baseball games, the other two showing surf movies. The music pouring from the speakers was a classic beach tune from Jan and Dean, "Surf City." The drink specials were Longboard beer and double mai tais.

Vance found seats along the railing surrounding the deck that overlooked the ocean. Behind them were the tables, most of them full. He didn't search the crowd for Layla.

Because Baxter was already surveying the knots of people. "I see them. Addy, Layla and Skye," he said. "They're back in the corner with girl drinks— something with rum, I guess."

Vance experienced a small clutch of worry. Layla could hold her tequila, but rum? Maybe he should go check—

No. God. She was an adult. She didn't need him supervising her night out. Sighing, Vance shook his head at the way Mr. Happy had perked up at the idea.

After ordering beers, he and his cousin both stared morosely into the distance. The waves came in long shallow spreads, fanning like spilled milk against the sand. The music switched to The Beach Boys' "Wouldn't It Be Nice."

"I hate that song," Bax muttered.

Eyebrows raised, Vance glanced over. "Okay. Does that mean you're ready to talk about what's eating you?"

"I blame it on my parents."

Vance stared at him in shock as the longnecks were delivered. Baxter had always got on well with his folks, just like Fucking Perfect Fitz. Vance had been the family's only agitator. "What did Uncle Roy and Aunt Alison do to ruin an iconic song of the 1960s for you?"

"I don't mean they ruined the song for me. I mean they may have ruined *me*. Consider how badly they've skewed my worldview. They're devoted to each other. Your folks, too. "

"How dare they," Vance said, his voice mild.

Baxter pointed at him with his beer. "You can laugh, but I'm right. All that marital bliss can make a man expect things. Want things for himself."

Vance groaned. "Are you going to tell me about the BSLS again? I already know you have a wedding with all the trimmings inked in on it somewhere."

"Not before thirty-one," Baxter said.

"There you go," Vance answered, and clacked his beer bottle against his cousin's. "You don't need to stress about that for another couple of years. You can be the freewheeling happy bachelor you've always been for quite some time more."

His cousin sent him a fulminating look, then glanced over his shoulder in the direction of the ladies. "I'm not happy."

Vance followed the direction of his gaze to where the three women were gathered at a round table, including the spritelike blonde. Well. He'd sensed undercurrents that first day at Captain Crow's and now it was clear to him. Baxter had something going with Addy—or rather, Baxter wanted something going with Addy but had been shut down. Beach House No. 9 was quite the hotbed of romantic tension this month, wasn't it?

"I'm sorry, cuz," Vance said. "You should be more like me. Unmoved by the influence of our parents' marital accord. Embracing the single life with gusto."

"Oh, really." Baxter narrowed his eyes. "Wasn't it you who were engaged not long ago?"

"Yes, but—"

"Are you saying it wasn't because you saw the example of your folks' marriage—"

"Blythe wasn't about that," Vance said, his voice going tight.

"Oh?" Baxter took a swig of his beer. "What was Blythe about?"

"Fitz." Shocked that his brother's name had come out of his mouth, Vance busied it by taking a long swallow from his bottle. Then another. When he finally set the beer down, he noticed Baxter was staring at him. "What?"

"You said Blythe was about Fitz."

Shit, Bax had heard that. Vance sighed. "The first time I met her, you know what I thought?"

His cousin shook his head.

"I thought she was just Fitz's type. He always goes for those impenetrable cool ones." He huffed out a short laugh. "Maybe I have a new career as a matchmaker."

"Yeah, the impenetrable, cool ones don't seem a natural fit with you."

Vance thought of Layla. Clutching at him when she had her bout of Ferris-fear. Slow-dancing, her warm body moving against his. Her simple enjoyment in the mani-pedi, pointing her toes for him to admire. *She* was a natural.

"You're right," he told his cousin, staggered for a moment by a truth he'd never allowed himself to see. "Blythe wasn't a good fit for me at all."

"So why'd you go for her then?"

"Fuck, I don't know," Vance admitted, still nonplussed. "We'd been dating awhile, though we never actually slept together." His motivations had not been driven by sex, and Blythe, in her still-waters way, had seemed fine with that.

"Oh." Baxter's eyes were wide.

"Yeah. Never went to bed with her." The confession made him feel uncomfortable and maybe even idiotic. He started to say something else, then stopped.

"Spit it out, V.T." Baxter nudged his leg with the edge of his rubber thong. "Because none of this sounds like you."

On another sigh, Vance tried again. "We were going along, dating slow and steady, and then I was called back up. I thought, 'Hey, why not?' I knew Mom and Dad would love her. They'd consider her a steadying influence—"

"Screw that," Bax said, straightening in his seat. "You had your wild times, but where you've been and what you've done since you enlisted…"

"The fact is, she was Fitz's type," Vance said, "so I think I saw her as my way back into the family fold." He hadn't been able to articulate that to himself at the time, but now, from a distance, he saw that it was true. Jesus. "Lousy reason to get engaged, huh?"

What had motivated Blythe to go along? She wasn't the only woman who acted on the impulse, though. He'd had army buddies who'd made the same impetuous offer and received the same impetuous agreement from ladies they'd not known half as long. Hell, more than one couple of his acquaintance had entered into a quickie, day-before-deployment marriage.

Thank God it hadn't gone that far for him and Blythe. And before long she'd realized Vance didn't have his older brother's chops and rejected him.

Baxter drained his beer and signaled the peace sign

at their waitress to order two more. "If I wasn't so miserable myself, I'd try to broker a settlement on your side of the family. Get some of you to wake up and others of you to start talking."

Vance laughed as the waitress put new beers in front of them. "God, you can be officious and arrogant."

"Prissy and pasty, too," Baxter muttered. "However, I have developed a bit of kink in my sex life."

"Whoa. Way better than talk of porn stars. Though I'm not sure I believe it."

"Believe it," Baxter said, then glanced over his shoulder toward Addy again.

Well, well, well, Vance thought. *This should be interesting.*

But his cousin's eyes had gone to slits. "Who the hell is that?"

Vance looked around. Addy was on the dance floor, laughing up at some dark-haired guy who had his hands on her hips and was trying to encourage them to move. "I don't know."

"I do. That's a firefighter. A dirty, no-good, fucking first responder. Teague something."

"They're just dancing, Bax," Vance said, and remembered with guilt how he'd pulled Layla away from another man on the Fourth of July at this very spot.

"A fucking first responder. Everybody knows that gives a guy an advantage."

Baxter had to be really upset, Vance thought, because he normally avoided cursing. Such verbal activity had never made it onto the BSLS. "Look, it's no big deal."

"Oh, yeah? Now he's got Layla out there."

Vance swiveled in his chair. His "natural" was certainly out on that dance floor, with her glowing, facial-ized face, her buffed fingernails and her moon-and-star toes. She'd changed into a rib-sticking tank top and a tight pair of jeans. The firefighter touched her like he'd been touching Addy, his palms on either side of Layla's sweet hips, encouraging them to swivel.

"Fucking first responder." Vance started to rise.

Then fell back onto his stool. *She doesn't need me supervising her night out.* He repeated it twice more for good measure.

The words, though, didn't do much good reining in his reckless instincts. They still urged him to peel that other guy's hands off the girl, then sling her over his shoulder and take her home to his bed.

"We should go to their table," Baxter suggested. "Give that guy the eye. Let him know they don't need some dude with a hose to put out their fire."

"I'm sure they'd really appreciate that," he said dryly, trying to remember he'd matured from the days when he'd bumped chests with a high school rival for Marianne Kelly's attention. In typical Vance Smith style, he'd brawled with the dude in the middle of biology class, instead of waiting until after school and choosing some off-campus location. They'd both been suspended for three days. For the remainder of the semester, his father had confiscated the car keys of his truck—though that didn't stop Vance from totaling it ten months later.

Now Vance turned back around to face the ocean, while Baxter had given up all pretense of not watching the object of his affection. "Hell," he muttered. "He's buying all three women more drinks now. They're smiling and laughing, even that serious one, Skye."

"The nerve."

"He's whispering something in Layla's ear."

Shit. Vance pretended he was glued to his stool as he tried to hang on to his cool.

"Now they're all getting up. It looks as if they're going somewhere together, drinks in hand." Baxter slid a sly look at Vance. "Do you think they're going to have a ménage?"

Vance rolled his eyes. "You're just needling me now, aren't you?"

"Kind of. But they all look damn happy as they leave through the front exit. A first responder might not get all of them, but he could get one of them."

And there was Layla, with her tattered heart. So lonely sometimes.

"Hell," Vance said. He tried remembering there was Super Glue on the top surface of his stool. It wasn't working. "I want her," he told Baxter. "And *I'm* the one who's going to get her."

But before he could make a move, Addy was there, her green eyes anxious. "I thought I saw you guys here. You'd better come quick."

CHAPTER THIRTEEN

UNDER THE BLAZING fluorescent lights in the Sunrise Pictures archives room, Layla fought to keep still. "Really, I'm fine," she told Teague the firefighter, who was gingerly sifting through the hair at the side of her head. "No big—"

"What the hell?" Vance exploded into the room, fingers catching hold of the doorway to halt his headlong run. His gaze zeroed in on Layla, then flicked to the man tending her. At that same moment, Teague found the knot on her skin and she flinched.

In a blink, Vance had pushed his way between her and the firefighter. "Don't touch her," he spat over his shoulder, then took her chin between his fingers so he could gently turn her face to the side. He blew softly on her hair to part it, and she shivered. His thumb caressed her skin. "What happened?"

A cacophony of voices burst into the shocked silence brought on by Vance's impromptu arrival. "Wait, wait." It was Baxter speaking now. "Slow down. One at a time."

Skye's quiet voice started the story. "Addy wanted to show Teague and Layla the archives room. I tagged along. When Addy unlocked the door, it was dark inside. As we walked in, a dark-clothed figure burst out, pushing through us and taking off at a run."

"I would have gone after him," Teague said, sounding frustrated, "but I heard Layla cry out."

"Sweetheart." Vance blew on the sore spot again. "How'd you hit your head?"

"When the…intruder…or whatever, ran past, he knocked me into the doorjamb. It's just a bump," she said, though now that she'd had some time to process, she couldn't suppress her shudder.

Vance made a sympathetic sound, low in his throat. "I'll be careful," he said, then probed around the spot, his fingers barely grazing the skin.

Still, Layla winced. "I'm such a wuss."

"Nah." He leaned close to brush a kiss on her temple. "You need an ice pack."

"Maybe she needs a hospital," Teague said.

Vance turned toward him, his earlier animosity dialed down a notch. He held out his hand. "I'm an army medic. Vance Smith. We'll just head out now and I'll take care of her."

"Great," the other man responded, returning a solid grip. "Some ice right away will help."

"I'm good," Layla protested. "We can't leave Skye here."

"It's okay. I've called the police," the woman in question said.

"We'll wait with you." Layla sensed Vance about to say something and shot him a look. "I haven't had my tour yet."

"We don't want to touch anything," Skye remarked. "Addy, I'm sorry, but it looks as if your work has been disturbed."

Vance moved, and without his or Teague's shoulders blocking her vision, Layla got her first clear view of the room. *Oh,* she said, in soundless dismay. Hung on the walls were colorful movie posters and black-and-white glossy stills. Their frames were askew now, as if someone had been searching for something behind the advertising pieces. Even more messy were the floors. Papers were strewn all about, presumably from the tumbled cartons that sat on a long table.

"What would someone be looking for?" Teague murmured. "Addy, what did you say you were researching again?"

From his place at her side, Baxter answered for her. "She wants to find out the truth of the relationship between the actress Edith Essex and her husband, the head of Sunrise Pictures."

Addy glanced at him sharply. "That's just a sidebar. I'm...I'm chronicling the rise and demise of the movie company."

"You want to know if love survives," Baxter murmured.

The blonde sucked in a breath, her green eyes widening.

Teague frowned. "How does that translate into something intruder-worthy? Maybe it was a vagrant looking for a warm place to spend the night. Or a burglar hoping for a way into the art studio next door. There's a cash drawer there. Maybe a safe."

Layla ignored the slight throbbing in her head. "Didn't you say something about a famous jeweled piece, Addy?"

"Yeah, but it's definitely not in here. I would have found it." She gestured to the paper-covered floor. "And I've gone through all of this. Haven't found a clue to its whereabouts, either. It was a famous piece, priceless—

imagine one of Elizabeth Taylor's incredible jewels—so you'd think there'd be a record if it was sold or turned up in someone else's collection. But there's been nothing."

"Just rumors," Skye said, "that have been around forever."

"But the story gets new energy every so often. It popped up again a year ago. That's when my interest was piqued," Addy confessed.

Suddenly, Skye sat down heavily on a chair. Vance patted Layla's shoulder, then crossed to the other woman. "Are you feeling all right?" he asked, his brow furrowed. "You're pale."

She waved him away. "Take Layla to No. 9 for ice. The police will arrive soon. I can handle it."

Vance shot a look at Baxter. "Staying," the other man said. "I'll be here as long as I'm needed."

With a nod, Vance strode back to Layla. "No argument now. Let's go home."

In this mood, he was impossible to dissuade. She walked from the room, Vance's protective arm around her waist. With a little wave, she sketched a goodbye to the others. But when she crossed the threshold, Layla had to glance back. "Maybe I hit my head harder than I thought," she told Vance.

He glanced down, gaze alert. "Why?"

"There might be something wrong with my vision."

His concern showed itself in the tighter way he held her against him. "What makes you say that? What do you see?"

"Baxter. Looking rumpled." She took another look over her shoulder. "And whiskered."

Vance laughed. "Your eyesight's just fine. He's got woman problems."

Back at No. 9, Layla decided she had problems, too. Since having sex with Vance—well, since the morning after—she'd been strict with herself. Though she'd understood his urgent wish to leave California had to do with his confrontation with Fitz, she couldn't help but be a little hurt. Still, that sting had served a purpose. It had reminded her there was no point hoping for more, no point hoping for another night when the guy couldn't wait to get away. Even a woman who didn't count on forevers didn't make that mistake.

But now Vance was holding her, touching her, assessing her with those electric-blue eyes. When he held a dish towel of crushed ice against the side of her head, she worried he might detect that her little quiver wasn't a reaction to the cold, but to his nearness. They sat close on the living room couch, his thigh against hers.

"You're cold," he said, brows drawing together.

"A tad," she lied. Their little ritual. He misconstrued her trembling, and she went right along with it.

He rose to his feet, making her regret the fib, and headed toward the fireplace. They'd not bothered with it before, although the air could be quite cool in the evenings. Wood was already stacked on the grate. A key built into the white-painted bricks lit the gas, which in turn lit the kindling and logs.

More quickly than she would have believed, the room warmed. Or maybe that was because Vance was sitting beside her again. "Are you okay holding the ice?" he asked. "Or would you rather I did?"

She squirmed, trying to get more comfortable. "Maybe I could trade places with you. Then I can prop the unbruised side of my head on a pillow and the pack will stay in place."

"Why don't you lean on my shoulder instead," Vance suggested and, without waiting for her answer, put his arm around her and arranged her so that she was snuggled close to him, her head resting on his chest, the cold weight of the ice pack soothing the last of the throbbing ache from her scalp. He'd had her swallow two pain relievers earlier and apparently they'd kicked in, too.

Using the remote, he clicked on the TV across the room. Baseball. They hadn't even tossed a coin, but she didn't mind. There was no way she could follow any kind of storyline with her cheek absorbing the beat of Vance's heart. She closed her eyes, breathing him in, and her bones seemed to go lax, while her blood stayed at that whenever-I'm-around-him simmer.

As minutes passed, though, she could feel the growing tension in his body. His hard chest turned rigid, his short breaths more shallow. Uneasy, she shifted a little and the ice pack slid down her bare arm, making her twitch. He plucked it away.

"Done?" he said, his voice low.

"Sure." She watched him toss it onto the tray that was centered on the coffee table. Uncertain if she should move, Layla remained in an awkward half-raised position until she heard Vance sigh and he pulled her back against him.

But she couldn't relax at all now, not with the way the walls seemed to squeeze inward. The noise of the baseball game didn't permeate her consciousness. In her head she heard only Vance's breaths and her own, a syncopated, unsettling rhythm. Layla's temperature climbed. Growing up, she'd had a dog, a mutt named Stewart. He'd had the softest ears and the sweetest disposition and had positively craved human attention. When you petted him, he'd warm in that exact location—the pink stretch of his belly, the dip between his shoulders, the top of his head. Layla felt as though she was doing that now, every point of contact with Vance its own singular hot spot.

She cleared her throat, searching for something to say that might ease the strain. "So…Baxter has woman trouble?"

"All men have woman trouble."

Her mouth curved. "Not Uncle Phil." The dedicated bachelor stayed *way* clear of it.

"You're wrong. He worries about you." There was a hesitation. "*I* worry about you."

Uh-oh. Slowly, Layla straightened to a sitting position and met his gaze. "Why did you go to Captain Crow's tonight?" She'd be annoyed if he was playing big brother again. "Were you worrying about me then?"

His expression didn't flicker. "We're out of beer. Baxter wanted a drink."

"Oh," she said, somewhat mollified. "But that doesn't answer my question. Why are you worried about me?"

His gaze slanted to the side, avoiding hers. "I don't want you hurt, Layla."

More uh-oh. Why did that sound like a patronizing *I don't want to hurt you, Layla?*

She glowered at him. "I don't want you hurt, either, Vance."

"We should call it a night." Pushing off the cushions, he rose to his feet. When she didn't follow suit, he huffed out a breath. "Look, I'm in a mood."

Layla raised an eyebrow. "A mood for what?"

For a moment he went still, and then his lips pressed together. "Don't push me."

Half thrilled and half wary, Layla found she wanted to do just that. For days and days, he'd been so controlled and polite and…civilized. He didn't look that way now, he looked bigger than usual, edgy and impatient, as if some force inside him was ready to spring loose.

God, please, spring loose on her. A woman didn't have to want forever to want that. Because the chemistry between them had never gone away. "Or what?"

He sent her a quick glance. "Or what, what?"

She licked dry lips. "What happens if I push you?"

His electric eyes shot to hers. Held.

The visual contact came with a physical jolt. Then that sexual tether snapped into place, hook-to-eye, the connection made, the two of them engaged in a torrid tango without moving a muscle. Frustration, irritation, caution crossed Vance's face and he narrowed his eyes at her. "Stop," he said.

Lifting her hands, Layla shrugged. "Green flash."

The room's temperature jacked up another few degrees. Though she held herself still, her nipples contracted to aching points. She glanced down reflexively, worried he might be able to tell, but then she knew he could.

"Layla," he groaned. A flush ran across his high cheekbones and the bridge of his nose. "Look, I'm trying to be noble here, but my temper's pointing away from white knight and sliding straight toward hell-raiser."

She shivered at the thought. That restless energy of his, unleashed.

"So…I think you should just head to your room."

That restless energy of his, wasted. As if she'd sleep,

thinking of him down the hall. "What about what I want?" Layla asked, rising from the couch.

His chest rose up and down on hard breaths and his nostrils flared as she came toe-to-toe with him. "You're in a vulnerable place. You don't know—"

"I'm not so fragile." It infuriated her that he believed differently. Colonel Parker's daughter had a spine of steel and a better understanding of the world than Vance gave her credit for. "All my life I've lived with the knowledge that things can turn on a dime. Which means I enjoy the moment I'm in—because I don't expect anything to last forever."

His nostrils flared again. She saw his fingers flex beneath that cast. "The other night, that wasn't the real me," he warned.

"How so?" Shivering, she remembered a very real kiss he'd pressed to the small of her back. The scrape of his whiskers up her spine.

"I'm not a gentle man," he said. "And definitely no gentleman."

She reached forward and crumpled his T-shirt in her fist. Yeah. This felt right. "I can handle whatever you dish out, soldier boy."

And on her next breath, he yanked her close.

Be careful what you wish for, her head said. Her blood just sang.

VANCE DROVE HIS MOUTH against hers. Their teeth clacked and he pushed between hers to bury his tongue deep in her wet heat. His heartbeat was unruly, his blood rocketing through his system. His control was unraveling.

She melted against his chest and it almost calmed the beast in him. He'd gone a little crazy when he'd heard

Layla was hurt, and then even crazier when he'd seen another man's hands on her. A primitive compulsion had surged from the depths of his belly once again. *She's mine.*

He speared the fingers of one hand in the hair at her nape, guiding back her head so he could taste the line of her jaw and the smooth, tender skin of her neck. She moaned and the sound spoke directly to his animal lust. He sucked on the tender flesh, wanting to taste more of her, wanting to mark her.

Maybe he should feel ashamed—but he'd warned her, hadn't he? There wasn't anything of the soulful lover in him tonight. She could run if she wanted, he'd let her go the instant she balked, but until then she was getting Vance, full throttle.

"No softness for you tonight, baby," he murmured as he ran his mouth back to hers.

She shoved her hands under the hem of his T-shirt. Her touch on his bare skin made it jitter and his cock jumped in his jeans. "I didn't ask for soft," she said against his ravaging lips.

He angled his head to deepen the kiss, surging into her mouth at the same time as he caught the tight jut of her nipple between scissoring fingers. She bowed into the little pain, her hips pushing hard against his. He caught one round ass cheek in his other hand and held her to him as he ground his shaft against her, not trying to be pretty about what he wanted.

This is who I am, he was telling her. The man in the tea shop, the sensitive lover who coaxed instead of demanded that first time was a facade. Vance's training made him a warrior first, a medic second and, before that, he'd come out of the womb restless and ready for action.

He released her nipple, only to pinch it anew, her needy moan gasoline to his fire. She tugged at his shirt and he managed to let go of her long enough to strip it off. With a little noise, she moved into him again, her mouth pressing here, there and everywhere.

Jesus. He felt like a tuning fork, vibrating in short jerky waves, each of Layla's kisses a new strike.

He buried his face in her hair and breathed in her scent. Shampoo, salt air and baking notes: vanilla, cinnamon, a hint of lemon.

She found his nipple and licked the scrap of flesh. Vance shuddered and his fingers shook as they reached for the skinny straps of her top. Time to get this off. Time to get her naked.

He stripped off the stretchy cotton. She was naked beneath it, but there was a faint red line below her perfect breasts where the shirt's elastic liner had pressed her skin. With a flick of his hand, he tossed the fabric away. "Don't wear that again," he muttered. "It hurt you."

"No—" she started, but then her mouth and eyes closed as he bent to trace the stripe with his tongue. He followed it to the side of her body, lifting her arm to not miss an inch of it. Layla was breathing hard, her fingers curled around the waistband of his jeans. "I'm going to fall," she whispered. "You're making my knees melt."

He straightened to pull her close then, groaning at the goodness of her soft breasts and hard nipples meeting the hot plane of his chest. His arms held her tight, and she pushed her hips into him again, ratcheting up the crazy.

"Bedroom," he said, suddenly remembering Baxter and Addy. They could have company at any moment.

Their fingers tangled, he drew her toward the hallway and the master bedroom. At the threshold, he hesitated. The room was unlit, and he imagined them in that darkness, bodies writhing on the bed. His blood was pulsing close to the surface of his skin, the head of his cock was beating as if it had its own heart. When he got her flat he was going to be all over her.

"Are you sure?" he whispered. Even to his own ears his voice sounded smoky and hot, like his desire. A dragon wanting to devour.

In answer, Layla pulled up their linked hands and rubbed his knuckles against her swollen breast, over her beaded nipple. Vance squeezed shut his eyes, waiting for the words. "Sure," she said. "Very sure."

He didn't remember getting her to the bed. But she was on it, her back to the mattress, his fingers already fumbling on the clasp of her jeans. He muttered a curse, the cast always in the damn way, so she took it over herself.

The zipper was loud in the quiet, and he was already yanking the material down her long legs. Then he crawled between them, the denim of his pants sliding against the silkiness of her panties. He stroked there, a teasing rhythm, as he bent to take her mouth again.

She wound her hands in his hair and opened for him. Their tongues tangled, eager friends, and then she sucked on his, her fingernails tight against his skull. Vance pushed into that sweet heat at the juncture of her thighs, grinding hard into her softness as she continued to feed on him.

He broke away from her mouth, needing air, and

sucked in oxygen, staring down. The darkness was so absolute she was just a deeper shadow in the shadows, but he didn't need to see her to *see* her. Like the scents of this summer month, she was etched in his brain. There would be no freedom from the memory of her frilly lashed brown eyes, her oval-shaped face, that mouth with the upper lip just made for sucking.

He did so now, finding it with his own and tugging at it rhythmically. It had her pressing her hips to his, her whole body writhing when he gave that lip a delicate bite. The friction against his cock made heat flare up his spine.

"What do you like?" he heard himself demand. The beast was clamoring for action, and it certainly didn't want to pause for direction, but Vance suddenly needed to make her feel the crazy as bad as he did.

Her hands clutched his shoulders. "You..." she moaned. "Your skin, your mouth. Your voice."

His voice? He smiled, and it felt feral. Did Layla Parker like a little dirty talk in bed? His skin shivered at the thought, then tightened against his bones, making it that much more sensitive. He licked her bottom lip and felt her quiver.

"I thought you were sugar and spice and everything nice," he said, then kissed his way down her neck. She turned her head to give him easy access and she undulated as he sucked on her again. "But maybe you have a naughty side."

Her body stilled, but under him he felt the temperature of her flesh spike. He chuckled against her throat, the sound almost devilish in the heated darkness. "Let's see if I can find it."

Her breath was ragged, and her breasts rose and fell

against his cheek as he rubbed his evening whiskers across them. "I love your nipples. They're such a pale pink but they blush to red when I suck them into my mouth, when I tongue them all shiny." He touched the tip of one, lapping at it until she made a frustrated sound and buried her hands in his hair.

"Greedy girl," he whispered, then opened to take a soft bite of her areola, his teeth pulling up to scrape the jut of flesh.

Layla groaned and he did it again, the lap, the bite, the scrape. Her lower body pushed against him in slow rolls, and her taste, her body, her need, they all enticed the beast, teasing it without mercy. But Vance held on and moved to the other breast, playing with that one, too, listening to her little cries.

Finally, he needed something more. "Greedy girl probably wants something hard inside her," he said. "I've got it pulsing and ready right here."

And she stilled again, shocked, he thought, then aroused, because her hands shot down to his pants to divest him of the confining denim. He laughed, low and uncivilized, and rolled away to take care of the issue.

She made another of her frustrated noises, an appetizer that fed his animal as he struggled with the jeans. His erection wasn't making things easy.

"Vance," she breathed, anxious.

"Shh," he said, and rolled his head on the pillow to kiss the warmth of her cheek. "Settle down. I'll fill you up soon enough."

Her mutter sounded like a curse and a plea.

Vance threw his pants over the side of the bed, then yanked at his boxers. Again, the cast and his cock made the process more labor-intensive than it should be. Suddenly Layla's hands were on him, and she was tugging at the material, too, shoving it down his legs.

Then he was naked and Layla was on her knees beside him. "Oh, I like this," he whispered, touching one flank with his knuckles. "Straddle me, sweetheart. Put your breast to my mouth."

Her breathing hitched, but then she obeyed. With a knee on each side of his hips, she leaned toward him. He lifted his head and caught her nipple, feasting, suckling, hard and deep. His hands found her hips and he held her there, drawing her in to slake his hunger.

"Vance," she whispered. "Please."

"Now the other," he instructed, and she shifted her weight. "Offer it to me, Layla. Let me have you."

She was shuddering as he pulled on her second breast now, and her glorious bottom dropped so that the juncture of her thighs kissed his cock. She was wet there, hot and wet, and the moisture bathed his shaft.

He sucked harder on her, ravenous for her taste. But when her wetness slid over him again, his mind clicked. "Condom," he said, releasing her nipple. "We need a condom."

His hand reached blindly for the bedside table. Now it was his turn to curse as the drawer's knob eluded him. Every moment of delay aggravated the raging appetite inside of him. His cock was throbbing, his pulse was pounding, the blood racing around his body was scalding and he was primed to go off. So ready to shoot.

Sweet Lord, he tried telling himself as the drawer squeaked open. *Take it easy.* The beast was on a short chain and despite the warnings he'd given Layla, he didn't want to scare her. But then his fingers found a foil square. When he lost it again he almost screamed.

"Can you reach into the drawer, honey?" he asked, his voice tight. "I'm a little desperate here."

"You're desperate?" Layla said, the edge to her voice making him laugh despite his urgency. "Let me get it."

She was more efficient than he. A triumphant sound and the tearing of foil. He meant to protest but from his mouth came only inarticulate sounds meant to represent words—*I can put it on oh my God your touch is going to send me over sweet baby what are you doing now oh yeah oh yeah like that. Just like that.* What she was doing now was sinking down on him.

His head pressed back into the pillow. "You're so slick inside," he muttered. "So damn tight."

And then she had taken all of him in. He was rooted deep and they both stilled, absorbing the sensation. His hands were on her hips, the sleek insides of her thighs on either side of his.

She shivered and then he felt her muscles gather. His fingers tightened on her. "Don't move," he said. "Give me a minute."

Another shiver ran over her skin. "Have to move," she said, her husky voice breathy. "Have. To. Move."

Then she did, rising off his cock. The beast inside him groaned, but Vance managed to let Layla set the rhythm. Her hips rolled as she rode, her sweet bottom high in the air as she came down on her elbows in order to kiss him. Vance went full crazy on that kiss, the meeting of their mouths and tongues carnal and wicked.

He caught her nipples between his fingers as her plunging hips became more frenzied. She broke their kiss, her breath frantic as he pushed into her wet warmth and said, "Touch your clit, naughty girl. Touch yourself and come for me."

The dirty words put a hitch in her pace.

"Lick your fingertips," Vance encouraged, his voice low and deeper than the dark. "Get them nice and wet and then circle yourself, honey. You know what to do."

And she did it. He could make out the gleam of her arm in the dark, imagined the swipe of her tongue against skin. Her hand moved low and she hesitated. "Ride me," he said, and he reached to the place where they were joined, farther spreading the soft layers to expose the small bud above. "Touch yourself right here and ride me. I want to feel you come all over me."

With a little sound of surrender, Layla obeyed. Her body moved on his, her hand touched her clitoris, and Vance gritted his teeth at the absolute pleasure of her hot center surrounding him, sliding wetly on him, up and down, up and down, up and down.

There was no tenderness, no gentle sweetness, just the slap of their bodies and the harsh rasp of their breaths, and that animal hunger that rose and rose and rose. His body strained, desperately holding the beast at bay until Layla cried out and her internal muscles clamped on his cock, telling him she was at the precipice. He grabbed her hips then and jerked up into her in short, urgent jabs. Her moan was low, ratcheting his need for her body, for her response. He grunted, grinding up and into her one last time.

"Now," he said, riding the edge. *"Now."*

His need shattered as she did, fragmenting into a thousand points of sharp bliss that hurt so good. Groaning, Vance squeezed shut his eyes and let the delicious ecstasy of violent release pulse through his body.

Minutes later, he came to awareness as she rolled off of him. His head was spinning and he felt half-drunk and whole-certain. The beast was a possessive bastard that was no longer willing to be caged. "Don't go far," he said in its devilish voice. "This is your bed until the end of the month."

CHAPTER FOURTEEN

IT WAS NEARING MIDNIGHT when Baxter walked along the sand toward Beach House No. 9. As promised, he'd waited for the police, listened while Skye reported the incident then stuck around a little longer to help gather up the papers on the floor. Now he could collect his car from No. 9's driveway and go straight home.

But instead of walking between the cove's last cottage and its neighbor in order to reach his Beemer, he climbed up the deck steps. Addy had left the archives room before him, anxious to check on Layla. Baxter, in turn, found himself anxious to check on Addy.

It looked like everybody inside the cottage was already asleep, though. The windows were dark and—no, there were two small, odd glows coming from the living room. Curious, he strode toward it and peered through the glass of the sliding door.

A smile curved his lips. Addy. Curled up on the sofa. He knocked lightly.

Her head jerked up and she pressed the book she'd been reading to her chest. Damn. He'd scared her. He waved, hoping to ease her fear.

It worked. In seconds she was on her feet and at the door. She unlocked the thing and slid it back. "What are you doing here?" she asked, her voice low.

Without waiting for permission, he slipped into the room. "Making sure you're okay."

"Apparently," she grumbled, "I survived the heart attack you just gave me."

He grimaced. "Sorry about that. I peeked in to see if anyone was awake and was a little startled myself by your twin points of light."

"Oh." She put her hand up, touching the glasses she wore. A beam emitted from each side of the frame. "I was reading."

"In the dark?" He sat near her spot on the cushions and patted her place. "Come sit down."

"Why?" There was a frown in her voice. Suspicion.

"So we can have a conversation."

"I was into my book."

Ouch, Baxter thought. Hostile. "We can start with that." He patted the cushion again. "Come on, sit with me."

She took the bait, approaching the sofa and dropping down. He noticed she still wore the zipped hoodie and formfitting jeans she'd had on at Captain Crow's. It struck him again how petite she was, her waist tiny, her bottom appealingly round.

"So," he said, as she drew her bare feet up beneath her. "What's your book's title and why are you reading it in the dark?"

"I always read in the dark."

Baxter blinked. "Always?"

"I mean when it's night. A habit I started as a kid. I'd hide under the covers with a flashlight so I didn't get caught staying up past bedtime."

"Ah." This was what he was after. More Addy information. "Strict parents?"

She hooked her finger in the glasses, removing them and switching off their beams. The room was very dark now, except, he saw, some barely glowing embers in the fireplace across the room. "They wanted me tucked away so they could hold rabid arguments without worrying about a witness."

The bald way she said the words didn't hide the pain behind them. And he'd been right, he thought, back there in the Sunrise archives room. He'd said it from instinct, but he knew it was true now. She wanted to believe that love could survive. "I'm sorry," he began. "That must have been—"

"What's the point of you being here, Baxter?"

Jeez. She didn't give a guy an inch. "I don't know. I just like talking with you. Being with you."

Leaning toward the coffee table in front of the sofa, she grabbed up a plate. Then she sat back and picked something from it, taking the object to her mouth. Before she bit down, she paused, releasing a little sigh. "Would you like some of my snack?"

In the dark, it looked like pretzels—or worms. "What is it?"

"Green beans. Steamed, blanched, drizzled with a little low-calorie Italian dressing."

"You call that a snack?" He remembered what she'd carried on her hike. Water and a handful of raw nuts. "Woman, do you need an introduction to ice cream? Can't Layla hook you up with some cupcakes?"

Her green bean was still crunchy enough to snap when she bit into it. "If you don't like vegetables, just say so."

"I actually do. Even Brussels sprouts."

"Figures," she said, sounding disgusted.

"What's that supposed to mean?"

"You need a flaw, Baxter," she muttered. "Your bathroom appeared sterilized. I noticed that your pantry was organized alphabetically."

"I've shared my self-diagnosis. Slight case of obsessive-compulsive disorder."

"Yeah, and when it manifests as tidiness and cleanliness, it's only another asset."

"I think you just said you like me," Baxter replied, smiling. "Which is convenient because I'm serious about the two of us dating."

"I told you—"

"I remember. France." The knowledge of her impending departure had walloped him when she'd first shared it, but he'd decided not to give up so easily. "We still have time, though."

She bit into another bean. "Time for what?"

God, Addy the Obstinate. "There are things I'd like to know about you. I remembered something interesting you said the other day. I want to understand what it means."

"Not a good idea," she said, putting the plate aside.

His gut tightened. Was she going to kick him out? Because he could tell she was shoring up her defenses like mad and if he walked out that door without her softening a little, he'd never find a way back in. He reached over, took her hand.

Of course, she tried tugging it away, but he held firm. "Two people, here in the dark. A perfect time for secrets."

She jerked a shoulder.

"The other day you said, 'I pretended I was pretend

people. I could pretend I was pretend people for days on end.'"

"So?"

Belligerence, thy name is Addison March. He threaded his fingers through hers, and they were as delicate as the rest of her. A perfect match for his pixie in the yellow dress. "I should have asked you why, Addy. I should have asked why you needed so much to pretend."

Her shoulder jerked again. He rubbed his thumb over hers, soothing her. "Can you explain that, Addy?"

"I told you about my parents. They vacillated between icy disdain for each other and red-hot rage. Unfortunately, they didn't divorce until I was almost out of high school. So I found ways to comfort myself... and to escape. I read books. I watched TV. I became mad for the movies."

All of which she could do in the dark, he thought. Meaning she must feel comfortable in the shadows, so he took a chance and scooted closer, slipping his hand from hers to draw her against him with an arm around her shoulder. "I wish it hadn't been that way for you."

Though she didn't pull back, her body refused to relax against his. Stifling his frustration, he toyed with the ends of her feathery hair, twisting a piece around his finger then letting the curl spring away before doing it again with another lock. Finally, she broke the silence between them. "Look. I really, really, really don't want to date you, see you, whatever you want to call it, before I go to France."

Three *really*s, but he continued playing with her hair. God, she was killing him. "Why?"

Another beat of reluctant, weighty silence. Then she finally said, "I don't want goodbye to hurt."

Now, Baxter thought, relieved. Now they were getting somewhere. He turned his head and placed a kiss on her temple. "Addy."

Her face turned toward him and then the kiss was lip-to-lip, sweet. He thought he tasted a yearning inside her. It couldn't be all on his side. He touched his tongue to the seam of her mouth and she opened, her own tongue brushing his. With a little moan, she broke away.

"Baxter, no." Her voice sounded strained. "I told you, I don't want goodbye to hurt."

He captured her hand again. "Won't it already?"

"No," she said, pulling free again and swinging around on the cushions in order to face him. "Because I'm still certain, here—" she thumped her fist on her chest "—that I don't get to have you."

"Wha—"

"An Addy March doesn't get a Baxter Smith."

He stared at her, trying to decipher the puzzle of her words. This close, even without any light, he could see she was serious. Determined. Near furious.

"Honey, I don't understand what you're trying to tell me."

She huffed out an impatient, irritated breath. "How many ways do I have to say this?" she asked, lifting her arms. "Here's how it is— You're the golden guy. I'm the plain fat girl."

His brain couldn't keep up. What? What, what, what? She could fit in a thimble. "I'm having trouble here."

Her feet thumped on the hardwood as she jumped up. "You don't remember me as a kid."

"Uh…" Not really. He remembered her as a concept—until That Night. As a kid he'd known the couple down the road had a girl, younger than himself and his cousins. Just with that, she had been dismissed from his consciousness. "Maybe I saw you passing in a car, or…?"

"It doesn't matter." She was pacing. "I told you, I developed ways to deal with the ugly atmosphere at my house. Stories in every form. Pretend. Food. I've burned every picture of myself between the ages of eight and nineteen."

Oh, Addy.

"Home was hell. School was hell. Then, for a high school graduation present my dad offered me a summer at fat camp."

Baxter couldn't think of one thing to say. But his heart was giving him grief, squeezing so hard that it seemed to constrict the beat. "That…that couldn't have been the gift you wanted."

"Are you kidding?" She rounded on him. "It was a great gift."

He should keep his mouth shut. He really, really, really should. "Okay."

"I had a chance to get away from my toxic household. I had a chance to think about me and what I wanted. I deferred college a year—I told you that—and I found new ways to cope. I learned some healthier habits."

"That's good."

"*Damn* good."

"Damn good," he echoed. "But why can't we—"

"Because when I see myself in the mirror, more than half the time I don't see this me." She faced him, and even in the dark he could see her vibrating with emotion. "Instead, I see the old, miserable me, unhealthy, unhappy, and I'm just a breath away from hiding from my reflection in those former habits."

"Honey—"

"I can't do it." Her voice sounded tense. "I can't spend more time with you and then leave the country. It's bad enough that I might come to...miss you, but to be emotionally brittle and living in the land of croissants and chocolate?"

"Addy..."

She shook her head. "I just can't do it."

It still sounded as if she liked him, though. Baxter couldn't dismiss that. He didn't want to dismiss that—he cared too much. Rising off the couch, he approached her. She didn't try to evade him, even when he curled his fingers around her upper arms. "It doesn't have to be disaster. The way I feel—"

"You don't get it!" She shook her head. "We're not suited. We're that kids' game made literal. You know, One of These Things Is Not like the Other."

"Bullshit." He shook her a little. "That's just bullshit."

"God, Baxter." Her voice went hoarse. "Tell me something about yourself that's less than perfect."

His stomach sank. Not because he thought he was flawless by any means, but because he didn't think there was anything he could say that would appease her. Still, he tried. "Addy, I'm going to suck at this." The BSLS didn't have a line item for self-examination.

"Give it a try."

"Uh...I hardly ever floss." He thought harder. "I can't work up an interest in ice hockey."

She made a disgusted sound. "I knew it."

Desperate, goaded, Baxter opened his mouth again, hoping something persuasive would fly out. "I hate my job." It wasn't until he felt her new, rigid stillness beneath his hands that he heard his own words. *I hate my job.*

Had he said that?

Had he really said that?

To escape answering his own question, Baxter dropped his hands and strode from the house.

THE MORNING FOLLOWING the break-in, Layla meandered her way from the Karma Cupcakes truck back to Beach House No. 9, aware she was—literally—dragging her feet. Glancing over her shoulder, she saw the physical evidence in the skid marks in the sand. She'd slipped from Vance's bed at dawn, while he was still asleep, and now she'd have to face him in the glaring light of day.

The shift in their relationship worried her.

The shift in *herself* worried her.

I thought you were sugar and spice and everything nice. But maybe you have a naughty side, after all.

A shiver wiggled down her back as she remembered his dark, drugging words. And then his other words, the ones that were graphic and…and crude, except they hadn't felt crude, they'd seemed just another element of the hypnotic spell he'd cast with his deep kisses and knowing caresses. His demands.

Straddle me, sweetheart. Put your breast to my mouth.

Touch yourself and come for me.

How was she supposed to look at him after that? After she'd done exactly as instructed and then been blissfully rewarded?

But she'd been the one to start it, hadn't she? He'd suggested they head to separate beds and she'd decided not to waste that sizzling sexual force that existed between them. It was gratifying to remember how little it had taken to persuade him.

She slowed even more as she began mounting the steps at the bottom of No. 9. Vance wanted her in his bed for the rest of the month now. Nerves jittered in her belly at the thought. Deciding to sleep with a man a single night at a time was one thing. Going into it as a sort of…of living arrangement, no matter how fleeting, felt like something different altogether.

What if that somehow left her wanting more—despite knowing never to count on such a thing? Maybe she'd better run back to Uncle Phil and ask for one of his vaunted lectures on the Buddhist principal of non-attachment.

She was so intent on her thoughts that she blinked as she arrived on the deck, startled to see people there she didn't recognize. Her head whipped around. In her distracted state, had she approached the wrong beach house? But there was Vance, breaking away from a couple of strangers to come her way. "Hey," he called out. "There you are."

He caught her fingers in his and drew her farther onto the deck. "Are you okay?" he asked softly.

"I'm great," she replied, going for bright and confident instead of embarrassed and unsure of her next step. "You have visitors?"

"Our predecessors, in a sense," he said. "Jane Pearson and Griffin Lowell."

Layla shook hands with the woman first. She was sandy-haired and her light gray eyes picked up the blue in the sleeveless shirt she wore over cropped jeans. "Cute shoes," Layla told her, taking in the wedged espadrilles that were dotted with small seashells arranged in the shape of flowers.

"My librarian's trademark," Griffin said, grinning. He was dark and lean with piercing blue eyes and a strong grip. Then his smile died. "I knew your father. And admired him. I'm very sorry for your loss."

Layla's throat tightened. "Thank you."

Vance rubbed her arm with the back of his knuckles, a gentle, sympathetic touch. "Remember? Griffin was embedded with us. He brought with him some photos from that time—of your dad and others—if you'd like to see them."

Would she?

"Even one of your favorite combat medic, too," Griffin added. "They're in the house."

A photo of Vance. *Vance, at war.*

Before she could respond, Skye arrived from the beach, wearing her usual sloppy pants and sweatshirt, a black Lab at her heels. "Private rushed me along. I guess he's excited about the wedding, too."

Layla looked at the couple. "Is that why you're here? You're really going to say 'I do' at No. 9 next month?"

"Any longer might give my honey-pie time to come to her senses," Griffin said.

Jane smiled at him. "I keep telling you, chili-dog, with a ring or without one, I'll still be your grammar girl." Then they both laughed as he pulled her into his arms and kissed her hair.

Vance shook his head at them. "I'm too polite to retch at those nicknames, Griff."

"They started as insults," Jane confided, "but now they've kind of grown on us. More Beach House No. 9 magic, I guess."

"Speaking of which," Griffin said, turning to Skye, "we're sure this place will be available on the wedding date, right? Have you heard any more from the mysterious August tenant who went AWOL?"

"Yes. The balance was paid, finally. And I informed Mr. Fenton Hardy that I'd waive his late fee in exchange for the use of this place on the last weekend in August."

An odd expression crossed Griffin's face. "Did you say Fenton Hardy?"

Skye's brows came together. "Yes. Do you know him?"

He glanced at his fiancée, who went still for a moment and then opened her mouth. "Isn't that—"

"A really fortuitous turn of events," Griffin said over her, and then he turned to gaze about the deck. "I'm sure we'll have enough room here. It's going to be very small. A few friends, family."

Jane nodded, her smile aimed first at Griffin and then at Skye and Layla. "And we're accustomed to small, since we're living together in my tiny one-bedroom until we find the perfect bigger place—we hope near the beach." Her voice turned more casual. "Have you heard from Gage lately, Skye? We don't have a clue as to whether he'll make it back for the nuptials."

The other woman blinked, and her hand crept to her stomach. "You…you think there's a chance he might be in the States next month?"

Jane flicked a glance at Griffin, then shrugged. "You hear from him more than anyone. What's your opinion?"

"His last letter didn't say a thing about it." Skye bit her lip. "He mentioned he had a new contact, was hoping to take a trip into territory he hadn't been to before. Nothing about returning here."

"Well—" Griffin began.

"He can't come to Crescent Cove." The words rushed from Skye. "I mean, he'd never like it here. Not anymore." Then, clearly flustered, she sped toward the steps and was gone.

"I don't think I understand," Layla said.

Jane grimaced. "I don't think any of us do, including Gage. He's been exchanging letters with Skye for months. She's clearly smitten—but clearly terrified by the idea, too."

"Why?"

"For good reason," Griffin said. "My twin lives for hard-edged excitement. Skye has too much of a soft underbelly. She'll get hurt."

Jane sighed. "People warned me away from you, too."

He lifted an eyebrow. "People? Like who?"

"Oh, that's right, it was you." She grinned at him.

"A man can change," he grumbled.

"So might Gage," Jane pointed out. "Especially if he's exposed to the Beach House No. 9 magic."

Vance groaned. "Feeling the need to retch again."

Jane laughed and threaded her arm through Griffin's. "We can't have that." She tilted her head toward Layla. "Would you like to see the photographs? They're inside the house. You can keep any you like."

"I…" She swallowed. "Okay."

The couple moved toward the sliding glass door, but Vance held Layla back. He turned her to face him. "Really. Are you okay? Last night…"

Heat flowed up her neck to her face. "Do we have to talk about it?"

A smile slowly spread across his face. "'Talking about it' seems to work well for us."

"Vance."

He leaned in and took her mouth in a searing kiss. Then his fingertips floated over the small bump on her scalp. "Head okay?"

At her nod, his hand moved lower, his thumb exploring beneath the open collar of her shirt to touch a place low on the side of her throat. "Did I leave a bruise?"

The heat was everywhere now, prickling beneath the hair on her head, tickling the sensitive backs of her knees. She took hold of him, tucking her fingertips under the waistband of his jeans at his sides so she didn't fall to the deck where her melting body would slide between the cracks in the floorboards to be lost forever.

Maybe that would be best. It would certainly be better than falling for Vance, a soldier, like her father. A man who'd be gone from her life in less than two weeks.

"Do you really want to see the photos?" he asked now. "They'll understand if it's too much."

Colonel Parker's daughter could face them, Layla told herself, and straightened her shoulders. No more melting, under any circumstances. "I do. I want to see them."

Vance touched his lips to hers, just brief contact. "I looked already. Smiles and laughter. Nothing upsetting."

He'd looked at them for her, she realized. Checked them over, so she could feel confident there would be no image that would startle or disturb her. She leaned up on her tiptoes and kissed his chin, touched by his consideration. "Let's go."

Inside the house, there were a dozen or so photographs spread across the coffee table, most five-by-sevens, some larger. Layla sank to the cushions, her gaze moving slowly over them. "Oh," she said, with a little smile, and glanced at Vance, who took the seat beside her. "There's Dad playing chess."

"He did it often," Griffin said. "With anyone who'd take the other side of the board."

Her father looked so handsome, she thought. Tanned, hair regulation short, a little thin, perhaps, but he'd always been a little thin.

Another showed him bent over a battered desk. In a different shot he was throwing a horseshoe. Each one showed Colonel Parker at work or at rest, looking his usual capable, calm self.

Her hand moved to reveal one picture that was half-hidden. Vance. Her fingers froze. In the shot, he was kicked back on a bunk, laughing. His face was a little dirty, his hair a little sweaty, but it was him, finding humor even though there was a gun slung from a peg just within reach.

Vance, at war.

"Layla, what's the matter?" he asked.

"Nothing." She kept staring at the photograph. "May I have them?" she asked Griffin. "May I have them all?"

"Of course. We brought them for you."

She stacked them carefully, putting Vance's on top. The visitors were preparing to leave, calling for their dog, Private, talking to Vance about the war memoir Griffin was currently writing, which apparently had brought him and Jane together at Beach House No. 9

in the first place. Only half listening, Layla finally returned to the present as the engaged couple bid her goodbye.

She stood and, with Vance, walked them to the front door. When they made it back to the living room, her gaze immediately fell on that image of him. The dirty face. The laughing grin. The gun.

Vance, at war.

She was definitely too smart to fall in love with him. But that didn't stop her from suddenly reaching for him. Putting her arms around his lean waist, she hugged his big body close.

"What?" He smiled down at her. "What's up?"

"Nothing." She was safe now, wasn't she?

His mouth met hers in a kiss that went from warm to wild in mere seconds. Gasping, she had to pull away. "Vance."

"I like the way you say that, all breathless and needy." He gave her another knowing smile. "You're blushing again."

"It's ridiculous of me, I know. There's nothing wrong with enjoying a healthy bout of consensual sex," she said, knowing she sounded prim but unable to help it.

He laughed. "Is that what we're calling it now?"

"I'm annoyed with myself for feeling embarrassed."

Vance laughed again, dark and low as they both saw Addy push open the glass slider. "I'm going to embarrass you again as soon as I can get you alone," he said in her ear. "And then all night long."

Feeling her flush deepen, Layla sketched a wave at Addy and turned back to collect the photos. She'd weathered this morning-after better than she'd thought. The pictures would make sure she remembered not to fall for a soldier. So nothing had changed as a result of last night, after all. Feeling eyes on her, she glanced back. Vance, watching her, with definite lascivious thoughts in mind.

All night long.

Yes, nothing had changed…except, she thought with a delicious, dangerous shiver, for the sleeping arrangements.

CHAPTER FIFTEEN

THE SETTING WAS PARADISE: blue sky, palm trees, golden beach and gentle surf. The soundtrack worked, too, a pleasing combination of waves hitting sand punctuated by seagull calls. On the deck of the beach house, Vance basked in good cheer that was as warm as the sunshine, even though the woman he'd have in his bed that night was standing in front of him, arms crossed over her chest, shaking her head. "I'm not going to do it."

"Jeez, Layla," he said, proffering the hair clippers again, "you're a soldier's daughter. All I'm asking—"

"Not going to do it. Nuh-uh."

He ran his fingers through his too-long hair, managing to avoid clunking his skull with his cast. Hey, progress. "Baby..."

"I like that it's longer," she said, coming forward to touch it herself. "Another inch and I think it might have a wave. Even curl."

"Bite your tongue." He batted her hand away. "My hair wouldn't dare do that again."

"'Again'?" Layla's eyes narrowed. "You had curls at one time?"

"Of course not," he lied.

She smiled, clearly delighted, and sidled closer, pressing her sweet body to his. "Vance Smith. I bet you were the cutest thing."

He copped a feel of her butt with his free hand and couldn't help but smile back. "It was a crime, what she did to me."

"Who?" She leaned up to kiss his stubbled chin.

It tickled, and he made a mental note to shave before bed so he wouldn't whisker-burn the soft and tender place between her thighs he meant to explore for at least half the night. She bussed him again, and he slid his hand to the back of her head, holding her in place for a real kiss. Lips to lips. Tongue to tongue. God, he loved that lemon icing taste of hers.

"Who?" she said against his mouth.

He lifted his head. "What?" Damn, the woman distracted him. "Oh, who. My mother."

"So it's her DNA that's responsible for the ringlets?"

Vance kept his arm around Layla, pleased to have her pretty face so close. "Probably. But what I meant was how sneakily she cultivated my head of hair."

Layla smiled again. "Do tell."

"You know what an active kid I was. Sports, bikes, you name it. Go, go, go all the time. So when I was in the sixth grade and she didn't hound me to go, go, go to the barber, I didn't complain or question, because it gave me more play time. Didn't give a thought to why I wasn't seeing scissors even though Fucking Perfect Fitz kept regular appointments."

"Fucking Perfect Fitz has hair straight as a stick."

He loved how his brother's nickname just rolled off her tongue. So he had to kiss her again, and tongue that tongue, and generally just enjoy the hell out of himself for a few minutes. Who knew something so fine could come out of that battlefield promise?

Maybe there was something to this Beach House No. 9

mystique, after all. Griffin and Jane certainly seemed to think so. The man was different than he'd been overseas—his smile more ready, his restlessness calmed.

When Vance's kiss for Layla ended, she was still fixated on the subject of his long-ago style. "So, Rapunzel, your hair just kept growing…"

"Into ringlets, like you guessed." Huh. He hadn't meant to confess that to her, but he'd told her so many things about himself. Maybe more than he'd ever told anybody. Certainly any woman. "Fat ringlets."

"To his shoulders," a new voice added. "And when our family went on vacation that summer, every day someone mistook him for a girl."

Vance whirled to confront his brother, climbing the steps to the deck. He looked as put-together as ever—not as *GQ* as Baxter, but pure dean's list in khakis and a sports shirt. His face looked tired, though, a strain around his eyes.

It only pissed Vance off more that he noticed the change. "What the hell is with you, Fitz?" His day had been so damn happy. "Rain on someone else's parade."

"Is that any way to talk to the guy who saved you from a rattlesnake?"

Stepping away from Layla, Vance glared. "That's such crap. You were wrong—it was a garter snake, which someone with your IQ should have realized."

Fitz managed to look down his nose at him, which was quite a feat considering he was shorter. "Isn't it the thought that counts?"

"When you shoved me away, I landed on my chin." He tapped the scar. "Five stitches, bro."

"It just furthered your romance with the intake nurse in the E.R." Fitz shoved his hands in his pockets.

"Should I be jealous?" Layla's voice broke into the tension.

Fitz shifted his gaze. "She knew his insurance number by heart. One look at those curls and the ladies were charmed." A small smile curved his lips and he looked younger, almost like the 14-year-old who'd believed he'd been saving his little brother.

It twisted Vance's gut. Sometimes Fucking Perfect Fitz made it almost impossible to hate him. "So what do you want this time?"

His brother looked away, then looked back. "The other occasions… The first time was to urge you to contact Mom, the second to return the ring. But now…I'm here for myself, V.T. To make things right between us."

Vance just stared at him.

"You're my little brother," Fitz started.

"It's not like I've forgotten," Vance said, impatient. "I'm the screwup, the can't-be-trusted, the not-good-as-you."

"Those are your words, not mine." Fitz frowned. "And I'm not here to insult you, dammit. I'm here to make sure you understand about…about me and Blythe."

"Not that again. Jesus, go find another dead horse to beat, will you?"

Fitz wore a familiar dogged expression, however, the same one he used to have when digging into an extra credit problem set for Advanced Calculus. "I swear that I didn't make any moves on her before she broke your engagement."

Vance rolled his eyes.

"Sure, I thought she was beautiful and I couldn't believe—"

"She'd tie herself to the black sheep of the family? But that didn't last, did it?"

Fitz sighed. "It just happened, okay? But not be-fore—"

"Oh, for goodness' sake," Layla interrupted, surprising them both. She stomped over to Fitz and he retreated until the small of his back smacked the railing around the deck. Her forefinger poked him in the chest. "Just apologize to your brother."

Fitz blinked. "Wha—"

"I'm an only child," Layla said right over him, "but even I know there's a no-poaching rule between siblings, breakup or no. So tell Vance you're sorry and maybe you have a chance of him forgiving you."

Vance's mouth twitched. God, she made him want to smile, for championing him yet again, and for humbling Fucking Perfect Fitz for perhaps the first time in his life. Because, yep, his brother just stood there, his mouth half-open, the dumb look on his face saying he didn't know what to think or do next.

A few minutes of silence passed. Finally Fitz looked from Layla to Vance. "She's right, V.T. I...I beg your pardon." Then he held out his hand. "Are we good?"

Vance strode forward, for all the world appearing as if he was intent on sealing the peace with a handshake. At the last second, though, instead of meeting Fitz's palm, he shoved at his brother's shoulders, hard, sending him toppling over the railing and onto the sand four feet below. Then he peered down at the other man through narrowed eyes. "You ass. It's not going to be that easy."

Fitz lay flat on his back, his hair disheveled, his button-down shirt askew, his gaze on the blue overhead. A sudden memory flashed in Vance's mind. Two young boys, shoulder to shoulder, finding shapes in the clouds. Usually something so tame would bore restless

Vance, but Fitz had found a pirate ship in the sky and was spinning the tale of two buccaneer brothers who spent a lifetime together fighting side by side, gathering riches and helping the poor. Figured Fitz's sea bandits were Robin Hoods, Vance mused now.

Though different from each other, they'd been close as kids. Later, when Vance was semi-estranged from their parents, Fitz had tried to retain the brotherly closeness—when Vance wasn't deployed he'd called on a regular basis and dropped by for a beer on occasion, no matter how cool a response he'd received in return.

Fucking Perfect Fitz, always doing the right, responsible thing.

He'd counted on that, Vance realized, and had been shocked by his brother's hooking up with Blythe. It had sliced deep, he realized now, much, much deeper than being dumped by his fiancée. And he'd been grieving over that break with Fitz ever since.

It just happened, his brother had said, referring to falling in love with Blythe. And Vance remembered saying similar words to Layla, too, explaining their instant combustible chemistry. Sometimes things just happened.

"What now?" Layla asked, coming up beside him at the railing to peer curiously over the side.

He glanced over at her, and it brought to mind her uncle Phil and his Buddha voodoo. He'd talked to Vance about grief. You could use it for the positive, the aging hippie had said. It could give you an understanding of how quickly life passes. Then you'd appreciate the world more. Then you'd be kinder to your fellow man.

To your brother.

"Now?" he said to Layla on a sigh. "Now I guess I better get ol' Fitz off the sand. Offer him a beer."

His brother still looked a little dazed as Vance stood on the beach, staring down on him. "You breathing?" he asked, his voice a bit gruff.

It was Fitz's turn to sigh. "I've got enough air for another crack at that apology I owe you."

Vance reached out a hand to help Fitz up.

"I think I'll stay here, if you don't mind. You might just knock me down again."

Without a word, Vance kept his palm outstretched.

After another moment, Fitz met it with his own. His grip was strong and even after he was on his feet, his fingers stayed folded around Vance's. "I'm sorry." Fitz swallowed. "What makes it worse was that you were going through a bad time and my involvement as part of it meant I couldn't be there for you."

"Yeah," Vance replied, his voice still gruff. Losing his brother had been much worse than losing Blythe.

"Like I said from the beginning," Layla interjected cheerfully. "He's not so fucking perfect, after all."

Vance had to grin. "Hey, the lady's right. And that puts me in a much more forgiving mood."

"Do that," Fitz said, serious. "Forgive me. Please."

"Okay." Vance nodded, then clapped his brother on the shoulder. "We're okay."

Then he got out the beer. And pretty soon he and his brother were shooting the shit in the sunshine with cold brews at hand and a pretty girl who just looked at them with an enigmatic smile in her eyes. Before the sun went down, Fitz had grabbed up the clippers and turned his perfectionism toward Vance's hair.

Look, Vance thought, in sudden surprise. His damn happy day was back.

It won't hurt to say goodbye, Addy reminded herself as she made her way to the door of Baxter's highrise condo. She tugged on her light cotton tunic, then flicked a piece of lint from her jeans. It *won't* hurt to say goodbye.

Of course, she'd already thought she'd said goodbye—wasn't it twice now?—but here she was, on Baxter's turf. That damn carton of ledgers, she thought. She should never have let him carry it away. But when he'd called about getting the stuff back to her, it had seemed smarter for her to make the collection herself rather than suggesting he come to Crescent Cove.

This way, she'd control the situation.

Leave when she wanted. As in, immediately upon receipt of the box.

Baxter answered the door dressed in a pair of jeans and a Superman T-shirt. She stared, surprised by the casual attire. He'd been in similarly relaxed gear the other night at Captain Crow's, she now remembered. It had seemed somewhat out-of-character then, but still, it had been after work hours. It was noon now, though. A weekday. Why wasn't he in one of his elegant suits?

"I'm sorry," she said. "I didn't think when I said I'd meet you at home. You could have brought the box to your office and I would have picked it up there."

He shrugged. "Come in."

Still, Addy hesitated. At his workplace, the handover could have been totally businesslike. But now she was going to have to walk into his living space, raising the memory of the last time they'd been together in these rooms. The bed. The tie. His body. *Oh, God.*

Better to avoid that, she decided hastily. "I'll wait right here while you get the box."

"Addy—"

"I don't want to be a bother."

Baxter gave her a wry smile. "You've been bothering me for six years."

What to say to that? "Really, if you'll just give me the box, I'll get out of your hair. I'm sure you're eager to return to work."

An odd expression crossed his face.

I hate my job. He'd uttered those words that night in the darkness that he'd said was safe for secrets. She hadn't gotten the chance to delve into the statement— he'd run as if he'd found the sentiment as startling as she did. But now wasn't the time to discuss it with him, either. It was none of her affair, after all, even though she felt a pang of sympathy for Golden Boy Baxter for the first time in her life.

If it was true, he had to be suffering. Where did job dissatisfaction fit on the Baxter Smith Life Schedule? It wasn't as if he could just up and leave the family business.

And now guilt stabbed her, as well. He might be in distress and she wasn't even gracious enough to walk into his home. With a grimace, she took a step forward. "Okay, I'll come in," she told him. "Just for a minute. Just long enough to collect the ledgers."

He followed her into the living room. "Don't you want to discuss what I found?"

She turned, eyebrows rising. "You looked them over?"

"I told you I would. I'll keep all my promises to you from now on, Addy."

Oh, she wished he wouldn't say things like that. And she wished that the navy T-shirt didn't turn his remarkable eyes an even darker blue and that when she saw the *S* emblazoned on the cotton covering his broad chest, she didn't think of *Sexy* and *So Good in Bed*.

She curled her fingers into her palms, hoping the bite of her nails would get her mind back on track. "Could you glean anything about the state of Sunrise Pictures' financials? When Max Sunstrum closed the doors, could you tell if it was in the red or black?"

Before Baxter could answer, she lifted her shoulders in a self-deprecating little shrug. "And please, make it simple. Because I'm going to confess I don't actually remember which one is better, even though I took an accounting elective in high school. Mr. Finney was a complete tool. The only thing I actually know about red and black is that I don't look good in either one."

His mouth twitched. "No?"

"No. Too harsh for the pale hair and the pale complexion. I once tried cherry-red, which is supposed to be okay on blondes…" She subsided, realizing she was chattering about nothing. "Sorry, I'm on full babble. Used to be that I'd eat when I was nervous. Potato chips are good nervous-eating food. Or cookies. Now I talk."

He smiled.

Had she just confessed she used to gorge on junk food? "Oh, God, I'm still doing it, aren't I?"

"Why are you nervous, Addy?"

I'm worried it's going to hurt to say goodbye. She looked away from his gorgeous face and bit her lip. "Please put me out of my misery. What did you learn?"

He took her hand and led her to the sofa. His fingers were warm and sure, and she remembered them playing with her hair. She remembered being curled against him the other night in his bedroom. Then, she'd closed her eyes for just a moment and had let herself pretend again, pretend that he was hers.

Which was no way to prevent the hurt when she said goodbye.

So she slipped from his hold and perched on the edge of the cushions. The box of ledgers sat in their carton on the coffee table in front of her and she gestured with the hand that was missing his touch. "So…?"

"I'm no forensic accountant, but I'm pretty good at reading a balance sheet. From what I can tell, the company was in solid shape."

"Oh." Addy slumped back on the cushions. "So…so Max shut it down in order to shut Edith down."

"Well—"

"Are you sure?" Addy asked. It was silly of her to feel such disappointment—thanks to her mother and father, she knew firsthand about lousy marriages. But…poor Edith. "Maybe you misread them. I imagine you went through them late at night, after a long day at work—"

"I've been a part-timer since two days ago, Addy." Baxter was focused on her face. "I quit my job."

"Oh." She blinked. "I… Well… Wow."

"Yeah, that pretty much sums up the response of everyone in the office and in the family. I went to work there out of expectation, not any interest of my own and I'd never given myself enough time off to realize that until…until you."

"Me?"

"Until you made me start thinking with my heart, I didn't look inside of it." Then he scooted down the sofa and picked up her hand. His head bent, he idly played with her fingers.

Her own heart started to pound at that casual touch.

And it made her absurdly proud to think she'd played some part in his change of direction if that's what he truly needed. "Keep me posted on your next adventure then, will you?" She smiled as he looked up. "That's what it's going to be, you know. Now that you've given yourself permission to enjoy life instead of just working through it."

Baxter stilled, and then he smiled, too, his head shaking ruefully. "Once again, I can only wonder at my idiocy of six years ago."

"You should forget about that."

"I can't. Not when I need you near to remind me of abstract ideas like adventure and enjoyment." His gaze turned serious. "Listen, Addy. I'm...I'm in love with you." She jerked, and her hand almost slipped from his hold. But he firmed his grip and said those words a second time. "I'm in love with you, Addy March."

Her mind was reeling, her heart was knocking around in her chest as if it was trying to get away. "But...but. You can't. The BSLS says you have to be dating someone for a minimum of six months before that can come up."

He lifted her hand to his mouth and kissed it. "Honey, we both know I've been a fool about that. The BSLS is just B.S."

She'd kind of thought that herself, but... "No, Baxter. Please don't say that. Please don't say any more of this."

"You don't feel anything for me?"

She felt so much that it scared her. But this wasn't pretend time, this wasn't fantasy. "Addy March doesn't get the golden guy," she whispered.

"Not so golden," he replied. "Think about it. I don't have a job, I don't know what my future holds. I only have wishes. That you care for me. That you might be in love with me, too. That you'll let me start my adventure by going to Paris with you."

Paris with her! She closed her eyes at the thought and images flashed through her brain. Hand in hand on city streets. Holed up in the back row of a dark cinema. A sidewalk café table for two. Swallowing hard, Addy opened her eyes. "Do you speak French?"

He shook his head. "Can't even claim that. I'll have to rely on you."

"Baxter." She was whispering again, as if a normal voice might burst the hope that was building in her chest. "Baxter, I…"

"If you're in love with me, say it," Baxter urged. "Or if you aren't, go ahead and tell me. I can take that, too."

"Well, of course I'm in love with you," she told him, a bit annoyed that he might doubt that. Yes, he'd been her go-to crush for years, but she was a grown-up now who knew the difference between made-up emotions and real ones that were lodged in her heart.

He grinned, and she realized he might have been a bit nervous himself. "Addy." He pulled her close and kissed her.

She came up for air some minutes later, breathless and thrilled and…scared all over again. "Oh, my God," she said, and tried scooting out of his arms. "This is going to be a disaster." She was whispering again.

Baxter put his forehead against hers. "Now what?"

"It's really going to hurt to say goodbye now."

"I told you, I'd like to go to Paris with you." His mouth pressed against hers once more, a quick firm kiss. "If you'll let me."

"I mean, when it ends. When we end."

He groaned and pulled her into his lap. "I'm not looking for endings. I'm counting on forever."

She turned her face into his neck, breathing in the spicy male scent of his skin. Yes, her feelings for him were real, but to believe in a relationship… "I'm afraid that it won't last."

"Addy, people *do* find lasting love. My parents are devoted to each other and happy. My aunt and uncle are the same."

"I know," she mumbled. But her parents' marriage had been so ugly and the divorce no prettier.

"My darling pessimist." Baxter's arms tightened on her. "What if I could show you a sign?"

"What kind of sign?" she asked, suspicious.

Without answering, Baxter kissed the top of her head and then reached toward the carton of ledgers. "I found some of that personal correspondence you've been searching for when I was looking through the business records."

She stared at him. "I didn't give them more than a glance."

"Then it's a good thing I took longer with them than you did." With a little flourish he pressed a paper into her hands—a delicate sheet of stationery covered in blue ink.

Addy swallowed and glanced at Baxter. "It's dated 1927. That's when Sunrise stopped making movies."

He nodded. "Read."

Addy turned her attention to the handwriting, which was feminine, though not particularly elegant.

Dear Max,
To commemorate this day you are closing Sun-

rise for good, I wanted to tell you all that is in my heart.

I know you loved the movie business and you'd be happily making pictures into the future, but you've given it up for me and I'll be forever grateful. I couldn't take the rumors and backstabbing any longer. I felt as if the critics and gossips had found a loose thread and were pulling on it harder and harder, faster and faster, until soon I would be naked and exposed, with no protection whatsoever. Perhaps I could have survived that with you as my buffer, but then came the rumors of the affair and the cruel way you were portrayed in the papers. It made me desperate to leave the business.

You are a generous, good and loving man. The speculation that you might hurt me or my career became intolerable. We should never have made *The Egyptian!* It all started with that picture and that ridiculous piece of jewelry the papers call The Collar. I've decided against selling it, thinking that would only add to the already unsavory notoriety I have received because of it. Drat Nicky! He refuses to take it back. I think he's using his so-called unrequited love for me to fuel his latest brooding performance (another of the Aston Agonies, as the critics like to call them). The public will be lined up to see it, eager to know if his looks have suffered due to the "Edith Essex Affair." Don't think this isn't part of his scheme.

When I looked out at the ocean this morning, I thought about throwing The Collar into the water, but you know me. My childhood makes it impossible for me to squander something so valuable. So I've put it safely away—we won't have to look at it or think about it any longer.

Which means our life will have no more pretense or pretend in it. All will be real now, our love and our beautiful cove. Just you and I tucked away in the beach house, alone except for any additions that might happen to arrive (and yes, that's a clue to the surprise I've been hinting about!).

I am ever grateful to you for discovering me and making me a star—and then unmaking me into nothing but the woman who loves you with all her soul. You once called me your beautiful dreamer...now, finally, my greatest dream has come true.

Always Yours, Edith

Addy looked up, a smile stretched across her face. "Edith and Max *were* happily married. He gave up Sunrise because it's what she wanted."

"You got your happy ending, Addy."

At that, her smile dimmed. "But she died only a little more than five years after writing this."

"Maybe that's a sign, too," Baxter said. "A sign that we shouldn't waste time worrying about what-if when we can be loving the heck out of each other instead."

A tear fell onto Addy's cheek and she quickly moved the letter aside. Baxter linked his hands at the small of her back and pulled her forward to lick away the moisture. "No crying, honey, unless it's from exhaustion."

"Exhaustion?"

"Yeah," he said, getting up from the couch with her

still in his arms. "I'm going to make love to you until we're both too tired to get out of bed."

Oh, Addy thought, a little punch-drunk on emotions. She wasn't going to be leaving, after all.

CHAPTER SIXTEEN

IN BAXTER'S BEDROOM, though, Addy's doubts returned. He'd set her on her feet and she stared at the bed and its smoothly ordered covering. The pillows were stuffed in shams propped at precise intervals against the head-board. His slight OCD in evidence.

Her right foot stepped back. "I don't know if I can do this."

He had the hem of his T-shirt in his grip and he froze in the process of removing it, half his six-pack revealed. "Why not?" he asked, frowning at her.

"You make your bed with impeccable hospital corners, I can tell. I'll...I'll never measure up."

Baxter let his shirt drop and his voice softened. "This isn't about hospital corners, is it, Addy?"

She made a face. "Was it the Freudian 'measure up' that gave me away?"

He came toward her, the bright light of day hiding nothing of his face and killer body. "You know," he said, his voice casual. "There's one good thing about my OCD. It means I'm very, very detail-oriented."

"Does it also mean you'll consent to keeping your eyes shut whenever the clothes come off?" She thought of the underwear she wore today, a pale green cotton set sprinkled with darker green frogs, little golden crowns perched atop their heads. It was her story, gender-reversed, wasn't it? The handsome prince kissed the ugly frog, transforming her.

His hands on her shoulders, Baxter lightly kissed her mouth. "Addy, I want to look at you. All of you. You're beautiful."

Still worry crept in, stiffening her muscles. Damn her body issues!

"Shh," Baxter said, then kissed her cheek, her nose, her forehead. "This is me. Just me."

Just him, the most gorgeous man she'd ever known. Her crush of a lifetime.

With stinging eyes, she looked up at golden Baxter. Even swimming in her tears he was leading-man material. "I told you before, we're the embodiment of One of These Things Is Not like the Other."

He closed his eyes for a brief moment, as if in pain. "Addy, no…"

"I mean it," she insisted.

"Addy." He moved his hands upward, using them to cup her face. "No job. No French."

She let that sink in for a moment. Finally she heard herself add, "No taste in superheroes."

"What?" He glanced down at the big *S* on his chest.

"Superman," she scoffed, feeling her mojo on the rise again. "So banal, Baxter."

He scowled now, but she knew he was just playing along. "I'll add that to prissy and pasty."

She laughed. "I'm sorry. That was my defense mechanism talking. You're hunky and so handsome that it was hard for me to handle."

"Handle me now, Addy."

And she heard it as a plea. He wanted her. He needed her touch. So she applied herself to getting him naked.

Superman shirt gone—note to self, get him into an edgier crime fighter before hitting Paris—he stopped her hands on their way to his jeans.

"Time for you to get naked, Addy," he said, his voice guttural.

She stalled again, her hands returning his tight grip. *Be brave,* she told herself, closing her eyes and breathing in the scent of his warm skin. Intellectually, she knew she wasn't that little girl who had lived in the dark. She was a woman, *a loved woman,* getting ready to have sex with the man she wanted in her bed for the rest of their lives.

I can do this, she thought, stepping away from him in order to shuck the rest of her clothes. *I can do this.*

Then, over his shoulder, she caught sight of herself in the mirrored closet doors across the room. She shuddered. It didn't matter what the size label said on her clothes. It wasn't even about size.

It was about feeling loved. Her parents hadn't loved her enough to stop the shouting, to end the rounds of stabbing criticism, to find a way to make the world feel safe for their young daughter. Her only security had been in an episode of *Saved by the Bell* and a Snickers bar. In *Dances with Wolves* and a bag of Doritos. In *Little Women* and lemon bars.

Baxter glanced back, saw what she saw, she supposed, because he moved, coming behind her, holding her back against his front. He crossed his arms over her waist, this hold not so much sexual as cherishing. His gaze met her reflected one.

"I love you," he said. "I love you."

She leaned her head against his shoulder and inspected their images in the glass. Despite his words, the sincerity in them, it still wasn't easy. Did the frog prince still see his old warts once he'd been kissed by his beautiful lady?

"Shh," he said again, and then bent his head so he spoke against her ear. "Screw mirrors, honey, if they bother you. Just look at yourself in my eyes."

That did it. That got her turning away from the reflection and toward the man of her dreams. Her comfort crush. The freakin' love of her life who could make her believe in the lasting power of what was in their hearts.

Addy March got to have Baxter Smith.

"So many happy endings today," she told her guy.

Smiling, he touched his absolutely best male nose in the world to hers. "Still got no job, no French, no taste in superheroes."

"But we've got each other," Addy said. *Je t'adore.*

Layla slapped at Vance's hand as he tried sneaking one of the cupcakes from the plastic carrier she'd brought home from the food truck. "Those are for dessert," she said, pushing the container farther down the kitchen counter.

"But it's my party," he said, a wheedling smile on his face. His hips pressed closer to hers as he pinned her against the bullnose tile.

She laughed up at him. "You're in a mood."

"Mmm," he agreed. "Getting all his limbs in order can do that to a man."

The final cast had been removed. Though he wore a soft splint in its place, he'd come home from the doctor's upbeat and energized. Likely already thinking of his return to active duty.

That thought threatened her own mood, a little melancholy creeping in at the idea of their time together coming to an end. But she wasn't going to think about the future. Not tonight.

With a saucy smile, she tilted her hips, pressing into the thickness she felt between his legs. "This limb seems to be in fine form, too."

He bent to her ear, his hot breath sending chilly tingles down her neck. "You are such a naughty girl."

"But I don't have time to show you just how naughty," she said, shoving at his shoulders. "Remember? Addy and Baxter called to say they wanted to have dinner with us."

His big body didn't move, even when she tried shoving again. "Is it too late to phone and put them off for—"

Vance hadn't even finished his sentence before the other couple was walking into Beach House No. 9, both of them carrying grocery bags and wearing high-wattage smiles. As Layla helped unpack the groceries, Vance snatched a magazine from Baxter's hand.

"What's with the *CarBuy* mag?" he asked his cousin. "You in the market for another car?"

"Research," Baxter replied. "I need to find the right price to ask for my Beemer."

Vance blinked, and then he stumbled back and fell into a chair at the kitchen table. "Is it just me, or are there pigs flying around this room?"

"Ha-ha," the other man said. "It's not a miracle that's making me sell the roadster...it's marriage."

Addy made a little noise, half distressed, half pleased. "Baxter. We talked about this. It's too soon to be throwing around that word."

"You like my self-confidence," he said, and snagged

the blonde with an arm around her neck to bring her close. "And you love me."

Layla felt her eyes go round. Vance looked equally startled. "Um...is there some news we should know?"

Addy's face was pink but she hadn't moved away from Baxter. "Yes. It's so cool. We've solved the mystery of Sunrise Pictures." Then she told them of a letter Baxter discovered that made clear it wasn't an affair that had ended the company, but Edith's own wish to be out of the business.

"So now you know," Layla said.

Addy nodded. "But not everything. The Collar is still missing. Edith put it somewhere for safekeeping... I think here at the cove. Baxter believes it's in an undiscovered bank safe-deposit box, but that's because there's no romance in his soul."

"My soul has romance," he protested. "But my brain says no man would hide a priceless necklace in a beach cottage."

"Ah, but no *man* did," Addy pointed out. "And shortly after Edith took action, there came the Great Depression. People didn't hold a great deal of faith in banks. I bet she thought it was just fine wherever she'd stashed it."

"But wouldn't she have told someone where that was?" Vance asked.

"She didn't tell Max in the letter she wrote him." Addy sighed. "And then she died a few years later, unexpectedly, of pneumonia. Perhaps she never had a chance."

"Or perhaps some visitor to Crescent Cove found it," Vance said, "and took it home with him or her, never knowing that it's a real treasure."

Layla frowned. "I don't like that ending to the story."

"All of that is old news, anyway," Vance said. He turned his gaze on his cousin. "I didn't forget the new news you just dropped five minutes ago. Selling the Beemer? Did you actually use the word *marriage?*"

Baxter stood behind Addy, a hand on each of her shoulders. "We're official."

Layla's brows rose. "Officially…engaged?"

"No," Addy said at the same time that Baxter mouthed *yes*.

"I promised I wouldn't buy a ring for two weeks," he added.

Still, their officialness called for handshakes and hugs and congratulations. Vance got everyone their beverage of choice, which they took out to the deck to enjoy with cheese, crackers and crudités. The men gathered near the grill at one corner, preparing it for the steaks they were serving for dinner. Layla and Addy stretched out on side-by-side lounges.

They both gazed on the cousins, so similar in size and coloring. There was a lot of trash-talking bouncing between them, the insults coming fast and easy in the way of men who are close. It brought to Layla's mind the recent afternoon she'd spent on the deck with Vance and Fitz. That relationship seemed on the mend, and she was glad for them both.

"Penny for your thoughts," Addy said.

Layla glanced over. "Right this second? That the smile you're wearing is awfully smug."

"Really? I feel more surprised than smug." Then Addy pursed her lips, seeming to consider. "But smug works, too."

"I can't believe it happened so fast."

"We had a...I guess you'd say a one-night stand, six years ago. I hadn't seen him since, but once we met again, the feelings were there. Again. More. Better." Addy lifted her hands. "Best."

"Just like that?"

Addy slanted Layla a look. "Why do you sound so amazed? It's not as if I haven't noticed there's only one downstairs bedroom currently in use."

Now Layla was the one flushing. "Well...ah...um..."

"See? It happened to you, too."

No, Layla reminded herself. Addy and Baxter had become a couple with a future. She and Vance were a couple with an end date. As gloomy as that sounded, it was the truth. So no sense in wishing for sunnier prospects. The best thing to do was to enjoy today's sunshine—something Uncle Phil was always reminding her to do.

Attachment is the source of suffering, he'd say. It only hurt to wish for things you couldn't have.

So when Vance and Baxter approached them, she forced her heart to lighten and smiled at the pair. How wonderful that they could all be here, at this moment, she thought. *It's enough.*

When Vance nudged at her legs to make a spot for himself on her chaise, she shifted, bringing up her knees. His back was warm against her shins as he leaned against her. Even though they had no future, she didn't stop herself from reaching out and tracing the curve of his heavy biceps.

"So, Addy," Vance said, patting Layla's shin in an absent but affectionate gesture. "What's your secret? How did you get Bax to drop his precious life schedule and commit to his lady a couple of years early?"

"Paris," she said promptly. "I told you guys about my upcoming year of study there. He didn't want to lose me to some man who can actually speak French."

Baxter tweaked her nose. "I would have missed her too much if she went without me."

Layla would miss Vance, too, no matter how often she told herself about end dates and nonattachment. Without thinking, she curled her fingertips under the waistband of his jeans. He glanced back at her, a question in his eyes, and she hurriedly removed them. But then his own hand reached back and caught hers, even as he questioned his cousin.

"*If* she went without you, Bax?"

The other man had straddled the second chaise behind Addy and she was now sitting between his legs. He toyed with her feathery hair. "Didn't anyone tell you?" he asked, frowning.

"Tell me what?"

"I quit. Two days ago I quit Smith & Sons Foods."

Vance's fingers squeezed down on Layla's, in shock, she imagined, at the news.

"I didn't know you hadn't heard," Baxter continued.

"Why would I?" Vance asked. "I'm not involved in the business."

And it so clearly pained him that he wasn't, Layla thought.

"Well, *I* shouldn't have been, either," Baxter said. "My heart was never in it."

"If Granddad was still alive he'd be sad to see you go."

"If our grandfather was still alive, lots of things would be different," Baxter said quietly.

"Yeah? You think?" Vance looked off toward the horizon, then drained his beer. "Anyone want something else to drink?"

Layla saw the set expression on his face as he rose and turned toward the house. He was gone for longer than it took to grab another beer. His face was calm when he returned, but instead of sharing her space, he leaned against the railing, putting distance between them.

Ignoring the urge to go to him, she closed her eyes and willed herself to appreciate the warmth of the setting sun, the smell of the briny air, the ceaseless rush of waves on the beach. *Stay in the moment. Enjoy the moment. Stay in—*

Baxter's voice interrupted her mantra. "There's going to be some reorganization in the company with me leaving."

Vance grunted.

"You have any ideas about that?" his cousin asked.

"It's none of my concern."

"I think they should move Fitz into my place. That would open up his spot on the growing and distribution end and—"

"Grove management. Get somebody in-house to do that. Get rid of those bloodsuckers from GreenWise."

"Why?" Baxter asked. "They do a good job."

"They do the job for too many growers in avocado country. It's better to have someone focused on our single interest."

Layla opened her eyes. Did Vance realize how he'd slipped from indifference to expressing an opinion with an *our* in it? Baxter was studying his cousin, too, his eyes narrowed.

"I see your point," he said. "I still say it's a good idea

to move Fitz into the business end. Then you take his spot and add in grove management, as well."

"What?" Vance asked.

"Yeah, it's twice more work than what Fitz is doing now, but he's gotten lazy in his old age. And you'll want to prove yourself to everyone."

"You're nuts." Vance looked a little nuts himself. "They'd never let me in."

"How do you know unless you ask?"

"I've asked before," Vance said bitterly. "We know how that turned out. It would be the same this time, too."

"What if you say it's what you want? Because I can see that it's the truth."

Layla held still, afraid to breathe because she could see it was true, as well. And she could see something else…her traitorous self considering there might be a future with Vance, after all.

Don't go there, she commanded herself. *No.*

Then he echoed her thought, shaking his head with finality. "No."

Baxter sighed. "But—"

"Let's just enjoy the evening, okay?" Vance said. His glance moved from his cousin to Layla.

"Great idea," she agreed, adding a bright smile. She was nothing if not a good soldier. "I'll get on dinner."

As she walked toward the house, Vance caught her hand. "And I'll help."

She twined her fingers with his. *Stay in the moment,* she whispered soundlessly. *Stay in the moment.*

It's enough.

CHAPTER SEVENTEEN

THE DAY AFTER BAXTER'S surprise announcement, Vance accompanied Layla and the Karma Cupcakes truck to a farmers' market held in a parking lot a forty-minute drive from Crescent Cove. Phil had gone to an afternoon lecture on global travel at a local community college, so Vance had tagged along with the baker to help her sell her wares.

He didn't want to be alone.

Which was nuts because he'd spent months living inches from a bunch of half-clean guys at a remote outpost and expected to be rejoining them soon. He should be reveling in solitude while he still could get it. But being without Layla at Beach House No. 9 gave him too much time to think.

There was a spot opening up in the family company.

He was not going to get fixated on that, he reminded himself. "You want the bistro chairs and tables set up?" he asked Layla as she moved cupcakes from the boxes to the display cases.

"Yes, please. Then we can check out the other merchandise if you like. I usually take a turn down the aisles before the market opens."

Sounded good. More distraction from family matters.

He took Layla's hand as they strolled through the

parking lot. There were a couple of other food trucks, but also many small booths. Some featured homemade jewelry, one offered salsa and hummus, another had bread from a local artisan bakery for sale.

He fed Layla a sample chunk of fresh peach, then licked away an errant drop of juice from her lower lip. She smiled at him, and he leaned in for a kiss. This brown-eyed girl was sexier and sweeter than he deserved.

"Vance. Vance Smith."

Startled by a man's voice, Vance swung around and found himself grinning. "Cesar!" He held out his hand to the wiry older man, dressed as usual in jeans, boots and a battered straw cowboy hat.

A strong grip brought him in for a brief hug. "You're home, but haven't called me?"

"Just here briefly, Cesar." He turned to Layla and gestured her near. "Layla, this is Cesar Ochoa. I used to work for him. Cesar, this is Layla Parker, a friend."

"A good friend, I see," Cesar said, a twinkle in his eye.

Vance ignored that. "What are you doing here?"

"My niece sells some of our produce here. She came up with the idea a couple of months ago. She wants money for a new computer. I brought the boxes in my truck."

"How is Adriana? And Blanca and everyone else?"

"*Bueno.* You must come out to visit. Blanca will make your favorite tamales."

"If I have time before my leave's up, I will."

Cesar glanced at Layla. "I understand if you're too busy, of course. But we miss you."

"The feeling's mutual," Vance said, smiling. "That

doesn't mean I won't kick your ass in darts the next time I get a chance."

The older man laughed, then sobered. "You know you have a job if you want it, Vance. When you return."

"I…" He sighed. "Thanks, I'll keep that in mind."

They said their goodbyes and Vance watched Cesar head toward his truck, his bow legs making him rock side to side as he strode off.

"What job?" Layla asked.

"Huh?" Vance said, still gazing after his old boss.

"You used to work for him?"

"Oh. Yeah." He took Layla's hand again, and they meandered by a booth that sold varieties of cacti in small pots.

"When?"

"Between getting out of the army the first time and going back in this time." In the next stall were tables filled with a selection of fruits and vegetables. His hand was drawn to a pile of avocados and the narrow-shaped one on top.

"What's that?" Layla asked.

"It's a genetic error. We call it a cuke. A pitless avocado."

"That seems convenient."

"Maybe," he said, placing it back on the pile. "I always feel a little sorry for them, though. It's like they're not living up to their full potential."

"Oh, I get it," she said knowingly, "because they have no stones. You're such a guy."

"Brat." He grinned at her, then ran his thumb over a plump and bright beefsteak tomato.

"That's what you want to be doing, Vance," Layla

suddenly remarked. "Working at an avocado ranch. Growing things."

He frowned. "No, I don't want to go back to Cesar's. The Ochoas are great, but…no."

"That's not what I said."

The conversation was taking a turn he didn't like. "Well, I say it's time to get back to the cupcake truck."

She opened her mouth to speak again, but he popped a nectarine sample inside, then led her away while she chewed. Once at their spot, they were busy throughout the afternoon. He left her alone for a few minutes while he went to buy them each a hand-squeezed lemonade and when he got back, Layla was engrossed in conversation with a woman in a wide-brimmed sun hat. It only took him a second to realize her identity.

Jesus Christ. His mother.

Gritting his teeth, he strode up to the food truck's window and passed Layla her plastic cup. Then he frowned at his mom. "Do I need to take out a restraining order?"

"Vance!" his mother and his lover said together.

"You're not going to tell me your car is broken down again, are you?"

"Of course not. I drove it here," Katie Smith said.

He sipped at his drink in order to cool his temper. "So it's just a big coinky-dink that you ended up at this particular farmers' market?"

His mother hesitated and Layla jumped in. "No, she happened to check out the Karma Cupcakes website and noted we would be here today. Because she was in the area, she decided to stop by."

"There's some excellent apricot preserves being sold

just over there," his mother added, pointing across the aisle.

"Mom—"

"And I wanted to see the inside of the cupcake truck, since I didn't get the chance on Picnic Day."

She was as subtle as a battering ram. Vance didn't have the heart to really yell at her, though, because he knew that the rift between him and the family—mostly now just between him and his father—upset her. From his bad spills to his bad grades, Vance had been upsetting her all his life.

"Well, what's stopping you?" he grumbled, then led her to the door and held it open while she climbed inside.

He sat on one of the bistro chairs during the tour, though he could hear the two women chatting and laughing. Finally, drawn to the sound, he peeked in at them through the window. His mother had a wet cloth in hand and was working on removing a smear of chocolate on the wide strap of the pale green dress Layla wore.

It was a maternal activity, and as he took in Layla's bemused expression, he remembered she hadn't had a mother for most of her life. This kind of attention was probably unusual to her. He couldn't see Phil or the colonel caring much about getting out a stain from a favorite garment. While he knew she'd been well cared for growing up, he doubted there'd been much TLC.

I should be gentler with her, he thought. *I should think of more ways to please her during these last days that we're together.*

"Vance?" his mother said, casting him a glance.

"Hmm?" Layla was still on his mind, and he was

surprised by a sharp little pang at the idea of sleeping without her on the next pillow.

"I asked Layla if you two would come out to the house for dinner tomorrow night."

His focus sharpened in an instant. "What? No. We were just there for Picnic Day. We're already coming again for Fitz's engagement brunch."

"But this would be different. This would be about the two of you."

She was definitely a battering ram. A sneaky, manipulative battering ram. He opened his mouth to refuse, but then she set aside the wet cloth and reached up to brush at Layla's bangs. "These look good on you," she murmured. "I was always too leery of grow-out issues to have them myself."

Layla just smiled as his mom continued to smooth her hair. And damn, it was the smile that got to him. A little more mothering would please the colonel's daughter, he could see that.

"Vance?" his mother prompted.

He sighed. "What time?"

THE SUN HAD LONG SINCE SET when Layla and Vance returned to Beach House No. 9 following their afternoon at the farmers' market. The night was clear but chilly, so she changed into a pair of jeans and a sweatshirt as she tried ignoring the melancholy that once again surged.

Hoping the ocean breeze would clear it away, Layla wandered onto the deck and leaned against the railing. The view of the sky was unobscured by city lights and she gazed up at the glitter of a thousand stars and the silver disc of moon. She shivered a little, noting its wavering reflection in the endless blanket of ocean before her. How small she was in comparison. How alone.

While the cove felt delightfully secluded during the day, tonight it seemed oppressively isolated.

It's just you and me, moon, she thought. The stars were too distant to be considered companions.

Soft music started floating through the air, a woman singing something slow and sultry—no, now it was slow and sad. *The man was gone, the day was done, yeah, baby, night instead of sun.* Layla glanced at the house to see Vance pulling back the glass slider. He walked onto the deck, a beer in one hand and a glass of white wine in the other. The moonlight illuminated his rangy body and handsome face, and her gloomy mood deepened as the woman's voice swelled into the chorus.

She should stop sleeping with him, Layla decided. It was time to put distance between them. Then maybe the upcoming goodbye wouldn't weigh on her so. If she told him he snored, he'd probably see through it as the excuse it was, but he wouldn't challenge the assertion because it was an easy way out for them both. They needed to start uncoupling and he would recognize the wisdom in that.

He pushed the glass of wine into her hand. Her fingers curled around it. "Thanks."

"Hungry?" he asked, taking a spot beside her at the rail.

"Not after that pizza." They'd stopped to eat on the way back.

The song that was playing ended and a new one began, another woman's voice. Another woman left behind. God, where were the cheery, upbeat tunes that celebrated summer? "What is this, heartbreak radio?" she grumbled.

"Hey, I'm just happy to say I finally figured out how to turn on the outside speakers. Means I retain my stud status."

She smiled a little at that. He'd been stomping around all month, his masculinity challenged by his inability to figure out the complicated stereo system. "Figures you'd solve the puzzle just days before we leave here."

They lapsed into silence, the only sounds the wet rush of water and the soft music on the stereo. Vance's feet shifted and she could feel his gaze on her. "Tell me about your real life," he said. "So I can picture you and what you're doing when this is over."

Oh, good. He was thinking about uncoupling, too. She opened her mouth to answer, but those dark feelings rose again, filling her chest and making it hard to breathe.

"Layla?"

Swallowing hard, she set her untouched wine on top of the railing. "I've told you. I live in a little duplex inland and north of here. What I do there is pretty much the same as I do now. I get up early, bake cupcakes, go out with Uncle Phil to sell them. Get up and do it again the next day."

"What about friends?"

Her seven-days-a-week schedule didn't leave a lot of time for a social life. "I'm in a baking group," she said. "We met in a food handling class, actually. About once a month we get together and have dinner, share recipes, just chat."

She should spend more time with them, she decided. Once a month was too long to go between girlfriend fixes. They had busy lives, though, and would likely find it hard to fit her in. Angelica was a new mom, Patsy was planning a wedding, Gretchen and Jeanette lived far enough away from Layla that meeting them couldn't be arranged spur-of-the-moment.

"But I admit I'm left with a lot of empty evenings." And the thought of them stretching ahead only made her lonelier. "Uncle Phil once told me I should join an online dating service," she added.

"Really?" Sounding surprised, Vance turned to face her. He was silent a moment. "Would you do that?"

She shrugged.

A heavy silence followed. Vance frowned through it, as if arguing with himself. Then he took a long swallow of his beer and met her eyes. "If you want, I know some guys I could introduce—" Breaking off, he looked away. "No. Sorry, but no."

Was it her expression or some compunction of his own that had halted his offer? It didn't matter—she couldn't bear to have this discussion. "No," she agreed, and forced some cheer in her voice. "Anyway, when I think about it, I'm going to be pretty busy. Uncle Phil is eager to start on that trip of his. I won't be surprised if he leaves as soon as this month is up. Then I'll be Karma Cupcake-ing all by myself."

All by herself. Didn't that sounded pitiful?

To Vance, too, she supposed, because he grabbed her by the arms and turned her to him. "You're going to be okay. Wherever I go next—I'll write. I'll email you. Even overseas I get a chance to make phone calls on occasion."

"You have your family to contact then."

"I have you, too," he said, giving her a tiny shake. "I'm going to be your friend, Layla."

"That's nice, thanks," she said, stepping out of his hold. She took up her wine again and hoped he wouldn't see her hand was trembling. God, she was a mess tonight.

At least the latest song was coming to an end, the woman's wail about bad luck in love hitting its last note. Through the speakers, a new voice drifted into the night and Vance gave a soft laugh. "Hey, it's your song."

The slow, acoustic version of Eric Clapton's "Layla." Her chest went heavy again. "My dad called it that."

"No surprise," Vance said, and plucked her wineglass from her hand to set it beside his beer bottle on the railing. Then he pulled her into his arms.

"No." Layla resisted. "What are you doing?"

He ignored her protests, drawing her closer. They were chest to chest, hip to hip, and he lifted her arms to circle his neck and crossed his at the small of her back. Then his feet shifted to the beat of the music.

Layla was stiff in the embrace. This wasn't uncoupling. "Vance—"

"We gotta dance, pretty girl."

"We've danced before," she pointed out. "On Picnic—"

"That was *my* dance."

She frowned at him. "And this one—"

"Is on the Helmet List."

Layla stared up at Vance, the moon behind his left shoulder, the stars twinkling overhead, like diamonds tossed on dark velvet. He'd not mentioned the list lately, and she'd been content to just enjoy time in his company.

"This dance is for you and your dad," he said now.

And with that the melancholy surged, growing from that heavy weight squeezing her lungs in her chest to a black shroud wrapping her entire body, trying to crush her to nothing. Her mouth opened, but she couldn't speak, she couldn't inhale air, she could only release a soundless scream of sorrow.

This dance is for you and your dad.

"Layla." Vance stopped moving, his eyes narrowed. "Layla, what's wrong?"

With a wild shake of her head, she broke away from him and ran, leaping down the steps to the sand and speeding up the beach, legs churning. Distance, she thought, desperate for it. She needed distance. Not from the cloying bleakness and the clawing pain—she carried that in her heart and on her back and tangled in her soul—but distance from Vance.

He couldn't see her in this state.

She ran out of breath before she ran out of beach. Her vague idea of making it to the cupcake truck wasn't possible. But her gaze snagged on a build-up of sand ahead, a sort of dune at the base of the hillside, and she dove for it, dropping into its dark shadow. Drawing up her legs, she wrapped her shins with her arms and pressed her forehead to her knees, clutching herself tight—a human knot of sorrow.

No sound reached her ears except her harsh inhales and exhales of air. She was breathing again, and she supposed that was good, but the oxygen coming in only put more pressure on a chest already filled with unshed tears.

"Sweetheart," a gentle voice said. "Layla."

Vance! She jerked, then tucked into herself more

tightly. "Go away," she told him, the words muffled against her knees.

Even though her eyes were squeezed shut, she sensed him settling on the sand beside her. She felt the brush of his hand on her shoulder and hunched away from it. "Go away."

His touch disappeared, but his voice remained. "Not a chance."

Her eyes pinched tighter and she pressed her lips together to hold back a frustrated scream. *Just be still,* she told herself. *Just keep it together.*

"You know about the five stages of grief?" Vance asked.

Ignoring him, she rocked a little for comfort.

He groaned. "You're killing me," he murmured. She heard him take in a long breath. "The five stages of grief. The first is denial."

That's what she'd been in, Layla thought, denial—until moving into Beach House No. 9. But she'd been facing the truth since then, hadn't she?

"The next are anger and bargaining." When she didn't reply, he spoke again. "Do you hear me, Layla? Anger and bargaining."

Suddenly, his little lecture struck her as condescending, and temper added to the roiling mix of emotions inside her. "I know about anger and bargaining," she said, her voice sounding rough. "I've been through those many times. Every time he left, don't you think I was angry? Every day he was gone don't you think I bargained with the universe?"

She was rocking again, the ache behind her eyes excruciating. "I didn't step on cracks when I was little. Later, to get on fortune's good side, I offered up prayers for drivers who cut me off instead of flipping them the bird."

"Okay," Vance said. "Okay. So that leaves just two others. Depression and acceptance."

Why wouldn't he go away?

"And I don't think acceptance is possible quite yet, Layla. I really don't."

She turned her head to stare at him. "Oh, great. Are you telling me I'm stuck with depression? What kind of pep talk is that?"

"It's not any kind of pep talk at all, sweetheart. It's permission to feel bad. And it's permission to start letting it out."

Her eyes closed again and she shook her head. "No. No letting it out. A soldier's daughter doesn't cry."

"When her soldier dad is never coming home again, I think she should."

"No." Her head went back and forth again, her hair swirling in her vehemence. *No, no, no.*

"Yes, Layla." Vance reached over and grasped her, hauling her into his lap even as she fought him. He curled himself around her, ignoring her struggles and slaps. "I'm not letting go until you do."

She opened her mouth to shout at him, to yell and scream and curse him. But instead, to her horror, a sob released. And then another. And then she was wailing like the women on the stereo, the notes of her sorrow a song about grief and loneliness and feeling as if she'd lost her roots.

Vance turned her into his body and she buried her face against his chest. "I'm so alone," she said through her choking tears. "I'm so alone."

"I'm here," Vance said, a hand against her hair. "I'll always be here."

The lie only made her cry more.

Exhaustion finally quieted her. Maybe fifteen minutes had passed. Maybe three hours. Vance's sweatshirt was wet and she shivered, suffering from an intense emotional hangover. He brushed a kiss to her hair.

"Let's go back to the house," he said.

She started to shake her head again.

"Shh," he said, kissing her once more. "You'll be better now. It'll be easier."

"Vance…" She needed to tell him they'd be sleeping in separate beds. She needed to make sure he understood that things had changed now. He'd been too close already and now he was the only man who had seen her fall apart. That kind of intimacy was unbearable.

He helped her to her feet.

"Vance…" she began again.

"I'll hold you all night long," he said.

And Layla was too worn out to resist.

Back at the house he washed her face with a warm, wet cloth then undressed her like a child. One of his T-shirts was pulled over her head and he tucked her under the covers. He spooned her, his knees curled behind hers, his arm across her belly to hold her against his wide chest. It was a Vance she hadn't experienced before in bed. No seduction, no demands, but a solid source of strength and comfort.

This is temporary, Layla reminded herself. *Impermanent.* If they were not yet uncoupled, she had to hold on to the thought that it would never last.

CHAPTER EIGHTEEN

LATE THE FOLLOWING afternoon, Layla and Vance made the drive to avocado country again, with him expertly managing the tricky turns in the road. Since waking alone in bed that morning, Layla had moved around Beach House No. 9 in a listless state, but Vance hadn't pushed her. He'd been quiet, too, likely preoccupied by the thought of another uncomfortable visit with his family.

His hand was on the small of her back as he pushed open the front door of his childhood home. She decided it was nice that he hadn't knocked or pressed the doorbell first. It meant he still felt, at least in some small way, that he belonged here.

It was heated summer outside, but inside, pleasantly cool, probably due to the home's thick plaster walls and polished terra-cotta pavers on the floors. The rooms were painted in earth tones and the furniture was oversize, the dark blues and golds of the upholstery matching the Persian area rugs.

The foyer opened into a spacious living room, empty of people. But a delicious smell permeated the air. Vance looked down at her with a quick grin. "Lasagna. My mom made my favorite."

Through an archway came the distinct clack of bil-

liard balls. A movement caught her eye. Fitz. Both the
sound and the sight had snagged Vance's attention, too.

Layla gave him a little push. "Why don't you go play
with your brother?"

"You come, too," he said.

She shook her head. The sound of female voices
could be heard from the opposite direction. "I'll find
the kitchen. I bet your mother is there and I can give
her the wine we brought."

Handing over the bottle, he studied her face. "Sure?"

"I'm good," she said firmly. It was good for them
to go their separate ways. Even after last night, *especially* after last night, it was a priority to end this attachment to Vance.

Inside a large and charming country kitchen she indeed found Katie Smith. Huddled with her at a granite
island was another woman who had to be her twin—
Vance's aunt Alison—and Fitz's fiancée, Blythe.

At Layla's "Good afternoon," all three heads popped
up. Vance's mother and aunt smiled, while Blythe
quickly closed and pushed away a magazine the three
had been examining.

"You're here!" Vance's mom cried, coming forward.

Layla held out the bottle of wine, but the older
woman merely set it on a counter and kept coming,
close enough to wrap her in a warm hug. At the unfamiliar maternal act, a hot pressure built behind Layla's
eyes. After a second's hesitation, she responded with
a short squeeze.

Then she drew away, embarrassed by her reaction
to the welcome. Pinning on a smile, she nodded at the
other women in the room. "I'm Layla," she said, reaching out to shake the hand of Vance's aunt. Next she ad-

dressed the cool blonde. "It's good to see you again, Blythe."

It would be better if the other woman didn't look so elegant. She was in silk again, a thin, ice-blue T-shirt tucked into buff-colored tailored slacks. Clearly, she didn't eat cupcakes.

Definitely one of those low-carb dieters.

Layla smoothed the cotton skirt of her dress and smiled again when Vance's mother asked if she liked lasagna. "Absolutely. And it smells fabulous. Is there something I can do to help?"

"Oh, no, it's all taken care of for the moment," Katie said, with a wave of her hand. "We ladies are hanging out in here so that we don't make the men nervous with—" She broke off, her gaze shifting in Blythe's direction.

Layla looked there, too.

Fitz's fiancée wore an embarrassed expression and she had her hands spread wide over the magazine cover, as if she wanted to mask its title. But Layla read it, anyway—*Bridal Boutique*—and understood the situation. "Were you working on your wedding plans?"

Blythe's face turned pink. "We can do it another time…"

"Don't stop because I'm here."

Vance's mother was beaming at her. "I'm so glad this doesn't have to be awkward."

Which, of course, it wasn't, because none of this nuptial business had anything, really, to do with her. Even if she had been Vance's actual girlfriend, there would be no need for self-consciousness.

And she wasn't Vance's actual girlfriend.

So she bellied up to the island and grabbed one of

the magazines off the stack that Blythe pushed forward. "We're looking at dresses," the other young woman told her. "Trying to decide between mermaid, princess, empire, column or ball gown."

It was like a foreign language to Layla. She must have worn her confusion on her face because Vance's aunt shot her an amused glance. "You don't watch any of the wedding shows on television? Never gone gown shopping with a friend?"

She shook her head. "I admit to being ceremonially challenged. I was raised by two very unsentimental, unromantic and deeply entrenched bachelors."

"But your baking is divine. And you always dress so pretty," Katie said.

"Thank you." The compliments warmed her, which felt a little dangerous, too. It was no time to be bonding with Vance's mom. "My inner girl eventually found its way."

"A very lovely way at that," the older woman pronounced.

The kindness flummoxed her again, so Layla directed her attention to the glossy pages, turning them one by one. Blythe would look beautiful in any number of dresses.

"Are you sure you're okay about this?" the bride-to-be murmured for Layla's ears only.

"Of course." A smile tweaked the corners of her mouth. "Think about it. I'd rather you be planning your wedding to Vance's brother than to Vance himself, right?"

"Oh, right." Blythe laughed, her shoulders relaxing. "Absolutely right."

The atmosphere in the kitchen loosened up considerably after that. Katie served up four glasses of a very cold and deliciously crisp chardonnay, along with a tray of chilled grilled asparagus and prosciutto-wrapped cantaloupe on skewers. A half glass in, Layla found herself agreeing to provide white-iced champagne cupcakes for Blythe and Fitz's upcoming engagement brunch. Vance's aunt got a little teary about losing Baxter to France for a year...but she seemed sincerely pleased her beloved son had found true love.

Katie slanted Layla a look. "That seems to be going around the Smith family these days."

Instead of answering, she pretended an avid interest in the magazine pages in front of her. She studied the two-page spread of a wedding party—an entire family gathered around a glowing bride and groom. It looked as foreign to her as the language of bridal gowns. Maybe she'd never daydreamed about a Big Day because she didn't have a large family with whom to celebrate.

Now she didn't even have a father to walk her down the aisle.

Oh, God, the tears were stinging again.

"Layla?" Vance's mother patted her arm. "Are you okay, honey?"

Blinking rapidly, she held the back of her hand to her nose. "Just a tickly nose," she said, aware her voice sounded scratchy, too.

"Everybody gets those sometimes," Katie murmured. Then she placed her palm between Layla's shoulder blades and rubbed a soothing circle.

The touch brought her back under control. She hauled in a steadying breath, then picked up her wine. "You're very kind," she said to the other woman, just as Vance's dad came up behind his wife.

"And beautiful," he added, grabbing Katie's glass from her hand and taking a swallow.

"Moocher," she said fondly. "You remember Layla."

"It's good to see you again," she started—and then found herself at a loss for words when William Smith took her outstretched hand in both his big paws. He smiled, and it was devastating, just like his son's.

"Welcome," he said. Then he leaned close. "I appreciate what you shared with me about my son on Picnic Day. I've thought of it often." Then he smiled again, and she realized that he was definitely a charmer when he wasn't at odds with Vance. He stayed in the kitchen with the ladies, offering groan-worthy opinions on wedding regalia and teasing his wife about their wedding day until she whapped him with a dish towel.

His brother came into the kitchen next, and Layla met yet another handsome Smith male—though he was about three inches shorter than the quite tall William. Apparently the elder Smiths had been joined in a double wedding and Roy told them how his brother's tuxedo had been delivered to him and vice versa, causing a four-alarm panic until they managed to get control of their groom jitters long enough to figure out what happened and swap clothes.

Then it was Fitz who wandered in. He made his way to Blythe and laid on her a lavish kiss that turned the pale blonde's cheeks pink again. She made an embarrassed protest, which he ignored as he went on to enthusiastically buss the cheek of his aunt, then his mother. Finally, he grabbed Layla and squeezed her in a bear hug.

Vance had mentioned in a grumpy tone that Fitz

could be impossible not to like, and she had to admit that was true.

Katie scolded him, though. "Son, are you sure Layla wants to be manhandled like that?"

Fitz met her gaze with laughing eyes. "She thinks I'm perfect. Just ask her."

Pressing her lips together, she let her eyes laugh back. Fucking Perfect Fitz. Yep, impossible not to like.

Conversation continued in the crowded kitchen, topics rambling and circling while the last details of dinner were completed. Layla found herself smiling and laughing and feeling entirely comfortable as they included her in everything from a squabble about a recent movie to tossing the salad.

When it was nearing time to sit down, Katie wondered aloud about Vance's whereabouts. Fitz said he'd gone up to his old room, so Layla was dispatched to retrieve him from "upstairs, first door on the left."

On her way out of the kitchen, a burst of laughter had her pausing to glance back, a smile on her face. Her gaze roamed the small crowd who had welcomed her in, a warm feeling running through her.

They were so nice, she thought. So nice, it was quite likely she might be a little bit in love with Vance's family.

But surely that wasn't the case.

She hadn't fallen for the family any more than she'd fallen for Vance.

WHEN LAYLA REACHED Vance's room, she hovered in the open doorway, her eyes going everywhere. The floor was like the rest of the house, polished pavers covered with expensive-looking area rugs. Under the windows directly across from where she stood was a massive desk fitted with little drawers and black iron pulls that gave it a Spanish flavor. To her left, flanking a dresser that matched the desk, were two doors, presumably leading to a bathroom and closet. On her right was a heavy, queen-size bed with a navy coverlet.

Lying atop it was Vance, who appeared asleep.

She rapped her knuckles lightly on the doorjamb.

He blinked, rousing, then lifted onto his elbows to peer at her through drowsy eyes. "Hey," he said. "Where've you been?"

"I think that's my question for you."

His brows came together, and he looked about, as if puzzled by his surroundings. After a moment, he sat up and rubbed a hand over his face. "Sorry," he said. "I came up here in search of my old softball mitt. Just stretched out for a second…"

The night before, she'd slept the deep sleep of emotional exhaustion. But perhaps he had not had a peaceful eight hours. Maybe *she* snored.

"I'm disturbing your rest, staying in your room at the beach house. Tonight I'll go back to my own," she said. The relief she felt at getting out the words let her know it was the right move. Self-protection was clearly in order. Separation from him a first priority.

His brows came together again. "I sleep with you just fine. As a matter of fact…" He crooked his forefinger. "C'mere."

She clutched at the doorjamb. "I'm supposed to be bringing you down for dinner."

"Not until you come here for a minute."

On a sigh, she stepped into the room. "What?"

He smiled at her, the charming smile he'd inherited from his father. "Come a little closer, baby."

The coaxing tone ran down her back like a seductive caress. Cursing her wilting willpower, she approached the bed, then yelped when he lunged forward to grab her wrist and pull her onto the mattress. "Vance!"

"Layla." With a villainous laugh, he rolled so his long body loomed over hers.

"What do you think you're doing?"

"I'm fulfilling a lifelong fantasy. I can't tell you how many times I thought about getting a girl in this bed."

"You thought about getting your high school squeeze, Marianne Kelly, in this bed," Layla said, and promised herself her lower lip wasn't pushing out in a pout.

Vance gave it a light bite, anyway. "I wasn't mature enough to imagine the vision that is you," he said, framing her face with his big hands. "You are so stunningly pretty, you know that? I'll be seeing these big brown eyes in my dreams for the rest of my life."

Because that's the only place they'd be together—in dreams, she thought, but dismissed her sadness. She'd gone into this with big brown eyes wide-open, hadn't she? Temporary lovers...*because sometimes a person just needs to be held*. Her very own words.

"Stunningly pretty," he said again, his voice going softer.

Her melting response was a clear warning, and she tried pushing at his shoulders. When he didn't budge, she frowned at him. "Are you telling me you didn't sneak girls up here? I thought you were the resident bad boy."

"Even I had a line I wouldn't cross," he said. "Once out of high school I moved into the bachelor house on the other side of the oaks and my bedroom rules were my own." He bent as if to take her mouth.

She turned her head to the side, so he kissed her cheek. Separation, she knew, meant curtailing the lip to lip. Her gaze caught on the one wall she hadn't seen while standing in the doorway. It was covered with shelves that were packed with trophies and photographs. "What's all that?"

Vance glanced over his shoulder. "Souvenirs of my misspent youth."

"Misspent? The trophies seem to tell a different story." She pushed harder at him now so she could disentangle her body from his.

With a sigh, Vance let her up, then followed her off the mattress to inspect the memorabilia, starting at the left. A collection of little silver-and-gold baseball players perched on top of foot-high faux-marble pillars. She slid him a glance. "That looks pretty tame to me. America's favorite pastime and all that."

He just shrugged, and she moved farther along the shelving. Two hooks held a selection of medals suspended on ribbons, one for downhill skiiing, another for snowboard racing. Beside them were framed pictures of Vance. In each he bore the evidence of injury: a casted foot, a splinted set of fingers, a shaved patch of skull decorated by stitches.

"I think my mother put these on display in hopes they'd slow me down."

"And did they?"

Instead of answering, he gestured to the right. Now it was trophies and medals for motocross and dirt bike races. They were partnered with more photos of a young Vance. In two he was in leathers and sporting a cut lip.

A third showed him holding his arm in an odd position across his chest. She peered at it, then glanced at him.

"Broken collarbone." Then he picked up a shark's fin–size fragment of bright yellow fiberglass. "My first surfboard—or what's left of it after we both wound up hitting some rocks. Damn, I loved that thing."

At the end of the shelves was another trio of enlarged photographs. Each depicted a spectacularly crashed vehicle. A truck in a ditch. A sports car against a fire hydrant spewing water. An overturned SUV resting on its side like a dead bug.

"Vance." Layla had to stop and suck in a breath. The accident scenes made her a little sick. "These are—were your cars? Your mom framed pictures of these, too?"

He was staring at them as if he'd never seen them before. "No," he said slowly. "That was me."

She widened her eyes. "Why would you take the photos in the first place?"

After a hesitation, he grimaced. "I...I was proud of them."

She blinked. "Proud?"

He rubbed his hand over the lower half of his face. "Proud that though I totaled the car I walked away without a scratch."

The tense note in his voice had her placing her palm on his back, stroking it in a little circle like his mom had done to her in the kitchen. She could feel the stiffness of his spine and the rigid muscles surrounding it seemed to vibrate.

"Can you believe that?" he muttered. "I was an idiot."

"Vance..." she said, her voice soft. "You were a kid."

"A waste," he said, still staring at the photos. "I was a fucking waste."

"You were a thrills and chills kind of guy," she countered, troubled by the growing darkness of his mood. "Some people are."

"It's no excuse for what I put them through. No wonder..." Shaking his head, he retreated from the shelves, stumbling on the carpet until the back of his legs hit the bed. Then his butt.

Layla crossed to him, sitting close so they were thigh to thigh. "Are you all right?"

His eyes still focused across the room, he didn't appear to have heard her. "Vance?"

With a sudden movement, he turned his head, his gaze pinning her. "Any one of those should have been the end of me," he said, his face going hard. "Why the hell did I survive?"

The question chilled her. He was right. He had cheated death, it seemed to her, any number of times. As a child, as a young adult. Again as a soldier at war. She swallowed, hard.

"None of us can know—" she started.

"I know that I was careless with things," he said, pointing to the automobile photos. "I know that I was reckless with my life."

But he wasn't that careless and reckless Vance any longer, Layla thought. As a combat medic, he needed calm control, gentle hands and a compassionate heart for those wounded and hurting. Qualities, she suspected, that were the unforeseen yet fortunate consequences of those very youthful escapades he seemed now to despise.

Turning to him, she took his face in her hands. Her gaze bore into his. "But you're a good man now," she told him. "Such a good man."

The man I've fallen in love with.

Everything inside her stilled. *Oh, my God. I...*
I'm in love with Vance.

The understanding didn't come as a thunderbolt. It didn't feel like an anvil had fallen on her head. There was no pain in it—that would come later, she supposed, because he was still just temporarily in her life. For now, though, it was like the sunlight parting coastal clouds, bright and sure and impossible to ignore.

Did something show on her face? Because Vance's eyes suddenly narrowed. "Layla—"

"Hey, you two!" It was Fitz, calling from the bottom of the stairs. "Come down for dinner!"

She popped up, grateful for the interruption.

"Layla, wait." Vance made a grab for her shoulder, but she shook him off. His brother's directive gave her an excuse to make an escape from Vance—though not, she was certain, from her newly acknowledged feelings for him.

CHAPTER NINETEEN

GUT ROILING WITH EMOTIONS, Vance hesitated in his room while Layla headed for the stairs. Something was going on with her, but the something that was going on inside of him was overwhelming his ability to read her. His gaze returned to those damning photos and he seethed, so angry at himself that he could hardly breathe.

He'd always blamed his father for the falling-out between him and his family—not understanding why the man had broken the promise of a position in the family company—but Christ, he'd been wild and irresponsible. Exactly how wild and irresponsible, he hadn't realized until seeing these photos again. No wonder they'd cut him loose.

That he was different now…well, how could lost trust be regained?

With a last look at what he now thought of as the Wall of Shame, Vance steeled himself to go down to dinner. It wasn't easy, not after looking at that damning proof. Christ, he couldn't wait for this night to be over.

At the top of the stairs, he spied Layla on the landing below. Fitz was nowhere in sight, likely already in the dining room. As Vance took his first step, a tremendous noise from outside the house filled the foyer—the screech of brakes, a squealing slide, then the unmistakable crunch of metal meeting solid object.

Car crash.

Vance froze. His imagination? Had the sound been conjured from his memories and triggered by those photos? But even before his mind could filter the truth, instinct kicked in and he was flying downward. "Call 9-1-1," he ordered Layla, who'd come to a halt. "Get Fitz, my dad, my uncle. We need blankets and a first-aid kit."

Wide-eyed, she ran off.

The blood in his veins burned like ice as Vance stepped onto the front porch. *Oh, God.* The scene was straight out of a Driver's Ed shock film. His heart slammed against his ribs as adrenaline surged through his system. The last time he'd faced blood and injuries, it had ended in death. Still, he raced across the courtyard and toward the road, cataloging details. Red pickup on its roof, resting against the trunk of a giant oak. Windshield shattered. Front end crumpled. At least one inside; no airbags deployed. Another unmoving figure was sprawled nearby, on the side of the road.

He dropped to the ground by the driver's window. It was broken, too, the safety glass scattered like teardrops on the truck's headliner. As he reached to turn off the ignition, he noted the driver was a teen boy—who appeared unconscious—with a seeping scalp wound. There was a teen girl on the passenger side, eyes closed and moaning.

In his peripheral vision, he saw Fitz and his father approach at a run. "You two need to divert any oncoming traffic," he said, and leaped to his feet to rush toward the body lying on the ground. Another teenager, male, face pale, though his eyes were open and slowly blinking at the sky overhead. Vance knelt down. "Hey," he said, his voice gentle. "I'm Vance, I'm going to help you."

When the kid didn't acknowledge him, Vance tapped him lightly on the shoulder. "I'm Vance," he said again. "How many were in the truck?"

This time, the boy's eyes shifted to his face and he started blinking rapidly. "Wha—?"

"You've been in an accident. How many were in the truck?" He needed to know if there might be other injured persons unaccounted for.

"Th-three," the kid said. "Where's...?"

At that moment, Uncle Roy appeared at his elbow, blanket in hand. "Great," Vance said. "Cover him, will you? And find a way to elevate his legs. He's in shock."

On his feet again, he raced back to the truck, this time going around to the passenger side and bending low. The girl was still moaning. "Hey, I'm Vance," he said. "Can you open your eyes?"

She did, then immediately started struggling against the bonds of her shoulder harness and seat belt. "Need to get out."

Vance touched her cheek. "No, don't. You might have hurt your neck or back. The paramedics will be here soon. Try to stay calm." Layla arrived with another light blanket and he did his best to drape it around the girl's neck. In her upside-down position, gravity was not his friend.

"Let me do that," Layla said.

Without a word, he left her to it and headed back around the truck to the driver. Dropping to the ground, he noticed the kid's head wound was bleeding more profusely. Vance stripped off his shirt, then used his teeth to rip a manageable piece of fabric that he wrapped around the cut on the boy's forehead. As he tightened the knot, the teenager regained consciousness, lifting an arm to bat at Vance's hands.

"I'm here to help," Vance said. "Just relax." He introduced himself again. "What's your name?"

"Oh, God, oh, God," the teen moaned. "My dad's gonna kill me. I crashed another car last month. He's gonna kill me."

Vance's father thrust another blanket at him. He glanced up. "Someone's watching for oncoming cars? 9-1-1's been called?" Out in rural avocado country, it could take a while for emergency responders to reach them.

"Yes—"

"Wait!" the driver said in a sudden panic. "I can't move my legs! I can't move my legs!"

Vance stretched supine on the asphalt so he could reach in and palm the boy's shoulder. "It's going to be all right. We've called for help."

"Don't leave me," the boy said, and wrapped his fingers around Vance's wrist.

"I'm not going anywhere. Can you tell me your name?"

"Marshall," he said, his hold not relaxing. "Marshall Richter."

"Okay, Marshall Richter. The two of us will sit tight until the EMTs arrive." From what Vance could see, it would probably require the Jaws of Life to extract the kid from the twisted front end of the car. Whether his legs were badly injured or just trapped, it was impossible to know.

"Vance." His father crouched beside him and spoke in a low voice. "The gasoline's leaking."

Shit. He could smell it now. Even as he took in a sharp breath, he could feel the liquid beginning to puddle under his body. *Oh, shit.*

"Dad, do you think you can get the girl out?" Between risking possible further injury or frying to death if the vehicle caught fire, it was a no-brainer. "Put her down on a flat surface a distance away from here. Keep her covered and calm."

"Vance—"

"A safe distance." He turned his head to meet his father's eyes. "Get *everybody* a safe distance away. You understand?"

"Yes," William Smith said, his jaw tightening.

"Good." He hadn't wanted to say the word *explosion* and freak out the kid.

The teen was no fool, however, and his fingers bit into Vance's flesh. "You can't leave me," he said, his eyes going wild.

"I'm not going to leave you. I'm right here." On the other side of the truck, he could see his brother, father and uncle making quick work of releasing the girl from the harness and belt. The door on that side wasn't crumpled like the driver's door, so when she dropped into Fitz's arms, he was able to ease her out. The girl cried throughout the entire process and it was Layla who reassured her, her husky voice telling her it would be fine, she was almost free, everything would be okay.

Then the girl was gone. Vance let out a long breath of relief as he sensed the others retreating toward the house. His gaze remained on the kid, though, maintaining eye contact to bolster the boy's confidence.

Footsteps alerted him to the return of someone. He glanced over, recognizing his father's shoes. Then there was Layla, the little moons and stars on her toenails giving her away.

"Dad," he called, new worry making his voice sharp. His jeans had soaked up the gasoline like a sponge. More of it was wet beneath his bare back. "Dad, please move back. Take Layla. Take her and yourself away *right now.*"

There was a hesitation. "Son—"

"Right now."

Layla made a small sound of distress and he closed his eyes, not sure if it was the smell of gasoline or her fear that was making his stomach churn. "Go, Layla," he said, making the order harsh. "Go on."

The footsteps retreated again and he blew out another long breath. Marshall was making panicky noises in the back of his throat and Vance reached in to cover the fingers that were still curved around his wrist. "So, Marshall, where do you go to high school?"

"Say you won't leave me," the kid said. "Say I'm going to make it out of this."

Words echoed in Vance's head, the ones he'd told every wounded man he'd ever rushed to help. *I'm going to get you out of here, soldier. I'm going to get you to the best doctors and nurses we have available.*

"Promise me," Marshall entreated. "Promise me."

Promise me.

The desperate tone sucked Vance straight back in time. Colonel Parker, lying in the dirt, life leeching out of him. Vance going a little nuts, knowing the man was dying and knowing there was nothing more he could do about it but endure the heat, the dust and the sick helplessness of not being able to save such an outstanding officer.

Not being able to save a father, whose last thoughts were focused on his daughter. *Why not me?* Vance had thought then, furious at fate. Estranged from his family, recently dumped by his fiancée, he'd wondered why it hadn't been his turn to die.

Why not me? he thought again now. *Why didn't I die that day or when I crashed those cars or when I flew off a ski jump and landed on my thick head but didn't break my stupid neck?*

Sweet Jesus. Now here he was, offered salvation from his youthful sins, it seemed, through the act of lying in a lake of combustible fuel, holding the hand of a kid who possessed his same reckless spirit. But now Vance didn't want it to be his turn. Seeing him blown sky-high would demolish his family. And Layla…

God, Layla. He hadn't fulfilled all the promises he'd made on her behalf, either.

But there was no way he could abandon the boy, this shadow self, and scurry away to safety. Karma, he thought, with a wry grimace, could be just like payback. A bitch.

"Vance?" Marshall said, his voice cracking.

"I promise." The back of Vance's head was soaked with fuel now, the fumes making him a little dizzy. "I promise. Now, tell me a little about yourself. We gotta do something to pass the time."

And the time passed slowly. The kid fixated for a while on the accident, telling Vance that he and his best friend had been taking the girl to her grandma's but they'd gotten lost on the rural roads with their hairpin turns. "My dad's always saying I drive too fast," he mumbled, his eyes starting to roll back. "He's going to kill me. He's really going to kill me if the truck doesn't blow first."

Vance distracted the boy from that thought, working to keep him conscious and talking. The gasoline fumes stung his eyes and tasted acrid on his tongue, but still Vance didn't stop talking. How about those Dodgers. Had Marshall been to the beach lately. Could the boy explain the appeal of watching golf on TV. The kid's answers were slurred by exhaustion by the time approaching sirens finally squealed in the air. Seconds later, they were surrounded by safety boots and turnout pants.

"Nobody light a match, okay?" he called, trying to sound casual, though the words croaked out. Relief was almost as dizzying as the fuel smell, he discovered. But you couldn't blame a man for being happy he wasn't going to end up a human Molotov cocktail, after all.

"You're good, you're safe," he told Marshall. "We made it."

When he stood to allow the EMTs to assess the situation, he went lightheaded. One of the responders grabbed his upper arm. "You okay, pal?"

"Yeah." He stiffened his knees, determined to keep watch over the extrication process. "I'm good. Take care of the boy."

The firefighter flashed him a grin. "Looks like you already did that."

While he was grateful that he'd been on hand to help the victims, Vance didn't feel his usual satisfaction. Maybe he'd been on scene at too many emergency situations, he thought, a wave of fatigue swamping him. A moment like this one used to juice him up. Still, he stood by until the teen was pulled from the truck and secured on a gurney.

Then Vance stepped close again, meeting Marshall's pain-filled eyes. "You owe me, kid," he said.

A ghost of a grin moved the teen's mouth. "I won't have a penny after my dad makes me pay for the cost of the crash."

"You just remember how good it feels to be alive," he advised. "And don't go scuttling your second chances."

As the ambulance took off, followed by another that held the other two victims, Vance finally turned toward his childhood home. His family was gathered in a small knot by the gate.

Adrenaline crash further added to his sense of fatigue, but he took a resolute step toward them. Earlier this evening he'd been reluctant to face them over a meal. What he knew he had to do now was going to be so much harder.

DINNER HAPPENED, though much later than originally planned, after Vance showered and changed into borrowed clothes. Preoccupied during the meal, he didn't participate much in the conversation around him. Perhaps sensing his mood, the others at the table left him alone.

He stacked plates when it was over, but his mother shooed him out of the kitchen when he brought them to the dishwasher. "Go relax. Your aunt and I will take care of the dishes."

"Sounds good, Mrs. Cleaver," he said, managing to send her a little teasing grin. His mom didn't usually stick to gender roles when it came to household tasks.

With a wave of her hand, she pretended to smack him with her dish towel, and his grin widened on its own. She'd cried some after the ambulances drove off, but she was back in control.

So it was time to seek out his father, he thought, sobering. His uncle and Fitz were playing pool in the billiards room, Layla looking on. William Smith stood by the French doors leading to the back terrace, his hands behind his back, staring into the night.

As Vance hesitated in the doorway, considering the best approach, he felt a light touch on his shoulder. He swung around, found himself looking into Blythe's blue eyes.

"Can we talk a minute?" she asked.

With a nod, he followed her into the deserted living room. Shoving his hands in his pockets, he noted how nervous she looked. "Hey," he said softly, guilt pinching because he'd been avoiding this talk. Stupid of him, when he was past the hurt. "It's okay. It's all right."

A half smile eased Blythe's tense expression. "I'm starting to think so, since you and your brother have made amends."

Vance nodded again. "We did. We're good."

"I never meant to come between you and Fitz."

"Understood," Vance replied. And he meant it.

A silence welled. "I liked you," she said suddenly, breaking it. "I liked you a lot."

"I liked you, too."

"So when you told me you were going overseas, going into danger…" Her fingers were clutched together at her slender waist. "It felt a little bit patriotic and a lot…a lot romantic to get engaged."

He smiled this time. "You're such a girl, Blythe."

"I know, huh?" A blush crept up her face. "It's embarrassing, what a dork I am."

"No." He laughed, realized how little he'd really known her. Elegant Blythe thought she had dorkish moments? Still waters indeed. "I shouldn't have asked you to marry me when I was on my way back to combat. I should have realized the situation might compel you to say yes."

Her head tilted. "So why *did* you ask me?"

"Truth?"

It was her turn to nod.

"To impress my parents. And, if I'm completely honest, because you are such the right woman for Fitz."

Her eyes widened, and one hand flew up to cover her heart. "Really?"

He could see that his answer had, in some odd way, pleased her. "Really."

"So, I don't have to feel so terrible about being with him though I broke up with you?"

"Don't feel terrible about that for another second," he said. "Fitz is the right one for you, too."

Wearing a bemused expression, she just stared at Vance. "He loves you, you know."

"Yeah." Vance smiled. "He also loves you."

"Yeah." Her smile was just as wide as his. "So... we're okay now?"

"Not quite. I've still got a page or two of sorrys I need to express. Because face it, beautiful lady, without me you wouldn't have met the chump—and now you're stuck with him for life."

She laughed. "Why don't you save all that for the wedding toast? Something tells me you're going to be tapped for best man."

Grinning at the idea, he watched his brother's fiancée walk off toward the kitchen. That had gone well, he thought. Really well. Then he turned back to the billiards room, hoping his next conversation would meet with the same level of success. William Smith hadn't left his post by the French doors.

"Dad?" Vance said, and his father turned around. "Can I have a word?"

By tacit agreement, they stepped outside.

They paced in matching strides away from the house, stopping at the low wall surrounding the terrace. In front of them was the black hulk of the hill planted with the first of Vance's grandfather's avocados. In the warm darkness he could feel the trees growing, their roots spreading to lick at the well water pumped into the irrigation lines, their leaves relaxing after a day soaking in the sun's heat. Though he'd never told anyone this, Vance swore he could hear a humming coming from the swelling fruit, a contented sound of health and goodness.

As always, it calmed him.

"You should have let Pinkerton Elementary School put my desk in one of the nearby groves," he mused aloud. "I probably would have learned a lot more and been a hell of a lot less trouble in the classroom."

"You weren't that bad," his father said.

"Yeah, I was."

His dad laughed. "You got your high school diploma. I breathed a lot easier after that. Your GPA wasn't even terrible, though at the end of every semester you were facing a D in at least one class."

"Would always find a stack of homework in my backpack I'd forgotten to turn in."

"Yet you made it out." His father was quiet a moment. "I'm still a little sorry you didn't get your bachelor's, though."

"But I did."

Even in the dark, he could see the other man's head whip toward him. "What?"

"After I came back from Afghanistan the first time." Vance wondered why he'd never mentioned it. Though they'd been at odds, he'd still maintained occasional contact with the family over the years. Stubborn pride, he decided, was another of his failings.

"I thought you worked for the Ochoas."

"Turns out I'm a multitasker. I didn't get a degree in business like Fitz and Baxter, though. It's agricultural management."

"Ah," his dad said, rocking back on his heels. "I'm pleased for you, son. Congratulations."

Avocado country was quiet at night. Vance took in a breath and it seemed to go more silent, the insects hushing, too. *Just get it out,* he told himself. *See if you can get your life back on track.*

"Dad," he said, at the same moment his father turned to him.

"Vance."

Their laughter sounded strained.

"Let me say my piece first." Vance took in another breath. "Dad, I want to apologize."

"Apologize? For what?"

"For my thoughtlessness when I was growing up. I know I was a pain in the ass to monitor as a young kid." He thought of those photos. Of those three totaled vehicles. "And worse when I was a teenager."

His father sighed. "Your mother couldn't sleep most nights from worry."

He was going to have to face her down, too, Vance thought, but he thought she'd forgive him. What he wanted from his father would be more difficult to obtain. "I suppose it didn't get any better when I joined the army."

"No."

"It was good for me, Dad. I can't apologize for that because—"

"I wouldn't ask you to," the older man interrupted. "Today…" He stopped speaking for a moment to pace away, then pace back. "I've been angry at you for scaring the hell out of me all of your life, Vance. But I saw with my own two eyes the value of that fearlessness of yours today."

"Oh, I was sweating plenty out there. I've been scared any number of times in the army, too."

"But you did the job. With confidence. With compassion. That's how you were with that boy out there. That's how I'm sure you were with the soldiers you worked to save."

"It's what I was trained to do."

"And I'm proud of you for it, son." He hesitated again. "I admire you."

God. Blowing out a breath, Vance shoved his hands in his pockets, strangely nonplussed. "I…I don't know what to say." He hadn't expected to hear anything like this from his father, so the script he'd worked out in his head wasn't right any longer.

"You don't have to say anything."

But he did. His days as a combat medic had done wonders for him as a man, but that career hadn't been his first dream…nor was it the one he had now. In order to attain it, he'd have to do as Baxter advised and say what he wanted. Vance took his hands from his pockets, spread out his fingers then curled them again to shove them back in his pants. Okay, he was stalling.

Don't scuttle your second chances.

All right. He'd take his own advice. "I'm going to ask again, Dad. It's been a few years and I'm hoping your answer will be different this time."

His father stayed silent, but tension radiated from him.

Vance felt his own muscles tighten. His chest hurt a little as he sucked in another breath. "With Baxter leaving, Smith & Sons Foods is down a son. I was hoping you could find a place for me in the company."

A long moment of silence passed. "You see Fitz moving into Baxter's work and you doing Fitz's—as well as the grove management tasks?" his father finally asked.

"Bax," Vance muttered, like a curse. Clearly he'd been talking to the family about this already. "Well, I did the management for the Ochoas. GreenWise is okay, but—"

"They're not a Smith. They don't have Smith & Sons Foods as a first priority."

"It would be my first priority." It was what he'd wanted since he was first following Granddad around, begging to be lifted high to pick the first fruit of the season.

"It's hard to be one of a pair of brothers," his father said slowly. "Don't think I don't realize that. Remember, I was raised with your uncle Roy. You get labeled within your family. Within your community. It's not always fair."

Bemused, Vance narrowed his eyes, trying to see

his father's expression in the dark. "What label did you get?"

"That doesn't matter," his dad said. "What matters is…is that this family heals. That we bring you back home, son."

Vance wasn't sure he'd heard right. "Does that mean I'm in?"

"Your uncle and your brother and I already discussed it. Frankly, Baxter insisted we consider the possibility you'd join us. But I wasn't convinced it was something you wanted."

Only all my life. "I do, Dad. I do." He hesitated, then got the last item off his chest. "And I want you to know I understand why you refused to let me in all those years ago. I was a screwup and I couldn't be trusted. But I won't let you down now."

"Son." His father hung his head. "I think *I* let *you* down. There were other ways I could have handled that moment…and many after. Your mother says I have a stubborn streak."

"Like father, like son."

And this time when they laughed, it wasn't strained.

Vance slid his hand from his pocket. "Shake?"

His father's palm met his and then he reeled Vance in. The hug was hard, and his father's free hand gave his short hair a brisk rub. "We'll be ready for you when you're free to come home."

"I don't have to go back to the army."

The older Smith pushed away. "What? Really?"

"I *could* go. But I was told that my injuries would allow me a medical discharge if I asked for it. I will." He wasn't conflicted about the decision at all, he realized. It was time to get out. Helping those kids today had opened his eyes and maybe even given him the permission to do so.

And there was that new, clear path ahead. He was more than ready for a smooth ride.

His father yanked him into another embrace. "Your mother will be over the moon," he said gruffly. Then he added, "I love you, son."

Vance breathed deep of the dark night and let the sense of rightness put down roots in his soul. This was the life he was meant to live. His future was settled now, and a new calm settled over him. He and the avocados would hum well into the future, he thought, healthy and strong.

They headed back a few quiet minutes later. As they approached the French doors leading to the house, Vance slowed, absorbing the tableau provided by the well-lit billiards room.

His uncle and brother were still gathered around the play table, but they had turned their backs to it as his mother and aunt came in bearing trays of coffee and dessert. Blythe moved to take a plate that she apparently planned to share with Fitz—they, Vance thought, would be fucking perfect together. His uncle was bent over the offerings, probably trying to decide which was the largest slice of chocolate cake.

"Dad," Vance said, still watching. "I gotta know. How were you and Uncle Roy labeled?"

"Uh…"

Vance elbowed the older man. "C'mon."

"Fine." William sounded disgruntled. "I was the serious brother, while Roy was known as the funny one. The life of any party. And it ticked me off, okay? I had this great impression I did of Robert De Niro—" He broke off when Vance hooted with laughter.

"Sorry, Dad," he said, trying to stifle it. "But you? Robert De Niro?"

"All right," his father conceded. "It was actually a terrible impression. Still… Hey, where's your girl?"

Vance pointed to the farthest corner of the room where Layla was curled up on a leather chair, a magazine on her lap. Shit. That wasn't a happy expression on her face, he thought. He shouldn't have left her by herself for so long.

"I like her, Vance," his dad said. "She's a very good choice."

Vance opened his mouth to come clean about Layla, too. They weren't really anything to each other…but then he saw her head come up, her attention shifting across the room to where his family stood in that tight group, laughing together over something his uncle, the funny brother, had said. The yearning on her face was easy to read—and pierced his heart.

It cracked open as he watched her, sitting alone, apart, outside that small circle of people. *Sweet Lord.* His palm pressed, hard, over his unlocked and aching heart as a new, insistent need surged in his chest. He wanted to give them to her, Vance realized. He wanted to give her his family.

He wanted to *be* her family. Tied to her forever.

Because the idea of parting from her was excruciating. Her natural beauty, her joy in things as simple as cupcakes and sandcastles, the way she made him laugh—so often at himself—lightened every day. She'd become his sunshine, he thought, her warmth and brightness making him damn glad to be alive.

And on those occasions when her ordinarily sunny nature was shadowed by sadness, he wanted to be the one to hold her, comforting her during the darker times. He knew he'd be good at it, just as she was so good for him.

His breath caught. *Damn,* he thought, astonished, *I've gone and done it.*

I've gone and fallen in love with her.

"Are you going to tell everyone tonight?" his dad asked.

No! God, no, Vance thought, panicking a little. Being in love shocked the hell out of him. His mind could hardly believe the words, let alone say them. His pulse rocketed. "I don't think—"

"Your mother will be so relieved to know you're staying home and joining the business. I predict double desserts."

His heartbeat slowed some. "Oh. Okay. Yeah. We can talk about that."

Would he have a talk with Layla, too? A private, cards-on-the-table conversation? But maybe it was better if he didn't—he was just at the beginning of a new phase of his life, after all, and he could give it some time, see how he felt in a few days, weeks, months. Wait a while before putting his heart on the line.

Yeah, he told himself, almost relieved. Being in love didn't demand declaring it.

Except...

Except when it did.

Maybe Baxter was right again, Vance thought, watching as his aunt kissed her husband's cheek and Blythe fed Fitz a piece of cake from her fork. All that marital bliss made a man expect things. Want things for himself.

And he wanted all things with Layla, his brown-eyed girl, to the marrow of his bones. When had she found her way so deeply inside him? Last night, when she'd mourned for her father in his arms? The day she'd come out of the spa and pointed her newly painted toes in girly pleasure? Or was it the morning after they'd first made love, when they'd shared a moment of quiet companionship and a cup of coffee?

Whatever the case, his future wasn't going to be complete without her in it.

Wouldn't you know? he thought, with a rueful shake of his head. Just when the track ahead appeared clear and smooth, his life had gone right off the rails.

CHAPTER TWENTY

RIDING BACK TO BEACH HOUSE NO. 9, Layla regretted the two glasses of champagne she'd tossed back after Vance had announced his impending return to the family business. She'd already had wine with dinner, hoping that alcohol could smooth her jagged emotions. Under the circumstances, who wouldn't be feeling more than a little rocky? Minutes after acknowledging she might have fallen in love with Vance, she'd almost been witness to his death.

Maybe she made a little sound of distress, because he glanced over at her. "Are you okay?"

She would be, she told herself. Just as soon as she managed to reclassify her feelings for him. It wasn't love, she'd decided after that first fizzy glass of champagne. It was infatuation. By morning, after a night's sleep alone in bed, she'd be sure of that.

"Layla?"

"I'm…I'm just thinking of those kids," she lied. "I hope they're all right."

"I thought you were there," he answered, puzzlement in his voice, "when the driver's dad called and reported that his son and the other two are going to fully recover. They have bumps and bruises and Marshall broke a leg, but all of them will heal."

"That's right," she replied, resting her head against the back of the seat. "I remember now."

"You're tired," Vance said, and he reached over to caress her cheek with his thumb. "Close your eyes and take a nap until we get to Crescent Cove. I'd like us to have a talk when we're back at the beach house."

Talk. With a mental groan, she closed her eyes, pretending sleep had already struck. She wasn't about to agree to a talk. Having a conversation when she felt this vulnerable could be a disaster. What if she let slip the fanciful idea that had invaded her heart? By tomorrow she'd have the roots yanked free, but tonight she didn't have the strength to do the job.

Pretense turned into reality, she discovered, because she did doze off. For how long, she wasn't entirely sure, but she was roused from sleep by Vance's hand on her shoulder. He had her passenger door open and was leaning in. "Layla," he said, brushing her hair off her face. "Wake up."

Still groggy, she got to her feet. He wrapped an arm around her waist to lead her into the house. She allowed it; the quicker she got inside, the quicker she could be alone behind her own bedroom door.

But instead of releasing her once they crossed the threshold, he continued holding her tight as he guided her into the dimly lit living room. Then, finally, he dropped his arm. Immediately Layla started edging toward the staircase. She'd take Addy's room, empty now that she was staying at Baxter's. A floor away would be a good start at distance.

Would Vance let her go without a word, or would she have to define her reasons for sleeping alone? Snoring, she thought again. There was always the excuse that he snored.

He crossed to the fireplace, going to his haunches to turn on the gas. Blue flames ignited, catching the kindling stacked on the grate. "You were pretty quiet about my decision to leave the army and join the family company," he said, glancing at her over his shoulder.

She froze. "Uh…I'm so glad for you." She hadn't expressed that? His announcement had been met by happy exclamations from his family, followed by even happier tears coursing down his mother's face. Layla hadn't considered it her place to comment then. Because…because she'd known it had nothing to do with her.

Though relief couldn't even begin to describe how she'd felt at the idea that he'd seen his last of combat. Emotion tightened her throat. "I'm so truly, truly glad."

"That's good."

The fire crackled, and he stayed low, staring into it. Unnerved by his stillness, she spoke to his broad back. "So I think I'll just—"

"I really want to talk." He rose, but didn't turn, and there was a new tension emanating from him.

Layla frowned at his stiff shoulders and rigid pose. Talk about what, exactly? Then the answer came to her in a rush. Talk about goodbye, of course. Without his return to the army, he'd feel it necessary to reestablish they still had one of those coming. And soon.

"There's no need," she said, trying to sound offhand. Her feet restarted their shuffle toward the staircase. "I'm going to bed upstairs."

His body turned in an instant. "What? Why?"

"I… Well…" *The goodbye,* she tried to tell him with her eyes. *I get it. We don't have to discuss it to death.*

But then he was in front of her, his big, warm hands cupping her face. "I don't want you to go, Layla. Stay with me."

No! Because then she'd want to stay with him forever. Still, her traitorous body swayed toward his. He gathered her close to his wide chest, then leaned down to press a gentle kiss on her lips.

"Yeah," he said, his breath warm against her face. "Stay with me by the fire and we'll talk."

Where had her willpower gone? But it had started the day squishy, and all the emotional events had only pummeled it into further submission. Resigned, she let herself be drawn to the couch and pulled down on the cushions next to Vance. He kept her close, though his gaze focused on the fire.

He'd been tense a moment before, but now she felt his...hesitation? Uncertainty?

Yeah, it wouldn't be easy to remind someone she shouldn't harbor false hopes. That they were both moving on, that this monthlong interlude was a mere pause in their real, but separate lives.

As his silence continued, the night seemed to wrap around them. There was the crackling fire, the background shush of the unceasing surf, their breaths, mingling like they would never do again. Layla's eyes stung and if there was one thing that she'd regret most about her stay at Beach House No. 9, it was how the weeks had peeled away her outer layer of strength. Tears were so close to the surface now.

Yet she didn't protest when his arms gathered her closer. She found her cheek pressed against his chest, his heavy heartbeat in her ear. Steady. Sure.

She could have lost him today. That moment when

he'd been lying in the puddle of gasoline and looking at her with such anxious urgency was burned forever in her memory. *Go, Layla,* he'd said. *Go on.*

Those could have been his last words to her.

Those could have been his very last words ever.

Her heart seized, her veins filling with a cold horror. She'd been almost numb before, and the wine and champagne had helped, but now the fear overtook her and her body began to shake.

She reminded herself he was fine. His heartbeat was unchanged. But she splayed her hand on his chest, trying to convince herself he was as warm and solid as always. Another person she cared for hadn't been lost.

Panic continued to rattle her bones.

"Layla?" Vance turned her in his arms so he could study her face. "You're shivering. What's the matter? Cold again?"

"Not this time," she said, certain only one thing would quell her sudden anxiety. "Take me to bed."

"Layla…"

"It doesn't have to mean anything," she added hastily.

He winced. "Layla—"

"Other than you're alive. I want to feel that you're alive. I *need* to feel you're alive."

His thumb ran over her mouth. "Let's talk first."

"No." Words weren't her friend tonight. She didn't need a discussion of their nonfuture and she didn't want him teasing her with his raunchy routine in bed. She loved that, he knew she did, but if Vance took her down, took her too deep into desire, *she* might say the very wrong thing.

This time, she wanted to drift atop the emotion and

only use their bodies to reassure herself that he was whole and here and hers this one last time.

"Please, Vance."

Instead of answering, he used his thumb on her lips again, and she nipped at it, then took it fully in her mouth. She sucked, swirling her tongue over the pad, and felt his body tighten everywhere.

He tasted good, and she felt dizzy with the flavor of the man. Her shivering stopped as her skin heated under her clothes, the cotton feeling too rough against the tender skin of her belly and at the hollow that was the small of her back. She'd zipped a hoodie over her sundress and she unfastened it now, still using her lips and mouth to suckle Vance's thumb.

His nostrils were flared, his cheekbones pressing hard against his skin, its color a soft rose-gold in the firelight. His gaze followed her as she released him to stand, then he watched in a clearly stunned silence as she shed the sweatshirt, kicked off her shoes, whipped the stretchy cotton sundress over her head.

Even the panties were too much, so she shoved those off her hips and felt the fire's warmth on her bare bottom.

"Jesus, Layla," Vance said. "Sweetheart…"

But the word drifted to nothing as she knelt between his knees and went to work on opening his jeans. He looked astounded, but then she was, too. In their sex she'd never been the aggressor, and maybe it would balance the scales. She wanted to have him at her mercy now, as she'd been at his since the very first time they'd touched.

Her hands fumbled with the denim and soft boxers beneath, but she caught her lower lip between her

teeth and persevered. He was hard and hot beneath the
material, she could feel him. She wanted that! And she
made a little sound of frustration as she couldn't find
a way to bare him.

He laughed a little, the sound male and indulgent,
and then, shifting his hips, he reached down and made
the proper adjustments until there it was, his erection
lying against his flat belly. Her heart pounding, she
stared at it, then kneed closer to take the shaft between
her palms. Ah. His power at her fingertips now. Then
at her mouth.

When her tongue touched the soft skin at its head, he
groaned, and his long fingers sifted into her hair. She
laved him, circling the thick knob, sliding down the
shaft, breathing in the scent of his skin and breathing
out against his flesh so that their essences merged this
one last time. Her hands curled around his denim-clad
calves, and she rose higher in order to take him deeper
into her mouth. He groaned again, arching against the
cushions, and the sound made her nipples tighten to
aching, greedy points.

She started a rhythm, a sexual, purposeful retreat and
advance, and her heart took it up, like a military drum-
mer's beat driving the pace of the march. Vance's palm
caressed her cheek, and she glanced up at him, struck
by the keen glitter in his half-mast eyes. It stalled her
a moment, and she just held him in her mouth, sucking
lightly as she took in the aroused flush on his face, the
stark beauty of his features.

Her heart squeezed in her chest, the rhythm falter-
ing there, too, and she swayed on her knees, dark spots
swirling in her vision.

In a second, Vance had pulled her up, taking her

into his lap. "You have to breathe, silly girl." His fingers gripping her chin, he tilted her face toward his. "Breathe."

The air she sucked in made the black spots disappear—and then she was struck by her vulnerability. She was trembling again, and naked, surrounded by a mostly clothed Vance. She made to climb off him—time to gain the upper hand!—but he tightened the arm about her waist. His other hand lifted to cage one swollen breast.

She moaned.

"Yeah," he said, blowing aside her hair so he could press a kiss to the side of her neck. "My turn now."

Pinching her nipple, he moved his mouth upward, ignoring her desperate wiggles. "Vance…"

"Hmm?" he asked, the sound humming against the hollow behind her ear.

"Please…"

He lifted his head and his fingers eased up on her breast. "Please harder, softer? Please more kisses? Please more touches?"

Her mind reeled, thoughts not coalescing. "Just please," she finally said, aggravated.

His smile was almost sweet. "Of course." Then he stood, lifting her in his arms.

The bedroom was dark, the sound of the ocean bouncing off the walls. He'd left the windows open, she thought, because the air was cool against her skin and smelled soft and wet. He placed her on the mattress, then came down over her a moment later, his elbows on either side of her head. His body was naked now, his skin delicious against hers.

"Oh, Layla," he said, framing her face with his hands. "Shall I tell you what you do to me?"

"Don't say anything," she begged. "Don't talk." If he did that, he'd ratchet up her desire and she would lose herself in the heat and need, lose her control over her thoughts and her voice and then it would be she who was talking, telling him the truth she hadn't yet eradicated from her heart. It was only loosely rooted, it had to be, but it was there now, and dangerous to her pride and to her future.

Instead of answering, Vance kissed her, long and deep and drugging. Yes, she thought, thankfully this wasn't talking, and reveled in the sensation of his tongue sliding against hers. She sucked on it, open to his flavor, letting the heat and weight of his body sink into hers. Her arms went around his neck and her legs twined his hips.

More kisses. A thousand kisses. A night of kisses.

But then he lifted his head to move down her body. Layla panted in the ocean-scented darkness, arching her back as the flat of Vance's tongue swiped across her nipple. "Look what I've found," he murmured, and then he traveled to the other, greeting it with another wet velvet caress. "You're hard for me, baby, just like I'm hard for you."

Oh, God, yes, she felt it. She felt his length against her thigh, the tip of him wet and that made her wetter, too. One hand tried to find purchase in his short hair, but there was only the silky brush of it against the hollow of her palm. How could that be so sexy? But it was, and even sexier in contrast to the way his thick shoulder muscle bunched against the grip of her other hand.

His mouth sucked her nipple deep. Layla tightened

her fingers on him, riding the exquisite bliss of the pull. Her mouth opened, and she moaned, the pitch of it turning higher as he paid attention to her other breast, too, kneading the soft flesh, rubbing his thumb against the tight tip.

"I'm thinking about making you come just like this," he said, lifting his head to blow cool air on her damp flesh. "I'll just kiss and lick and tug on your pretty breasts until you give it all up for me."

No, no. She couldn't give it all up for him. Alarmed, she thrashed under the weight of his body, but that only brought her more exquisite sensation, her hard nipples abraded by the hair on his chest. Her mouth opened on another cry.

"Shh, shh," he said, trying to soothe her by trailing wet kisses back up to her mouth. He took her there once more, his possession slow and sure, sending her mind careening off again.

Her control spun away with it. Now it was only Vance's touch that kept her body centered. He swiped his palms down her belly and along her flank. He reared back, lifting one of her legs so he could trail his tongue up her calf, along the inside of her knee, and on to the twitching flesh of her inner thigh.

He opened her, using his broad palms like blades and then he bent over her, his hot breath the only warning before he was taking her there with his mouth. She jerked at that first velvet stroke and he lifted his head. "You taste so good, Layla, why do you taste so good?"

But he didn't wait for an answer before he dove low once more and applied himself to savoring her flesh, to exploring every pleated layer and slick surface. She was thrashing again, but he had her hips in his grasp and it was even better to struggle against his strength, his masculine power an aphrodisiac as potent as the gentle stroke of his tongue.

The scent of sex mixed with the scent of ocean. The sound of the waves was louder in the room and as Vance took her up and up, she felt herself tumbling in another direction, slipping against sleek surfaces, twisting and turning toward some elemental center.

Like sliding into a seashell, she thought. The conch, the Buddhist symbol representing the awakening of disciples from ignorance. Because she would never be the same, not with the way Vance was turning her inside out. He flicked his tongue against that most sensitive spot at the apex of her cleft and her skin rippled, every nerve ending responding to the touch. Then he slid two fingers inside her, and they both shuddered. "So hot," he murmured against her wet flesh. "So soft."

He turned his hand, penetrating her with a twisting motion that had her arching again. "Vance," she cried out, protesting, because it was too much or not enough or just wonderful, and she was sliding faster now, into the heart of the spiraled shell.

His touch destroyed her, tearing down all her defenses, until she was just flesh and bone and tissue that yearned for his touch, his lips, his penetration. His mouth was greedy on her hot center, eating at her, the edge of his teeth scraping the sensitized flesh, his tongue piercing the wet channel, making her writhe and shake and beg him for more.

His tongue turned gentle then, soft and adoring on the delicate tissue, licking upward until he could lap at the little bud. She moaned and he lashed it now, holding her still while her voice went hoarse with need. And then…then, he sucked, taking it between his lips and relishing it with a thoroughness that drew all the pleasure from each cell in her body toward that small point. She felt herself sliding again, spiraling, until she was surrounded by soft light and the ocean's pulsing breath and—bliss…bliss…bliss.

It was as if her climax unleashed something in him. He went almost ferocious, his teeth grazing her hipbones, his mouth burning her belly. His hands were hot, too, cupping her breasts and squeezing her nipples until she was writhing on the sheets again, his wildness contagious. His mouth fell onto hers and the kiss was wet and desperate and she sucked on his tongue again, tasting herself and him, a heady combination.

Her hand slid down his chest to find his erection but his hips reared back. "God, too close," he muttered.

So she let him put on the condom and guide himself into her body, her sex open and welcome. They both groaned as he infiltrated, a sensual assault by degrees, until he was fully inside her. One arm came under her hips, tilting them up so he gained another searing degree. Then he began moving, in powerful and deep strokes from which she had no defense.

"Layla," he whispered, his breath hot against her ear.

She wound her legs around his hips, allowing him everything, her body his, her heart the same. It terrified her, this feeling that she'd unlocked her own doors and thrown them wide for him to ransack. Yet she felt herself rising to meet him again, another climax building.

Still thrusting, Vance slid a hand between them and stroked her, playing over the sensitized knot of nerves. She gasped, and then the orgasm crashed upon her like love had—without permission. Her cry was echoed by

Vance's groan, and he shuddered in her arms, his own crisis shaking the entire bed.

In the aftermath, his arms gathered her against his chest. Layla's heart still pumped in an unsteady rhythm, and then, oh, God, and then what she'd been dreading happened. The words whispered into the room. "I love you."

Appalled, her mind froze. How could she have let that go? She hadn't even felt the phrase on her tongue.

But it was out now, and there was only one thing to be done.

She'd already known it was past time for goodbye.

THE KARMA CUPCAKES truck was back in its usual spot in Layla's duplex driveway. The familiarity should soothe her, she thought, but she'd lost all hope for serenity somewhere between Crescent Cove and home two days before. Trying to ignore a churning stomach and a throbbing head, she settled onto a stool and contemplated the bottle of champagne on the countertop beside the mixer. Lost in misery, she almost fell over when Uncle Phil suddenly pulled open the door and stepped inside. He was in his usual counterculture garb: cargo shorts, natural-fiber shirt, braided bracelets, but the expression on his face didn't look the least laid-back.

He appeared…determined.

It wasn't a familiar Uncle Phil state of mind.

Layla's brows drew together. "What's wrong?"

"Staring into space won't get those cupcakes made, you know," he said, gesturing at the champagne.

Alarm tickled her again. He'd never been a harsh taskmaster. As a matter of fact, he'd never been any kind of taskmaster. And managing Karma Cupcakes was her baby. His had always been a supporting role. "Uncle Phil—"

"Don't you have an order to fulfill? I thought you planned to deliver it today."

"I've been considering, uh, reneging on that," she confessed.

His eyes narrowed. "Layla."

He'd never scolded her, but that's where it sounded as if he was going. "I'm sure no one's even counting on them," she said, her voice defensive. "When I moved out of the beach house, the note I left behind said goodbye. Vance will have understood all that it means."

She'd written it so fast, and in the dark, she hoped he could read her handwriting. Panicking in the aftermath of those three words, she'd pretended instant sleep. Then, once Vance had dropped off, his slumber heavy, his body boneless, she'd bolted from her place next to him. For twenty minutes, she'd dashed about, packing her things, penning her brief explanation, leaping into her car for the race home.

Uncle Phil looked dubious. "You really think Vance understands?"

He hadn't called her, had he? "Believe me, things are better this way."

"What way is that?"

No longer able to meet his gaze, Layla let hers roam the snug interior of the truck. It snagged on the ridiculous Teddy bear Vance had given her that first day. With a silent groan, she glanced upward, her eyes settling on the statue of a seated, half-smiling Buddha in its resting place. That's how she wanted to be, a tranquil carving of stone without wants or regrets. Without expectation or disappointment.

"Layla?"

"Craving results in suffering," she suddenly said. "Buddha says so, right? Hurt comes if you want something too much."

"How does that relate to you running from Crescent Cove in the dark of night?"

She frowned. "It was closer to the gray of dawn. And it relates because I departed the cove—" not run from it, she'd left that note, right? "—in order to work on my attachment issues."

Her uncle took his own look at the figurine above then met her gaze. "I don't think Buddha meant—"

"Look, I need to stand on my own two feet!" She did that now, rising from the stool and crossing her arms over her chest.

"Why?"

"Dad's gone." The words made her stomach take another unpleasant dip. "And you'll be taking your trip soon, too. I need to learn to count on myself."

"That doesn't mean cutting yourself off from everyone else."

Layla shook her head. "This time, it does."

With a sigh, Uncle Phil leaned against the countertop. "So does this independence of yours allow you to avoid situations you don't like?"

"Such as…?" she asked, wary.

"Doing your job, Layla. Taking orders for cupcakes and then delivering them."

She glared at him. Uncle Phil was supposed to be always laid-back! Not incisive. Not probing. "Don't you have an excursion down the Amazon to plan?"

"I've never tried to be your father," he said, ignoring the jab. "I've never thought it was my job to form your character."

Her anger faded in an instant. "Oh, Uncle Phil—"

"But I do *know* your character. You might be on your own two feet, but you won't be able to live with the woman in the mirror if you break your word on this."

"C'mon." Her chest felt tight. "It's just cupcakes."

He raised a brow. "Is it?"

On that first day at the cove, she'd wondered if her uncle had hatched his own secret matchmaking plan, and the suspicion now rose again. "Uncle Phil," she said, pinning him with her stare, "did you actually go along with this whole Helmet List vacation in the hopes that Vance and I might pair up?"

"Would I interfere that way?" His expression turned pious. "Buddha said, 'Three things cannot be long hidden. The sun, the moon and the truth.'"

Layla frowned. "Meaning what?"

"Meaning bake the cupcakes," her uncle replied, and turned to leave.

Layla reached for the bottle of champagne, resigned. No one could dodge the tough questions as successfully as Uncle Phil. Fine. She'd bake the cupcakes. Vance's family had been kind to her. Vance himself had been generous in so many ways. She was obliged to see this through, despite her discomfort.

Fiddling with the metal cage at the top of the bottle, she promised herself she'd keep her own cork tightly seated. Every emotion would stay inside until the damn desserts were delivered.

The door shut behind Uncle Phil, then it opened again and he stuck his head back inside. "How long have I been planning my around-the-world expedition?"

Surprised by the question, Layla glanced over at him. "I don't know...all my life?"

"And longer." A rueful smile curved his lips. "If I was ever really going to leave the west coast, would I have waited until I have arthritic knees and an addiction to *Storage Wars?*"

She stared. "But...but why all the guidebooks?"

"There's more than one way to enjoy a journey, Layla. You've got to decide if you want to do it my way—only on paper and in dreams—or if you actually want to step onto the plane and fly."

CHAPTER TWENTY-ONE

After Layla's abrupt defection, Vance spent the days alone at Beach House No. 9, brooding over why she'd gone and concocting plans to get her back. Oh, he'd considered accepting it for the rejection it seemed to be and forcing himself to move on. Time would expunge the pain, right? He'd get busy in the groves and losing her would no longer feel as if winter had descended five months too early.

But the stubborn, hardheaded part of him wasn't ready to surrender. And he found her early morning escape highly suspicious. If there wasn't something profound going on, he figured, she'd have had the decency to say goodbye to his face. So he curbed his innate impatience and listened to his instincts. It would be better if she returned to him.

When the knock came on the door around 7:00 p.m. of the third day, the evening before his brother's engagement brunch, he knew who stood on the other side. Schooling his expression, he crossed to the entrance, determined to remain calm.

His heart stumbled, however, when he caught sight of her on the doorstep. Her hair in a ponytail, she wore ancient jeans, a sweatshirt and a pair of flip-flops. Two oblong pink bakery boxes were balanced on her palms.

She looked determined, but so exhausted that he wanted to snatch her up and hold her close.

His own sharp yearning startled him. Somehow she'd dug herself deep, and without her in his life he'd been left empty and aching. *Never again,* he whispered to her silently. *I won't let you run from me ever again.*

She didn't appear to notice her effect on him and just shoved the cartons forward. "Here," she said, her low-pitched voice huskier than usual. "Best wishes to Fitz and Blythe."

"That's it?" Despite his effort to stay cool, his temper sparked, and he deliberately stuck his hands in his pockets and stared at her. "You're not even going to come in?"

A huff of breath ruffled her bangs. "Why?"

"I need to talk to you," he said.

She frowned, her arms still upraised, offering the cupcakes.

They were at a standoff. Though his nerves stretched tauter, Vance refused to give an inch. But he should have known the little soldier facing him wouldn't crack easy, either, and several strained minutes passed.

Finally, she huffed again. "Just move out of the way and I'll put these in the kitchen."

Stepping aside, he let her go by. Relief buckled his knees and he braced an arm on the wall to keep himself upright. Okay. *Okay.* At least he'd gotten her this far.

After a moment, he took a breath and followed her into the kitchen. She whirled as he approached and pressed back against the countertop. He didn't hesitate to get into her personal space.

The woman had wormed her way into places he hadn't planned on, hadn't she?

Layla touched the tip of her tongue to her top-heavy upper lip. "Uh, I hope you weren't concerned about the cupcakes."

"I knew you'd keep your promise."

She flushed. "Still, I didn't want anyone to worry. I called your mom and explained that I'd be dropping them off to you."

"So she said."

"Oh." Her head bobbed up and down. "That's right. You're, um, patched up with them now, aren't you? Did I tell you how great I think that is? It's great. Really, really great."

"It is," he agreed, "though it's only half of what I want."

Her brows pinched together. "I'd think you have everything now. Is something wrong with the job at Smith & Sons?"

"No."

She studied his face with her big brown eyes. "Well, I would have thought you'd be in a better mood then. Is it Fitz and Blythe's engagement—"

"I'm ecstatic for them."

"You don't sound like it," Layla said, frowning. "Though I can imagine it's hard to get over—"

"If you mention another word about Blythe I'm going to strangle you."

"Well, you were the one engaged to the woman," she said in a snotty voice.

Her tone made him ease a little more. "I was stupid about that," he confessed, and figured he owed her a better explanation. "I didn't care about her for herself… I saw her as my ticket back into the family—and also as a poke at Fitz."

"Oh," Layla said.

"And I've apologized for it." He smiled a little. "All's forgiven, even though she's signed herself up for a lifetime with my fucking perfect big brother."

Layla made a face. "You don't fool me. You love him."

"Yeah," he agreed. Then they stared at each other for another long minute. His nerves cinched again, going so tight he heard a high whine in his ears. "So—"

"I've got to be going," she said.

"No." He cleared his throat. "I mean, I have something to give you. Don't take a step." Not trusting her to do as bid, he hurried away.

And she did move. His stomach swooped at the sight of the empty kitchen, but then he found her in the living room, her gaze focused out the glass slider. The sun was hovering at eye level in that odd, breathless manner it had of seeming to stay glued in place before taking its last precipitous dash for the horizon.

He came up behind her, close enough to smell the sweetness of cupcakes on her skin. "Layla," he said, putting a hand on her shoulder.

It made her jump and before he could stop her she was out the door and onto the deck. Gritting his teeth, Vance stalked behind her, following his prey until her belly was pressed against the railing.

Impatient now, he grabbed her by the arm and turned her to face him. "Here," he said brusquely. "This is for you."

She glanced down at the frame he pushed into her hands and then her gaze came back to his. "What?"

Was she blind? "It's the Helmet List. The one your

dad gave to me. I had it framed, along with a couple of photos. One is the picture of you he always carried."

Her head bent again as she studied the item. The art shop had mounted the simple lined notepaper on a special backing. It took center stage, the crease marks and smudges of dirt and sweat still apparent. On the upper left, he'd had them place a photo of her father, something he'd taken from Griffin's stash. On the lower right was little-girl Layla, the child he'd expected to host at Beach House No. 9.

The woman he'd fallen in love with looked up. "I…" She lifted one hand from the frame and made a helpless gesture. "Thank you. I…I've got to go."

All his muscles and tendons seized. He opened his mouth, trying to recall a single one of the speeches he'd rehearsed during her absence. Not a word of them came to mind. *Hell,* he thought. *What now?*

A seagull swooped low, and his eyes shifted, his gaze once again landing on the sun. "We haven't ticked off the green flash yet," he said quickly. "Don't you think—"

She shook her head, her refusal emphatic.

Vance's mouth dried. It was like waking up to that empty bed all over again. The alarm he'd felt upon opening his eyes and discovering her gone had turned to dread when he'd read the note she'd left. *Thank you, thank you so much for everything,* she'd written, *but now it's time I go. Goodbye.*

Maybe she'd really meant it, after all.

"Why did you leave like that?" he asked baldly. Those few words had felt a thousand times worse than Blythe's long-winded Dear John. He swallowed, then forced out the question that had to be asked, though it put his pride on the line. "Is it because that night I told you I loved you?"

Her Bambi eyes flared wide. "What? That was me."

He frowned. "No, I said it. I wasn't sure you heard me before you fell asleep." His heart started thumping, hammering in his chest, his throat, at the ends of his fingers, for fuck's sake. Had she just implied she loved him, too? "I'm in love with you, Layla."

Her knuckles went white on the frame, and then she shook her head again, clearly panicked. "I thought we were clear we didn't want that."

He laughed a little, trying to ease his anxiety. "Yeah, well, sometimes it just happens, remember?"

"That was chemistry," she said, edging toward the stairs leading to the sand.

"Layla, stay put."

Instead she kept moving. "I didn't plan for anything like...like love."

He held himself still, worried about frightening her away. "Well, it's not something you plan," he said. "Just ask Baxter. Or Fitz. But if you're ready, and in the right place—"

"I'm not ready!" she cried out. "I'm not in the right place."

"Sweetheart, what's the matter?" Concerned by her distress, he took a careful step toward her. "Would the two of us...would love be so bad?"

"Yes."

He blinked.

"Because it's weakness," she said. "And dependence and...and..."

"And what, honey? And what?"

"And heartbreak!"

"Heartbreak?" He blinked again.

"My mother didn't make it to my third birthday." She swallowed. "My father was in and out all my life and now he's gone forever."

Oh, sweet girl, Vance thought, as a crack crawled over the surface of his heart.

"So how do I know that what you say you feel will last beyond…beyond the next moment? Or the one after that? I can't trust it." Her brown eyes were as big as he'd ever seen them, and so, so serious. "Because the fact is, Vance, I've only ever been loved in very small doses."

Oh, God. The fracturing organ in the center of his chest made him slow to react, so slow that when she whirled and leaped down the steps and onto the sand, he missed his chance to catch her. Keep her.

And this time he worried he might have lost her for good.

LIKE THE OTHER TIME SHE'D run from the beach house, Layla sprinted northward, frantic to outdistance herself from Vance and the confusing and conflicting feelings he'd provoked. He said it had been *his* whisper in the dark. He said he loved her.

The idea of it terrified her even more than knowing *she* loved *him.* If it was true, how could she ever leave him? And if she didn't, how could she ever be safe from pain? *Attachment is the source of suffering.*

Her eyes and lungs were burning when she finally dropped to the sand, all breath gone. Her resting place was at the base of the same dune where she'd stopped before, the night he'd danced with her on the beach house's deck. Air heaving in and out of her chest, she tried directing herself to calm, but the order wasn't working. Realizing she still clutched the frame Vance had given her, she dropped it to her lap and buried her face in her hands.

"Layla? Are you all right?"

Her head jerked up. So unnerved was she by her confrontation with Vance, she hadn't noticed that Jane Pearson was sitting on top of the dune, beside Skye. The brunette's focus was out to sea, her arms wound tightly about herself.

"What are you two doing?" Layla asked, picking up the frame so she could clamber to her feet.

Jane glanced at Skye's set face then looked back at Layla. "We're getting some fresh air."

"Something's happened to Gage," Skye said, her voice colorless.

"What? Your pen pal Gage?" Layla looked to Jane for confirmation. "Isn't that your fiancé's brother?"

"Twin." Jane grimaced. "And his twin-sense has been tingling for several days. Then Skye called and said it's been too long between letters from him."

"Mail can be erratic from that part of the world," Layla said. "Believe me. Even the military postal service isn't always reliable."

Skye shook her head. "He's in trouble."

"I…" Layla let her next platitude go unsaid. She knew how useless they were. People would tell you it would be all right. Have faith, be strong, think positive thoughts. None of that changed a thing.

You could avoid the cracks in the sidewalk, bargain with some higher power or just your inner fears, and the unthinkable still could happen. A mother would leave her husband and her small daughter. A man's letter would fail to arrive. One day there'd be a knock on the door and the sight of the uniform on the other side told you everything you needed to know but never wanted to hear.

Loving someone meant you set yourself up for hurt.

"Do you want to come sit here with us?" Jane asked. "You look upset and like they say, misery loves company."

Layla stared at the other two women, shaking her head. She didn't want upset. After already losing people in her life, she didn't want to position herself for miserable again. Her hands tightened on the frame until the edges dug painfully into her flesh. Glancing down, her gaze landed on the Helmet List, and then the last item listed on the notepaper.

That wasn't her father's writing, she thought with a frown. The others were in his precise, spare hand, but the last line was not. Someone else had written the final words: *Keep Layla safe.*

She stared at them, her earlier roiling emotions coalescing into a heated ball that burned in the pit of her stomach. Instead of feeling vulnerable and insecure, she glanced at Skye, then at the frame in her hands, and experienced a righteous rage.

Murmuring a quick good luck to the other women, she spun around and marched back to Beach House No. 9.

Her feet sounded loud on the wooden steps. Coming to a halt on the deck, she saw Vance rise out of a chair, his watchful gaze on her face. She hesitated a moment, tripped up by *his* face, that arrangement of tanned skin, masculine bones and blue eyes that would be almost pretty without the accompanying heavy musculature of his rugged body.

She thought of those long, hair-roughened limbs sliding against hers in the dark, the hot rush of his breath against her neck, those sinewy hands cupping her breasts and sliding between her thighs as he unraveled her in bed.

I love you. I'm in love with you.

He'd said that.

The liar.

Her ire rose again and she stomped across the painted wooden planks to confront him. "What's this?" she said, shaking the framed list in his face. "What's all this about 'Keep Layla safe'?"

Rubbing the backs of his knuckles against his whisker-stubbled cheek, Vance regarded her warily. "Do you mean because it's in my handwriting?"

"Hah," Layla said. "So it *is* yours."

He frowned. "Yes. On that last afternoon…he asked me to add it, and about that—"

"Well, I don't need your pity promise," she shot at him. "I know you, Vance Thomas Smith, and if you swore to my father you'd keep me safe, then you'd do whatever you must to make that happen."

"What are you talking about?"

She poked him in the chest. "Telling me you love me…that's your way of giving me the security my father wanted for me, isn't it?"

"I keep telling you, I'm no hero. I wouldn't—"

"You were going to be my friend, you said. You'd write me, email me, call me. But that wasn't enough to appease your conscience, was it? Instead, you decided to tell me you love me and—"

"Jesus Christ, woman." Vance scowled. "I *do* love you."

He'd said it again, and those four words brought her up short. She'd thought he'd back down if she called him out on his game. It made her anxious again, her stomach roiling, her palms sweating. She stared at him, unsure how next to proceed.

"Sweetheart," Vance said now, his expression softening, his voice gentle. "I love you." He put his hands on her shoulders. "I'll tell you a thousand times if I need to. I'm in love with you."

She wrenched back. "That's not keeping me safe!" Her whole body felt on fire now, her tongue a flame. "That is *not* keeping me safe."

"I know," Vance said. "And if the colonel was here right now, I'd have to admit that's the one promise I made that I can't keep. Love takes risk, Layla."

She shook her head, aware her anxious voice was rising higher. "I don't want any more risk. I can't take any more risk without breaking into a million pieces."

He stared at her a long, long moment, as if assessing her state of mind. "All right," he said slowly. "I understand."

The lump in her throat made it hard to swallow. "Okay. Good. You don't love me. That's better."

"Oh, I still love you," Vance said, with maddening calm. "And you can walk away from it if you want, if that gives you the protection you think you need. I won't fight you on that—but it won't extinguish my feelings for you, either."

Layla wanted to tear out her hair. What was she supposed to say to that? Didn't he get it? "Attachment is the source of suffering and—"

"No. Attachment is the source of joy. Parent to child. Brother to brother. Man to woman."

Panic turned her cold then hot again. He was speaking of his family, and how could she deny what he said after meeting them? But still…

"How can we count on something we didn't get to choose? Love—" and she put scare quotes around the word "—forced us—"

"No." Vance interrupted her again. "Love didn't force the two of us together, Layla. The two of us together *create* the love."

Oh, it sounded pretty. But it would hurt so much to hope and feel and then someday to have it disappear or die. She opened her mouth.

"Wait." His gaze had jumped over her shoulder. "Turn around," he ordered. "Turn around right now."

At his urgent tone, Layla spun. Her gaze swept the beach, uncertain what she was supposed to notice. Vance came up behind her, his big body crowding hers. His head bent to her ear as one hand landed on her shoulder and the other pointed to the horizon. "The sunset," he whispered. "Watch the sunset."

Layla stared westward, holding the framed Helmet List to her breasts. The sand had lost its golden luster and was a dark shadow spilling into the gleaming, silvery blanket of the ocean. Beyond that, the orb of the sun was more than half gone now, its curved edges distinct between the water and the thin clouds above that had taken on its orangish glow.

There was an orange reflection on the water, too, a narrow-to-broad cone that reached toward shore, but then pulled farther and farther back as the sun slid lower. The orange turned to yellow as the sun seemed to flatten. It became a disk, thinner than a dime, lying on top of the water. In a half breath it was almost gone, just the smallest spot of light. Then even that shrunk in on itself, going smaller…smaller…smaller—

Until shafts of green shot from the tiny point, a deep emerald flash.

Awed, Layla gasped, then gasped once more, as a dolphin leaped high from the water, its sleek body arcing as if to catch the jewel. Then it dove back under, and both were gone.

Vance squeezed her shoulder. His other hand crossed her waist, holding her to him. "Make a wish," he said against her ear.

To be brave, a voice inside her whispered. Then it was Uncle Phil she heard, presenting two choices. *You've got to decide if you want to do it my way—only on paper and in dreams—or if you actually want to step onto the plane and fly.* And then, finally, it was Vance's voice. *The two of us together* create *the love.*

She spun again, out of his arms, to stare at him, mouth dry, blood rushing in her ears louder than the waves on the sand. "Do you…do you really love me?"

A smile played at the corners of his mouth. "What did Jules Verne say again?"

"That a person who has seen a green flash can't be deceived. That they've gained the power to read others' thoughts."

"So you tell me," Vance said, reaching out to brush a lock of hair behind her ear. "What am I thinking?"

As always, his touch thrilled and burned and made her shiver. She swallowed. "That…that you love me and that you know I love you. And that I should stop being such a coward and instead be a little reckless so we can start being happy together."

He tilted his head. "So…"

Her heart lurched as she gazed upon this beautiful man: soldier, healer, nurturer. Lover. As her father had said, there was something special about him.

Thinking of her dad, Layla felt herself smile, and for the first time it wasn't tinged with the bittersweet pain of loss. She glanced over her shoulder, wondering if that green flash truly signified his soul had crossed over.

"So…" Vance prompted again.

Maybe it meant it was time she crossed over to a new life, as well. Heart rising to her throat, she turned to face her future. "So," she said slowly, "I've decided I want to start being happy right this second."

Then she launched herself forward and he caught her to him, his mouth finding hers to spread heat and magic all through her system. *Yes, there's definitely something enchanting about this place,* she thought, before her mind misted over with happiness.

LATER THAT NIGHT, when Vance was sleeping, she slid from his possessive grasp and crept out of bed. Unlike the last time she'd sneaked away, this time she went no farther than the dark kitchen. His laptop sat on the counter, and she used it to log on to her mail service. After clicking Compose, she stared a few moments at the blank screen and then wrote:

Dear Dad,
As usual, you picked the right man for the job.
Love, Layla

Closing the computer after hitting Send, she gave it a pat before returning to bed. Vance half awoke as she crawled under the covers. Opening his eyes, he looked at her face as he pulled her close again. "Why are you smiling?" he murmured.

She kissed his throat. "Because tonight, the ether doesn't seem all that far away."

* * * * *

From Layla's Karma Cupcakes Recipes File

CHOCOLATE CHAI CUPCAKES

---

*You can create your own chai spice mix according to
your tastes by adjusting the ingredients below and/or
adding others. Like a little more cinnamon? Go right
ahead! Don't like cloves? Just omit. Cardamom is one
of the most expensive spices on the planet by weight,
but it provides a glorious, exotic base note. Well worth
the cost.*

Chai Spice Mix

½ teaspoon ground cinnamon
½ teaspoon ground cloves
½ teaspoon nutmeg
½ teaspoon ginger
1 teaspoon ground cardamom
Combine in small bowl.

For Cupcakes

Makes about 12 regular cupcakes

3 ounces bittersweet chocolate
(at least 60% cacao suggested)
½ cup all-purpose flour
½ cup cake flour
½ teaspoon baking soda
¼ teaspoon salt
1 tablespoon chai spice mix
¼ cup unsalted butter, room temperature

½ cup sugar
⅓ cup light brown sugar, packed
2 eggs at room temperature
½ cup buttermilk

Preheat oven to 350°F. Line a muffin tin with cupcake liners.

Break up chocolate and place in microwaveable container. Melt in microwave, taking into account the particularities of your appliance. Start slow! Once complete, set aside.

Using a whisk, stir the flours, baking soda and salt together in a bowl. Stir in the chai spice mixture.

Cream the butter and both sugars together in a mixer on medium speed until soft and creamy. Add in the chocolate and mix. One at a time, add the eggs, beating each in completely before the next. Alternate adding portions of the flour mixture and the buttermilk until they are completely incorporated.

Fill the cupcake liners about 3/4 full. Bake in oven for 15 to 18 minutes, or until a toothpick inserted in the cupcakes comes out clean. Take into account your own oven and keep a close eye! Cool before decorating.

These taste wonderful without any icing (don't miss taste testing at least one from the oven!). But the Whipped Spiced Chocolate Icing will make it a truly decadent treat. Can also use Milk Chocolate Frosting.

Whipped Spiced Chocolate Icing

4 ounces semisweet chocolate, broken into pieces
(chocolate chips work just fine)

½ cup heavy cream
¼ teaspoon nutmeg
½ teaspoon cinnamon

Place chocolate into a medium heatproof bowl.

Put cream, nutmeg and cinnamon in a saucepan, stir, then place over medium heat. While continuing to stir, heat just until it comes to a simmer.

Pour cream mix over chocolate. Let sit for a few moments, then stir until chocolate is completely melted and mixture is smooth.

Put bowl into refrigerator and chill until firm *(approximately an hour—can be left there until ready for next step)*.

Using a mixer, whip the cooled mixture until it is light and fluffy. Be careful not to overwhip!

DHARMA DULCE DE LECHE CUPCAKES

NOTE: THE ICING FOR THESE CUPCAKES REQUIRES A CANDY/OIL THERMOMETER.

Dulce de leche can be loosely translated as "milk candy" and is milk that is cooked until the milk sugars caramelize. It has a lighter taste than caramel and there are a variety of methods for making it (you can also purchase it in a jar). Leftovers can be used to drizzle over ice cream or to jazz up plain slices of pound cake. The oven method for making dulce de leche requires little attendance and results in a beautiful, honey-colored sauce. One can of milk will make enough for the cupcakes and icing below, but you can use additional cans to make more dulce de leche as desired.

Oven Method Dulce de Leche

Preheat oven to 425°F. Empty one can sweetened, condensed milk into a shallow baking dish or pie plate. Cover tightly with aluminum foil. Place foil-wrapped dish in another, larger dish and fill that with hot water until it reaches halfway up the container holding the condensed milk.

Place in the oven for 1 to 1 1/4 hours, checking every thirty minutes or so and refilling water if necessary.

Carefully remove pans from oven. Remove pan now holding dulce de leche from larger one and allow to cool completely. Using a whisk, smooth out cooled mixture.

For Cupcakes

Makes about 12 regular cupcakes

¾ cup all-purpose flour
¾ cup cake flour
1 teaspoon baking powder
(make sure there are no lumps!
Push through fine sieve if necessary)
⅛ teaspoon baking soda
¾ stick unsalted butter, at room temperature
⅔ cups sugar
½ teaspoon salt
¼ cup dulce de leche
2 large eggs, at room temperature
⅛ cup vegetable oil
1 teaspoon vanilla extract
⅜ cup buttermilk, room temperature

Preheat oven to 350°F. Line a muffin tin with cupcake liners.

Using a whisk, stir both flours, baking powder and baking soda in a bowl. In mixer, cream together butter, sugar and salt on medium speed until light and fluffy. At a low mixing speed, slowly add the dulce de leche until incorporated. Add eggs one at a time, beating well, then the oil and vanilla. Again at low speed, add the flour mixture and buttermilk a little at a time, alternating between the two. Don't overmix.

Fill the cupcake liners about 2/3-3/4 full. Bake in oven for 15 to 20 minutes, or until a toothpick inserted in the cupcakes comes out clean. Take into account your own oven and keep a close eye! Cool before decorating.

Dulce de Leche Buttercream Icing

2 large egg whites
¾ cup sugar
pinch of salt
1½ sticks unsalted butter, at room temperature
¼ cup dulce de leche
½ teaspoon vanilla extract

With a mixer, beat the egg whites, sugar and salt together in a heatproof bowl. Set the bowl over a pan of simmering water and heat, stirring with a whisk the entire time, until the mixture registers 160°F on a candy/oil thermometer.

Using the mixer again, beat on medium-high speed until stiff peaks form. If outside of mixer bowl is not yet cool, rub ice along the outside until the surface no longer holds any heat. Next, at medium speed, gradually add the butter, a tablespoon or so at a time. Then, at medium-high speed, beat until the frosting is thick. Add in the dulce de leche and vanilla and beat until incorporated and frosting is smooth.

AVOCADO CUPCAKES WITH
MILK CHOCOLATE FROSTING

This dense cake has the color of a pistachio nut and a slight tang. Goes well with a sweet icing!

For Cupcakes

Makes about 12 regular cupcakes

1 large, ripe Hass avocado, pitted and sliced (when held in the palm of your hand, a ripe avocado will yield to gentle pressure)
¾ cup low fat or skim milk
⅓ cup vanilla or plain low fat yogurt
1 teaspoon vanilla
½ cup white sugar
1½ cups all-purpose flour
½ teaspoon salt
1 teaspoon baking powder
(make sure there are no lumps!
Push through fine sieve if necessary)
¾ teaspoon baking soda

Preheat oven to 350°F. Line a muffin tin with cupcake liners. Using a fork, mash avocado slices in a bowl, then transfer to a large food processor or blender. Add milk, yogurt, vanilla and sugar. Mix until a smooth puree is formed (you don't want any chunks of avocado).

Using a whisk, stir together flour, salt, baking powder and baking soda in a bowl. Use a hand mixer or whisk to gently add avocado mixture. Mix until just combined yet smooth.

Fill the cupcake liners about 2/3-3/4 full. Bake in oven for 18 to 22 minutes, or until a toothpick inserted in the cupcakes comes out clean. Take into account your own oven and keep a close eye! Cool before decorating.

Milk Chocolate Frosting

½ cup heavy cream
6 ounces milk chocolate, broken up

Pour cream into a small saucepan. Put over medium-high heat until the cream begins to boil. Remove pan from heat, add the chocolate. Let stand until chocolate is melted. Using a large spoon, beat the mixture until it is smooth. Let cool to room temperature. Once cooled, use an electric mixer to whip into a thick frosting that forms gentle peaks.

**Sometimes the best man
is the one you least expect....**

New York Times **Bestselling Author**

KRISTAN HIGGINS

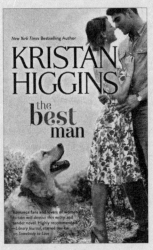

Faith Holland left her hometown after being jilted at the altar. Now a little older and wiser, she's ready to return to the Blue Heron Winery, her family's vineyard, to confront the ghosts of her past, and maybe enjoy a glass of red. After all, there's some great scenery there....

Like Levi Cooper, the local police chief—and best friend of her former fiancé. There's a lot about Levi that Faith never noticed, and it's not just those deep green eyes. The only catch is she's having a hard time forgetting that he helped ruin her wedding all those years ago. If she can find a minute amid all her family drama to stop and smell the rosé, she just might find a reason to stay at Blue Heron, and finish that walk down the aisle.

Available wherever books are sold!

REQUEST YOUR FREE BOOKS!

2 FREE NOVELS
FROM THE ROMANCE COLLECTION
PLUS 2 FREE GIFTS!

YES! Please send me 2 FREE novels from the Romance Collection and my 2 FREE gifts (gifts are worth about $10). After receiving them, if I don't wish to receive any more books, I can return the shipping statement marked "cancel." If I don't cancel, I will receive 4 brand-new novels every month and be billed just $5.99 per book in the U.S. or $6.49 per book in Canada. That's a savings of at least 25% off the cover price. It's quite a bargain! Shipping and handling is just 50¢ per book in the U.S. and 75¢ per book in Canada.* I understand that accepting the 2 free books and gifts places me under no obligation to buy anything. I can always return a shipment and cancel at any time. Even if I never buy another book, the two free books and gifts are mine to keep forever.

194/394 MDN FVU7

Name	(PLEASE PRINT)	

Address		Apt. #

City	State/Prov.	Zip/Postal Code

Signature (if under 18, a parent or guardian must sign)

Mail to the Harlequin® Reader Service:
IN U.S.A.: P.O. Box 1867, Buffalo, NY 14240-1867
IN CANADA: P.O. Box 609, Fort Erie, Ontario L2A 5X3

Want to try two free books from another line?
Call 1-800-873-8635 or visit www.ReaderService.com.

* Terms and prices subject to change without notice. Prices do not include applicable taxes. Sales tax applicable in N.Y. Canadian residents will be charged applicable taxes. Offer not valid in Quebec. This offer is limited to one order per household. Not valid for current subscribers to the Romance Collection or the Romance/Suspense Collection. All orders subject to credit approval. Credit or debit balances in a customer's account(s) may be offset by any other outstanding balance owed by or to the customer. Please allow 4 to 6 weeks for delivery. Offer available while quantities last.

Your Privacy—The Harlequin® Reader Service is committed to protecting your privacy. Our Privacy Policy is available online at www.ReaderService.com or upon request from the Harlequin Reader Service.

We make a portion of our mailing list available to reputable third parties that offer products we believe may interest you. If you prefer that we not exchange your name with third parties, or if you wish to clarify or modify your communication preferences, please visit us at www.ReaderService.com/consumerschoice or write to us at Harlequin Reader Service Preference Service, P.O. Box 9062, Buffalo, NY 14269. Include your complete name and address.

ROM13

Harlequin More Than Words
Where Dreams Begin

Three bestselling authors
Three real-life heroines

Each of us can effect change. In our own unique ways, we can all make the world a better place. We need only to take that first step, do that first good deed and the ripple effect will be life-changing to so many. Three extraordinary women who were compelled to take that first leap and make a difference have been chosen as recipients of **Harlequin's More Than Words** award. To celebrate their accomplishments, three bestselling authors have written short stories inspired by these real-life heroines.

SHERRYL WOODS captures the magic of pretty dresses and first dances in *Black Tie and Promises.*

CHRISTINA SKYE's *Safely Home* is the story of a woman determined to help the elderly in her newly adopted community.

PAMELA MORSI explores how literacy and the love of reading can enrich and indeed change lives in *Daffodils in Spring.*

Thank you… Net proceeds from the sale of this book will be reinvested into the **Harlequin More Than Words** *program to support causes that are of concern to women.*

Available wherever books are sold!

www.Harlequin.com

CHRISTIE RIDGWAY

77740 BEACH HOUSE NO. 9   ___ $7.99 U.S. ___ $9.99 CAN.

(limited quantities available)

TOTAL AMOUNT $ _____
POSTAGE & HANDLING $ _____
($1.00 FOR 1 BOOK, 50¢ for each additional)
APPLICABLE TAXES* $ _____
TOTAL PAYABLE $ _____

(check or money order—please do not send cash)

To order, complete this form and send it, along with a check or money order for the total above, payable to Harlequin HQN, to: **In the U.S.:** 3010 Walden Avenue, P.O. Box 9077, Buffalo, NY 14269-9077; **In Canada:** P.O. Box 636, Fort Erie, Ontario, L2A 5X3.

Name: _____
Address: _____ City: _____
State/Prov.: _____ Zip/Postal Code: _____
Account Number (if applicable): _____

075 CSAS

*New York residents remit applicable sales taxes.
*Canadian residents remit applicable GST and provincial taxes.

HARLEQUIN® HQN™
™ www.Harlequin.com

PHCR0312BL